PAN THE LOW WATERS

PAN THE LOW WATERS

By Arnold F. Rothmeier

Four Seasons Publishers
Titusville, FL

Pan The Low Waters

All rights reserved
Copyright©2000 Arnold F. Rothmeier

This is a work of fiction.
All characters and events portrayed in this book are fictional, and any resemblance to real people is purely coincidental.

Reproduction in any manner, in whole or in part, in English or in other languages, or otherwise without written permission of publisher is prohibited.

For information contact: Four Seasons Publishers
P.O.Box 51, Titusville, FL 32781

PRINTING HISTORY
First Printing 2000

ISBN 1-891929-25-9

PRINTED IN THE UNITED STATES OF AMERICA
1 2 3 4 5 6 7 8 9 10

To Lynn, my wife, whose kind urgings
and helpful criticism helped to make
this story a reality.

*   *   *

Also, to Dr. Kenneth Fox D.D.S. of
Auburn, California has graciously granted
the author permission to use the books cover
picture of the Claude Chana statue.

Table of Contents

Arrival and Loss 1
The Brawl 10
The Levee 16
Interview and Slave Auction 20
Stave Boy 28
Cooper Again 34
Jacques 43
Double Disaster 51
Paddle Wheeler 59
St. Louis 65
Chouteau 74
The Trading Post 83
First Winter 90
Soiree 102
Pikes and Settlers 113
Second Winter 120
Covillaud 127
Decision 131
Upriver 137
Blacksnake Hills 140
Coup de Charles 145
Working Again 150
Settler Meeting 155
Enigma 161
The Storm 173
Independence 178

Tug Westward	182
Mary - Part I	192
On the Trail	215
Savages	226
Sicard	232
Eddy	242
Assistance	246
Sutter's Fort	256
Mary - Part II	266
Marshall	275
Cordua	278
Nemshas	288
San Jose	292
Mine Test	296
Agriculture	305
The Gold Bite	308
Nemshas Purchase	322
Mary - Part III	325
Land Commission	333
The Monitors	341
The Bear	345
Defeat	351
Epilogue	356

Chapter 1
Arrival and Loss

Huge leaden-bellied clouds seemed to press the schooner *Zotow* deeper into the water, making it veer alternately to port and larboard. Ominous gusts flapped its reduced rigging unpredictably, and the captain cursed his landfall weather in filthy brown epithets.

Loud though they were, it was neither the bawled curse, nor the scudding feet of sailors overhead that caused me to stir. It was not the nasal gargle and whine of a dozen snoring bodies, or the mixed odor of feces and vomit which, in the dawdling weeks of the ship's passage since L'Harve, mixed with a briny smell of a gray and turbulent ocean.

Sleep, for most souls aboard the emigrant ship, had been fitful and hard to woo the night before. I alone, of the seventy-four passengers, had paced the deck until late, speculating upon the coming morning, for the harsh rules of the open sea and curfew were relaxed here, in the South passage. The others, tired from a long day of staring at the stringy, characterless headland, had gone to bed early and unsatisfied.

Arnold F. Rothmeier

That which had caused me to stir, that which I heard above strain and creak of the mainmast, was a secretive and rhythmic movement of figures I knew to be unmarried emigrants. I turned my head and sought again the sleep I had missed. A light, feminine moan, then the pair became silent. The moaner would soon rise and steal silently to the draped section aft. It would be her last clandestine visit—at least aboard this schooner—for the ship bid fair to end its run by nightfall, despite threatening weather and the ship's slow crawl up a hundred miles of treacherous delta.

By mid-morning, stagnant odors of seventy-four emigrants and piping shrillness of a dozen young voices has sufficiently shocked most of the hold to wakeful expectancy. With landfall now imminent, and with little thought of breakfast other than a mouthful of whatever remained from the voyage, there began a general, noisy stacking of boxes, pans, and luggage in obedience to the captain's coarse commands.

Soon, the gloom of the dingy hold filled with acrid fumes of vinegar, and sand bit into oak flooring as the first mate sprinkled it for scouring. Seventy pairs of feet began to shuffle in grotesque ballet. A madder throng of gritty, gliding dancers, to a more unorthodox verbal accompaniment, in a more ludicrous setting, would have been hard to imagine. This one had only curses under his breath for the enterprise, though he had fouled the floor most frequently; another mouthed simpering prayers for safe deliverance at New Orleans; yet another called a child across a whirling throng; one held his silence and skated arm-in-arm with his mate, pantomiming decorous promenade.

By noon a warm drizzle played about the deck, offering only discouragement to any who wished to watch a low, dark, tree-fringed island slip by. A captain's edict, also, had damned them to an acid-fumed hold, for the decks now belonged to the bare and obedient feet of sailors.

Pan The Low Waters

It was late afternoon when bawled commands and padding feet ceased to be heard, and the mate arrived, escorting an officious-looking customs official and health inspector. The deck was bathed in the crimson sunset glow of a storm, which had failed to materialize. We were all informed that a lighter was alongside, the first off would be married couples and children, then single women. All would have to take their chances with accommodations ashore, since the ships tardy arrival had caused hawkers, who preyed upon emigrants, to remain away.

Since I, Claude Chana, would be amongst the last to quit ship, I gathered blankets and satchel of cooper's tools, and found berth on deck to watch the debarkation. It was a slow procedure, noisy and profane, and accomplished almost without incident.

A general free-for-all became the method used in debarking. Two rough sailors descended to receive parcels and chests, and to guide unsteady feet onto the heaving lighter. Two hempen ladders attached to the *Zotow's* larboard side provided precarious exit from the ship, which had been our prison for almost two months.

A florid expression of extreme jealousy lit Herr Meier's face as a sailor aboard the lighter found it necessary to grasp his wife's ankle when she missed her footing and cried out. I thought to assist, but was deterred by the memory of verbal and bloody battles begun for similar reasons earlier in the voyage. I wanted no such end to a trip that had left me weak and in need of good food. The ship's meat, heavily salted as it was, had for weeks smelled and tasted of decay, and the old oil casks rolled aboard at L'Harve had never contained a water that satisfied thirst. From time to time its flavor changed, the captain pouring in gunpowder one day, treacle the next. In the end, he had spoiled good wine and rum in an effort to make water potable.

Arnold F. Rothmeier

The sun was low, and firing the bay with a golden-red luminescence as I descended from my seat on some spare rigging. I had studied the city and its waterfront was waiting turn. From our position, a hundred yards offshore, I noted a closely-knit border of large buildings, most uniform in height, and not unlike those of my own waterfront at Rouen. Their monotony of size was punctuated here and there by a dome or spire. Several cargo smacks, a brig, four cargo ships, and a brigantine lay near at anchor. A dozen river steamers unloaded cargo. I had often boarded those kinds of vessels at home, but my interest was piqued by a curious kind of flat boat with a severe, box-like superstructure. A thin bearded man, attempted to navigate the craft by means of a long rudder pole. Much later, I would see many of these flatboats–the lifelines for up-river produce– and learn that they were drifted down, unloaded, then broken up for their lumber.

Here, too, were smart packets of French registry, their sails hanging limp and square, imitation gun ports painted black on a white stripe. They had arrived, perhaps weeks ago, with their fine freight and mail. The passage, forty guineas, had simply been too much for my slim purse.

Curious, I thought, I could not tell when the odor of the sea had been replaced by river smell. At sea, salt air had made me ravenous, for I had exhausted my supply of cheese and sausage long before most. Now the dank odor of stagnant bayous and a rich, heady air-wine of unknown flowers stirred again my appetite. All these impressions were but a moment in my existence, yet they were strong in their stimulation.

When my turn came, I slung tool satchel strap across chest, tossed blanket roll into the lighter, and clambered aboard as quickly as my weakened condition would allow. The few guineas yet in my pocket from sharpers at L'Harve docks felt lean, but good.

Pan The Low Waters

My need for good food and rest was a prime concern, and guided me almost reflexively to a small restaurant near the broad levee. It was a small, mean enclosure at the foot of the short flight of treacherous steps. The aroma of its menu of fried foods enveloped me as I waited for a garson.

At last the owner's " Vous desire" ... and my impatient, "Quelque chose a mange et a boire," brought to the bare, wooden table a bowl of clam soup, a plate of small, fried lobsters, a tear of bread, and some wine. I ate greedily, almost without control. And, when the plates were empty, I ordered another bottle of wine. When that, too, had been drunk, I sat long with battered pipe, and with an occasional feel for my precious tool satchel, took inventory: strange country, little money, no friends, no home.

The low flicker of drafty candlelight, the warm, secure odor of good food so long denied, the low alternation of male and female confidences indistinct and palliative, and the tranquilizing fullness of a stuffed belly soothed by four glasses of Burgundy, fused me to a pleasant drowsiness. The room, if any were available, would have to wait. Accumulated lack of sleep overpowered me. Placing head on arm, I slept, and, in my dreams I saw each of my tools, draw knife, shaper, then plane, dance maddeningly out of hand and away. They assumed absurd shapes, became fluid and then formless by turn.

It was the subtle absence of ship sounds and aroma of coffee that awakened me. My first act upon awakening was to reach down for my bag of tools. A shocked confusion engulfed me as I bent in disbelief to see what my searching hand had established: my beloved tools, my livelihood, were no longer there! I rose and wildly searched the place, and questioned all present. I established, in the end, only a "Yes" from the proprietor. "Yes, there was one. He sat and drank near your table, then left, carrying something, and I do not recall his appearance."

Arnold F. Rothmeier

With an effort to control my despair, I continued to search the dimness and litter. There remained only two others in the room, either tired and drunk, or simply drunk, who lay hunched over their tables, hands and hair coated with the sticky dregs of a last brandy. There was no sound in the room, only that which came from beyond a soiled canvas sheet veiling the working area to the rear. I was conscious of a vile stench of vomit as I pushed the cloth door aside. There a black worker, hands deep in a tub of fresh fish, had "Seen nuthin' and new nuthin' about a bag."

Still reeling from the combined effects of my debilitating sea diet, from the drink, and now from shock of loss, I shouldered my greasy blanket role and stepped into the morning, a sun-shot haze of March, 1839, New Orleans waterfront. The loss, I considered, as the cool of the morning revived me, was severe, though not fatal. I breathed deeply and felt again the security of a money belt that no deft fingers could remove. I cursed aloud at my foolishness in failing to safeguard my tools, and swore it would never happen again.

That another might steal from me was not a strange thing. Indeed, I recalled my mother saying, after loss of purse or toy, that the price of the article was a reasonable fee for learning one of life's lessons. The memory of her words, however, did little to lessen my regret, for the tools had become a part of me. It was as though a portion of my body had been amputated, reducing my capacity to function, diminishing my self-image, reducing me to peonage. My tools had been evidence of the pride with which, for years, I had labored in my father's employ. Then, as I had finally taken leave of the small Chana vineyard to live closer to the docks at Rouen, my tools had acquired an even higher status symbol, and I had daily inspected, sharpened, and oiled each, knowing that my skill depended upon this lavish care.

The tools were gone now, their theft accepted. I was shocked to lucidity, perhaps even to self-pity. As a concession to my sense of loss, I sought solace in the physical: I breakfasted on crayfish and hot bread peddled by a small, swarthy negress on the dock, and washed it down with pale, dry wine. Afterward, standing on the wooden sidewalk, as my outlook ebbed back to normalcy, it occurred to me that, since the theft was made for private gain, the thief would sell at first opportunity. If he had not yet sold, he might trade for an offered reward.

Thinking thus, I spent the day laying a foundation for a legitimate exchange of tools for reward of fifty francs. I revisited the scene of my loss, made known to the restaurateur my willingness to pay a reward, posted a series of brief placards about the docks in both French and my best English, and inserted a small ad in the *Picayune*.

It was late afternoon when, after engaging a small room, I returned to the dockside-eating house to await developments. Now, despite a loss of tools, I felt a small surge of confidence with possession of address. It was the first step in an orderly progress to a feeling of worth and belonging. The levee was a confusing scene of vendors, voices, and odors that attracted and repelled, but the very variety of its sensual distractions erased my deep sense of loss and a sudden onslaught of homesickness.

By nightfall there had been no response to my advertisements. Nor did I longer expect one. The hopelessness, which had earlier overcome me, no longer cut as deeply. The handful of warm salty prawns on which I munched served to alleviate my early dismay. At twenty-nine I was not given to self-pity. I simply had not been without my bag of prized tools since the age fifteen when I had chosen trade school instead of lycee. Like a child whose parents divert with new toys, I found myself diverted by a thousand sights, sounds, and odors: thick-lipped, shuffling black dock men working to a tight, rhythmically moaned tune, spinning it to the end of the gang way, then sluffing off their shoulder-load and pivoting for a return to the hold without missing a beat; quadroons and octoroons of light beige beauty clothed in plumed hats and riding with an old seamed-faced mammy so black and shiny as to make the girls skin appear white; Indians in gaudy blankets trailing a squaw and an odor of rancid sweat and raw alcohol; and grinning, turbaned negresses shouting incomprehensible names of the hot foods they carried upon their heads–ducking to catch the descending tray when a customer motioned.

That night, the third since arriving, I spent in my spare sleeping room not far from the scene of my loss. Several times during the next two days I returned to the restaurant to inquire after the tools. At the last inquiry, the restauranteur ignored my question. The matter, I knew, was closed and I resigned myself to the loss.

It was raining heavily when I returned to my room. Never had I felt more desolate, more alone. Even the ecrevisse at a great market beyond the docks where I had attempted to dine had tasted flat. I had thrown the lot to a mongrel who had swallowed them, skins and all, in one swift motion. Like my bag of tools, I thought, they had been gobbled up thoughtlessly and would do their new owner about as much good and as the unpeeled, unmasticated crayfish would do the cur. I dismissed the incident, walked to my room, pulled a mental curtain over my troubles and fell asleep to the toneless drone of a downpour.

Mellow tolling of the church bell aroused me. The late March rain had spent itself and through a small window high on the north wall I could see the reflected glow of a fresh, warm sun. I flung lengthening black hair from my eyes, dashed a handful of water onto my face, and rubbed vigorously with a shirtsleeve. It had been four days since debarkation. I had not bathed since departing Rouen nearly two months ago. True, I reflected, I had done no work to raise a sweat, such as was required at the great cooperage on the Seine. And, so far, I had not become host to crabs and lice which, I knew by their scratching, others aboard had had. But, I knew I stank, and I felt, rather than saw, my encasement of bodily filth.

Pan The Low Waters

Bathing was accomplished with dispatch and at no expense. Half a mile out of town and beyond a levee thick with flatboats and vendors, I moved to a side path and cleaned myself with mud and water of the Mississippi. And, with the cleansing, seemingly, went my troubles. Afterward, I basked and dried in the brilliant Louisiana sun and even washed my shirt, going bare-chested as I returned slowly along the levee, swinging and waving the shirt for faster drying.

Arnold F. Rothmeier

Chapter 2
The Brawl

The New Orleans levee was a milling tide of shoppers and vendors as I crossed from the path to a high open plain above the river. First signs of excitement greater than that which already teemed began with high-pitched shouts of a youngster calling a friend to come and see the event. Then, off to the right, I was attracted by braced shoulders and wide-swinging fists of a levee brawl between two burly boatman of equal height and weight. If there was an advantage on either side, it could not be detected. A blond headed brawler sidestepped cleverly and avoided wild charges of the brown, who mixed unexpectedly swift kicks as well as blows in his attack. Nor was the fight all physical, for there was an apparent deep-seated grievance between the mauling and flailing men. It was expressed in a snarling, grunting speech and seemed to fuel the battle and to stir both to wilder exertions as they slugged and kicked, grappled and danced.

This was my first viewing of a serious fight in the New World. So far it had not differed from the usual fist fights I had seen, and even participated in, at the Rouen quayside. True, the vicious kicking was an innovation, but this seemed not to affect the outcome, since both were now using feet with stunning effect.

Suddenly, after working in their hates for perhaps twenty-minutes, the blond one effected a trip. The other went down, closing his legs vice-like as the other fell on top of him, grunting verbals which changed to something resembling, "Gotcha this time, you bastard!"

And now, as the two shapes rolled in their cloud of dust, there was a sudden bending of the blond atop the writhing, grizzled head beneath, a motion that struck me as most strange among fighters, since it was common in France for men to greet another with the cheek kiss. At once a hideous cry of pain welled from the man underneath, and in strength born of pure agony, his body whipped around the other with reflexive snake-like effort until he was atop the blond. And, as he managed this assent, a low, throaty cry over something infinitely pleasurable welled from the circle of spectators. The brown head, which earlier numbered two ears, now had but one in position; the other hung grotesquely against a bloody neck, almost severed by the bite. A musk sweet-smell of new blood now tanged the waterfront and a new sound rose from the rabble, shrill and confused, like the voices at the Seville bullfight to which my father had taken me on vacation so long ago. Such flashes of memory came to me in lightning-like bursts as my eye recorded the growing desperation of the struggle.

A slavering, animal-like grunting now replaced muffled, nasal curses. The scene, bestial and wild in the extreme, held a growing crowd with vice-like fascination. And now, as they rolled in their dust cloud and smote each other's face, the brown hair, from a rider-like position on the belly of the other, suddenly leaned forward. To a cry from the crowd, whose satisfaction rose to new heights, he came away, in a savage twist of the head, with the bloodied flesh of the other's nose in his jaws. This he spat over his shoulder even as his own bloodied ear dripped into the eyes of the other. His eyes had taken in the nameless terror of the man beneath, who now blew small balloons of blood through a nacreous stump once large and aquiline.

With both beasts now hideously bloodied, the circle of baying humans seemed to press inward, to slowly implode upon the contestants in their own growing madness. Neither the bloody blond, with his reddened chin and chest, nor the darker, grizzled fighter showed signs of slowing or of surrender. Both now regained an erect position. They paused and glared, the grizzled one pointing and jeering at the other, whose face seemed so oddly altered, so crimson. Then they began anew the pounding.

With blows now landing on gristle, the blond slowly became unrecognizable. His face was a streaked crimson mask, over which hung long strands of hair that stuck to the drying blood, which made him appear as a wild scarecrow caricature.

But, as though sensing vaguely through a screen of shock that he must destroy or be destroyed, the blond fighter now sought to trip the other – anything to escape the smashing fists of the dark grizzled one. His chance came as the latter momentarily lost balance after a misjudged swing. In the half second it takes a pair of heavy bodies to fall, they lay in the heavy dust, clutching, writhing. Now, to the increased roar of the onlookers, some of whom made noise only because of their frustration over not being able to see the fight above the other's shoulders, it was the blond who sought again to maim. The almost imperceptible duck of his dead and a blow aimed at his opponent's nose was frustrated. The nose of the other was not there. But, another target presented itself, and the blond's teeth closed around an ear while his head and upper frame strained to tear it from its owner's head.

I would gladly have left the wild circle, but escape was no longer possible, so tightly pressed was the audience. Blood-smell and the accumulated rancid odor of clamoring, sweating bodies washed over me. A sense of unreality enveloped me, for, as I looked anew at the brawlers, I saw why screams of the crowd had increased. A left eyeball of the dark one hung outside its socket, suspended by a single sinew. Now came a sudden pause in the fighting and it seemed there must certainly be suspension in a contest that had already consumed so much energy, drained so much blood.

But there was no lengthy rest, no truce, only a moment to regain breath for further struggle. And, as the ragged and bloody figures renewed their circling, it became evident to all that the brown-haired one had received a fatal handicap. While he had, it seemed, a store of energy greater than that of the blond, it was also apparent that the latter was pressing his visual advantage. His breath now a rasp, he fought with cunning, telling blows to the other's blind side. Unable to direct blows accurately and mad with pain and frustration, the brown one resorted again to holding and kicking.

A last scene in the struggle began as the two again went down with an audible grunting thud, feet, knees, and fists flailing to effect a blow that would stun the other. A groin shot from the blond's knee brought forth an instant bay of pain and, as his opponent doubled in dusty agony, the blond clawed at the other's face. It seemed to me inconceivable that, now with the opponent prostrate and in paralyzing pain, there should be further effort to maim. Yet now, with a slow and deliberate movement, the blond rose, grasped the other's hair, and jerked the head violently backward. As it struck the ground, he placed his heel upon the man's neck, bent, and with a crowning show of bestiality dug out the other's remaining eye and flung it into the dust.

The circle of rabble had seen their quarry splayed, had been thrown their piece of the kill. There was a gradual stunned lessening of tension in the crowd. Opponents occupied the ring from which sunmotes rose and swirled. But the action was over. The noseless one felt gingerly of his cartilaginous stub, turned, an odd faceless form, and stumbled an uncertain path through the crowd. The other lay on his back softly moaning and weaving slowly from side to side, his eyes sightless sockets, hands at a groin which had received the most painful blow of the affray.

I turned and made my way through the crowd that seemed loath to leave. Already there was aid for the fallen one. Whether relatives or helpful bystanders, I never knew. My introduction to one element in new America had been a stunning one, bizarre and grotesque beyond imagining. The few angry threats and brawls aboard ship had been as peace offerings compared to the compulsion of the two Kaintucks (I was later in Missouri, to know them as Pikes or Pukes) to reciprocally mangle each other. Already I could sense the wildness which was all about me and I retired within myself. I shuddered and felt suddenly and truly alone for the first time since leaving France. I knew that I must never come close to Americans in this sort; that risk of their anger was too great, their unpredictability of temperament too great a menace for me, a foreigner, to risk. Yet I felt I must have friends, must enter into the life of the new nation, must function in ways other than those of a spectator.

It was late afternoon. Drays and hacks crackled over cobblestone pavement. Here and there a vendor of prawns or crawdads called her wares, aromas advertising the food long before its name was called. I purchased a handful of crayfish handed me on a large plantain leaf and cracked and munched them as I walked. But my thoughts were on the Pikes. The two were not born vicious. Nothing was worth the loss of body members, and sightlessness was tantamount to a death sentence. These tall, shuffling, bearded giants wore their anger on their cuff, especially when drunk, but were keyed-up most of the time, ready as a gun to explode. And yet they had their families, some of which were much in evidence on the long keelboats crowding the levee. But most of the giants – or so they seemed to me, a five-foot-eight-inch Frenchman – were in their early twenties, loud of mouth, forever spitting at a fly or at a dog, and chewing much more than talking, as though the jaw were a pump for the priming of the brain; as though the act pumped an unseen fuel to light eyes continually darting and defensive.

The ecrevise were succulent and inexpensive. Were they not so reasonable, I would surely have caught and cooked some myself, for I had often seen them dart beneath rocks and debris wherever stagnant water stood. My belly tightened against the money belt and I sensed again a small, secret thrill of security. For yet another week I would play the part of a visiting baron, then perhaps I would…

Chapter 3
The Levee

The levee was a paradise of odors, sights, and sounds that quickened and captivated my imagination. From the misty dank of the river came the aroma of fruits, vegetables, and kegged unknowns. From the hundreds of keelboats and barges arose ethers tantalizing and smothering. Each made its impress, then was replaced by another. The variety was endless. They mixed and fused; they existed in the air in a kind of sandwich form and, like everything else in this amazing America, the delicate scents seemed to waver, then recede. It was, however, the sharp, acidic odor of mule dung that monopolized my air, for the levee was a highway to dozens of carts and drays with mules pooping away their steaming green loads every few feet. It seemed, I thought, America was like this, in its infant growth. It required the roughness, the strident and the callously persistent. There was no room for the hothouse citizen in a country so new so raw, and zealous. The delicate man, as with the delicate odor must grow stronger or be overpowered.

I reflected upon my susceptibility to fragrances. Each essence seemed to contain a message of its own, and gave of it freely, just as

Pan The Low Waters

an opera or play gave of its message, or as a game gave of its satisfactions. I would still be a cultivateur in my father's small vineyard, or at best only another obscure laborer in Mssr. Durand's cooperage had it not been for the mysterious and heady perfume that arose one day from the workplace – that of the white oak staves. Yes, it was the enticement of the source, then the fruity, resinous seductiveness of the naked oaken staves that had tempted me to take one step after another towards the thing called emigration.

One of my first duties had been to drive the cooperage dray to the wharves and load the fragrant staves, fresh from America. I never tired of this job, but then I had been allowed, between loads, to practice with a knife. And when my care and success with a drawknife was observed, I had been schooled and given tools of my own.

I loved work that immersed me in the fragrant oaky smell. I labored under a blanket of odors; it clung to my clothes and I was counted pleasant to be with for I carried the woody perfume wherever I went. Sometimes, in the company of a fellow cooper, I would attend the local opera and sit and stamp my approval, or, on occasion, troup instead to one of the town's bawdy houses. Oak was my trademark. It was always fresh and woodsy, and its strength masked the odor of my sweat. And at the opera, the warm tonal waves of melody, the mystery of the orchestral build-ups, the releases of tension, the passion of the vocalese, and the pealing climaxes, all expressed the phallic in tone. The tang of oak became a symbol of the distant, the elusive, the forever new.

But even a skilled and successful worker will always try to better his lot – or perhaps only change it. I had risen quickly to become one of the most skilled workers, but seemed to require challenge or diversion. It was a perceptive Mssr. Duran who one day felt that I should have a change. I was asked to drive a dray of finished barrels to the dock. It was an enviable task, for the job provided me with an hour or two in which to browse about the busy wharf, inspect ships, and dine while the dray waited its turn for unloading. One might even drop a line and fish, or even board one of the ocean-going steamers.

The day had been one of the loveliest of a mild summer. The dray was loaded. I took reins, released brake, shook the leads against sleek brown backs, and hunched forward professionally for the two-mile trip. I liked horses, they with their wild, sub-human docility. In their surging, swaying backs and flanks I sensed a dumb gentleness and horsey sense of pride in their tension against black leather; their ability to pull the enormous load by sagging forward and walking. Their poly-rhythmic clopping against the hard, yellow roadway lulled me, and I enjoyed a moment's doze until sound of steel wheels cracking against paving cobbles nudged me to wakefulness. I swung the team onto Rue de la Paye and wound slowly into yards near the docks where other wagons stood and leather-aproned packers filled casks with pork and salt and the air hung heavy with vinegar.

"Bon jour, Claude! Vous ne travaille aujourd'hui?", from Jean, a driver, who also waited his turn. "Pas aujourd'hui", I replied, "Je suis roi du grand chemin!"

I leapt lightly to the platform and sauntered into an adjacent docking facility. It would be several hours before my dray could be unloaded. Newly arrived ships nudged the wharf: A packet from New York, flying a gay banner of stars and red and white stripes, loaded French calicoes, the bright newness of its material much in evidence; a large four-master, also from America, unloaded barrel staves, lumber, and hemp. The air was heavy with white oak, its odor seeming even more penetrating here at the river front, freer, more virgin, more mysterious. It was the instant which beckoned. It was the moment, the particular second from which dated all my plans and hopes in a new world.

There was here a subtle, quick synthesis between odor and ship, and a sudden feeling of lack of challenge at Mssr. Durand's cooperage. That brief morning exposure, uniting sights and odors of the new world, produced in me a zeal born of this synthesis, and I knew at the moment that I would one day board ship for America. I would see the country where grew an oak with these wondrously seductive scents, where lived a people who wore my country's fine materials. I would see ports from which sailed the huge cargo ships – they that spawned uniformed crews who lined the rails and then swaggered like proud kings through Rouen.

By the end of the second week of my stay in New Orleans, I could feel a growing apprehension about the thinness of my money belt. The opera, food and rent had reduced its size alarmingly. To my dismay, upon counting, I found there remained less than two hundred francs and I knew I must find employment.

Chapter Four
Interview and Slave Auction

It was the area between Camp Street and the levee, where large wholesale concerns did their packing, that I first applied. Here I had already seen mountains of containers – both wet and dry hogsheads – being filled, and knew their workings must be near. After watching a group of shirtsleeved laborers, I determined which was the contremaitre, and when the man appeared free for a moment, I said in my best French: "I am Claude Chana. I am a cooper from Rouen, and need work."

The foreman sized me up long and intently. He was not French, and seemed impatient to get on with his duties. He apparently understood, but did not wish either to speak or to be spoken to in French.

"Say it in United States, garcon," he demanded, his words sliding past an unlit cigar clamped between yellowed teeth. I repeated my remarks in English and again waited. There was an apparent belligerency in the man's tone.

"Wher'r your tools?"

"They were stolen just after I arrived in New Orleans two weeks ago."

"Unh. You do wet or dry coopering?"

The terms confused me for a moment, and in the time it took for me to sort "wet" into "tight" and "dry" into "slack", terms which I had once known and used, I could sense the man's mounting impatience.

Impatience spoke: "What's d'matter, don't'cha know what kind a barrels yuh make?"

The remark and its tone only served to embarrass me further. The man, now seeing me in confusion and about to walk away said: "Tell yuh what ahl do. Yuh can take it or leave it. If yuh want to bring in the staves for the regular coopers and keep shavings cleaned up for em, I'll try you out for regular after yuh get some tools, an if yuh really can make barrels."

Then, seeing me still hesitant, he went on: "The pay is five dollars per week to start. Come around tomorrow at seven if yuh want to work." He walked away shouting: "Hey Sam! Bring it an put it over here!"

The foreman had terminated the interview by remarks to another worker. I turned and walked from the yard.

"Les Americain. Mon Dieu!" What an impatient lot they are! Everything must be business: The only things that matter are buying and selling! There is room only for the practical – that which brings in one more dollar. The French Creoles are different, seem to enjoy life more in their passage through it. They too, treasure the dollar, but also they treasure the feelings of others and seem to enjoy the game of life. One has the feeling that with them the game is more enjoyable than the possession, like the old proverb that Grandpere sometimes recited so long ago: "C'est ne pas le but; c'est la route" ("It's not the arrival that is interesting and important, but the experience had while getting there".)

The New Orleans Frenchman, the Spaniard, even the Choctaw and the black vendor seemed to relish their existence more day-to-day than did the American.

"Yes, tomorrow I must go back to work", I thought. "It will not be as it was in Mssr. Durand's cooperage, but I must not expect it to be. I must not expect it to be as in Rouen."

It was yet midday when I turned away from the river and strolled thoughtfully again up Canal Street. Time to enjoy an afternoon in the new city once more before surrendering to necessity and obligation.

The day was sultry, one that made perspiration at the same time necessary and yet impossible. I turned in at the entrance to Banks Arcade with the thought of enjoying a glass of wine in the cool lobby. But there was no serving, nor was it cool. Instead of relief from temperature, a cloak of warm, fetid air hung over the large rotunda-like space. On a raised, circular, stone block stood a large, well-built negro incongruously clothed in stovepipe hat and black suit. His eyes were cast down, and though nattily clothed, his whole demeanor spoke of dejection and shame. It was the interval between slave sales, for the only sound was an almost inaudible buzzing among some of the eighteen or twenty observers and buyers. Presently the man in charge approached the patient, hatted black.

"What am I bid for this fine specimen of a work hand? Gentlemen, do I hear two hundred? This darky is strong as a horse, and obedient. The only reason he is for sale is that his owner no longer needs him."

The man continued, seemingly enthused by the sounds he made. Judging from the posters about the room, the man was Joseph A. Beard. He droned on, saying nothing which cattle or swine salesmen might not have included in a sales talk.

Presently a spare, athletic man in shirtsleeves and dirty, wide-brimmed straw hat approached the auctioneer. They spoke in low tones, each gesturing toward the cast-down black.

An agreement apparently reached, the slave was escorted brusquely to the side for closer inspection.

The block now received another – this time a negress with child in arms – and the auction continued. To the side, the planter-buyer proceeded to remove slave's coat and hat. He grasped the black's arm, flexing and examining it; he stood behind and pressed rib-cage and abdomen, which hung in a great fold over rope belt; he raised the slave's eyelids and received the subject's cooperation as he grasped the black jaw to inspect his teeth. Then, livestock inspected, the planter retired to a small group at the side to await the business of the auction.

Following a short spate of bidding in which only one other participated, the planter received slave and papers for two hundred dollars. Their exit was curiously like that of a farmer leading his cow, slack rope about the neck, a stupid stagger of unclad feet, the outward jutting of neck, seeing first where it would go before the rest followed; slack fullness of paunch quivering and swaying.

And so it was with a kind of dazed detachment that I watched the sale of humans, my mind unconsciously comparing the negro's lot to my own. What was the essential difference? Was it color; a distinct facial configuration, flared nose, pendulous lips? Was it the unseen thing called freedom, the deprivation of initiative, rude substitution of an owner's will for one's own; a cancelling out of all individual desires and making owner's wishes suffice for both?

The auction now continued louder. A mother and infant with diarrhea went for three hundred dollars – two souls for the price of one the man had said, and gotten a laugh. My thought tangled with emotions and sights, and I made my way to the door and to the brilliant New Orleans sunshine. The scene, with its smells of rancid sweat and feces, had clothed me in a profound depression.

For I was a creature of the senses. Odors cajoled me; sounds and rhythms stirred me deeply; colors swayed and entranced me. I had been an early and eager riser in my father's household and had gone unbidden to the fields and to duties. It was in the pre-dawn hours that I found the world virgin, rested and washed of the sights and taints of man. The habit had persisted in my apprentice days, and I had walked early in a world cleansed by night breezes and dews; in a new world before it was defiled by the odors of man and his waste, by noises and engine sounds.

Street lights were being lit when I left the Arcade. I did not go directly to my room, but instead, made directly for the levee. Streets withdrew their crowds grudgingly. It was the hour of preparation. Soon most would be dining, then hacks would clatter and parterres would again fill roadways and plunge toward the tumultuous maw of the opera. Or, they would wind in packed, sinuous cords toward odd, theatrical diversions marqueed for those who had a brandy-soused evening to give away.

The levee in April was stridently, brilliantly busy. It had not withdrawn its hordes and seemed, now that night had come, to increase its activity. Towering torches lighted the passageways and the brown, undulating snake-like folds of the Mississippi beyond. I had seen the crowded levee before in the humid glare of the sun, the seeming

Pan The Low Waters

miles of triple-tiered up-river "arks" and its sloops and its brigantines; its confusion of produce, cotton, and curses. Now, with bulge of season upon them, boss and black crew must work through the night, slave to the harvest of a land beyond dreaming. They loaded; they unloaded; they drove their miles by the light of tall, smoking torches stuck in boxes of sand; they seemed possessed of an eternal itch that made them shout and curse and sing.

As far as eye in nighttime could reach, the smoke-clouded vista along the levee was the same confused hive of shadow-mottled figures. Faces and torsos of the slave gangs gleamed a sweaty, flickering black, their mouths milky bars when thick lips curled back in anger or in mirth. Then, periodically, and without apparent prompting, their voices would erupt in rhythmic song and their labors would take on a new vitality and plunge. This was the invisible whip their master knew how to use – a whip often bought or hired for voice as well as muscle.

The crescent levee was a flickering ring of fire and ships and fortresses of cotton bales and barrels. I sat apart upon a cask, my mind and eye drinking in the view. The city was as a constriction in a mighty pipe line. All passed through the pipe, but here, at the constriction, activity accelerated and friction and heat generated. The port was a magnet for those who shipped much, as well as for those who shipped a few hams and barrels of whiskey. All was drawn downstream to the New Orleans levee where spectacled and bearded men catalogued and sent it to far ports and on larger ships. A short way off, ne'er-do-wells lived in flimsy cabins at the swamp's edge and fished or trapped alligators.

The variety of yield emerging from keel boats, arks, and rafts was a continual wonderment. From more than one came the stamp and whinny of mules, and the stench of hogs. From some came the cry of children, and many rough decks were strewn with corn and apples and stacked with barrels marked "wisky". On the scores of flatboats and keelboats wedged between and flanking larger ships, one item of cargo caught my attention. It was the single article which most seemed to bear: furs. Furs in large, flat bundles tied with strips of rawhide or rope; precious furs of rippled luxury. All this I saw as one in a theatre, the stage the more wondrous without curtain and without admission charge, with extras, principals and effects without number, a continuous drama with all its stage hands and actors forever visible.

And above the confused babble and toot and whinny, beyond the aroma of bulging hold of apples and piles of steaming mule dung, rose the unbelievably metric and melodious "coonjine", tonal stimulus for another ounce of strength to heave a bag, shuffle, grasp another, heave, shuffle. Where the dusky, soothing melody and its river-like flow of rhythm was heard, loading went smoothly, and where the black man sang not, there was friction, cursing, and delay.

Huge torches cast their twisting, intermittent glare on glistening backs and groping forms magnified to giants against sail and ship. As the night sky deepened to indigo, then coal, a thin gossamer of river mist crept over boats and laboring figures, and movement and sound grew soft and indistinct and unreal. For periods of several minutes there would be a time of no sound, a ceasing even of the coonjine and noisy winch. Then flares would brighten and pain of labor need a balm, and song and cursing would resume.

It was in one of these lulls that, from my perch atop a whisky barrel, I observed a vignette of water front life. To my right and in an area of many barrels, squatted another spectator, one in rags and possessed of a gargantuan nose that showed red even in the flickering half-dark. During one of the periods of confusion and noise, Rags had deposited himself in shadows between two casks. He was half concealed by a scrap of canvas and, with some small object, was drilling a hole close to one bottom. When next I looked, Rag's mouth was pressed against the cask. Half an hour later, as I rose to leave the scene, Rags lay sprawled upon his back, a look of drunken stupidity upon his face and a thin rill of whisky pouring its potency onto a grizzled cheek and slowly puddling his head.

Tomorrow the whistle would sound and I would answer it as I had at Mssr. Durand's cooperage for five years. Vacation had renewed me and I would be glad to have the responsibility of a task, satisfaction of doing, of having the good, tired feeling that brought deep slumber. I made my way through high cotton and barrelled aisles, dodged a plunging team of mules and reached my room just as the nine o'clock black curfew tolled.

Arnold F. Rothmeier

Chapter Five
Stave Boy

I was awakened by a tropical sun that played its flat brilliance against bare walls. I dressed hurriedly, for it seemed I had slept late. I stuffed bread and cheese into my mouth, more into pocket, and hurried to the cooperage. The Gobin Barrel Works was similar to that of the old country. A long, wide shed fronted a warehouse yard stacked with casks of all sizes. About it wound a high plank fence of unsure stature, seemingly little more capable of letting barrels out than of letting outsiders in. In the yard a dray was being loaded.

I was not met by the impatient American, nor did any of the several yard men seem concerned that I was there. I waited. Half an hour passed. Suddenly from behind.

"You!" It was the forced gravelly shout of the foreman. "Load a cart with staves yonder and keep the bins full inside! Make sure none of the coopers run out! That's your job. Clean out the shavings, too! Look alive! See what's to do!"

Not the kind of greeting and respect that a master cooper had been accorded where I was known, but I was working again. It was a beginning. No where to go but up. Time enough to show the quality of my work. The heady waves of white oak seemed fresher here. Their odor bolstered my ego, anchored me to the country, caused me to feel I belonged. I went to work with a will and handled the rough, split staves with a hasty reverence. I had arrived; my world was again scented and pure and indescribably sweet despite the foreman.

As I worked, steadily doling from my cart the needed staves, I noted method and cooper. Of the fifteen workers shaving and fitting along the windowed side, I saw that most were Frenchmen. Only here and there were seen a small tub, high with suds, from which a portly German dipped his pint, wiped moustache, and grunted a low throaty satisfaction. My countrymen seemed the busier, taking hold of their bottles only after long intervals of fitting and testing.

But, I missed the feel of the froe, the draw-knife, the plane, the champfering knife. I felt somehow deprived of an earned and God-like gift; I felt a waste. A feeling of unworthiness welled within me each time I paused to see the slow pull of another's blade on a naked white edge. But I was not an impatient man and I knew my chance to work as a master cooper would come again.

The cooperage was not as large as Mssr. Durand's had been, yet a steady output of casks left daily for sugar plantations where brandy and molasses butts were needed. There were other shops where smaller five to twenty "drys" were made, but here only the tight premium barrel was fashioned. And on Friday, late, the large, drafty factory flickered red with the charring for a large whisky still up-river.

As the weekend approached, workers lit the barrels, quenching them afterward in a black, scum-laden tub. On Saturday it was the barrels that lit the coopers. Especially did the large, moustached

Germans, with their "goose egg" kegs of beer, echo the cooperage with their shouts and songs. At one end the Germans, at another the French and Creoles. Songs, too, but a more withdrawn jollity; bottles of wine; songs pensive and artistic. Nostalgia flowed from the French throat, though here in New Orleans more sights reminiscent of France greeted one than did those of any other nation. So, souse it up, you sons of Dresden; ring the air with tonal bits of homeland! Sweep aside the fragile foam and glut the lunch pail tankard! Hold it high 'til all its eager drops apply and ease the lonesome soul to sweet befuddlement!

Here, at last, at the Saturday get-togethers, the fetters of strangeness and unfamiliarity fell away and I eventually emerged from the cloak of foreignness. Not with Americans did this emergence take place. But did one distinguish the American by his swagger, loud, talk, and inclination to differ and fight? The process began here, all French coopers perched on barrels, sharing the bottled happiness of the fields of France, piping into their nostalgic throats the essence of her loveliest grapes.

We sat thus on barrels for the better part of the afternoon, neither group hearing the other and, as heels smote their individual drums, drowning out lyrics, our voices became thicker, indistinct, more unrecognizable as words; more felt, however, as a lonely bridge built of songs and memories was flung across the ocean with all the savage, drunken weight of our homesickness.

We had worked our weekly stint, not for the few sous to pocket, not because of the obligation some had to send a portion to loved ones left behind at L'Havre, Marseilles, or other ports, but to dull a gnawing ache for the old ways left half a watery world away. So now we sang and stamped and slapped one another on the shoulder for no reason but to delay the hour when we would pocket our cooper's pay and leave this, the palliative of our lives.

It was in one of these pre-payday convivialities that I became acquainted with the cooper Jean, questioning to draw out bits of a personal history that form mosaics of mutual understanding. He was visibly older than I, heavy-set, and with a face which showed perhaps even more buffeting than the floundering sloop which had brought him to America several years ago. Especially noteworthy was his proboscis – an unbelievable enormous, red, cucumber-like appendage with tremendous tax of blood coursing close to its surface. He seemed not self-conscious of its tumidity; indeed, he handled it lovingly, and with a soft, silk handkerchief which always failed just short of engulfing it. Yet, despite the huge quite ridiculous bulb, or perhaps because of it, he was one of the more respected of the master coopers (The *Boomers*, as they called them), the true, the recognized artists of the stave and header.

"Then you will send for you wife and son as soon as you are able?" I asked.

"Yes, soon, when I have a suitable place here, and after I am sure there will be no *Bronze John*. I do not want her to come the same way I did – not steerage."

There was a pause, the minds of us both recalling an interminable voyage, its filth and senseless quarreling, the beastiality of the crew, the water cask whose cloudy contents were disguised from day to day with a new and stronger flavor.

"There is talk that the cholera will not visit us again this summer", he said. "Four years before I arrived – that was in 'thirty-four – there was a plague here such as they hope never to see again. Too horrible to talk about. And yet, there have been a few deaths every summer since. No one knows why. So now you hear talk of the rich, and even the not-so-rich, leaving town, going north for the hot, sticky months to escape it. But they don't leave until early June. That's when the rains and the heat make this old cooperage an oven.'"

Arnold F. Rothmeier

We lifted our bottles again, as though to dispel imagined discomfort.

"You are lucky to be outside so much. Did you do this kind of work before?", he asked.

Then I had my chance to tell of Mssr. Durand's cooperage, the loss of tools, and about hopes that I would soon be allowed to work at a cooper's bench. Jean was patronizing, but by now he was in his cups and weaving a light circle from the waist up. He listened, but not intently, and his eyes wandered. A short while later his eyes glazed and I knew he no longer heard my story.

Presently, a young office worker was among the group, tapping first one, then the other on the shoulder, a sign, seemingly in order of seniority, that their pay was available at the office. So, one by one, each left (the Germans had been first to be paid) and flung a hasty "Portez-vous bien" and an arm toward the group. Since I was lowest in seniority, I was the last to be called for pay. In the office I confronted the same tall yellow tooth and unlit cigar:

"Like the work? Ain't had no complaints about your work, so you can stay if you want." A pause then,

"Oh yea, you was wantin' to do bench work. Well, there ain't no room yet, so…" He shrugged his shoulders. The man had a good face, I thought, only he seemed to want to express himself belittlingly, with demeaning gestures, as though he were frustrated with his own work and wished others to share in his disappointments. He struck me as another of the driving Americans whose characteristics I was beginning to note: their intense activity, their ingenuity and imaginativeness and, sadly, their tendency to allow frenetic activity to displace concern for others.

I pocketed the several gold coins shoved across the pay table, thank-you-ed, and quit the yard.

    A heavy, humid cloak of saturated air awakened me the next morning. A warm drizzle had fallen through most of the night. I rose, donned jacket and shoes and cleared my throat with a few swallows of a thick brandy I had come to require. Its sweetness countered the host of unpleasant tastes in my mouth and I felt again its warm, anaesthetizing vapor. Then came the characteristic warming of the gut, and simultaneously I was stunned, refreshed, and comforted. This morning my brandy had the peculiar effect of opening the drawstrings of thought. Again, I raised the bottle and, without swallowing, lay back upon my pallet. Breakfast could wait. This morning I had vague feelings of dissatisfaction. To go outside meant to risk a soaking. I waited. Rain changed to a heavier drizzle, and I slept. Though I was tardy to work, my absence was not noted.

Chapter 6
Cooper Again

It was mid-May before a change occurred at the cooperage. For weeks the routine and non-exertive monotony, the fragrant white oak essences and Saturday convivialities had lent me strong feelings of belonging. Early spring breezes and sunshine had permitted windows and doors to be left ajar, and there was a newness and brightness to even the heaviest of labor.

This particular Monday was different, however, not simply because it meant a resumption of routine following a week-end of debauchery and excess, but because few had been able to invest in a laborer's much needed sleep. Warm rains driving in from a thousand miles of beach and headlands had kept most Orleanais inside, but these, as well, had suffered from a stagnant, supersaturated humidity. It brought to every home, store, and factory a change, one recognized by older residents as signs of a premature July weather.

By noon there was no change, but there was full sun and a rising skein of mist. Inside the cooperage tempers mounted with the humidity and temperature. It was during these muggy periods that fetid, rancid odors from piles of rotting garbage and slops penetrated to the cooperage. Then even the resin, and pitch, and the wondrously cleaning ethers of white oak could do nothing to cleanse the air, and it lay thick and leaden and must be breathed.

"Pretty bad stink, hein?" Jean noted as I filled his nearly empty bin. "Hey! Don't bite so hard!" He had dropped his champfering knife and slapped smartly at the mosquito on his neck.

I gathered a handful of the thin, oak shavings and daubed at the amazingly large red smear.

"There, that one won't bother you again", I said. "I've never seen them so big. Do they get large like this every year?" Jean's answer was lost in the racket of a darky outside, cursing a contrary mule team and I passed on to the next stave box.

At lunchtime Jean and I were joined by another cooper who volunteered information that there would soon be a change to slack barrels. These were needed to meet a demand for flour containers.

At quitting time this news was general and brought a near-unanimous reaction, for dislike for the slacks was in proportion to the length a cooper had been away from the old country. For most it was a point of pride to finish and head a tight cask; to know, even before bands were tightened, that the barrel would never leak, that it could not be improved upon. Those who had been longest in New Orleans felt a violation of pride when put to this menial apprentice's task.

That evening I lay awake once more, pondering the strangeness of New Orleans, the mixed feelings which the French coopers (for it was rarely that a French cooper exchanged views with a German or an American one) voiced toward a slack barrel. I, myself, had been through slacks in my apprenticeship. With these one worked with the poorest of woods – soft pines and sycamores. No artistry was involved. Feelings of pride, satisfaction, challenge were not possible. The making of slack barrels – for however a short a period – was an affront, just as the sound, coming from beyond the curtain was an affront to my ears. It was a whine, high and insistent. I had heard it before, this treble buzzing annoyance. But this one's life must be short. I hunted it and noted its bloody streak. The Rouenais insects had been pests, I recalled, but these had a disagreeable language, one of persistent voracity. Sleep was late in coming. The tormenting whines beyond the veil penetrated dreams from which I awoke many times – always to the same monotonous mosquito sound.

Just as predicted, an announcement was made the following morning: "There is early need for slack sixty-gallon hogsheads; change over will be immediate". Crisis need for the new barrel was so great that already new material was at each bench. There was no mention of how long the change would endure. What the announcement did not accomplish in depressed-worker spirits, the weather did. As morning sun burned through the heavy mist, the humidity rose to near-unbearable heights. Several shed their shirts, then wore them again when the mosquitoes returned.

The staves which I distributed were lighter, easier to handle. Like husks they were, thin, lacking in substance, and so difficult to work with that curses hung heavy about each bench. By mid-morning I noted two changes. One was loss of the odor of split white oak – without which the overpowering stench became apparent; the other was the empty bench of Jean. He had not appeared and was badly needed. The foreman's face mirrored his irritation.

Nor did Jean appear for work a second day. It was then that I determined to pay him a visit. The cooper's room was an attic high on the rear of a *briquet entre bateaux* on Rue Dauphine and was approached by a rickety outside stepway. There was no response to my knock. I rattled the knob. Now came a response from behind the closed door:

"Are you related to Jean Boudet?"

"No."

"He died of cholera this morning. They took him away around noon."

There was no more to discuss. A lone immigrant was dead; his wife and family, whom he had not seen for three years, waited. Now they would wait even longer for news of his death, for no one would enter his room, let alone rummage for address in the pockets of another cholera victim.

I was to learn that, although there might not be a cholera outbreak such as had occurred in 1837, there were, each year throughout the summers, small outbreaks and isolated deaths attributable to it. Of this they had not told me, neither the sailors at Rouen, nor the coopers at New Orleans.

At work next morning I was approached by the foreman. In tow was a tall colored man.

"Show Ollie here what to do with the staves. You go make slacks at Jean's bench. You can have his tools; he won't be back." He turned abruptly. That was all. Word got about when the cholera began to visit. Jean had been the first of this summer's crop. Other would sicken and most of these would die.

Jean's tools were the finest and moulded to my hands even better than had my own. And though for days the image of Jean, the amiable cooper, lingered on and caused a tear to fall now and then, it was good to feel the fine balance of the champfering knife, the keen, almost exuberant bite of the new drawshare. These were truly fine steel and kept their edges well. My work went fast and I was almost glad my own tools had been stolen.

Though I was now working with slacks, or "dry" barrels, as I must call them, I took such pains to make a tight stave fit that my barrels – with all their unreliability of edge, warp, knots, and susceptibility to moisture change – were almost water-tight. I worked with a kind of frenzy to prove myself. So happy was I to be back at the cooper's bench that I even forgot the demeaning job of having to work with inferior materials. Truly, I was succeeding far beyond even my own expectations with the unruly sycamore staves. They posed no problem, so quickly did my old feel for steel and wood return.

"Don't try to make a wet fit with that lumber!" The foreman had approached and observed me. He had done so surreptitiously, just as he seemed to do everything. His sudden interruption caused me to mar an otherwise well-champferred stave. No reply was necessary. I nodded. The boss seemed satisfied that his new man was a cooper. All he wanted was more barrels, always more. This was the essential change I must adjust to , I mused. Here was no old world solidity; only belief in more product and more money. At Rouen there had been little of the present urgency and none of the disregard for detail and quality which I had met since landing. It would be hard to sluff off those years of attention to fine work. Enough that I must assemble barrel components which no self-respecting French cooper would touch. And my thoughts dwelt upon the words of a man who would prostitute my skill and reduce pride of workmanship. I would work faster then, but I would keep the feeling which always came over me as I assembled well-bevelled edges and watched them press together as the winch created bulge and fit.

Toward closing time of the same day I began to notice an increase in the number of inferior staves placed in my bin. Wood of such inferior quality suddenly appeared that I was hard put to assemble it in any form resembling the crude slacks which would tolerate a frame to hold a lining. I became frantic, wrestling with first one stave, then another, as they bent and unbent like devils challenging and mocking me, clipping, cracking, refusing fit even when assembled and under pressure. Beads of sweat streamed down upon the hated, unpredictable sycamore. It was a living thing that defied me as it sagged here, gave there, gaping at seams so recently champferred. I was turning a clamp with my knee while holding winch and staves with my freed hands when suddenly I became aware of several fellow coopers grouped about. Sly smiles wreathed their faces. The new binboy, Adolphilus, and even the foreman – the latter from a distance – were enjoying my ridiculously frantic efforts to join unjoinable staves and headers. There was laughter and shouting now, as, realizing the good-natured trick that had been played on me, I released my holds. The miserable material flew as an exploded bottle to the floor while my audience howled with glee.

"Say, Claude, if you can't manage with these staves, what will you do when the new sycamore and fir get here?", asked one. Another confessed he had collected all the rejects and near rejects and had had Adolphilus fill my bin with them. Another patted me on the back, saying, "Eef you hadt finally hooped dat von, I vas going to suggest dot de boss put eet oudt front to show dat only de best coopers vork here."

I left the cooperage that afternoon in the company of two of the most respected coopers, and after a bottle of the best vin rouge in a nearby dining area, we parted. It was a different Chana that sought sleep that night. I was at one with myself. I had arrived. Old securities and the feeling of warm comradery had returned. I knew now they respected me. They knew they not only had a master cooper, but that the old unquenchable fire was beneath it all – the thing called principle. it would be the last to go. I felt good, too, about my tools, for now they were mine. And I was flattered that the coopers should accept me and demonstrate acceptance with the creation of a humorous scene. So long, I mused, as I had "les amis de Gaul" about me, the new, the raw, the unfamiliar America would not be so bad.

In the sweltering, mosquito-punctured weeks that followed, a change came over me. I noticed it and welcomed it for it seemed to bring a kind of liberation, as though the presence of so much of it in America bestowed upon me, too, its mantle. The fear and reticence with which I left my native land, I now saw exposed in its contrast with the freedom and fecundity of the new country. I shed my timidity, at least inwardly, as an old garment. Indeed, I bought new clothes, that I might not feel and appear as an impoverished newcomer, but as a proud and skilled craftsman. I moved to quarters less humble and, at length recognizing a vulnerability, opened an account at the handsome Bank des Citoyens and discarded my greasy money belt.

On Sundays I loved to set abroad in the early morning and explore a new section of this fragment of America. One morning it would be a part of the Second Municipality, the new American portion of that curious three-way pie split of a city which in its growing pains besected itself until the sharp split of its language and customs became less frictioned and more assimilable. Another Sunday it would be a long stroll through the park or Congo Square. Once I even made so bold as to mix with the throng boarding a train marked *Carrolton*, and ride, for the thirty-seven and one-half cents, to a lakeside where, in an outdoor concert, the musicians from the St. Charles and Camp Street Theatres performed.

I would walk about the city probing, noting, even when the summer sun was merciless. For the most part, however, I avoided the dirty, congested sections, for the town was lower than its levees. Stagnant ponds, which multiplied even after short rains, reeked of slops, garbage, and small dead animals. One could choose more aromatic routes by passing the great French market, the levee, or the coffee and spice warehouses on Jacquiline Street. Too, now that the warm season had arrived, the wharves were nearly deserted, and for miles one might stroll upon the great bruised timbers and take the clear river airs.

Long Sunday walks, before the street and banquets came alive with church goers and vendors, furnished me with time and mood for laying plans. Captivating as the great town proved, I felt now only as a spectator standing to the side while evidences of the wealth and adventure of America's interior flowed past – or paused to be baled and re-shipped. Daily I saw the representative bits of goods and people fresh from up-river. That they stayed only long enough to be sold, bore heavily upon my musings, and whenever opportunity occurred, I listened and read.

There was a vast and boundless grant of a nation upstream, one so vast and fertile it was humorously said to grunt a little in season, as a birthlike outpouring flooded the wharves and inundated the town. And I sensed an unknown there of succulence and beauty and mystery.

With repeated visits and wanderings, the town grew less strange and people lost much of their earlier coldness and hostility. The lazy slurrings and approximations of Cajun French I would comprehend in time, and what little necessity for English I experienced, I could handle, thanks to early academic proddings at L'ecolle.

The Norman within had stirred me to thrill at the thought of distance and newness. More recently my growing years at home had taught reverence for soil and earthy smells. Superimposed upon such foundations were the more recently learned skills of coopering, which encouraged patience and channeled into domesticity those flights of fancy now being called romantic. Skill now provided the time and leisure for contemplation. My bent was the contemplation of growing things, and I marvelled at the obvious richness of the land.

Arnold F. Rothmeier

My days at the cooperage were now an almost unbroken sameness. Though Jean's death had put a scare into the workers, and though there were other deaths talked about and listed in the *Picayune*, by the end of a torrid August, one which mercifully withheld the tepid, fever-laden rains, the plague, if it were to rise again, would wait another year. But the months of July and August were a trial by fire, and while wrestling with wretched sycamore staves my thoughts often wandered to the cool Seine and its high banks behind Rouen, which even in the warmest weather, steered steady ocean breezes through town. I longed for the cool Norman nights as I lay in a mosquito-punctured sweat behind the baire.

Chapter 7
Jacques

The return to crisp, late September breezes restored some of the old seasonal rhythm and renewed in me a feeling of time and change. Mosquitoes vanished overnight when a light frost slickened the banquets and cobbles in late October. But as the weeks passed, it became obvious that winter would be only a wet chain of months lashed together by flashes of sun and the languor of benign breezes. There would be none of the bone-chilling cold which formed so large a part of my memory of Rouen winters.

Despite the ease and interest with which life flowed at New Orleans, I was not satisfied. More and more inclination led me of a week-end to the wharves with their view of the great Mississippi and the often mist-clouded vistas upstream. Downstream I could see the equally misty way the *Zotow* had come, but this was not the route for me. Not only could I not contemplate a return trip, but the thought of ocean-going ships and their confinement repelled me, and I often looked steadfastly in the direction of higher ground – toward the source of the muddy restless waters.

Arnold F. Rothmeier

Was it the miserably weak change of season that caused this stirring? Was it a lonesomeness that cried out for something greater than companionship in a country reeking with companionship? Did the crowds in New Orleans, with their obvious gregariousness and hilarity make me feel conscious of my oneness? Or, was I restless because of the soul-crushing frustrations at my cooper's bench where I was compelled to relinquish all my inbred desire for satisfaction through perfect work and take, in its place, more and more of the same? Was I then, at thirty, so full of a restlessness that residence, for more than a few months in any one place, was stagnation and slow death?

The weeks at Mssr. Gobin's cooperage wore themselves into months. The humid, breathless season passed at last on the wings of a tropical windstorm of such intensity as to peel slate from roofs and pile huge ships in a sodden mass against lighter river craft and wharves. The cooperage lost many of its barrels to damage and kiting. The huge slacks fell from their neat stacks at first gusts and rolled and tumbled by the hundreds to a lot corner where successive batterings lifted them like so much chaff, sliding them over a wooden peneplain of other staves and debris and over the high enclosure. Mssr. Gobin recovered but a few of his wandering casks, and it was two weeks before the yard stacked again its barrels and staves. The city and wharves were even slower to heal, and stoven roofs and tangled ships remained a common sight for many months.

By mid-November a delicious hint of coolness filled my morning strolls to the cooperage. The sun no longer built its stifling wall of heat, but rose with a benevolent coolness as though penitent for past ravages. Then, by mid-December, a tropical winter set in , and for many months the soft, low gray swept in from the Algiers side of the river, drenching the town. The wharves were alive again. They had stood almost empty during the warm season, and the huge but incongruously dove-like steamboats stood massively elegant, glistening and steaming for their up-river boarders.

I paused often for these sights, as, heedless of the rain, my mind drew a veiled picture of the mysteries in the foggy distance. I saw myself again the traveler, standing on foredeck, waiting for new cities and sights that lay around a next meander.

Seasonal change also brought changes at the cooperage. The unusually abundant wheat crop which had been responsible, in part, for work in the slacks now had the belated side effect of creating a need for barrels to contain rum and whiskey made form the surplus. Overnight work benches were made ready for the fragrant white oak. Coarse drawknives disappeared and sharpening tools appeared to keep a good edge on fine steel.

A buoyant feeling of optimism showed among the coopers, who, not waiting for the busy stave boy to replenish their box, readied tools and brought in an arm load of the wood without being bidden. The good staves were placed gently in their boxes with a feeling close to reverence. Fine wood again; fine tools in the hand again; the stench of sycamore and gum replaced by the satisfying, penetrating fragrance of aged white oak.

Even the stave boy, tall and thin like a stave himself, seemed relieved and happy with the change back, as though to apologize for quality and odor these past months. A tune ventured forth now and then, the old lilting rhythms of the countrysides of Loire and Alsace. Occasionally one of the German workers would begin one of the more somber ballads of his countrymen and a passer-by might note more than one Gallic cooper impressed by the tune and humming it himself.

I was delighted with the change-over and radiated some of my feelings in conversation when room was made for a new bench and another cooper. The new worker was older then I, obviously French, heavily bearded, and walked with a decided limp.

Arnold F. Rothmeier

"This is your lucky day," I began. "You join us just as we begin again to make fine barrels. We worked with those sycamore splits and knots for three months in hot weather. Now we can all become coopers again."

The man's eyes reflected an odd animal-like intentness, an honest but shifting alertness. As we introduced ourselves and bent to our jobs, it became clear that the man, Jacques Dubois, was less skilled than most, that he knew and felt his lack.

Late in the afternoon as quitting gong sounded, Jacques turned to me and, in a tone almost supplicating, asked, "You will share a bottle of wine with me?"

A leanness, a hollow intentness seemed never to leave his face, even as I answered. Was the remaining stamp an impression from some great misfortune met with fortitude? Whatever the cause, its strain, mirrored in rigid facial muscles, rode his face like a plague.

"Avec Plaiser". I found I slipped more often back into the French now. I had fought the tendency and been rewarded with the feeling of naturalness and mastery while scanning the English side of the *Picayune*.

Then, as we left the cooperage, I was made conscious of my companion's decided limp, and slowed to accommodate to his labored stride.

We chose one of the cleaner bistros not far from the great French market and settled back. Our burgundy had a softness about it today as was so often the case on cooler days.

"Have you followed coopering long?", I asked.

"Only since losing my toes. It's hard being on my feet so long, but if my work is acceptable, I will get a stool to use part time."

He seemed, at first, reluctant to speak of his misfortune. But the wine warmed us and we approached a decorous loquacity. With Jacques the drink seemed a catharsis, but even though his voice slowly lost a hurried, furtive quality I had noted earlier, his facial mask remained one of expectant stealth, never relaxing. Indeed, it seemed to war with the relaxing effects of his drink.

"I was born in Quebec", he continued. "My mother and father were scalped and slit open by the Nez Perce and I was cared for by the mother of a large family. I helped by trapping and later, when eighteen and wanted to see more of the country, I helped load bales of fur and went to St. Louis. This is when I became a real trapper. I signed on with the American Fur Company and, after four years of helling up my take around the rendezvous, I had the bad luck to get caught in a bad snow. By the time I reached the camp I knew I would lose something." His face seemed to lose some of it rigidity. "But I'm glad it was my toes and not fingers." He stared at this open hand with a half fierce, half astonished look and flexed fingers worn and scarred.

"But you will go back to the woods, no?"

"Yes and no. This living is easy. When I got back to St. Louis I couldn't believe how the place had grown in five years. New little places had come alive farther west, too. I heard tell of settlements called Westport and Independence and Chouteau's Landing that hadn't even a name to spot their location a few years before. Yes, I suppose I'll go back." His eyes lost more of their concentrated fierceness and I beckoned for another bottle.

"But for a while I just want to work and live a little. Competition for beaver is getting' fierce and market is down. While I had my toes I could get around fast and safe. I would have to do it all on horse now, or hobble too slow. But, if I do go back, it'll be to coopin' or tradin'."

It was odd, I reflected, this blend of careless, backwoods speech and French inflection, made more curious by a growing thickness of alcoholic speech. The liquor had made both of us stupid and unsteady when we rose to leave, but the concentrated fierceness never left the trapper's eyes. We parted at the small river front boardinghouse near where I had lost my tools.

In the next few months I found I had much in common with Jacques. He helped me whenever there was opportunity. Though from widely different backgrounds, we both disliked (as did most of the old Creole element of New Orleans) the American tendency to put a fixed price on everything. The need to bargain, as generations for hundreds of years had done, ran strong in our veins. We revelled in the power and skill of our hands, and we shared a sense of accomplishment and pride in fine workmanship, and neither would leave a cask until its staves sheared precisely with each other. Too, we shared a love – infrequently mentioned, but intensely felt – for the forest and growing things, for the fecund earth and the bud, pregnant and naked on limb tip. We hared a love for the red-raw beauty of the tropical flower.

Occasionally we would visit the opera, sitting high in the uppermost balcony, enjoying the secondary drama, too, in which the audience showed its pleasure or displeasure. Stormy receptions of the singers were never dangerous, for things thrown, including bottles, were always cast down or across, never up. Then, if the opera was especially stimulating and the wine which we had drunk had sufficiently pickled our inhibitions, we would enter the halls of Madame Cheri and burn in the carnal charms of one of her harlots.

Neither of us had married, nor had either of us ever contemplated marriage. I, because in my France it had been unthinkable that a family could live supported in any other way than by the land. So I had surrendered early the hope of marriage when my older brother took a wife and assumed many of my aging father's duties. Jacques' reason was, as he put it, that he could take it from the squaw of his choice simply by pressing her into the grass.

But always, whether Jacques told of rutting or rattlesnakes, there was that look of intense, hunted fierceness in his eyes. It was as though, in forsaking his reeling from river to mountain, his soul had been invaded by the savagery of the animals, and as though he partook of their eternal alertness and gnawing hunger, their steel-like decisions and sudden action. And I wondered in secret if I, too, might not acquire that same repelling fierceness if I were, one day, to pry into this vast and private continent. I wondered and thought about the things I had seen come down river – the odd keelboats, the produce that seemed to gush from the unloading barges, the lasciviously bellowing, belligerent crowd of men, the pipe-smoking women, naked, unwiped children. And I pondered the slick, greasy deerskin clothing, the long rifles, and the Jacques-like fierceness of the bearded faces of those who held them.

I read the *Picayune* accounts of the trading trains to Sante Fe for silver and caught a vision of the staggering immensities of space in my new world; of the opportunities that lay upriver and westerly. Beaver, said Jacques, was yet to be trapped, but was thinning. Of course, Jacques' stories of all those buffalo was pure fabrication, but still, they must be very numerous – here and there.

Jacque's tales of Indians and their gullibility at lonely trading posts fascinated me. This I could understand, for the Choctaw were numerous in the streets of New Orleans, and their need for the novel and gaudy seemed never to cease. The ferment within me, caused by these stories, lent so prosaic an air to my occupation that at times it seemed I could almost wish that I had no skill at all. I felt ensnared, that life was outside the cooperage walls and ceased at the gate.

Arnold F. Rothmeier

There was an almost irresistible lure to distances up the muddy churn of the Mississippi, and I felt that their penetration would revitalize my life.

We returned to slacks and their hated sycamore staves.

Chapter 8
Double Disaster

In the end it was a double disaster that liberated me from the job I had come to loathe, and that sent me northward along an unfamiliar river where tests of strength and will and cunning waited.

The new summer, which so many had predicted would be another for *Bronze John*, arrived. With it came a shocking stench of decaying matter that accumulated along low edges of town and in sumps. Warm nights, the prison created by the barre, and the monotonous drone of angry mosquitoes just outside it made sleep a near-futile effort.

One night, to add to my restless discomfort, they managed to invade the sheltered space, and I itched myself raw. The following morning I looked, with vindictive satisfaction, at the long and bloody smears, where the heavily engorged devils had streaked themselves under my blows.

At any rate, I mused, there would be drinking and singing to end the work week. The lack of challenge with slacks had come to be a little less annoying. It had been more than a year since the change-over, and the job was now just a thing to get done. The flow of air after working a few hours in the morning was anticipated with relish. Occasionally, even the Germans joined in with the French songs, though from a distance.

By the time a Saturday quota of barrels was reached, it was later than usual and I felt the need of a bottle. I attributed my slight indisposition to the fact that we had worked on through lunch hour and drunk heavily. But song and banter were not in me today. I broke off, and without waiting for pay – which I could postpone – sought my room. There, on my pallet, I stared at the ceiling, thoughts spinning unaccountably; madly. Tools, vegetables, boats, barrels, trappers – all mixed in a confused miscellany of imagined pictures, yet none would focus save one: Through beads of sweat, which now coursed my forehead, my fevered eye could make out only the face of Jacques.

"Something told me to look in on you, Claude."

He clapped a rough hand to my forehead.

"You're sick of the fever. Hold on while I get something." Then he was gone.

I could never clearly recall occurrences of the next seven days. Jacques said later that I was out of my head and fought him, and that since he could not hold me for medicine, he had had to tie me, like a madman, hand and foot, and pry my teeth ajar.

"It was then that you fought me," he said. "You rolled and kneed me in the back while I sat on your belly and poured in the bitters. The whole first bottle went on your face, or you spat it up. You never drank any of the first, so I left and got another pint. Then I pinched your nose and you had to swallow." What Jacques didn't tell was the hopeless panic he felt when he tested my burning face, and fed me liquids as the black vomit came again and again, drenching the blankets to a sodden, stinking disarray. What he saved until I had fully recovered was his ultimate feeling of despair when, after a brief doze sometime during the second night, he awoke to find blood oozing from my nose and gums.

Around the ninth day of my confinement I awoke without nausea, but with a dizziness which, when I attempted to stand, sent me reeling against the wall. As though from a nausea-coated cloud, my maimed senses struggled to return me to old patterns. Long before my red and swollen eyes brought the room and Jacques into focus, it was the sense of smell that repulsed me, set up waves of revulsion that shook me willy-nilly as one shakes from prolonged cold. I lay in filth and vomit. Movement, periodic and violent, stirred old coursings of the blood within me, brought pressures and pain to bone and muscle needing a longer sleep. I would move a hand and find it so painful an operation that I would cease. The simple act of moving a finger was excruciating, and prodding thought in long-dormant mental equipment set my head throbbing with the effort.

Jacques said little, seeming to sense my myriad aches and the adjustments I must make in order to mend. Nor did I regain my former voluble self until long after I took, first, a little wine and thick broth, and later, much later, stood and staggered a few steps, only to fall exhausted across the pallet.

It was twelve days from the onset of cholera to the day when I felt steady and strong enough to descend the three steps and stagger a few, tentative feet. Then, it was several more days before I could note a faint promise of returning strength.

Jacques never told me all he did during my days of delirium: the forcible restraint, the retching that seemed to rend and tear the gut, the days of black vomit, or that his – Jacques' – hand was bandaged because a madman's teeth had bitten to the bone in frantic resistance to the liquids. Neither, for a long time, did he tell that on the very morning that I had opened my eyes and rallied, he had left to arrange for a pauper's burial. "Lord you was sick," was Jacques' simple statement. "And if it hadn't been for the medicine, you'd never a made it!"

In mid-September I returned to the cooperage. My tools were being used by another worker and were grudgingly relinquished, as though fate had not done right in allowing me to live. Those at neighboring benches regarded my return as something of a miracle, and they shook hands as though to pump me full of new life. For they knew how few lived to tell of their illness, and they knew of fewer still who returned to work. But there had been no other sickness at the mill, and there had been only the usual and normal hundred or so in all New Orleans who had been laid low.

The mirror showed me a cadaverous image and my pants were now slack in waist and legs. But it was the tool grip that frustrated me most. The one thing I needed most for long smooth edges was a firm grip. For weeks my hold would slacken and tool would clatter to the floor. There would be bevelled gouges to repair, and always, it seemed, neighboring glances were half-condescending. Were they hoping that I – that no one – could pass through such fires of fever and depths of debility and still find renewal at the cooper's bench?

But despite muscle pain and frustration I hardened. Each day began with the same nausea, as though promising relapse; each morning was a new encounter with weakness that required physical effort for standing, clenching, shoving, drawing, thinking. Each operation was a glutton, demanding more of my puny strength.

By the end of the third week, it was apparent to me, as well as to the others, that there would be no relapse, that my body had rebounded and that I was again fit. Appetite returned with the fierceness of a hibernant bear, and I brought to work, wrapped in

Picayunes, great quantities of bread and meat, and I worked them down each noon with a full quart of Burgundy, blood-red and full-bodied.

"That is how the trapper eats," said Jacques one noon. "He eats sometimes half a deer, and carries it in his belly instead of on his back. A few chips of dried meat are enough between times to keep the stomach from complaining, and dried meat runs low, he has a belt or moccasin. But the moccasins either warm the feet or the belly. They can not do both. I warmed the belly – and lost my toes."

"What is it like to live so far from people and towns? Is it…"

He interrupted: "Claude, out there you can get just as close or as far away from those things as you want." Jacques' fierce eyes lost their hunted look for a moment as though searching for something in the wilderness of his thoughts.

"They keep pushing farther west and bringing what they need – or think they need. And always there's somebody has more than he needs and starts a little store. Always there's somebody who can do what nobody else can, and starts a smithy or a bootery. But generally they live off the land, hunt, plant a little, have a few hogs. Folks come from a hundred miles to St. Louis to sell their truck – just like they come here. And as long as they stays near the settlements or trading posts, they can live like kings – and safe, too."

On he went. I listened, not with the ears of one hearing a curious tale, but now with those of a student, an apprentice. For, in the confinement and silence of the sick room, a need to go – to leave New Orleans – had been born. The new, the yet unseen reaches of the Mississippi touched and tugged at my imagination. They rose before my eyes in an irresistible newness and splendor.

The cooperage – with its monotonous quotas of slacks to assemble each day – now seemed a prison to which I returned each morning and from which, at the end of each dreary day, I received a reprieve. I knew that I would soon go, and that in my mind there was building such loathing for the prostituting of my craft that I might leave coopering forever. So now I talked to Jacques for information: How would I go, how far, what I should expect of the weather, the people, chances for employment.

Memory of the scent of the tired French soil came to me as I strolled about of a Sunday. It was now October, a time when my father's small vineyard and potato ground would be lying fallow, resigned to another winter, and gathering, in some mysterious way the growth needs for spring. But here, in New Orleans, spring was perennial! Planters were working now as though they expected no change, but that they would swing eternally from one growing season into another. The thought of a succession of crops to where man was chained to a land that burgeoned, fecund and lavish, season after season, seemed to me an imposing, masterful earth. It seemed one greedy and demanding, one that lacked normal, seasonal activity and rest. Yet, the very thought of an earth so demanding and interminable productive was, somehow, revolting; like a woman who demanded hot, successive love, the while giving forth progeny in ever increasing numbers.

The reek of the countryside's fecundity seemed present everywhere. It fumed daily from the marketplace in a thousand essences; it was present in the musty aura of the darky, laughing and sweating himself into obscurity as he threw his grunting weight against yet another bale; it came in the flaccid evening breezes that soughed across river and bayou and hung in airy layers like invisible aromatic sandwiches; and around misty bogs undisturbed by the river breeze, one might even choose which layer or scent he wished to enjoy.

There was here no awakening to spring nor slumbering to winter, but only an eternal burgeoning of growth and a constancy of temperature that palled, with its endless, unbroken suitability for growth. It was as if every leaf cried out for rest from division and multiplication; that always, below, in the teeming mould, was a black power that pushed grass and bush and tree into being before its due season with a kind of indecent subterranean urging. It spawned such a luxury of green that one could hardly recognize an area for growth, a week after passing. And of an evening, the juices massing within plantain and oleander were almost audible. To be surrounded by so much verdure, rampant and heavy, was like being imbedded in an enormous fragment of jade or emerald, veined by trunks and branches, and encased in a sky of the same gem-like intensity.

There was no one day when I can be said to have determined upon leaving. Indeed, I had little to do with the process. The weeks I had spent near death had caused me to hear the voices that speak in periods of crises and enforced inactivity, and I neither fought nor cooperated with them. But hour after hour as I applied my tools automatically to the hated slacks, my mind gently, insistently nursed the notion of moving on. The where was not the issue, but the name of St. Louis struck comforting chords in my Galic, Catholic nature. There would be other emigres, other Frenchmen there. They did not all remain in New Orleans. I would stand at times, staring at a particular warped or unsuitable stave, and tabulate, as upon a ledger, the merits of an immediate departure. It was mid-November. The weather was right, and even if it were cold upriver as Jacques had said, there would be quarters in town. My thoughts flew back to the comfort of the bank account. I had not paid much attention to it lately, but even with the monthly sending home of fifty or sixty francs, I must have more than a thousand dollars in the account. It was comforting, a small source of added security, a biscuit to be nibbled come famine. I put the thing easily from mind. I had no plans for expenditures, though vague thoughts of owning a small store or cooperage had crossed my mind as I had listened to Jacques.

In the end, the decision was made for me. Whether by poorly

extinguished coals on the charring line, or by a disgruntled incendiary, neither I nor anyone else ever knew. On Saturday night we sang and drank as usual. On Monday me heart sank at sight of the black, ashy desolation that had been a cooperage. I slowly unlimbered the bundle of small implements I had taken home to sharpen. They were all that remained of my tools – or those of others. Fire had destroyed their tempers and they would be discarded. I turned abruptly, walked to the bank. I withdrew my savings, tucked them into a new money belt, and tied drawshave and a few pans and clothes into a tight bedroll. At the Girod Street Landing my steamboat, the *Henry Bly* swung wide at precisely one o'clock and plowed a slow path upriver.

Pan The Low Waters

Chapter 9
Paddle Wheeler

A curious mixture of relief and uncertainty teased me as I stood on the baggage-strewn main deck, letting pulse of the motor spread into my feet and thighs. The *Henry Bly* was a stern-wheeler, and for a fleeting moment, gazing at the powerful drive and push, I recalled how the system worked in reverse in the mills near Rouen – the force of water used to drive a wheel - as here it pushed water from the vessel. Thoughts and schemes. They were as dreams; how few materialized! I was loose, floating in a new country, slowly approaching the center of a vast and only partially explored continent. I wondered at my audacity, took silently the blame, and succumbed to the pull of the unknown.

How different was this placid, forward throbbing from the uncertain trail of the *Zotow*! How different the accommodations! Presently all would dine at tables already being prepared. I had seen them from the gangway window, as had most of the other passengers while they strolled about on their new ship-world.

As odors of crab and venison filled the companionway, my memory

Arnold F. Rothmeier

locked upon a scene on the deck of the *Zotow* nearly two years past. It had followed a stormy, confining, but now windy and clearing morning. Many of the passengers, after two stormy days in a foul-smelling hold, were attempting to cook potatoes. The stoves were miserable benches of stones and sand on open deck upon which were placed bits of paper and cloth to ignite faggots grudgingly doled out by the first mate. No system of priorities had been attempted for mothers to cook first, and a jostling for place was accepted as the best method. One émigré a short distance ahead in line, who, like most of the rest, patiently balanced his food and swung unsteadily to the ship's pitch, imagined he saw an affront to the pale young lady ahead. There was a murmur, audible over the ship's creak and sail flap, and in a moment two men were seen battering each other. Since the ship's motion caused them to slip and fall, they were unable to accomplish much in the way of retaliation, and it was not long before the aggressor, a stocky Pole, became abashed and apologetic when the young lady, during a momentary pause in battle, was able to inform the Pole that her honor had not been sullied.

I wondered about those passengers. None aboard the *Zotow*, including the captain, had known exactly at which American port we would land. None had really cared, since, for most, escape was the thing, escape from a land which could no longer feed them, could no longer mete out land sufficient to support life. I had not seen a single shipmate in the two years I had been in New Orleans. It was as though they had all returned to Europe, died, or had been swallowed up in the immensity of America.

I slept to the sound of throbbing motors and to the soothing surge of water. Sleep stayed but a little while, however, for the new sound bore in upon me, tore me from my bed. I jacketed and left the stateroom. This was, actually, no more than a closet, built peripherally to a central dining room, and so abbreviated in length and width that a fall from the bunk would have entangled me in the tiny chair and chamber pot on a rail-like table against the opposite wall. Indeed, were it not for the bunk, raised to a point shoulder high, there would have been no room for activity of any sort.

Outside, on the boiler deck, an evening mood enveloped me, swathed my senses with a hundred fruity scents, clothed me in the bittersweet musk of trees bruised and torn by the massive current. There was little to suggest motion, for the boat had geared massively, and the moon, low on the river fringe showed an imperceptible forward motion on a ribbon of water so smooth it might have been a lake of mercury.

But for the secure rail beneath my hands and a solid deck floor, all was as it had been for untold centuries – primitive, changeless. But how changeable it must now become, I mused with steamboats bringing new life upstream to any point on a shore that stretched its thousands of miles to the very heart of the country at St. Louis. The act of leaving behind the civilization of New Orleans had not impressed me at first. But now the barrenness of the distant shoreline bore in upon my consciousness, and a feeling of being on the front line, the frontier, of the primitive unknown, smote me. Was I a wanderer, too, as so many of the Kaintucks and Pikes seen and heard on the levee? In time would I, too, boast and swagger with their sophistication?

Twilight on the Mississippi. Time to heave to and wait for a new sun. Time to light torches, to wood up! Time to watch the performances of the steerage crew – the alienated group on the cargo deck who earned passage by wooding up!

Ahead, around another wide, sweeping bend, a fire was burning. Dim figures rose like dervishes, shouting and waving brimmed hats. "Hyartiz! Hyartiz!" was all they seemed to be saying. Then as the boat edged toward the fire, I could make out the uniform cords of fresh-cut oak and gum. Below, a mate's voice range out metallically. "Turn out! Turn out! Wood lot! Turn out!"

Arnold F. Rothmeier

The *Henry Bly* swung easily into the firelight. A sound of chains, shouts and oaths brought stage planks smacking onto a muddy bank, and with still stronger oaths from the mate, a more organized dervish began. Sweat-gleaming bodies of the rousters sulked and swayed aboard with load after load until, hours later, from my bunk I caught the terminating bellow of the mate and slept again to the powerful paddle rhythm.

Despite the midnight interruption of my sleep I awoke early and went on deck. I was alone. Morning mist lay like an infintely soft shawl over the river and flowed in rent streamers behind the paddle house. A vagrant flock of red-winged blackbirds rose high to catch the sun which even now was lightening the river mist. The world was virginal, primordial.

Odors of the new continent overwhelmed me and I exhaled quickly for another heady breath. Yet, when I drew the second breath, the first wondrous odor faded, and subsequent breaths were sterile. Like so many of the sensations of life, I thought. We reel from one to the next, and none is ever like the first, but tarnished or utterly barren: so like the bittersweet musk of bruised willow that would not come again.

Standing thus alone, I experienced, with a pleasant shock, the realization of a new element in my personality: an ability to reflect and ponder had surfaced. I had just had the experience of having philosophic thoughts, and the effect was as heady as had been the bruised musk of the willows. But though I stood there before the awesome beauty of a new-breaking day, I could neither recall the wisdom of the revelation, nor call again the sense of pride which the philosophical pondering engendered.

I stood long on a gently surging bow that oozed slowly through interminable forests, and took stock of my position and of a life change upon which I had embarked. At no time before leaving L'Havre had I pushed myself beyond a point of no return. Even on the *Zotow* I had not felt beyond my depth. Now, I had embarked upon another voyage, known only to a relative handful of people since my countrymen rafted the Mississippi a hundred years ago. I experienced a feeling of letting go, a sensation of stepping out beyond depth, a pioneering that made me one with Jacques and the other rugged souls against whom I had brushed on the levee.

The sensation did not suggest in me a shrinking from danger or from the unknown; but rather the welcome possibiltiy of meeting many small dangers and surprises; the standing to test to see how I would react. Though not of the country, I felt immeasurably more in command than when a raw Frenchman from the *Zotow's* hold. There was an infection about in this new land; I had caught it, and it had subtly altered my way of thinking. I felt bold and self-reliant. And I could feel a deep, inner satisfaction in succumbing to the tug of the wilderness around me. But, I thought, I must stay out of the way of those who know what they are about, these others who have been here much longer that I. I must appear capable to all and be eternally alive to dangers, for those whom I have seen in trouble have ignored this caution; there is a conspiracy against the weak and I am not the strongest.

As it became light, the monotonous gray of the bank gave way to a green brilliance. A kind of ship's routine asserted itself, much as at sea. Bells sounded; there was a sleepy emergence of those who desired breakfast. It was pleasant to sample warm food and return to the open deck with a tart or two, a drink, and a pipe. Surprising how smoothly things went aboard. Word had somehow gotten about that one of the women riding steerage had given birth the previous evening and that both mother and child were well. I remembered my days aboard the *Zotow*, and had smuggled from the table a few extra pieces of bread and meat. Though the *Henry Bly* was not large, as Mississippi steamers went, there was an interesting fare.

I was often a listening post for talk of upriver towns, particularly

St. Louis. One could not help being informed of the town as we approached the upper reaches. Passengers were prodigal with their information and I listened to it all as though receiving the strictest of confidences. To a man, all spoke of St. Louis as the great repository for furs brought from mysterious distances to the north and west.

Chapter 10
St. Louis

Five days and four nights was the time frame necessary to deposit me on the docks of St. Louis. I immediately bought a newspaper and set about finding a temporary room. My determination not to repeat losses suffered at New Orleans amounted almost to a reflex. Afterward, I would walk about the let the town and its people make their impressions on me. The paper was all in English. I would have to try harder now, for there were no translations as in the *Picayune*.

Beyond its docks and wharves, St. Louis rose above the river on two bench-like levels, well drained and laid out. Though a town now as large as New Orleans, neither had it the sticky gumbo for streets, nor the smells of rotting refuse which had hung low in the streets and clung to the clothes. It was to this first bench-like strip that I ascended. It was not that the dock area rooming houses looked unclean, but that I wished to better my situation and felt that I could not do so were I to begin with quarters amid unpredictable transients.

Among the passengers on the trip up, the name of Chouteau had been often mentioned, along with the names of other Frenchmen. Not only were some of these said to be well-to-do, but they were said to have led out in the city's improvements, that they employed considerable numbers in trades and businesses, and that they encouraged an approved social life, with balls, musicales, and the theatre.

There were few negroes about, but many Indians, and both the streets and the landings were in marked neat contrast to those of the gulf city. Though I could hear French spoken now that then, it seemed that most spoke a hurried, slurred English with which I had wrestled so long. Too, there was an air of greater purposefulness, and less time seemed allowable for such things as dickering and buying. There was little of the distracted saunter that characterized Canal Street. Though phaetons and drays were about, here they pulled their loads or passengers with more reasonable speed.

From my perch atop a large rock, I could see much of the town. To the right and left ran Main Street, with its stores, beetling and squat, or with false fronts preposterously out of proportion. Did the one with the widest façade and display attract the most business, I wondered? I sought a rooming house address noted in the *Inquirer*.

The building lay one street removed from Market. It was a boarding house – the last room without board having been taken two days before. I was to have a small cubicle to the right of the front entrance and to receive a light breakfast and evening meal for twenty dollars per week. Though this was somewhat more than I felt I could afford, I agreed to board for a week. Leaving my bedroll I then promised to return with payment within an hour. Observation of life in the new country had made me excessively cautious, and I was anxious to deposit the contents of my money belt as soon as possible without displaying its contents. I was money-conscious, and perhaps justifiably so, for I had been frugal at the cooperage, and now carried close to eight hundred dollars – all in ten-dollar New Orleans dixies, and another two hundred in gold, so well hidden in the hollow handle of a tool that only its weight told it held the cache.

Pan The Low Waters

After having been suitably receipted for most of the one thousand dollars, I returned to Mrs. Sharp's boarding house, paid the week's rent, and was advised that the evening meal would be served at six. My arrival back had coincided with that of another boarder who opened the door and nodded me through. Then, proceeding along the bare, raw wood corridor, the man led me to a kind of waiting room filled with half a dozen chairs and the warm vapor of frying steak and boiling peas.

Expectedly enough, the stranger began with, "Been in St. Louis long?" I responded, and warmed to his manner and smile. He was a few years older than I and had stopped off in the city to make a few purchases, having come down river some days before on a flatboat with marketable abundance from his acres far up on the Ohio. Of these he spoke with lavish pride: of his bottom land and apples and cider press, of the seeds which he bought each year from a curious and excessively pious people called "Shakers", who sold and bartered along the river; how he filled his barns and cellars year after year with increasing yield; how they – his wife and two sons – lived upon the previous season's bounty, even after the next season's plenty filled barn and cellar.

The man so intrigued me with the fecundity of his farm that I had failed to note the entry of Mrs. Sharp's other boarders. By the time her little daughter came to tell us dinner was ready, I was in the midst of enthusiastic conversation with several other male boarders. How they could have entered, with their heavy boots pounding on bare, plank flooring, and have missed my notice, was a tribute to both the farmer's enthusiasm and to the chords within me upon which his narrative played. We continued to talk – rather, he to talk and I to listen – as we ate. But while I found that my fascination with the farmer's tale could exclude the thud of boots, it could not prevent my sense of taste from informing me there was something wrong with the way the cook had prepared her meat. And had I not been famished, I should have eaten but little. The food was tasteless, except for the penetrating rancidity of its cooking oil. Portions of the meat had been burned; the steaks though abundant and stacked high on huge platters, were stringy and tough; the half-cooked peas offered an unexpected and annoying resistance.

Though the food quality tempted me to try for a better situation, I had found the boarders fascinating. In addition to the plump and perpetually murmuring Mrs. Sharp, who seemed to feel no necessity to apologize for her cooking, there were a father with two hunkering, teen-age sons, a French trapper, and a trader shopping for his Westport post.

All were recent arrivals, each a transient, a passer-through, like myself, caught up in the newness and vastness about him, where few had, or seemed to want, roots; where only the thrill of uncertainty was real, and where life that reached not to the livid tip of the heated iron was no life at all. These were the men of that point, the ragged and the daring, the front rank and scouts, the first to seek and make contact. Each seemed one to breast a tide that shattered barriers to the new country. And I was now among them.

The boarders pulled me eagerly into their conversation – all but the taciturn father and his hunkering sons, who filled their mouths as though to somehow plug the exit of sound.

"Plenty of plew if'n you know whar to go. Me, I'm agoin after buffalo hides along the Platte."

"Wissht I knew something to do, like cooperin'. Is it hard to larn?"

"Winter's gonna be a hard one, an' early. Don't yet know whar I'm gonna stay, but…"

I listened, learned, and occasionally managed a question. St. Louis was just about the end of the road west. A few outposts lay scattered along the Missouri, stretching to a landing called Independence. But that was the very end. And no one went further, for no one was permitted even to trade beyond the Missouri without written government permission. Much of the talk, coming fast from one, slow from another, and all interspersed with woodsy idioms, was confusing. I was able to gather the broad picture and sensed general contours of the situation here and beyond, but that was all.

Of the eight, the trader was by far the most outgoing and informative. He seemed attracted to me, and I to him. This was in part, at least, because his English was more understandable than that of the rest. I noted also that he was listened to. He was more on the "Qui vive", heard more, was able to draw better conclusions because of information that came over the counter at his post. Through him emerged a confused picture of a brawling, teeming frontier space filled with entrepreneurs, soldiers, and malcontents, all bent on pushing back the Indians, some of whom had already been pushed back and resettled from hundreds of miles east of the Mississippi.

He drew a picture which brought malevolent glances from the old man and his sons – of intrigue and greed and advantage-taking not pleasant to hear – of the susceptibility of the savage to bad whisky, and of their resultant degeneracy. The whole picture, now that I was hundreds of miles closer to it, came into focus. In retrospect, my life in the sweltering, disease-laden atmosphere of New Orleans had been a troubled one, had had its share of uncertainties – nearness of theft and death. But with the recital of my friend the trader, all these took on a softness, a dim romantic color that was almost nostalgic. All about me in New Orleans had been the sharpie, the cut-purse. But the milieu had been one of sodden plenty and where all about were means for sustaining life.

Now, as the trader's words poured from him I caught, between phrases, a scene disconcertingly contrasting between the two towns. How, I thought, could a few hundred miles make such a difference?

Arnold F. Rothmeier

And, could whites actually have deliberately sown the seeds that destroyed half a nation of Arikawas? The old man and his two sons, in one of his garrulous moments had boasted of their record kill: three thousand buffalo – for five cents per tongue, and fifty cents a hide, with the remains left to create such a tide of stench as to make a breath of pure air an intoxication.

Creatures such as these fare badly in this life without that half of their personality, which deals in enlargements. Yet the brutality and blandness of their boasts left me with no alternative but to believe their gasconade. I found an excuse to go to my room. Upon returning I was relieved to find the trio gone and the other reading newspapers.

I should have sat in the dining room and tried to digest some of the impressions, had not the trader, who seemed anxious to continue my frontier education, been in his chair. Since my experience in the new country seemed prosaic, I smoked and listened. He chewed an unlit cigar, and from the other end of his valve-like lips came the words, cooly convincing, that would influence heavily the next two years of my life:

"St. Louis' a good place to get you a good start. Then, when you have a few thousand, you can set yourself up along the river where the Indians and settlers would rather come than go all the way into St. Louis and pole back, and make yourself a good living on the hides they take during the winter. Beavers are scarce, and beside, the east don't want 'em for hat felt no more. But mink and coon and deer still bring good prices. And theys so many buffalo, looks like they'll go on forever."

His description of prospects sounded good to me, and I sat listening to him far into the night. His voice – or one very like it – intrigued my thoughts long after I turned in, building possibilities. Like a skein of yarn were my thoughts in the morning when I awoke to the deep-throated sound of a departing steamboat. Only a slight mental tug was necessary to review the numerous possibilities which had occurred to me as I passed from wake to sleep, unravelling the trader's words.

They had stirred something within me – a chord of my Norman forbearers, perhaps. They had given me a glimpse of possibilities I had not seen before. I saw St. Louis as the waist of a nation stirring to press into country new and bright and westerly where canyon and plain stretched into mystery and inviting grandeur; where all was new and virgin as the great sea depths or the world beyond life. I was moved as by a dream and my life now began to rotate slowly about an as yet unformulated urge. The mists and odors of the river promised it; the brilliance of the morning sun and the carmine sunsets confirmed it. I felt as though a great promise lay to the west. And I resolved to seek that promise, wherever it led; however long it took.

After breakfast I looked about for a way to better my situation; for a way to secure a firmer financial grip on this ledge to which I now hung. At twenty dollars a month for food and lodging such as this, it would not take long to bankrupt me. I must work again, and either build a small cabin, or rent more reasonable quarters.

Neither the *Advertiser*, nor the *Herald* contained anything of interest and I found myself drawn to the wharves, where I sat upon a brandy cask to watch black dockmen roll small drums up the stage plank of a nondescript steamboat. It was apparent that the vessel was bound for posts further upriver for, besides the loading of casks, there was intense activity by others who stowed a variety of gear and stores. There were bags of canvas and burlap, all of which seemed to contain fragile material. A tall, bearded man in frontier dress was everywhere, cautioning loaders. One bag had developed a small hole; through it streamed bright colors of beads. A length of buckskin fringe quickly laced the rent. At the bow others were heaving aboard short, thick rolls of colorful cloth.

I was viewing stores which went to purchase fruits of the frontier –

the hides – which everyone assumed would come in a never-ending stream from the west. In another two months I would see pour onto the docks, hides of deer, muskrat, beaver, and stacks of thick, oily buffalo that baked and grew rancid in warehouses downstream. St. Louis was the nerve center of the frontier, the point of exchange, the port that spawned a thousand stories into an unknown, and from which one might not return.

I watched the loading as it progressed through the hot afternoon. In the eyes of the loaders I saw the same glint of eye that I had seen in Jacques – the hunted alertness that flashed a message of daring and cunning, eyes that seemed incapable of resolving from striking intensity to quiescent observation. That dark brilliance of their features matched the lithe power of their movements. There was no clattering of box, clang of chain, or strident shout; only muffled pad of bare foot and an occasional muttered oath.

I was caught up with the feeling that here there was a clandestine preparation for a sortie into Indian country, whose every preparation, a stone's throw from banks and business houses, must be carried on as though the law were within earshot. These were not the swaggering, argumentative Missourians and Kentuckians I had seen at the end of their keelboat run, but descendents of the Huguenots who had left my country for greater reasons than I could muster or comprehend; had sacrificed more, and now turned to a worship of the wild - and with the same fervor with which their ancestors clung to Protestantism. The taught cord of my memory tugged lightly, guiltily. It had now been nearly three years since I had heard mass. What had happened to me? I had attended early Rouen services at the cathedral for as many years as I could remember. The habit had died as though it were an outgrown and useless form; it was as though change to my new country sufficed, supplanting everything I had done as a youth in France. Here was the raw excitement of an unpredictable newness; the uselessness of form and formality. Here I was part of a new nation whose frontiers I could feel taught and stretched, whose borders had the bulge and bend of a woman before parturition. I had, without knowing, found a new religion: a formless, exciting state of mind and body.

Shadows and gathering river mist at length told me the lateness of the hour. As I rose and quitted the wharf, reflection of a rich, pink-mauve sunset colored the town above me, and a heady glow reflected within my being. Already the thought was forming, germinal, unexpressed, that I wished to push further into that sunset.

The evening meal had already begun when I reached home, and I was relieved to note platters of steaks and tongue done to a lighter tan that the day before. They were delicious – perhaps more because I had not eaten since breakfast than that they were skillfully cooked. The trader had checked out. I retired early, but slept fitfully.

A melange of sounds awakened me: horn of an early arriving steamer, a dog bark, a slammed door. An odor, piquant and penetrating, of frying pork in the landlady's quarters stirred action deep within my bowels and spread its awareness upward with a pleasant pressure. An early breeze was moving oak leaves that shaded my small window in a pattern of tremulous agitation. I felt chilled, for it was late December. In New Orleans, warm mists would have arisen. I had not felt the bite of winter since leaving Rouen.

Chapter 11
Chouteau

Today I would find another home. In the several days since arriving I had become accustomed to the city. Its situation on the Mississippi was probably responsible for the feeling of familiarity which I felt for it. The dependency of its people upon the placidly powerful river spawned a kind of reliance that all seemed to share. It was the tangible umbilical upon which their lives depended, the common liquid denominator that permeated the lives of all who landed here. From the barren sandstone cap on which St. Louis rested, the wharves, with their steam, keel and ferry boats reached for two miles in a northerly direction. West of the city an undulating, oak-covered prairie seemed to stretch to infinity.

The city was alive with people, throbbed with activity. Here, in the van of a new day, streets and boardwalks filled with a dusty jam of suited, jeaned, and leather-clothed men – so exclusively men – that it was as though women were banished.

Some of these men stood in groups of three or four chewing and spitting and squinting guardedly. I had the distinct impression that these activities were thought to be the height of sagacity, that he with the empty mouth was deemed witless. What they talked about I was never privy to, for, beside a chary, tightlipness, that, in contrast with the open gaiety I had been used to in New Orleans, they spoke with a kind of nasal twang. Though they talked slowly, their words were connected in such a way as to prevent my comprehension, and only rarely could I distinguish a word's beginning and ending. The many Yankee colloquialisms had never found their way into the lycee English I had studied for one year.

My need now was a purpose, a routine from which to plot a goal. I felt neither of these, and as yet saw no immediate possibility of gaining them. I did, however, feel a need for human companionship. It was like an appetite that commanded the gregariousness in me – a thing that had so far warred with my nature, repelled me from missing, even speaking, to those around me.

I walked the streets for hours thus, neither knowing what I sought, nor comprehending how to find it. At noon I bought my bottle of burgundy and retired to a café corner to drink and enjoy its pleasant confusion. The bistro was a low, smoky adjunct to a larger, popular eating hall, and a buzz of conversation drifted indistinctly through its connecting doorway.

The drone and the bottle lulled me and I had cradled my head on arms folded across the table, when voices, speaking distinct French, came to me from some new arrivals at an adjoining table:

"I will not go back to clerking at the store now, for I would be beaten by Chouteau's men. He gave me the key to give to the man's woman. But I will send it by someone else. I want to have nothing to do with the matter. When the key is delivered, I, too, will be on my way up the Missouri."

The conversation changed, and as their bottles emptied, their voices now filled the room with snatches of a suggestive French song I had not heard for many years. They stumbled from their tables presently, and out the sun-struck doorway, still singing.

I, too, was feeling my bottle and my mind made no connection between the conversation and my present needs. So, it was with a soggy memory that I wrestled when I awoke. But the name Chouteau had lodged in the corner of my mind and for a time there was no reasonable link, no two plus two. Still hunched upon the table in the torpor of slow waking from an unaccustomed nap, the embers of a dream emerged, flared, then died. I had drunk too much and my mind yet dwelt on need for a room. But had I dreamed, too, of the Frenchmen and their mention of what was now a vacant position? Of the man Chouteau? My mind, wading from present reality to possible phantasy, eventually made the muddy ford, and I stumbled from the dim interior into a cold afternoon sun. That another day of the fast-approaching winter had been wasted, disturbed me mildly. But shouldn't I at least inquire, and perhaps prove the strength of my own dreaming?

Thus began the first of several procrastinations which were to plague me and to provide me with misfortune. I had failed to learn the lesson that the deed must follow the thought, that the still, small voice which I was beginning to hear more frequently must be obeyed. I could have missed one of the best opportunities I had to establish myself in St. Louis had not chance lent a hand. Upon hearing the conversation I should have immediately inquired about employment with the man Chouteau. Instead, I had sat and brooded over the sick headache still pulsing; and finding it would not go away, had ordered and drunk another bottle – which afforded me an even larger headache.

I was in a belligerent mood when at last I re-entered the boarding house and ate again its overdone steaks. Feeling better with some food in me, I was able to concentrate, but was mildly stirred to hear the landlady direct her delivery boy to fetch some firkins of flour from

Chouteau's mill. So the group of Frenchmen had been real. I cursed my need for drink and went to bed resolving to investigate the possible storekeeping vacancy in the morning. A mill owner who also had a store must be an influential man. And he was French. I was cold during the night. I dreamed fitfully and again overslept.

The boarding table was being cleared when I appeared. My lot was lukewarm coffee and one slice of bread – grugingly given while the table was cleared. Inquiries regarding Chouteau were as sparingly answered by the mistress, but anyone could have told me where the man August Chouteau lived. He was a patriarch of St. Louis and had built on the *hill* – the tall second bank of fine homes where need for defense against Indians had once been great. His mansion was not far from my present quarters, and lay on a rounding, oak-fringed knoll on several acres of cleared land. Its style was not unusual, for it resembled many of the homes in old Rouen, but here in the wilderness it was an anomaly. It was a plastered, two-storied structure with hipped roof and dormers, about fifty feet wide and half as deep. Balustraded porches ran completely around the second floor. Its huge windows were expensively shuttered, and from the large square chimneys smoke dipped and swirled in cool December gusts.

Outside a heavy, evenly-faced rock wall that delineated street from mansion property, a group of robed and moccasined Indians grunted and gestured, flopping their hair feathers about in a ridiculous fashion. Inside the wall an occasional figure could be seen, mounting the several steps that seemed to lead to an office or side entrance. It would have been presemptuous to climb the broad front steps. I entered the office.

Inside the bare, box-like room two men conversed earnestly. One, a suited gentlemen who had just preceded me; the other sat cozied up to his desk, a long-stemmed pipe in a clutch of sensitive but strong fingers. Deep blue eyes of the latter were fixed upon the visitor. There was no shift of them in my direction as I entered, though I felt an immdiate scrutiny even as he gazed in concentration at his associate.

Presently, adieux were exchanged and the man whose visitor had called him Monsieur Chouteau turned to me.

"Hein. And how may I help you?"

This as he reposed the pipe, stood, and with extended hand, motioned toward the visitor's chair with his left. He placed himself now near the broad window, and I felt my whole being peeled raw under his studied gaze as I made known my name and need for a job. Then I waited. It seemed an eternity before he spoke.

"My forman informs me that one of my store keepers did leave precipitously, but that his vacancy was filled yesterday."

I silently cursed my delay as he continued:

"Just now many young men are leaving to try their luck on the trappingline and have little regard for the security of a steady position. May I inquire how you came to learn of the vacancy?"

My reply left no doubt in my questioner's mind that I could have applied the day before, and I sensed a mild paternal rebuke in his manner and tone as he continued.

"Do you read and write English as well as French? Would you take a laborer's job temporarily?"

His tone was fatherly throughout the interview and I sensed, in his words, a liking for me, one I had not felt since leaving home. It was as though he saw in me somehting very like a son. Much later I learned that his son had been slain by the Rickeraws enroute to a distant post only months previously.

Pan The Low Waters

The questioning was pointed, and intended, I thought, more to observe me through answers than for the purpose of gaining information. His gaze was penetrating, yet sympathetic, and I reflected afterwards, as I returned home, that my mind had been searched and my character weighed. After leaving I found I could hardly recall his physical characteristics, so thoroughly had I been held under his questioning gaze.

I was given the job, though not the position for which I had applied. While I had drunk my tyrant bottle the day previously, another had been accepted. I was to present myself to a Mssr. Picot at the hide warehouse near the bottom of North H Street. This I did early the following morning.

But had it not been for an unconscious regard I had come to feel for the man Chouteau, my first day in his hide warehouse would have been my last.

After ten hours of labor in a box-like building that housed the rancid pelts of a herd of buffalo, shock of drawing my first untainted breath was like a physical blow. Throughout the day I scraped and piled stinking hides, and at day's end staggered uphill to my rooming house too late for supper – and unable to care. Fatigue occupied my whole being, and I slept in my clothes until the bootpads of others awakened me and I knew I must gain strength for another day.

Had I looked at the faces of those who breakfasted, or glanced at the landlady's frown as she whirled quickly by, or interpreted the look of dark resolution with which she spoke to her assistant cook, I should not have been surprised at the curt note found pinned to my blanket that evening:

"Mssr. Chana, you will please have your goods out of this room by six o'clock tomorrow. It is being let to another boarder starting at that time."

Arnold F. Rothmeier

I had been too tired to bathe, too fatigued to rid myself of the offensive reek, and too anesthetized by its strength to judge its effect upon others. The putrid odor, like the powder glow of a ruddleman had expanded in the warm dining room to a monstrous intolerance. I took my things and left the next morning. Hopefully the rancid odor left with me. Though I had simply exchanged shelter for employment, I felt sure that there would be no objection if I were to ask for quarters in a room off the warehouse, for the nights were turning very cool. The habit of optimism refreshed me, and I was whistling as I descended to the warehouse.

Another day passed in a sweaty monotony of scraping and folding the odious hides. Most of these, I learned, had been stored for four or five months at posts along the upper Missouri. They had been brought by steamboat, keelboat, and even bullboat (a floating, bowl-like container, ribbed of willows and coated with raw buffalo hides) to this warehouse. A small and drier section of the warehouse contained small bundles of the more precious hides: beaver, mink, fox, deer.

Then, as the day ended and as I was about to inquire whether I might be allowed to put up for the night, the overseer informed me I was to present myself again at the Chouteau office. Had I failed to do my work satisfactorily? Had the overseer reported me as untrustworthy? Too slow? My mind scurried through a dozen reasons for the summons, but I could not see how my labor had been remiss. Stinking and filthy, bedroll and bag in hand, I returned to the mansion.

The outer door was ajar. I placed my things against the wall and knocked. Feet scuffled the floor, a chair moved, and August Chouteau opened his door.

"Come in, Mssr. Chana."

I entered and took the indicated chair. Whatever my tired thoughts were at the moment, they could hardly have anticipated the conversation that followed:

"I know you do not feel presentable. Think nothing of it. I, too, have stacked hides. Let me pour you a drink. You prefer a good wine, no doubt?"

He talked as he poured and I noted a softening in the slate blue eyes of our first meeting.

"The storekeeper hired a few days ago has not worked out to our satisfaction and had left my employ. He may have been dishonest as well as lazy. I had no way of knowing. But by hiring you for the warehouse I know, at least, that you are not lazy. I am also quite certain you are not dishonest."

He gave me no opportunity to reply, and I sensed that none was necessary, for he seemed to have thoroughly made up his mind about me.

"We will visit the store in the morning. I need not ask if you would like to bathe."

He left the office for a moment and through the door I could see him in conversation with a diminutive, tastefully dressed woman, whom I was later to meet as his wife.

Returning to the office, he informed me that I would occupy, for the night, the small bedroom across the hall; that a tub of hot water would be there presently, and that his man would bring food after I had bathed and dressed. I was not expected to appear until called for breakfast. How he surmised that I had no place to go is one of the mysteries of the mind of August Chouteau.

I found it comforting to associate with a man of my own race, to feel the security of the control he exercised over home and business.

Arnold F. Rothmeier

And in the days and months that followed I was to appreciate the quiet power and modesty with which he managed mansion, a large farm, mill, and several places of business in town – in addition to which, of course, he held partial reins, as clerk, of one of the most powerful companies on the frontier: The American Fur Company. He, himself, was the younger of a group of enterprising Chouteau brothers. I was to take charge of one of his larger trading posts on the outskirts of town.

Chapter 12
The Trading Post

Early the next morning, I was awakened by footsteps sounding on the floor above me and was already dressed when Mssr. Chouteau rapped and said that breakfast was hot. We ate a filling meal of meat, cakes, and coffee. I was ravenous, but ate as politely as I could manage, relieved that the eyes of my host were no longer upon me. It was as though he now knew he could trust me, that he approved of my character, and that this approval, once given, removed all hesitancy and formal barriers. As we ate I had an opportunity to study Mssr. Chouteau as he paused occasionally to gaze across the vista of roofs and the mist-shrouded river beyond. In his eyes there was a hint of the same intensity of gaze I had noted in Jacques', but also a steadfastness and omniscience which at once probed and commanded, pleaded and searched. He was a man perhaps no taller than my five feet eight inches, though the angularity of his jaw and high forehead seemed to lift him taller. There was also a hint of courtly grace about his movements as he offered platter and pitcher, a grace too strongly imbedded to be bred out of him by the life he had led on the frontier. Perhaps, though, he would carry forever a hint of this adversary in the slight hunch and droop of his shoulders. These, however, represented an anomaly; they were incongruous, for all else about him, even the forward-looking optimism in the tone of this voice – suggested an uprightness of character to which I reacted favorably.

"Claude", he said, as we approached the end of the meal and prepared our pipes, "you will have much to learn in your new job – or, rather, your new job will teach you much, if you will allow it. Your trading store is three miles from town, out beyond Prairie des Noyens, and the common field of Carondelet. This far the Indian will come to trade furs for what he needs, but no farther. A few of them come into the outskirts out of curiosity, but either they do not like what they see, or dislike the stares. At any rate, they seek their own level and they stay pretty much where they should. Trading is good most of the year, except in the hottest months and at the end of a long cold spell. You are to trade hard for the scrawny pelts. Watch your goods closely, for this is the beginning of the trading year. It is also the beginning of short food. There never was a provident savage – though they tell me the Pawnees across the river are getting the idea with their small cornfields."

At this point in our conversational walk we had reached the warehouse. Its stench still hung like a pall over the area. My employer entered to leave a message. I sat upon a cask nearby and watched docking maneuvers of a newly arrived steamer, so heavily laden that its decks would have been awash had it not been for a short railing. Casks of whisky or brandy ringed a cargo deck two deep and fifty feet wide. On the hurricane deck dozens of passengers in coats or shawls milled and pointed.

Presently Mssr. Chouteau emerged. We proceeded through town to its western outskirts. For most of the three-mile walk I silently followed on a barely descernable path over frost covered grass and around clumps of vine-covered beech, oak, and elm. It was most flattering and reassuring to reflect occasionally upon the confidence this man had in me and to feel that I was now to be given carte blanche control and trusteeship of a place of business.

The last half mile of our tramp took us to a narrow path around the base of some low hills and ended in a large treeless meadow through which a small willow-lined stream flowed. Long before we arrived at my new home I made out the outline of a squat, dark gray rectangle beneath a grove a hackberry trees. Beyond, from the slight rise of our approach, could be seen a portion of the meandering Missouri, which flowed within a half mile of the post.

A heavy chain barred the thick oaken door. My patron opened the lock with a deft turn and resnapped it shut on the two chain ends. The door swung inward and wedged itself open on a knot in the oaken floor. We entered a commodious, tightly constructed building, its timbers so solidly hewn and joined that I could perceive but little chinking. Its timbers rose to a height of ten feet and were joined and braced by six massive beams which formed a kind of overhead storage for numerous bales of furs and hides. Directly opposite the entrance stretched a long low counter of rough timbers, greasy and hair-tufted. The whole could be lit by a single oil lamp swung directly over the counter's mid-point, for there were no windows or spaces for them either with or without glass. The post was a fortress, as, no doubt, it had been in years past.

To the left of the entrance lay a hearth and fireplace; to the right a low bed of buffalo robes and pine needles. A single chair made by the simple expedient of sawing half-way through a four-foot log section, then splitting off that portion which would leave seat and back. There was no other furniture.

Behind the counter ranged a series of widely spaced shelves on which lay knives and bolts of cloth, boxes of lead shot, beads, mirrors. A few small drums, each half full of sugar, crackers, and salt stood behind the counter.

Arnold F. Rothmeier

Our boot steps resounded hollowly as we strode about the store, taking note of stock and surveying the needed articles of trade. Now that we were here, a thousand questions flooded my mind and, as if he knew the confusion within me, Mssr. Chouteau set about enumerating my duties and responsibilities. Beginning with the the fact that I was to trade high for prime pelts and that I was, as an employee of the American Fur Company, to bring into that company's coffers as much wealth of peltry as possible. He ended with an interminable volume of cautions: Until I felt confident, I was to avoid frictions, and for the time being I was to trade liberally, depending on it to become known that I, the new factor, was easy to trade with. This would bring in a more flourishing business, at which time I stood to profit considerably as the Indians brought in a greater volume of withheld hides.

The jugs of whisky, now pointed out to me in the far corner beneath some robes, were to be sold or traded only to whites and on request. Later I would, my patron said, learn to use it to separate, more easily, the pelt from the Indian. All these cautions pertained to trade with Indians, mostly Pawnee – who had, to a degree, been domesticated – or appeared to have been domesticated since their proximity to Leavenworth, Franklin, Independence, and St. Louis. My mode of handling and trading with whites, and particularly with unattached, argumentative Kentucky and Missouri trappers and floaters, would prove a matter far more challenging. The savage knows only that he needs the few things which nature denies him – salt, a good knife, a few chunks of lead. He is able to get the other necessities, including an abundance of food, by stalking or trapping, and places no great value on a hide, since his squaw does the scraping. The white buck, on the other hand, rarely failed to be argumentative and to trade tight, believing that the high value of his pelts, or the low value of my goods, should give him the edge in any deal.

On the counter was a long list of commodities in stock, together with their barterable equivalents. This, I was to commit to memory as soon as possible. It was understood that my trading would not at first

Pan The Low Waters

be that most advantageous to the American Fur Company, but I was expected to grow in astuteness, learn to judge values of pelts quickly, and the personalities possessing them. I was to keep books and inventories. I was to be aware of the thieving propensities of most Indians. I would be treated with respect because the Indian knew he needed me and because I obliviated his necessity to trade in town (which he disliked). I would have to set about gathering grass hay for the mare and completing other tasks. I might investigate the surrounding area, but must not be absent from the post for more than an hour at a time. The post must be tightly secured when I left (key around neck), and I must cut a stock of wood – or freeze this winter! When I ran low on any of the items in stock I was to ride into St. Louis and leave a list of shortages with Mssr. Bardot at the warehouse. I could expect delivery in a week or two depending upon weather condition and stock available.

It was mid-afternoon before Mssr. Chouteau seemed satisfied he had given me all the verbal help he could. We ate some dried venison, washed it down with a swallow of company whisky, and with a few reminders – repetitiously given, he caught one of the horses and rode away.

Warm feelings arise within me as I recall the tacit trust he placed in my ability. To be left in charge of such a place, by a man who knew my lack of experience, generated in me a large obligation – one which, of course, Mssr. Chouteau was not insensitive to. There would be no half-measures. I set out armed with his trust and backed by the knowledge that he was in a much better position to judge a potentially successful factor than I was.

It was late when Chouteau rode away. I had much to do to make my quarters comfortable, but set about first to enlarge my supply of firewood. For, once the heavy snow came, the effort of gathering it would be double. Dead and down was plentiful, and rather than cut it immediately to burnable lengths, I spent my remaining hours of twilight using horse to tow a quantity of dry logs and brush close to the post. By nightfall I had accumulated an uncut woodpile of considerable proportions. This would be my fuel source for weeks to come and would be supplemented later by driftwood along the river. Of food there would be little problem, for, in addition to quantities of dried venison on hand for trading, and the dried vegetables, melons, and seeds for which the Indians would barter, Mssr. Chouteau had assured me there would be more than enough fresh meat from the visiting savages.

One morning after a particularly cold, windy week, I awoke with a feeling of oppressive warmth. Throwing back my buffalo robe, I was conscious of a lightness in the air reminiscent of the balmy springs of New Orleans. I opened the door and stepped into shocking sunlight and four inches of white slush. The sun was hot and heady, and the early, unseasonable warmth seemed a warning for early spring, though it was yet December.

All that day and for several more until late at night, the post was filled with blanket-clad figures gesticulating and softly grunting. They stood by the fire; they lay on the floor with heads on small packs of furs bound in deer hide and thongs; they sat stolidly, backs against walls, watching intently with piercing brown gimlet eyes my transactions with others. I was the cynosure of thirty pairs of eyes and felt the drama, perhaps the danger of my position – though Chouteau, in his wisdom, had assured me that the last thing the savages wished was to plunder their supply source. This was the beginning of their long winter, the beginning of the period in which they would lie clothed and bundled with each other for weeks on end in their rush and mud huts or skin wickiups.

Each night when the last of the blanket-clad figures shuffled out and the oaken beam was laid across the door, I tallied my furs. First I separated them into small stacks of like variety and quality from the common pile where I had tossed them. Next, I entered these on my record book, together with remembered approximate amounts of traded goods. I appended small entries in the margin to help me remember oddities of transactions or price, and by the end of my first year I no longer needed this crutch. I then bound each labeled pack with a deer hide and cord and stowed it in the rafters.

There was no set date or routine for the collection of these, nor was there compliment or recrimination when I was periodically visited by one of the young half-breeds who had formerly sweated with me in the hide warehouse. I flattered myself that at the time I had noted his quiet efficiency, and saw now why, perhaps, I had been chosen over him to trade: other than displayed signs of company loyalty and the ability to do a job unsupervised, I had no advantage over him but one: he receipted me for each load of furs with a tally thusly: ⁄⁄⁄⁄ - X.

As the months passed, the previously impenetrable fog of money, pelts, language, and weights lifted. I was able to sleep without a tightness in the belly – the result of a fear of error-making. Rhythm and rest imposed by the weather and isolation put my mind at ease. I was able to study my books, to classify my pelts with increased accuracy, and good trading became a reflex.

For bartering, I came to depend almost totally upon a few signs which I learned from the Indians - and awkwardly at first. For many months the only sense I could make from their gestures and grunts was an auditory appreciation of their pleasure or displeasure. Happiness or eagerness was only a pitch higher on the scale, and silence, I came to know, was ominously worse that "unacceptable". All tribes - and there were eight or ten (all at first distinguishable to me only in their degree of greasiness) – upon seeing that I was conversant with only a few Spanish words, fell back upon the reliable and accessible hand signs.

Arnold F. Rothmeier

Chapter 13
First Winter

I came to respect the wet and shivering Pawnee and Oto who came at any hour, slapping the thick slab door with their hands or gun butts. They would enter behind great breaths of steam, shuffle to the fireplace and squat on the floor or sit on log or fur pack enveloped in their blankets and mist. At first they would sit in silent thaw. Then one would be distracted by an article in the room, and begin to talk and gesticulate. Never did they seem hurried about their trading, nor did I ever show, by gesture or glance, an impatience. And before I had traded for more than a few months I came to know that the Indian, savage though he was, entered the post with a kind of mental list; that he knew quite precisely what he was going to exchange his furs for, and that it was useless to force him with the gee-gaws of trade.

Few of the savages entered the post in their native clothing, seeming to regard the wearing of white man's material as a step upward in society. And always they brought their pitiful baskets of shelled corn and dried squash, strung on lengths of rawhide, to exchange for combs, beads, knives, or paints. Through the first months of my apprenticeship I thought much on the produce, and I would wonder how I would dispose of the piles of corn. Then, when I had determined to accept no more of these, in would come a wandering band that would take away the produce and deposit in their place, many fine furs. It went without saying that a minor bourgeois such as I was not to profit personally from the post transactions, and I never did. I maintained as strict an accounting of goods on my ledger as I knew how, even to the guessing of some amounts and weights which were necessary when large groups came. My own food costs came to be absorbed, naturally, in the daily accounting, for I had on hand always ingredients for the stew which, throughout the winter, hung simmering over a fire, and to which I added when it grew low. The pot was never emptied, and some of the ingredients were heated so many times that they became a delicious gravy. Often in addition to dried meat for barter, an Indian would enter, thump a bloody venison rump upon the counter, point to the article he wanted, then strike his right index finger twice across his left – the universal sign of a wish for trade.

As time passed I think I became rather expert at reading my customer, and found it always the best policy to allow the Indian – or white – to handle the initiative. Money prices for the latter were invariable, being set and dictated by a market over which I had no control, but prices, when trading for robes and furs, were bent or adjusted. Though the Missourian or Kentuckian sometimes had extravagant opinions as to the worth of his pelts, the Indian struck me as more than perceptive in gauging equivalent value. He seemed to have thought out the comparative worth of his pelts in store goods and rarely showed overweening opinions as to their merit, but traded a given pelt or pack in straightforward manner. He often allowed me the edge in a trade, and I often deferred and added more salt or flour to the already agreed-upon amount. How well I succeeded as trader and post keeper, I was to discover late in the season, following one of the severest winters on record.

My confinement, that first winter at St. Louis had some interesting consequences. There was not enough loneliness to drive me mad, but just enough isolation, perhaps, to help me examine the forces which had plucked me from the wharfs of Rouen and placed me at the edge of a frontier wilder and greater than I could have imagined.

Occasionally, a trapper, enroute to St. Louis from the country far up the Missouri would stop and leave hint, by some related commonplace adventure, of the mystery and wildness of the areas west and north. Or I would be visited by a party of hunters passing through to fetch game for town markets. These would sometimes tell what they knew of boundless forests or vast and beautiful lakes or prairies. The tales, sometimes ominous and wild, fascinated me. They were good stories – and, of course exaggerated.

On one of my stock-renewing trips to town I brought back a roving, ownerless dog for company. He was a lean, cream-colored mutt who seemed attracted to me from the moment he first smelled my heels. At first I gave him little encouragement, but when he continued to wait for me outside each shop, I became more attached to him. When his bluster discouraged another and larger bitch from a threatening approach, I bought a slice of meat and gave it to him. From that moment until a tragic incident far from St. Louis and years later, he stayed by me, answering to the name "Lait" – his milky coloring.

Of all the nights and days that arranged themselves endlessly that first trading winter, one returns to mind repeatedly:

Dense black clouds had cut short the afternoon. I had used horse and sled to bring a fresh load of driftwood from the river. As I turned the horse loose in the gathering dusk, I saw I had a mixed group of ten or so customers squatting near the post door. As usual, my horse had bolted for the dried grass and shelter which it knew lay waiting inside the small corral. I followed it to close the gate against wolf and bear, whose tracks I had often seen.

The pelts were prime: fox, martin, a few beaver. One becomes sensitive to the worth of furs after long trading. The older of the men traded first, while the others, as a sign of their lack of seniority, grouped about the fire. Next to trade would come those second in authority and bravery. Never was there any departure from this convention – unless drink clouded judgement, making them irritable and argumentative. After three of the males had been served, I noticed the right hands of the last. the eldest had left small trails of blood from an injured right hand, and now clumsily gathered his purchases with a left arm.

I was further mystified when it came turn for the squaws to trade. Not only were digits missing from both hands, but the hands of the oldest presented signs of both recent and earlier mutilation, and her efforts at sign language had the pathetic effect of a person attempting to converse with a half normal tongue. I simply could not read the meanings foreshortened by half or two thirds of a finger. Her's were, I saw, cut but one joint from the knuckle. She had lost an earlier crop from most fingers.

While we had been bartering, and while we were engrossed with one another's finger signs, the hour had grown late. All seemed reluctant to leave; the half dozen or so small children and two dogs dozed before the fire. It was not my policy to remain up so late; the business was at an end; a general movement generated itself in the direction of the door. But as it was opened, a blast of wind and snow drove the first back into the room. Without warning a severe storm had generated as we traded, catching even the natives by surprise. Temperatures had dropped to near freezing.

There was no help for it: I would be obliged to shelter the ten overnight. Number one Indian closed the door and turned to me with a look of confused concern. To a background of chattering he made, with sign and gesture, that they would sleep here. Though this was against my better judgement, as well as against Chouteau's policy, I thought even he would have made an exception under the circumstances. Since most had already chosen to crowd the floor about the fireplace, I pulled my own bedding to the far side of the room and resigned myself to a night of wakefulness for fear of thievery. Actually, I was prepared to lose a few articles. I even handed each a generous slice of venison ham from my inner room. What I was totally unprepared for was the resumption of an apparent mourning period. Sometime about midnight, while I lay half-wakeful, propped against the wall, a wavering, lowpitched moan arose from one of the figures silhouetted against the coals. In another moment a second and then a third female voice rose in a shrill, rhythmic keening that kept me wakeful through most of the night.

There was no attempt at thievery, and when at last daylight came and I opened the door, the sun shone dazzlingly, and as far as eye could see, on a two-foot blanket of snow. The Indians relieved themselves along the sheltered areas under the eaves then greased themselves thoroughly while gnawing and sharing with each other the remaining meaty venison bones. By the time they had finished their scant meal, great clumps of snow, loosened from the overhanging oaks were falling upon the roof, and they left quietly in a slow slogging single file pointed toward the river. The group had been one of the largest to visit the post. I still could not distinguish between the Pawnee – native to the area – and the Crow, Assinaboin, and Kickapoos who came in such numbers that spring. All came clothed in the same buffalo or deer robes, or in filthy blankets when it was cold, or in cloth shirts when sunny, and it was many months before I began to appreciate the varieties of facial contours and silhouettes that mark a given tribe.

The late storm marked one of several false ends of winter that year of 1840, for the weather seemed to have difficulty deciding which season to resolve into. As late as mid-April there were snow flurries and other un-spring-like displays. A day would be calm, even sultry, and at night the walls would sway under great cannon-like thunder that seemed to land and explode just outside. One week would bring sun that would almost dry the earth; a sleet might follow, coating the earth with a mighty ice sheet that would drive wood-gatherers indoors and split the larger trees from ground to first limb with an utterance of wooden pain. At other times the forest would be beaten by winds so mighty as to fling great living branches against the post walls. I could not help but wonder how the savages existed in these perverse seasons, how their minds ran to assess their shortcomings as they thought on some personal deed that had brought on such fear and discomfort.

That first winter, despite its harshness, was not unlike the one very cold winter I recalled as a youth when the Seine froze from bank to bank and there was ice skating after work for many nights; when huge fires along the shore lit the silver surface and kept fingers and toes from aching.

After a month or so of this wintry melange, a true clearing arrived. The weather seemed to have exhausted its range of possibilities. Signs of spring appeared in great, heady waves and with a rush that filled me with anticipation. It lined branches with bursting buds and song birds, and covered post acreage with a green carpet. There was a lushness about it, even as it sprouted, that re-awakened in me a desire, a need, to test it with plow and seed. As a youth, I had not cared for the life of planter and farmer – preferring instead to use tools – but the past winter had subtly altered my thinking, and I now looked forward each day to a few hours with a hoe or the wooden plow I had fashioned. I anticipated the time when I would be able to gorge myself on leaves and roots from the vegetable garden. Winter and its monotony of cold and solitude had played havoc with my constitution. It showed itself in the fatigue I felt after only a few hours in the new garden; my elimination had grown sluggish, due, no doubt, to a predominantly meat diet. Also, it was some weeks before an odd twitching of my left eye disappeared. This I attributed to the strain of reading old newspapers and working in the dim waver of lamps.

Spring's arrival too, was a wild, tempestuous thing. It was the dazzling blue slit of sky and slow roll of fleece overhead; it was the erratic wildness of wind that pushed and shoved trees almost to earth, then shook and twisted them as if trying to rid the boughs of their buds; it was a sable-like path in the knee-high grasses on open stretches beaten and tossed by a wind that seared down from a colder north in an unpredictable series of frigid breaths, frightening and quailing the rodents and birds as they gnawed and pecked and cowered; it was the hard beat and lift of a rain cloud, late and futile; and it was the relentless burgeoning of a thousand bouquets that rose from the morass of delicate mauve branch tips which seemed to have kept alive promise of spring when all was hard and dead.

With the opening of leaf-pod, during this odd early spring, my senses expanded to aromas that swirled about the little valley. Saps and barks and buds all had their own heady redolences, and presented me with shocks of wonderment. Whether it was the length of the brutal, cold winter, or the starvation I experienced for odors, I never knew. Through that first spring and on into early summer I was never without the enjoyment of heady essences wherever I went. Often, in the evening I would saddle the mare and ride in a wide arc to the cresting Missouri and back. I would sometimes pass through half a dozen strata of pungencies. The air was an aromatic cake and I had but to voraciously breathe my way through it, anticipating, sometimes guessing which breathed flavor delighted me most. Mint, bitter willow, pine resin, rotten oak, bruised laurel, and others afforded, with each breath I took, an ecstatic enjoyment I had never known. But, then, an odd phenomenon would occur: each time I would breathe a piquant odor, I would immediately re-inhale, expecting, hoping for an increased heady pleasure. But, instead of richer stimulation, there would be no odor at all. It was as though the first onslaught of stimulation were all that the odor contained; as though it were incapable of reconciling with the nature of man, which is to demand more, greater, and more profound effects from the senses; it was as though the total design of nature's perfumes was reticence and subtlety, and that once the subtlety presented itself, it dissipated; hid from repetition.

Pan The Low Waters

I was never to understand this, never to fully comprehend that the instant of the fullest enjoyment of any of the senses was the instantaneous "now"; that it could not be realized or amplified by mere repetition. The odor was there in all its intensity but once; it returned neither with the same intensity not at the bidding of the will. After lapse of a few moments, I might, perhaps, breathe again the illusive scent, and again greedily attempt to experience it more fully and repetitiously, but the aroma never returned in strength; often never at all.

Odd that this principle seemed not to apply to the other senses. My coffee, stew, or wine, my appreciation of the amazing beauties of the Missouri spring, of the notes of songbirds – these I enjoyed, seemingly, more each time I heard them. But never the odors. They came and went in too illusive a fashion.

The weather now allowed me much time out of doors. Trading was slow, for most pelts had been traded, and I gravitated toward a more farmer-like existence, trying all possible varieties of bulb and seed in the rich black loam so close to my door.

The twitch, so annoying through the darkness of winter, left my eye, and rectal pain vanished with a change of diet and the new-found enthusiasms of my garden. I resolved to never again be without berries, roots, and leaves that delivered me from the effects of my first Missouri winter.

There are two periods of high waters on the Missouri and its tributaries: one occurs in April, when spring rains are at their peak, and another comes in June when the snows in the north melt and glut down river banks. By riding half a mile I could witness these changes. This year there were no steamboats or keelboats on the river, only trees and debris rolling and tumbling in a menacing, dark brown tide that seemed to grow in size and power even as I looked. Only the bores of the Seine offered comparison to it. Where the Seine was a few hundred yards wide, here the far bank could not be seen. I came often, that spring, despite the new menace and annoyance of a new crop of mosquitoes, to view the muddy torrent and to respect its obvious power.

Despite the series of late cold rains that settled for what seemed an eternity over the valley, my vegetables sprouted and flourished. And even with the depredations of rabbits and squirrels, I used and then laid away great quantities of beans, potatoes, beets, and turnips in a cool cavern on the north side of the post.

Now that the trapping year was closing and summing-up of proceeds accomplished, it was time to plan for another year. I had touched but little of the capital earned from my two years in New Orleans, and was now able to add to it a considereable sum of American Fur Company wages. There seemed little, if any, outlay necessary for a comfortable existence here in America. As long as my services were adequate I was guaranteed quarters and use of all the rich land I was able to till. My leather clothing never wore out, and even the soles of my boots had an imperishable quality – due, no doubt to the soft, lush loam on which I trod – and the willingness of my mare.

As the season wore on, I think I tended more and more to play the part of a petty bourgeois. The years of spare living that had forced me first to the Rouen cooperage, then pulled me like a magnet to New Orleans, were gone, and I luxuriated in a warm Missouri summer, fed on squirrel, fish, and deer so plentifully close. I seemed but little dependent upon additional human companionship. My dog, horse, and an increasing flow of white settlers were all the fellowship I seemed to require.

I say I was but little dependent upon human companionship, yet I know I must have been. Had it not been for the pleasure of hearing the savage grunt of aye or no in trading, or of listening to the ever more potent and sometimes menacing tone of the renegade Pike, I should have been truly alone. The faces of my customers, whether they spoke words or used gestures and grunts, were alive with unspoken volumes demanding instant translation. The word was not the vehicle that abolished my loneliness; it was the silent glance that fired the thought faster than manipulated sound could have done; faster than the laborious and frustrating voweling of words, often tyrannous in their translation.

Further, summing up, as I habitually did each night before wooing sleep, I found I was developing a bias contrary to that acceptable to most frontiersmen and trappers: My position put me on the firing line, so to speak, in an area most sensitive to observation of both Indian and white. I was compelled by my position to judge. And I saw here, miles from St. Louis, not the wild, murdering, treacherous savage of the eastern forests, but one who sensed – whether he verbalized it or not – that he was losing something he possessed in direct proportion to his readiness to accept traded goods. I saw him – in his shabby attempts to emulate white dress (in which, by tacit agreement, all Indians felt superior) – as one who relinquished daily the very things that made him admirable: easy acquisition of arms reduced his sense of stealth and dependence upon wild and delicate senses; the substitution of things like boats and buckles and powder relieved him of natural and earned ingenuities; and finally, his growing attraction for bad whisky seemed to complete the undoing of his whole moral and spritual fiber; it furnished him with an excuse for relinquishing the stern stoicism that had been his heritage. When he fell prey to the bottle, he used it precisely for what it was – a tool for making the sordid and the brutal more endurable. Bad whisky seemed to weaken all the elements of a heritage that furnished him with pride; it dissolved, before his bloodshot eyes his savage, native self-confidence and left him with only a weak, rotting indifference to the future.

I saw it often in the gutters of St. Louis. For though it was forbidden by law to sell or give alcohol to an Indian, when both seller and buyer are determined to subvert a rule for their own ends, the rule remains only that.

Arnold F. Rothmeier

The final months of my first year as trader were the most idyllic I had spent in America. At times, while tending the garden, I would pause to survey the surrounding sea of waving green, the rows of leafy things that seemed sprung from the rich leaf-mold overnight, and notice the yet greener banks of tree-green that softened low hills across my stream – they that had been so stark and severe only a fortnight ago. It was in pauses such as these that I felt impelled into another level of existence, as though tugged gently onto the threshold of a promising future. I turned philosopher. Time, I saw, was consciousness of time: no consciousness of time, no flow of time. The woods and fields were full of an infinite variety of gentle movements, each, seemingly allotted their second or two for completion. Yet, since I was not caught up in a consciousness and awareness of their movement, time simply did not exist. The spring and summer of 1844 was a time of profound peace and wonderment. I was in limbo.

Then one sun-shot midday in July – what the Indians called the "silk on the corn" month – I measured some lead and powder for a settler. Over the man's shoulder, as I reckoned with him, I saw Mssr. Chouteau enter. He stood leaning against the opened door while I finished my business, then approached. I came from behind the counter and we shook hands warmly.

After a complimentary remark as to some re-arrangements and improvements I had made about the post, he suggested we sit outside on the stump chairs.

"My hospitality does not rank with yours, Mssr. Chouteau", I said, "but I have some passable wine which I brought back from town on my last trip".

I poured the two cups and we sat in silence for a few moments. One does not ride the distance he had come on a sultry Missouri summer day without cause; he came to the point quickly and surpisingly.

"Claude, you have performed well here at the post. The American Fur Company is satisfied as to your allegiance and industry. I feel the same degree of satisfaction, in that I am vindicated in my choice of a man to do the job you are doing. But I am wondering if you would not like to indulge in a more social life occasionally, meet some countrymen, broaden your horizons a little. One can get a very circumscribed view of America from behind the counter or the plow. You must know that one's view of the back of his plow horse in not nearly as attractive as the ankle and form of a fresh young dancer." I smiled. He paused for a moment, then went abruptly into the reason for his visit.

"In a few more days the "*St. Ange*" will return from upriver with several bourgeois and their season's packs. We have always had a soiree of sorts after our accounting – to wash off some of the bear fat – so to speak, to get acquainted, to exchange experiences. I can arrange for one of my men to tend your post for several days, and, if you like, you can join us."

He paused now, for longer seconds, waiting for my reaction. I was conscious that my services were valued and that a visit by a man of Chouteau's stature was highly complimentary. Then, for a fleeting moment, I sensed another thought poised to be spoken. But I had already formed an answer, and said I should be happy to accept the invitation. Immediately the words were spoken, I had the distinct feeling of having interrupted a further expression of his regard for me.

The moment passed with the impression. We finished our bottle and strolled along to view the garden. I picked and prepared a sling of fresh vegetables for his table, and he left shortly after thanking me for my hospitality.

What I had postponed or interrupted by too ready an answer to his invitation, I was to realize when next we met. It was late. I dismissed the thought and went to feed the horse and tend chores before dark.

Chapter 14
Soiree

It was almost a week before the arrival of the young Frenchman who was to tend post in my absence. The "St. Ange", he said, had run aground several times due to its heavy load of passengers and furs and because of the slack winter. This was the reason for the postponed soiree. I fed him some jerky and vegetables and, after showing him the shelves, their prices, what to feed the horse and dog, I cinched my saddle blanket and rode townward.

I had decided to take the river route because I had never ridden it yet. It was early – not yet noon – and a leisurely walk or jog-trot would bring me to St. Louis well before sunset.

But I misjudged both distance and terrain condition. Not only did the meaders of the river cause my journey to be lengthened by several miles, but the late snow melt at the headwaters had played havoc with the river banks and had deposited large tree stumps and dense tangles of debris along a shore that otherwise would have provided easy traveling. I cursed myself for not having asked the relief boy about this route, and, after several miles, seriously considered returning and taking the old trail - but I continued, sometimes backtracking, sometimes having to dismount and lead my animal. About dusk, just as I began to fear I would have to bivouac and finish my miserable trip in the morning, I saw the first signs of habitation and the white church tower. It was full dark when I made my way through the streets to the Chouteau mansion at the east end of the city.

On previous visits, I had transacted my business as usual in the Chouteau office, and had perhaps wondered about the rest of the mansion. Tonight, I would see the whole house. The front approach was illuminated by pitch torches, and numerous candles burned on large circular chandeliers in the salon that gave on the wide, house-length veranda.

I entered through a wide open front door expecting Chouteau himself to greet me. But there was no greeting. Several couples stood conversing; a group of five men in buckskin, tankards in hand, noisily occupied one corner, and in the opposite, more secluded corner, seated on the floor, huddled several squaws. A few servants made themselves noticed by seeking out and filling empty glasses.

I, too, was plied with drinks, and had more than one, but not before I had eaten a liberal serving of venison and cleaned myself with one of the cloths scattered about the table. Presently Mssr. Chouteau and two other well-dressed prosperous-looking men entered from the office door with drink and pipes. Upon seeing me, my patron left his two friends, crossed the hall, and greeted me warmly. I responded and was about to narrate my experiences along the river when he said: "Come, I would like you to meet some newly arrived countrymen".

"Claude Chana, ici Mssr. Paul le Clede et Charles Covillaud. Mssr. le Clede is a purchasing agent here on business for the the American Fur Company, and has brought along Mssr. Covillaud, whom he met on the steamer from New Orleans.

I was, perhaps, slightly repelled by Mssr. le Clede, who, beside being dressed like a business man, appeared almost twice my age. He fell to conversing with Mssr. Chouteau, and the two older men separated naturally, leaving Mssr. Covillaud with me.

As we chatted I studied the man Covillaud. I was immediately struck by the deep intensity of his voice and piercing gaze. He was not a large man, either by French or by American standards, yet there was about him a hint of aggressiveness which seemed to lend him immediate stature. It developed that he had made his voyage from Marseille in a stateroom of one of the new trasatlantic traders now coming into use, had landed in New Orleans at the height of cholera seasons and, fearing that he might contract the sickness, had quickly boarded for St. Louis. It was plain to see that physical want had not driven him from the old country. His talk was not picayune, but seemed to hint restlessly of goals to be reached and obstacles overcome. And as we talked – he, for the most part – my own little niche of business and garden seemed to lose some of its lustre and security, and the words of Covillaud built challenges and lent such attraction to the general movement westward, that I simply listened and was swayed by his words.

But ones circumstances do not long remain concealed. Although I could not help liking and being immediately attracted to Mssr. Covillaud, my first impression was that he concealed an intense need for the approval of others. I noted this at the time, and in later years was able to understand his actions in the light of this first impression. I do not criticize Charles – as he insisted I call him – because of this trait, for it made him somehow, an intense, likeable person who seemed to have chosen a direction for his life. The fact that this direction was as yet lacking in me, seemed to increase my attraction to him.

Charles was a year or two younger than I – perhaps twenty-six, well-built, a little stocky for a Frenchman, with cheerful, flashing brown eyes that peered through a full head of hair and a beard just coming into luxuriance. His outward-jutting chin accentuated and complemented the aggressiveness in his voice. His long, dun-colored coat and matching trousers fitted him handsomely, and his suit, together with expensive, worn, brown boots suggested he had worn the outfit long, hard, and exclusively.

As we exchanged experiences and impressions of the United States, I found myself doubting the validity of my first impressions of him, and when I related my experiences as a cooper, he was genuinely enthusiastic, for he, too, had worked in a cooperage in Cognac. I also noted that his hands were strong and capable, though I wondered that they should seem soft, while mine never lost their rough, gnarled surface no matter how long I remained away from the occupation.

Mssr. Chouteau was a gracious host and his soiree was memorable in the tradition of French opulence. Though he and his guests were not only ten thousand miles from the old country and surrounded by country lacking in the rudiments of culture, yet he caused mood of a courtly homeland to permeate the gathering. Even the brown-robed squaws seemed charmed by the brilliance of the oil lamps on the walls, the paintings, the long, flickering candles on the central chandelier, the deep, brown-red polished beauty of massive furniture, and the library shelves that dominated a wall opposite the cavernous fireplace.

In the course of the evening a young lady sang to the accompaniment of a guitar, servants plied us continually with wines and brandy, and a young man from a visiting troupe entertained with card and other tricks. The tables were continually replaced with new and different plates of spicy, exotic, and tempting meats and condiments – venison, lamb, fowl, smoked fish, and nuts, which were rare in these parts, and it was well past three in the morning when the guests (some simply fell asleep on the floor) took their leave. As several of us, including Charles and I, were house guests, a gracious Mlle. Chouteau showed us, in our half-stuporous state to a side porch liberally spread with rugs and buffalo robes. No coverings were necessary except to soften the floor, and we instantly fell asleep.

Light and warmth from the high sun awakened me the next morning. My head had the proportions of a pumpkin and, for a few minutes, I had difficulty focusing. Covillaud was gone. Nor was he present in the house when I entered and found Mssr. Chouteau and his wife seated at a table sipping coffee.

"Eh bien, and how did you sleep?" First, I paid my respects to Mlle. Chourteau, then, "Perhaps a little too soundly, Mssr., but then, at the post I am unused to late hours. And the trial of getting here apparently had to be paid for with a few extra hours of sleep."

"Oh, it is not late, Claude. I think it is only eight. Here on the hill we receive the first sun in St. Louis, and it is particularly bright this morning."

The servant brought cup and saucer. Mlle. Chouteau poured thick, soothingly aromatic liquid into it and, as Mssr. continued, she excused herself and left the room.

"Claude, you must know by now that I am very happy with the way in which you handle the business and adjust to new surroundings and work. Not every French emigrant could have learned as quickly as you the double art of trading with Indians and whites – a success which is apparent in both your records and furs. It was you I thought of first when, last night, I was informed of the need for a new bourgeois on the Yellowstone. The American Fur Company relies heavily upon men it sends so far. It tests and scrutinizes carefully before engaging them: do they drink to excess; do they possess an ability to direct men and show them how to perform tasks; would they be well-liked even though they must be stern; are they loyal when beyond a superior's observation; can they keep records. In short, do they have judgement and ability to be the law when they, themselves are beyond it in the wilderness?"

My head swam with prideful, even bloated thoughts when, that afternoon, Mssr. Chouteau at last sent me back to the post. I had indeed done well and, if it needed stating, I should say it too: I was honest – perhaps to a fault. For had I not detected in his recitation of the loneliness and responsibilities of a post bourgeois, a hint of the controlled corruption that is a part of the great enterprise of the American Fur Company. And surely that is a part of dealings where a customer or client is seen to be gullible, where large possibilties of gain are present, and especially where the opponent on the other side of the counter considers the new, the bright, worthy out of all proportion or reality. In short, and as my vanity resumed a more normal size, I recalled and weighed certain phrases used by Chouteau, and the manner in which he had said them (phrases loaded with subtle references to the necessity for convincing the Indian that he should part with his skins for the cheap conveniences and bangles – and perhaps alcohol).

Chouteau had furnished me with a new proposal. I was to give my answer within two months – before the middle of September – and in time, if my answer was negative – for another to be approached for the same station.

I paused in town for a few purchases and set out in the usual way to the post, and at a good trot. It was an effortless trip this time. But beneath the appreciations of Chouteau appeared small, nagging doubts about myself and my ability to cope with the larger managements. I was inclined to accept his evaluation, to agree that I did indeed possess the iron to manage a large post and to be law in a region where passion and inclination replaced natural laws. The intensity of my thoughts in this regard, the conjuring up of situations encounterable in the long, cold witner in a wild section far to the north seemed to erase time, and suddenly I was at the post clearing, my dog at my feet, barking, the substitute storekeeper at the post door.

As I dismounted and tended horse, I thought how pleasant it would be to have someone listen to a recounting of my trip. For, I reasoned, the young French helper would not be expected to ride back so late.

Etienne had tended the post well in my absence. He had swept, renewed the ever-present stew-pot with new potatoes, wild turnips, and calish roots and had pleasantly seasoned it with wild thyme and bay. Only one sale had been made – to a white man. It had been a quiet two days and so Etienne had walked up to the creek, located a large patch of blackberries, returned for a panier and filled it. Some we ate as fruit; most were now a tart-sweet jam simmering over low coals.

Etienne was in a talkative mood and proved to be a typically jolly courier de bois, who, after helping to keelboat a load of furs to the big city, remained a few months before returning to his wilderness post. Here was a man from the upper reaches of Missouri, and I lost no time in telling him of Chouteau's offer and interrogating him about conditions there.

After several questions, which Etienne answered with lurid tales and anecdotes, he turned to me and said:

"Mssr., if one must ask about life among the savages, he should not travel so far to find his answers".

"And why do you say that?" I asked, knowing full well why.

"Because one does not want to go there without first having acquired, through experience, all the answers to these questions."

His answer was so low and thoughtful and ended with a tone so charged with menace and warning that I put off any further questioning.

It was long past midnight and halfway through the small keg of wine which I kept for special times, when Etienne's head began to nod. Then, without another word he drained his cup, rose, shuffled a few steps to his buffalo robe near the dim orange cavern of the fireplace, humped, and began to snore. I, too, rolled into my robe. But it was hours before sleep came and when it did, I wandered intermiably and dazedly through a maze of flint-hard thickets in the Rickeraw country, tired, cold, and lost.

In the morning Etienne's robe was empty. Small wonder. I had drunk the greater share of our keg and awakened perhaps hours later then he. He had crept away rather than to awaken me. I rose and stood in the doorway. Scraps of conversation welled up in my half-drugged head: first the one by Chouteau, the ones which sent tremors of pride and anticipation of adventure through me; then the words of Etienne, with their mysterious caution. And yet there remained, ever, the inexplicable contradiction: here was a young countryman who saw only menace in the course proposed by Chouteau, but who yet planned on returning to the wilderness as soon as finances and weather made the trading and trapping possible and profitable. His eyes, I recalled, had had the same fierce glint I had noted in the eyes of Jacques, as though they had caught and still retained a vision of wonders and beauty, of hardship and horror too deep and compelling to express in words; experiences that recorded only in the eyes of the beholder.

I returned to my routine post duties still troubled and undecided. In the end it was I who would make the move, the decision. I recalled there had been no attempt by Chouteau to tempt me with promises and material rewards, no attempt to minimize the savagery of the northern winters, the dispositon of the savages; only the quiet conviction, mirrored in his words and gestures that I was his choice.

I cannot say that the two months remaining before I should state my decision were comfortable ones. The diversion at Chouteau's mansion, I found, had caused a change in my thinking. I now felt, without conscious egotism, possessed of a confidence that anything I attempted here on the frontier would succeed. Where did this super-confidence come from? I was the same Claude. And yet here, alone, and on the fringes of a wild land, vast and unknown, there welled up in me a ceritude of power, of curiosity, that animated all my waking hours.

The offer by Chouteau had liberated a part of me long in bondage. My reaction was a revelation, a personal, exciting discovery: I began to read more closely the French newspaper which occasionally came my way, and to question others concerning life far from civilization. I even shaved a smooth small square on one of the logs behind the counter and bisecting the area with a vertical line, labeled one half "OUI", the other half "NON". In the weeks that passed I queried each person who came to trade – Indian and white – about the wilds. And as the time drew near when I was to tell Mssr. Chouteau my decision, there was no single mark on the "OUI" half. I had no desire to risk life on the north frontier. Yet the knowledge that a man of Mssr. Chouteau's stature and reputation should feel that I could perform well at such a task remained with me, and was the seed whose germination caused me to become profoundly dissatisfied with my lonely post. The months of June, July, and August came in a welter of hot, humid days with little to distinguish them except that in some the mosquitoes bit deeper. I boiled leaves of a strong-scented and oily shrub and laved myself with the brown liquid for temporary relief. Fort Brule had been incinerated in mid-July, I was informed.

By September I had made up my mind: It was torward the west I wanted to travel, if I were to leave St. Louis. But I made up my mind to let Mssr. Chouteau down as easily as possible. One feels a certain mastery of control over a situation when it is his prerogative to make a decision and one day, as I rode, I rehearsed the words, the processes I would employ in affirming my appreciation for his confidence in me.

I left Mssr. Chouteau in a mood of deflated detachment. I knew there had been no lessening of the man's regard for me, nor of his convicion that I could perform to the Company's specifications. But even as I told him my decision I felt in a way cheated, wounded. Had I expected him to supplicate, to implore? No, both of us knew he had a second choice in mind had I been unwilling to accept. And yet a hollowness of spirit set in. My ego was bruised, yet not maimed. I rejoiced that I would remain at his post yet a while. One day after renewing my personal stock of wine in town, I set out to find Charles Covillaud.

He was not at the address handed to me by Chouteau. He was at work. I was directed by his landlady to a large cooperage near the waterfront where, as I waited for the workday to end, I could not help observing a group of nondescript laborers carrying materials and trash from the cooperage floor. One figure with a red band about his head stumbled and fell and received a storm of oaths for his clumsiness. In the act, his band came off and I saw, with a shock that it was my friend Covillaud. The man had impressed me as one far above the working class. Why had he taken a job so menial if he was a skilled cooper?

To wait, to meet him again under these circumstances would cause him much embarassment, since the impression he had left with me was so at variance with the present situation. I recovered my horse and returned to the post after a long, hot ride. Pondering as I was, it seemed but a minute. Somehow, Covillaud's apparent fall from high estate affected me and I felt a sudden deep sadness for a man who possessed such outward show of affluence and taste, but whose circumstances compelled him to work so menially.

The Missouri summer fled in a fury of business activity for the post. A veritable flood of people seemed to spring from nowhere. They arrived in battered wagons and squatted on the land in bustling, bold sullenness. Arriving when the planting and harvesting seasons had ended, they appeared at the post, shouted their inquiries from the wagon seat, and drove on or dismounted and bought little.

Arnold F. Rothmeier

At Chouteau's suggestion, I now wore a gun. With the influx of white settlers there was a diminution of Indian trade and an increase in cash sales. Though this made my business tasks simpler, since I had only to record the item and case intake, it withdrew the interest I had always had for dickering – the contest of wills over an item's value.

Not only did the intake of hides now diminish, but the Indians of late – members of eastern tribes not previously seen – now came to the post but rarely, and then, usually very early in the day, when there was little chance of being accosted by white settlers. Always present in their attitude was that low river of fear, just as there seemed always present in the white, a deep-seated conviction that everywhere, all Indians were the war-cry-whooping, scalping and skulking savage of the east. There was, however, little friction between the two.

I missed the deer which no longer poured in dun-colored packs through a hole in the forest wall and left only the impression of a quick, white-tailed twitch. They came to the clearing much less frequently and I never quite became accustomed to the daily sharp pound of a hunter's rifle.

The post came more and more to resemble a small store for notions and petty items. Trade now demanded the prosaic. Overnight my dealings went from contact with the wild man and his air of mystery and childlike dealings in furs and bright things, to the gruff suspicion of the settler and his pounds and cash.

Chapter 15
Pikes and Settlers

They came in droves that fall of '44, each wagon load of drab bonnets and red-faced sweating men pounding and cursing their ox teams. With the advancing fall weather the hillsides and valleys about the post beame dotted with small crude log houses. Why they should have waited until late in the year to make their move, I was never able to discover. Perhaps it was the necessity to gather in late crops at their old homes. Perhaps it was a delay in selling their old homes. Or perhaps it was simply that a desire to resettle came late, so that there was little or no plan to the whole thing, but only a need to seek an inexpressible something further west.

As the year progressed I came to know, too, the solid, independent, law-abiding, religious settler families. They were the early comers to the region. Many spoke a heavy German accent. They were cautious, and they were well established with small barns and a crop of wheat and vegetables before an early snow fell.

Others, though not so welcome as guests around the post fire, were those who were referred to as the "Pukes". They came, it seems, from a country known as Pike. Only much later, after I had left the area, was I to discover the derogatory implications of the synonym for them: "Puke".

They all came to the post for their few necessities, rather than to spend a good part of the day riding to St. Louis, and though none of them spoke more than a dozen monosyllables, I came to read in their faces, actions, and tones their common reason for being here; an inborn need, a compulsion to wander, to achieve self-sufficiency in isolation and to avoid, at all costs, the responsibilities that accompany life in a close-settled area. Not only did the new settlers avoid proximity to others in their choice of location, but their aproach to others and to me was cautious and moody, as though by conversing, something – perhaps their achieved isolation – might be taken from them.

Since the New Orleans days I had been struck by the fondness some had for chewing and spitting, but had given the habit little thought. Now, after lanky Missourians had purchased and departed, I found corners of the post coated with thick, brown spittle, and I was forced to contrive shakesided, earth-filled boxes for their habit.

More disturbing than this crude custom was a belligerence I detected in their eyes and swagger. One evening as the stew came to a boil, I was visited by a pair of tall, grizzled Missourians.

"You got any 'lasses?", the taller asked. I replied that I had some in the back room, and turned to get the jug. Both men turned and sauntered towards the fire. The jug was on a shelf beneath some material and I stooped to get it. There, unknown to them, and unavoidable for me, I overheard their conversation.

"Damned furriner. Ought ter run em all out of the country. Caint understan' their talk noways."

"Yeah", the other answered, "how'd he git this store innyway.

White folk otter run white stores 'stead of furriners."

The tones of the men were low and ominous and my flesh crawled at the though that, to their list of prejudices, they might add "eavesdropper".

Fortunately dim light and the high counter made it possible for me to seem to re-appear from the storeroom. I sold the article with as few words as possible, almost giving it away in order to shorten their stay. The taller one paid for the purchase with one of the the "bit" pieces then coming into use, pressing the sharp, pie-shaped point cruelly into my palm as he did so. I winced and peered into two unwavering, close-set eyes. Then he turned his head and spat, and the dark slime covered the new box side and oozed onto the floor. His laugh from the doorway contained elements of intolerance, irascibility, and pure idiocy. The other, silent until now, also began to laugh, and the sound continued even after heavy quirts sent their horses stampeding from the yard. These were Pikes, whom I was to meet with growing frequency.

I was shaken. Their explosive violence had unnerved me. I had detected no whiskey about either of the men. Would the encounter have let me off so easily had they been drunk? And what might they have done had they been provoked or opposed?

The incident was traumatic and its memory conditioned me for many years. Once, in a dream, I went hunting. Each deer I felled seemed to die from a bullet that left an empty eye-socket and a hanging ear. I awoke the following morning to the realization that my dream had been in English. I took this as a sure sign that I was at last becoming thoroughly Americanized.

I resolved now to go about better protected, and the Colt, which I had bought at Mssr. Chouteau's suggestion, became part of my daily wear. This was the second time I had observed the ugly nature of the

Pike. This time I had been a near-participant instead of a spectator. I could not help feeling that the animosity so frequently displayed was a natural response to personal, physical discomforts brought on by the sickening monotony of their diet of pork, and the frustrations of simple things like the ague shakes, the mosquitoes, and the no-see-ums that lit an exposed limb with a fiery sensation and left one bleary from a night of scratching. How many of the brawls – which were a common occurrence along the water-front – were only blind outward attempts to soothe aching guts or bruised and frustrated feelings?

Not all Pikes were as ill-humored and prejudiced as these were, however. As the valley became more settled, new arrivals would frequently enter the post with the obvious intention of passing an evening exchanging observations on the state of the country. I was glad for these occasions for they kept me current on the feelings of the settler, his government, the economy, and their feelings concerning the territory set aside for the Indian. And they wondered, too, as I did, what was contained in that vast land that lay across the Missouri. I saw myself – and them – standing tip-toe on the dawn of an epoch, which ended with fur trading, and began with something else. What that something was to be for the Indian, I could only guess. Its successor would be settlement.

What newspapers I saw served to confirm local, often monosyllabic harangues of the newcomers about savages. Though most of those who talked spoke of the farmer wronged by the savage, occasionally one seemed to peer beneath the flood of tiresome cliches that described the Indian and his land.

Early one memorable evening, as three or four "regulars" whittled and mouthed, we were visited by a customer of another stripe. He was an emigrant farmer like the rest, but more given to silent observation than to dogmatic speech. Declining my offer of a glass of wine, he sat for a long time on a log section just inside the door, listening to the others, and smoking.

Pan The Low Waters

A kind of running spate of diatribes against the lazy savage was receiving an airing. The quiet one chose for his entering theme one of those natural conversational lulls when there seemed no need for words, when all present were agreed and unanimous. Suddenly his voice rose like a wraith from the corner.

"The Indian will lose in the end, whether or not he has ever had any right to the land. His right to it is only because of having been here longer than the white man. What seems to me to be shaping up now is a battle of the government with the impossible: how to take the very sustenance of the savage – his land and his buffalo – without him reacting to the injustices done him."

The tone of the voice was even and deadly, and carried, in its clarity and simplicity, a purity of logic that held his listeners transfixed. While he talked, it was as unthinkable that another should interrupt as it was that the cabin walls should dissolve and vanish.

He continued, after a short pause, as though waiting for his words to fit into the niches of his hearer's prejudices. There was no response. He continued in the same expressive monotone.

"The skirmishes and frictions we see now are only bashful quarrels compared with the Armageddons to come. Two powerful forces are only jockeying for position on a plain of inevitability. The Indian can not adjust to civilization in time to avoid disaster to his nation, and the white man can no more stay his transgression of this land than the ocean its tide.

The Indian will see his hunting grounds decimated and feel the push and shove of the white. He will retreat in the face of the settler, thinking that the land and the buffalo will go on forever, and in the end it will be too late for him to solve his problem in the only way possible and retain his nation: by becoming tiller of the soil."

The man moved his head from side to side, and added, "Too late! Too late!"

The silence was eloquent at the stranger's pronouncements. It was strange to hear a settler play on the unpopular theme of the dispossessed savage; strange to hear from a countryman so contrary a point of view. His was an audacious observation and one that had no place in a frontier filling with families who had had, and whose parents had had, all romance and charity wrung from them by the hostility of both Indian and land. There was here no wish to re-examine an option already solidified into a way of life.

In the lush, red glow of a summer sunset I observed the effect of the speaker's words on the faces present. One bent with unwarranted zeal to his whittling, head lowered almost to his knife; another's eyes ridiculously scanned dimensions of the room, as though planning an addition, eyes nervously tracing lines from corner to corner; another spat his quid at an empty fireplace, raising grey dust that seemed to match something in his eyes, which, like the firewood, was already consumed; the face of a fourth, who leaned against a stack of buffalo hides, was seen to twitch uncontrollably as though pulled, like a puppet, by fine wires drawn by a force within the man's head.

I had no chance to examine my own reactions to the visitor's unorthodox opinions, but I had the distinct impression that however unpleasant their memories were of Indian depredations, none felt his justified imposition of the tragedy which he saw – through the eyes of the stranger – closing in upon, blotting out the existence of the savage. It was as though in a flash of insight the truth of an unavoidable catastrophe was revealed, in all its nakedness, and that each person present – myself included – shared a responsibility for its coming.

No sound stirred in the now softly rose-colored room. Outside, a bird sang in descending tones with an eerie lethargy, and in a register so low as to lend to its melody a contrived unnaturalness. There was

Pan The Low Waters

an inaudible crackling of something within the room, a stirring of mood or thought, as though in concert, all those present had psychically responded to the same stimulus. The tone and truth of the speaker's words had so surprised them that, willy-nilly, the parts of them which operated above acquired prejudice were stunned to silence.

It was a singular moment – if moment it was – for it was poised upon the loneliest conceivable spot in a man's nature – the searing aridity of his conscience.

There were other evenings that proliferated with a thick verbiage of proposed solutions, but there were none in which I was as moved as I was by the prophetic tones of the stranger. This was the only time in all the years of my apprenticeship that I was to hear a word of kindness or sympathy voiced in the Indian's behalf. Idle talk about the native – or even serious consideration for him – never seemed capable of rising above passionately derogatory words of those whose parents had sown the seeds of hate and revulsion.

Arnold F. Rothmeier

Chapter 16
Second Winter

It was in my third year of managing the post – the first mainly for Indians, the second almost exclusively for settlers – that I came alive to the rapid changes taking place in the country and noted, more than once, new changes within me. From conversations with an ever-increasing number of settlers, I learned of the smouldering resentment against those who denied them access to land farther west. I could, however, see little reason for their terrible recriminations. The land was fertile, and though more densely settled than when I arrived, there seemed room for many more farms before one could call his situation crowded. And then, too, those who cursed the loudest and damned government restrictions, were the single, more rambunctious men, those without responsibilities who simply wanted to move about, to see, and test, and debauch, then move again. It seemed an obsession, a compulsive American trait. Certainly no country, to my knowledge, had for centuries had so boundless a playground in which to roam, where land was had for the settling, and where food came so easily to hand.

Pan The Low Waters

For my part, I was happy. Never, even in the humid, fecund, proliferating days in the south, had my needs been so easily satisfied. Food was plentiful, and though I now had to range father for deer, my kettle was never wanting for a variety of vegetables, fresh and dry.

All was, in fact, as though I were living in Eden, with no compulsions, fear, or needs – except one; I was now at the height of my mental, physical, and sexual powers – if power be the correct word for such a need. But for the latter, I seemingly had no need, and few of the opposite sex were present to create a stimulus. It was indeed a bachelor's paradise. Every ingredient was present in it for the suppression of the mating instinct: an almost exclusive male company, and a vast variety of distractions, not the least of which was the food for thought, left by customers on the counter of my mind, just as bit-pieces were left daily upon the slick, greasy counter planks.

And as the winter of my third year approached, a series of events and rumors came crowding in upon me. There seemed never enough time to digest them adequately. The one which concerned me the most of all concerned the beaver market. I had come to St. Louis at the beginning of its decline. Now there was little incentive to trap them. Prices for prime beaver pelts, even in the short time I had been here, had sunk so low – about one half their former price – that few trappers bothered with them, but chose buffalo hides as the object of their hunt. The situation puzzled me until, one day I chanced to overhear informed settlers talking pelts. I had seen, on the streets of Rouen and New Orleans the wide floppy brims of the beaver hat, but since coming to St. Louis, had never taken the trouble to puzzle out why these so-called "beaver hats" simply did not resemble the lush, thrilling feel of the actual pelt, or possess its scintillating auburn hues. For the hat itself had a drab, grayish cast. Now I was informed that the only part of the pelt used was the downy, indescribably feathery undercoat next to the hide. This, after the stiffer, auburn-colored guard hairs were plucked, clipped, and sifted, and because of its almost magical power to coalesce, made the felt from which the hat was shaped.

But this was changing now. A force as unfathomable as religious dogma and doctrine had swirled against the tides of fashion, and within the period of my emigration, had almost banished the beaver felt and replaced it with Canton silk. The why of such forces I could mull over and inspect, but never attach a cause – except to lay the change to a movement which usually had an economic source. If the cause touched the purse, then a change would, somehow follow. This was the dominant fact of life I was observing – and perhaps the occasion of my being here in the employ of Mssr. Chouteau lent me perspective from which to see this motive more clearly.

The gathering of people on the northeastern shore of the Missouri was another phenomenon I was to note and ponder as winter closed in again. Often a settler would remain a night or more in the post before he could leave. And we would sit by a snapping fire and ponder the country's changes between exclamations over the force of the storm raging outside. We would sit and smoke, and the barriers between emigrant Frenchman and a foreigner-hating Kentuckian would vanish, and we would be just two souls standing in awe of the forces that shook and blasted the post timbers. We would talk about the fabulous trading then coming to a close on the Santa Fe Trail, the sea of Indian tribes squeezing westward, reeling from the shock of an overpowering white wave; the United States Forces which stood guard at Fort Leavenworth, lest a leak develop in that false dike and flood the forbidden land with settlers; the effect which the killing of so many buffalo – simply for tongue and hide – would have upon the savages who depended upon them for food, shelter, and clothing. What else was there?

The winter of '44 was an interminable monotony of snow-laden storms that kept me cabin-bound for weeks on end. These were times when not even the closest settlers – those half a mile away – came to the post. These were the lonliest months I had ever experienced, and though I was Norman French, and by nature self-sufficient, I unconsciously resolved that I should not be so isolated another winter. The peasant Frenchman, the gregarious in me, was beginning to show through.

Toward the end of March, when the heavy snows and cold were past, when even from a mile away I could hear the boom and grind of river ice, Mssr. Chouteau surprised me with another visit. He arrived one noon as I was bundling a few locally trapped pelts. There came a whinny, an answering neigh from my mare, and Chouteau descended from a small, delicately constructed equipage (for there were now well-beaten wagon paths). We greeted and went inside. As we sipped our wine, he came quickly to the point of his visit.

"Claude", he aside, "How has our business gone this year, compared with last year?"

I had no slightest need to falsify. The rafter racks, which a year ago had bulged with prime fur, now contained only a few small *plews*. I had had no need to remove what I had traded this past year, for they occupied so little space.

"Mssr. Chouteau, the Indians who brought in our furs last year have gone. In their place have come the settlers. But the needs of the two, and their furs, have made what you see before you." I gestured towards the rafters, then continued, "There will be a few more furs taken in trade before spring, but most will be shot, not trapped, and they will have bullet holes. As settlers come, the Indians remain away and trade where they are not bothered – perhaps at Black Hills, or at Westport." Mssr. Showed no sign of wishing to interrupt, and I continued.

"I now do a typical store business. There is cash on hand, but no trading; no furs. I see a future for the post, but not the one you would like for the American Fur Company." I paused.

Mssr. seemed anxious for me to continue, and for the first time in our acquaintance I noted about him a kind of hopeless expectancy, almost a craftiness about the eyes. It was as though he were willing me to say what I could not discern in the purpose of his visit.

I refilled his glass. A customer arrived; left with a minor purchase. Mssr. Chouteau had risen and stood peering through the doorway while the man bought. He now re-seated himself and reluctantly approached his purpose.

"You haven't mentioned it, Claude, but you must know, I'm sure, of the store and mill being built by Mr. Brandon out on Deer Creek."

I replied that I had not heard of such construction, but the implications of a competitive store were spelled out as he continued. No customer had made mention of this, although for more than a week I had had only a small portion of my usual thin business. Since there were few, if any, Frenchmen in the area, and because the store would be large, not to mention the handiness of the grist mill, most of what little trade I now had would surely be siphoned off. There simply was no excuse for keeping a trader on at this port.

And now Chouteau stated the purpose of his visit: it was to offer me the opportunity of purchasing the post and its five acres.

Before he left we opened another bottle and then, as if to reassure himself that his decision was for the best, we strolled about the grounds. He reiterated assertations that he was more than satisfied with the care I had shown for the property and the trade. I assured him that I would give the proposition my most serious consideration, and with that he mounted his buggy and wheeled away through the trees.

For some moments I watched the leaves fall back and grow still after his passage. A curtain had fallen upon a small drama of my life for, though I had not stated it to Mssr. Chouteau, I felt it only folly to continue here. It seemed, somehow, that a show of audience appreciation should follow. It came on cue: a raucous mocking nearby of two saucy jay birds.

I stood for a long time in my doorway. No one came to interrupt my thoughts. For two years I had been "Bourgeois" of a small company post. Though I had had no one under me, I had had functions to perform and responsibilties which made me master of valuable company property. Now I was to be a free agent again. In short, I was to be without a post and home. Realization of the rapid changes on the frontier struck me suddenly, and I quailed. In France there had been accepted routine and few, if any, abrupt changes. There the village and city life had seemed to thrive in a pattern which, like water, moved to find its own level, then wore placidly on.

But I was not without alternatives: there, in the corner lay my cooping tools. For nearly three years I had not opened the bag in which they lay, oiled and wrapped. I could always return to the skill I had learned so well, and which lay there embodied in a few turned and flattened pieces of fine steel. Memories of past satisfactions at my cooper's bench, remembered glances of wonderment and admiration from my fellows in Rouen and New Orleans passed pleasantly across my mind. I had always felt a keen pride as I bevelled my staves – as though guided by the Carpenter, Himself. Yes, I could return to this calling, the one that I knew so well.

But, again, the thought of city life, with its smoke, stench, and routine repelled me. My years at the post were compelling me to find myself, to discover the truth about myself. There was within me an instant revulsion for things unnatural, teeming and pretentious, and life in the city, especially the frontier city of St. Louis, represented all of these things.

There was little to debate. It would be foolhardy to continue here. One balmy May morning I packed ledger, bagged money on hand, slung my few belongings and tools behind the saddle, locked the post, and made for St. Louis. A chapter of my life had ended. How would the new one begin?

Pan The Low Waters

Chapter 17
Covillaud

I reached the city's outskirts in mid-afternoon and made my way immediately to Mssr. Chouteau's office to be relieved of the cash and paper I carried, and to collect monies due me. My mentor was happy to see me and not at all surprised at my decision to forego purchase of the post. It was, as he put it, "a thin investment" for anyone, in view of the potential area market. His mood, again, was one of concern for me, and as I enumerated my choices and said I had decided to look over the town more closely before making up my mind, he offered the names of two cooperages that might employ me – if a return to this was my final choice.

My wages for the third year were a handsome nine hundred dollars, and, with heartfelt thanks I left Mssr. Chouteau's employ with his best wishes and a most cordial handshake. I then proceeded to the Bank of St. Louis, where my spirits rose as I added to my earlier deposit. My account was now in excess of two thousand dollars, plus some pocket cash which would do until I might be employed again. Never had I had such a sum! And never did I feel such a thrill of independence as on that cool March afternoon upon leaving the bank.

Arnold F. Rothmeier

A room was available at the Navarre Boarding House. I took it, paying a week in advance after sampling lunch. Then I left my horse in the adjoining stable and strolled through town toward the wharves.

Again I sat on a barrel on the wide-timbered wharf, pipe in hand, watching the sweating engagees, enjoying the stunning, the overpowering scents – and my idleness – fully as much as I enjoyed my pipe.

Steamboats were like tethered beasts newly broke. They lay docile and low in the eddying brown water. Each time a bale or heavy bundle reached a deck, the boat would seem to shudder and plunge ever so slightly, as though resenting an additional burden. Each ship shook thus, the larger ones bearing up under the load with a patience that contrasted with the skittish rebellion of the smaller.

I observed more closely the work of the common engage' and dock laborer and was struck by the similarities between these and the black freemen I had seen on levees at New Orleans. Both, seemingly, had no limit to their strength and endurance, and gloried in the absurd demands made upon themselves. It was now late in a humid afternoon and the rhythm and suggestive lyrics of the French songs lent power and endurance to their backs and legs just as the southern coonjine had done. But while the latter songs had had a quiet, shuffling swing, a low bounce, the ditties of their counterparts here were full-throated. Almost as much effort seemed to go into their songs as into their carrying. Their raw heartiness and challenge matched, no doubt, the rough contentions and lonely country toward which they would soon be moving, and I sensed now something of that bleakness, loneliness, and danger.

My reverie ended abruptly. I was clasped around the shoulder and hand-shaken by Charles Covillaud. He, too, had been attracted by the bawdy songs, the suggestive French, and had been nearby for some time before spotting me.

"Eh bien! From the rear I took you for one of the ship's owners!"

It had been more than a year since we had met at the Chouteau soiree, and almost that long since I had seen him in the improbable role of common laborer. Now he was again dressed as a dandy. He lost no time in telling me about his position as clerk in one of the general stores in town.

"It seems my talents for coopering were not appreciated, and so I simply kept an eye on the paper advertisements. Life is never so good that you can't find a better job. Today is my day off."

He went on at a rapid rate about his prospects for becoming purchasing agent for a large store. I experienced a twinge of envy at hearing his good fortune, but then, at the same time, caught a note of false optimism in his nervous, rapid speech.

At any rate, Charles did look the picture of prosperity, and was a thoroughly likeable person, having more than a normal share of volatile enthusiasm and optimistic good humor.

As the conversation explored my own prospects, and as we continued to watch the quayside drama, a kind of revelation emerged, a wedding of ideas that seemed to suggest a path for me. While Charles talked on – I know not on what subject – my mind rapidly tried out, vicariously, the idea of a small store and cooperage somewhere farther west.

I suppose the idea and the desire had lain unspoken and unconceived somewhere about me ever since Chouteau had offered me his northern post. At the time of his offer my inclination for such was low. But today I seemed possessed by a confidence in my trading and mechanical skills, and everything – including the secure feeling produced by my bank account and the sight of these outward-bound engagees – stirred within me vague and daring prospects.

Arnold F. Rothmeier

Charles had noted an odd expression and manner about me as he talked, and said as much. I then had to tell my thoughts, which, as we conversed, kindled, also, his volatile imagination.

Part of our now rapidly developing enthusiasm, I am sure, was stimulated by the mystery of the scenes about us, and the wish to participate in whatever it was these men on shipboard were about – a wish not to be left behind.

Chapter 18
Decision

The day was one of sunny brilliance. A light breeze played about us, fanning the ships' flags and lending a romantic air to the picture. Not far from where we sat lay a steamer, low in the water, whose main deck was being filled with oxen and wagon beds – wheels removed and stacked to save space. Several men and boys – apparent owners of the gear – in addition to bare-chested crew – gee'd and haw'd. Chests and boxes were thrown roughly on board; a group of three women and an assortment of dirty, sallow-faced children squatted resignedly, watching the proceedings with frightened, sunken eyes, as though their turn to be herded aboard would come and they, too, would answer to the whip-crack.

Scraps of meaning: the bold "OREGON" scrawled on a wagon bed; a fragment of shouted oath about the "trail"; a hoarse phrase about "—maybe can be got at Independence" – formed a collage of hasty impressions of people on the move to somewhere beyond the pale of a frontier. These were not settlers I had observed who moved about, settling smugly on the fringes of another's daring and around already established cities. There was about the whole company a stamp of boldness. And yet the eyes of the children smouldered with a kind of terror-ridden uncertainty. The cocksureness of the men and the young boys contrasted vividly with the posture of the women and the very young. These radiated their dejection – an air compounded of surrender and panic.

As we watched the loading I became conscious of a growing assemblage of male onlookers about us. Patently this was no ordinary venture. Nearby could be heard opinions that ran the gamut of speculation from that of dire disaster to the opening of a trail to a place called the Oregon Territory. As I drank in these opinions and their implications, I observed Charles closely. His being contained a contradiction: there was about him yet the dandy I had noted when first introduced by Mssr. Chouteau; his carriage had about it a softness, incongruous in the surrounding ruggedness of St. Louis; and yet, as I caught him in intent profile, I saw a quiet power, a determination that one sees in heroic action.

Loading of the boat was accomplished by late afternoon after a troupe of small, sleek swine were driven squealing and grunting aft; women and children were seen to stir as though their cue had at last been spoken. Without knowing it we had witnessed the start of not only one small cluster of souls, but the prototype of many lumbering and probing parties, that, like the new-formed bird in its shell, must break out or die.

In a fleeting moment of understanding I felt the mystery, the sadness, and the unspoken promise of life at the end of the trail. And I thought, for a brief moment, I could hear a song in their hearts and feel the pain of leaving as the boat's whistle sounded and a slow slap of the great paddle drew them away.

The boat's departure created a mournful vacancy in the faces of those who watched. And did I imagine those guilty, half-abashed faces of the older lookers-on? Or was there something in the drama which caused me to expect them because I had empathized so deeply with the feeling of those now gone?

Our attention was diverted by feats of strength by a tall, burly, negro dock-hand. He was enjoying gasps of astonishment and the buzzes of disbelief as he loaded himself with thrice the burden of his co-workers. The stage-plank sagged and creaked under his every load, and his return for more was a stage-entrance, light and swaggering and so full of grinning confidence as to intimate the imbecilic.

My musings concerned the number of years such a man could expect to perform such sinew-testing work before nature dictated terms. The sweating bodies of the loaders seemed to suggest the bottle, and Charles proposed that we have a brandy, for chances of getting good wine were poor. I glanced again at Charles, and was struck by the change that had come over him since we last met.

I had early met a dandy, one who thought to bring facile, courtly ways and young, thoughtless years to this raw city. I had been adversely impressed by his facile, ready optimism, and had turned from him. But now I saw a different Charles, one who seemed enormously aged, as though the effect of the scenes just witnessed had been to blow the soft fuzz of youth from his cheek and raise a vision of grizzled manhood. His eyes, as we mounted to Pinod Street, were of steel and his shoulders had grown immensely broad and capable. My earlier opinions of him were further altered by his remarks as we sipped our brandy in a dingy waterfront café.

"Claude," he said, "I'm not ready to face the things these wanderers are going to face, are you".

Not ready! The words suggested a period of waiting, or preparation; a timidity, perhaps even a need for time or experience. But I know now, that had it not been for the thoughts of Charles, I should have remained much longer in St. Louis; perhaps for the rest of my life. I must confess that for many months now, in fact, ever since Mssr. Chouteau had suggested Yellowstone, the spectre of life in the wilds, and the thought of myself as a lone, free agent lost in forested vastness, had stirred me. The thought had been there in the background of my consciousness, like a challenge too big to acknowledge or face. It was like the bittersweet of a forbidden liaison. Now it burned constantly and deep. Not yet ready!

"What do you mean, you're not ready?" The question came forth unbidden, reflexively, and I could no more have refrained from putting the question than have stopped my heart from beating. For I was ready. I saw it now with crystal clarity. I was ready; had been. The readiness had grown like a tumor within me. I had not come to this new country to spin uselessly in the backwash of the wave of settlers. I now had a second apprenticeship behind me – one acquired on the docks at Rouen, and that learned under the tutelage of Mssr. Chouteau. Both had made me ripe-ready.

"Charles", I said, feeling the surge of sureness within me, "I think that you and I together could make it to the Oregon Country. Both of us have good health and a trade. I know what the Indians and the settlers need." I was, perhaps, as much urging myself on, as I was importuning Charles.

And we sat in the saloon half the night, drinking false courage and planning, somewhat as school children do before running away from home. But whether it was the brandy or the new camaraderie we seemed to feel for each other; the sight of those departing on the dock, or simply knowledge that there was a beautiful and dangerous country west, I could never be sure. We shared, that night, a decision headier that the cups we drank, and when the saloon closed us out we had made a vow to move soon. But we would test ourselves and the new country first. Charles would ask for a short leave to retain the security of his present position. We would book river passage west as soon as he had spoken to his employer.

The morning dawned clear and cool, and, for some strange and wonderful reason, I had an undeservedly clear head, a bland, sweet taste in my mouth, and a ravenous appetite. There were but few boarders at the breakfast table, and, after finishing a hearty and leisurely meal, I walked slowly down the hill in order to give Charles time to make his leave request.

Later, as I approached the store where Charles was employed I caught sight of him sitting on a stairway. He had been dismissed. His employer, a volatile, French-Hungarian, earlier fancying Charles as a handsome figurehead for a clerk, had turned on him. There had been words, and Charles had crossed the street to wait for me. Other than to explain his dismissal, he had little to say. He was not dejected, However, and seemed anxious to get on with our plans to board the steamer.

Up to this point I had not told Covillaud the state of my finances, though I believed he had little more than his two weeks wages, and thought it best not to. I could end up footing the bill for most of our expenses. I had sensed a disturbing improvidence about him, and determined that we should save as much as possible against real and unpredictable needs. So I was silent about my larger banked sum and spoke only of the smaller yearly wage I had earned at the post. I was not distrustful of Charles, but felt that we should depend upon what, ostensibly, we had in common – a sum of about two hundred fifty dollars.

I was, I think, the more optimistic about our move, and possessed more self-reliance and confidence. I was two years his senior and had spent three years in the near-wilderness toward which we were heading. My familiarity with the frontier had erased much of its mystery and uncertainty. I knew we would find fish, game, and berries at this time of the year and that at whichever one of the settlements upriver we would debark, there would be people and supplies and food. It was not as though we were summarily leaving for the ends of the earth. Furthermore, at this time of the year, there was no cause for concern about shelter, as the days and nights were temperate and storms rare. If the life at the end of this short upriver excursion proved not to our liking, the costs became impossible, or conditions became unbearable, we could simply return to St. Louis.

Truly, we had no plan. But then, I wondered at the time if any but men like Mssr. Chouteau and established men had plans. Trappers and hunters would hunt and trap, yes; deck hands and engagees would continue their backbreaking jobs, as long as their backs held out; the families moving up and down river and arriving from the east would settle where it seemed they might eke out a crop of corn; but few could rely on a planned permanence as was possible where cities stood for generations and the land was tilled and courts and law and security existed.

Chapter 19
Upriver

With no more planning or fuss than one would undertake for a *pique-nique* Charles and I were able to board a small steamer called the *Tamerlaine* after promising to help with the wooding-up when necessary. There was no decision made as to how far we would go. Though we shared steerage with some men of questionable appearance, the work was not excessively hard. Only three woodings-up were made, and pork was furnished. But, as it was tainted, I made as if to eat, but slipped mine overboard, for I feared what the other workers might think if they saw me refuse what they had eaten. Several pieces of jerky in my pack sufficed for most of the voyage.

After a second wooding-up and a brief exchange of parcels and barreled goods at a lively waterfront town called Independence, we hove to at Fort Leavenworth, where, for the first time, army uniforms became evident. Soldiers lounged about the small dock and Indians squatted on the rough timbers or stood, wrapped in ragged and filthy blankets, smoking.

There was no mixing or associating of the uniform and the

breechclout but all felt that the soldier was put there to rebuff the tide of immigration upon Indian land. A kind of bashful dependency could be sensed, a feeling that the harried savage sought security behind the blue uniform and blue guns.

Aside from the unusual cleanliness and order of the post, which gleamed whitely from the hill above, there was nothing about the post that suggested a temporary new home.

After a more strenuous wooding-up and purchase of more jerky, we again cast off. Earlier in our voyage I had imagined that our bags and packs had been disturbed. Now, when we again resumed our place in steerage, this evidence was too great to be ignored. My knife and tobacco were missing. I accepted the loss, for there was no recourse, and recognized the folly or our attempt to economize by roughing it in steerage. Our minds turned to the possibility of escape from the dubious company we kept. Charles had lost nothing, but had the same thoughts as I about leaving ship at the next port. There was much about our steerage companions that disturbed us both. I caught one looking fixedly at me as though to calculate the amount in my money belt; another looked away or past me when I happened to return his glances. Charles, too, had noticed these looks. We remained together and said nothing to antagonize.

When we reached Robidoux's post at Blacksnake Hills we had decided to ride no further with such company. The country was growing wilder and lonelier at each bend. We had already come nearly three hundred miles and were now in open Kickapoo country.

It was an uncomfortable, eerie feeling that possessed us as we worked our way upstream, one which set me to pondering why there was such malice shown toward the French. A generation had passed since the days of the infamous French war. Could it be that the illiterate class – here represented by four shifty-eyed laborers – resented us because our unconscious suavity of manner held up the mirror, so to speak, and made their beastiality more patent? Was it because the conditions of our birth made them feel their depravity more deeply and hate us in proportion?

We had been on the muddy, snag-filled Missouri almost two weeks, running only during daylight, when we coasted to another small, muddy cove for wood. Beyond a thick grove of beech a clutch of frontier houses and building was visible. This was the Blacksnake Hills post of the man called Robidoux. Neither of us had planned it as our destination, but the weight of circumstances compelled us to leave ship here and now. Perhaps is was the apprehension we felt under the eyes of the other travelers; perhaps we were tired of the monotony of the voyage; perhaps the realization that we were almost four hundred miles from St. Louis and another two hundred from the next post caused us to debark when we did.

Whatever it was, it made no difference, for after helping with the wooding-up, we picked up our packs, left the boat, and watched the stage plank swing aboard. To this day I remember the ill-concealed looks of frustration on the faces of the four steerage scoundrels as they saw their boat pull away without us. It is quite possible that had Charles and I not then parted company with the *Tamerlaine* and the quartet, we might soon have departed life. That fall, when the last boat came out of the north country and stopped at Blacksnake Hills, one of the tales it told was of four toughs who had been hung for murder and thievery near Fort Atkinson on the Platte.

Arnold F. Rothmeier

Chapter 20
Blacksnake Hills

Unlike Independence, whose cluster of wide streets and rough buildings were located at the top of a long, steep grade, and St. Louis, which mounted its metropolitan sprawl along a two-mile stretch of waterfront much as did New Orleans, Robidoux' Blacksnake Hills Post was situated on the left bank of the river at the foot of some low-lying hills just out of river reach. It was late and at the end of a warm afternoon. The swarms of insects through sun-slanting shadows seemed a normal accompaniment to the slow shuffle of a few mountain men and lightly-robed Indians about dusty areas between buildings, There was an air of repose, too, about the post and village, as though gathering, in its raw, unpainted spirit, potent and lusty power for a burgeoning growth. It lay now in a late summer torpor, seeming to gather strength for a leap into size and recognition.

Blacksnake Post was as far upriver as Charles and I wished to go, though as yet we had no thought that it held any more promise than Lincoln, Weston, Independence, or any of the seven or eight shy clusters of habitation between it and St. Louis. There had been one more port of call fourteen miles north – a settlement called Savannah, and another called Jeintown, halfway between, at which we might have debarked, had not the threat of the steerage toughs changed our minds.

Since joining forces with Charles I felt more secure that I had at any time since arriving at New Orleans. We were now two very self-sufficient adventurers in search of a "position" as we shouldered our packs and robes and went in search of food and bottle. Secretly we were happy in the knowledge that those working steerage on the *Tamerlaine* would have to load all the wood by themselves.

Venison, served at a small log house near the landing, was tender and savory, the hot bread warm and motherly, the brandy sweet and heady. It was nearing dusk when we finished the deer ham, for it was a temptation to keep munching on the slivers of succulent flesh shaved from the bone and sip a little more from the cup.

At last we could postpone leaving no longer, for a resting place must yet be found. Over Charles' objection I paid for the food, thanked the proprietor, and shouldered my pack. Whether the man had heard us conversing and knew us to be strangers, or whether he thought of us as potential customers, I could not ascertain. I know only how kindly I felt toward him for the splendid food and now for the offer: "There's plenty of room for you two to bed down over there in the corner, if you've got no place for the night."

There was a quiet light on his face as he made the offer as though he had been studying us and wished to encourage the right kind of people to remain.

We spread our buffalo robes in the corner and offered and thanked him. After a few more words he took his candles, latched the door, and retired to a rear room. Charles and I lay on our robes, the faint rose in the fireplace painting the barely discernable walls an infinitely soft tan. We spoke of the cordiality of the host, of the instant familiarity of the Black Hills Post, of our escape from the steerage, and dozed behind a deep curtain of sleep through which an occasional wolf-howl drifted.

Toward morning I was aroused by a need to relieve myself, and stole as softly as possible through the door. It was cool, but the warm feeling which had been with me earlier returned, and I looked down a main street toward the mist-shrouded river area. Charles was still snoring lightly. The cool early morning air had quickened my thoughts and I knew I would sleep no more. Outside I booted, donned gun and jacket, and strode along in a day refreshing and new. It was the moment that divided night from working day for most people. Just now in St. Louis the streets would be filling with men and wagons. Here the onus of frantic commerce had not arrived, though there were signs that some inhabitants were preparing to scar the day: as movement appeared on the single, sandy street which I descended, an essence of fried pork came from the scattered cabins and mingled with the tart, bruised willow I have always loved; a candle flickered here and there; from the misty river, muffled shouts. On my left a window sprang from dark to dim light; a figure moved within. From the misty shroud above the waterfront came the first vigorous curses of a new day, stinging the air and seeming to move the fog. The words penetrated the gray mist as though the frequently-mentioned Diety lent power and penetration to the profanity; made it go farther.

A few steamers and keelboats were plain now. Mists parted like a curtain as I strode through them, and the work dockside was revealed by a soft glow that preceded fullness of sunlight. Though it was barely daybreak and yet cool, laborers and deck-hands wore no shirts, and their faces and backs were aglow with sweat. Behind a barrel Indians scooped a dark sweet flood into an old felt hat, licking rapidly at their hands after each motion. The molasses oozed from a rent stave near the bottom. Most of it pushed into a slow puddle and slipped through space in the planked dock.

Nearby, ragged and near-naked children huddled around a small fire flickering in a sandbox aboard their flatboat. Everywhere the same leaden-heavy odor of fried pork hung like a cloak over the scene.

Now a light breeze sprang up, warm on my face. It pulled the shrouds of mist from the dock, and suddenly harsh details of men and their activity replaced the muted, foggy scene. Sounds and views stood forth starkly, etched by the cleansing breeze. Curses and grunts became more strident and penetrating; the Indians became more embroiled in the sticky murk they tried to capture; cries of children on houseboats became more piercing, plaintive. I turned and walked a short way upriver along a sandy path, skirted a patch of willows, and again turned into the main street up which we had come the previous evening.

Charles was having coffee and stew with our host when I arrived. Already three or four others were seated at the long puncheon table, helped by the proprietor's wife. I sat near Charles and was served by the owner, who then left, somewhat reluctantly, to serve other customers, as though his conversation with Charles had been interesting and hard to terminate.

Charles was in an expansive mood, and felt much as I did about the bustling little town and its raw newness. While I ate he spoke of news gathered from the owner, Mr. Starkey. It seemed that we had arrived on the birthday of a new town. Only yesterday there had been held at the dock, a brief ceremony and announcement to the effect that the Blacksnake Hills Post was no more; that henceforth the settlement would be called St. Joseph, christened for the patron saint of the town's chief property owner, Mssr. Robidoux. "And", continued Charles, "the new St. Joseph is just far enough west and north to make trading good. He says the Otoes and Kickapoos and Shawnees come across the river on a new ferry. They trade, and go back to their own side and never cause trouble – except sometimes among themselves."

I could see that Charles was enthused over our prospects in the new town. He continued relating his newly gotten information with the enthusiasm of a schoolboy.

"The town needs tradesmen of all sorts; opportunities are everywhere, Mr. Starkey says. And Mssr. Robidoux is selling his lots at a low price."

I shared much of Charles' enthusiasm, indeed, I had earlier resolved to give the town a try. Now, I thought it wiser to let him practice his selling arts on me, and remained, for the most part unconvinced.

After eating and settling for our food and lodging we thanked our host and set out again to view the town. Now, magically, it seemed ours, though we had spent but a night here. The streets, the widely-spaced rude cabins, the few blocks of false-fronted business houses standing beyond a wide docking area, all seemed oddly familiar and personal. It was as though I had lived here before.

Perhaps this intimacy sprang from the town's inherent loneliness, here hundreds of miles from St. Louis; perhaps it was the feel that St. Jo was itself a miniature New Orleans, fronting as it did, on a great river; perhaps it was the feeling of independence that came over me when I sensed the awesome distances stretching to the west, and the camaraderie that comes from risk and a need to share adventure.

Chapter 21
Coup de Charles

I had already begun to think in terms of an occupation, so far had my feeling for the town progressed. Already, early in this bright May morning, I could sense the solidity and progressiveness of the place. From the main dock-side thoroughfare several wide streets pointed at right angles toward the Blacksnake Hills, petering out to trails, but lined, each for a short distance, with store, warehouses and open workshops, smithies, a small cooperage.

I had disliked the teeming, almost visible burgeoning at New Orleans and St. Louis because of their impersonal nature, and because I had had no share in their growth. But here, in St. Jo, I was present when the town's growth pains began; I was part of the pain; would share in the increase; could feel accepted.

It was on an afternoon's tour of the infant town that an incident occurred which endeared us both to the town and held us here on the western fringes of the frontier so long:

Charles and I crossed the town from one angle, then re-crossed it from another, approaching the dock from upriver, then down, almost as though measuring it for purchase. There was an element of satisfaction in simply being here, an indefinable feeling of ownership, and yet we owned nothing but a few cooper's tools and blankets. We paused, I remember, where a group of four suited men seemed to be verbally examining merits of a small block of property just upriver, pointing and weighing its prospects for a business investment. Covillaud was fascinated, as he often was when he saw high finance in other's eyes. Though he had hardly the price of a month's lodging in his pocket, this did not prevent him from finding a position from which to eavesdrop. I was not so inquisitive, though I knew we would find opportunity in some form if we looked long enough. I was thinking in terms of a steady job, doing what I knew best – coopering. Charles, however, with the eyes of a neophyte capitalist and entrepreneur, had scented financial blood.

With hardly a word, other than that he was going to find someone, he left me, and turned quickly toward town. I sat for a long time watching the unloading and activity about several ships, noting the vast number of barreled commodities. Then I walked slowly back toward town. The main street at noon was filled with carts, mountaineers and a few businessmen. Some bonneted women and children jostled or avoided the Kickapoos and Shawnees, who stood about, blanketed, sullen, yet dignified.

I did not see Charles again until late in the afternoon, when, emerging from a saloon, he approached in the company of an elderly French gentlemen.

"Claude", Charles said as we met, "this is Mssr. Robidoux, whose new town we have the honor of inspecting."

We shook hands and exchanged pleasantries in the manner in which new arrivals will. Mssr. Robidoux expressed regret for a need to fulfill an appointment and left shortly. Now alone, and enroute to our temporary room, I was made privy to the thing Charles had done.

Noting immediately the property's value, and overhearing its desirability described, Charles had sought out its owner, Mssr. Robidoux. He had disarmed him with charm and seeming affluence, and had purchased the property for a light down payment and on exceedingly liberal terms.

As we walked along the roadway above dockside I was shown the property which Charles had acquired. We even went so far as to think in terms of a trading post or trading store with cooperage in back. As it was close to both wharf and the town's business, it would have been an admirable building site. This was not to be, however, for later in the evening, at Starkey's, we were visited by two dour-faced gentlemen – two of the four overheard by Charles. Following some wine and a brief conversation, Charles was offered so attractive a price for his property, one so out of proportion to what we might, with our limited funds, make of it, that Charles closed the deal. He accepted a check and the man left, content that though they had been bested, the property was now theirs.

But Charles now had, what seemed to me, a new and difficult task. I had, in the brief space of our acquaintance, sized up the man Robidoux, and felt him a man not to be cuckolded or crossed. This judgement had earlier been confirmed by a chance remark of Mr. Starkey, who spoke – as Chouteau already had – of Mssr. Robidoux as a shrewd trader and a man anxious to see his town grow. Charles had now to face this man who had acted kindly toward him and who had, in a sense, been tricked by him – or let Mssr. Robidoux find out the deception through a third party.

Late that evening we took up temporary residence in a small cabin just off the main street. Though we still took our meals at Mr. Starkey's tavern, I was anxious to have a place to cook and call home. Charles had made a killing with his land sale and we were elated at the turn of events that had brought so large a measure of security in so short a time. Candles guttering, we talked of our prospects until late.

Charles seemed little concerned about the prospects of facing Robidoux or the consequences of his duplicity and, try as I might, I could not think of the resale in another light. Mssr. Robidoux had extended the hand of friendship and assistance, and Covillaud had sold the gift for personal gain before it was hardly given. In my view he had masqueraded, engaged in a form of deceit – and this with the most wealthy and influential person in town.

But Charles slept well that night, and if he was conscience-stricken it did not show. He snored a deep, hungry snore, one of peace and fathomless ease, perhaps one even of rumbling anticipation.

This time it was Charles who was gone when I awoke to the sound of horses and wagons passing. I rolled from under my buffalo robe resolving to scour the town for some kind of employment. The resolve may have been the result of unconscious promptings of a conscience that reacted to Charles' streak of luck – and probably was. At any rate, a few bites of jerky, a swallow of stale coffee, and a dozen steps brought me into the full stride of another day in St. Jo. I could not help reflecting, as I passed down the puddled street (for it had rained lightly during the night), that here, on the frontier, man's search for anonymity was so strong that he would rage through country bedeviled by savages and go without even the barest necessities for it. I could see, in the eyes of men, under slouching hat brims, the furtive looks of successful escape from penalty or convention. And I averted my eyes, knowing that a raw, lurking hatred was there, for except among countrymen, the French were universally disliked on the frontier.

I had awakened with a kind of momentum about me, a feeling that my feet knew where to lead, that optimism ruled, and no discouragement was possible. My mind was clear, confident, expectant. What I

Pan The Low Waters

required was routing – some purposeful grind and rut in which to channel my efforts. I longed to lay my tools about me and feel the security or work – one that enveloped me as did the perfume of split white oak; I longed to have again the gratification that welled up in me when the bevelled edges of my staves drew flat and even against one another, and seams betrayed themselves in faint, thin lines – or not at all. I longed to experience again the confidence with which I estimated unerringly, bevel and croze. For I knew now – and the realization struck me forcibly – that the essence of life was indulgence in that thing which we do most skillfully, and which we always find, tantalizingly, possible to improve.

Chapter 22
Working Again

It took me but a short while to obtain employment. At this time St. Jo was finding itself in the position of having to repack foodstuffs and goods for conveyance to northern posts. For this it needed both dry and wet barrels for oil, meat, whisky, wine and gunpowder and the increasing acreages of wheat.

As I turned on one of the several short side streets running parallel to the dock, I caught the familiar odor of raw, drying white oak. I was drawn as by a magnet. The odor was sensual, virgin, irresistible.

There was no haggling. In the work yard I was literally set upon and placed at a broad bench inside a long, well-ventilated work room. I was given a crank-windlass and even supplied with a stool – both innovations I had never used or even seen in other cooperages.

Anxious to please so considerate a person as my new employer, Mr. Mallot, I set to work immediately on an unfinished wet barrel, and had tightened the staves with the windlass and inserted the temporary metal hoop when I became aware of a general movement of all workers to the rear entrance. Not having been asked to join them, I continued the closure of my barrel until called to the group by my genial employer. Here, in a cleared spot amid the fragrance of seasoned staves, the workers were enjoying the unheard luxury of hot lamb roast, freshly baked bread, and a large jug or red wine. In an atmosphere of congeniality, I was introduced to each worker as "Claude, the new cooper from St. Louis". Each hand that shook mine was massive and earnest, and so heavily calloused as to leave imprints of its horny hardness. One worker had but two fingers and thumb; another a knuckle that oozed redness, but in the eyes of each was a calm earnestness which I could interpret in no other way than a love for what he was doing – making barrels.

Of the seven or eight men (I seemed to be the youngest), only one was French; the others were either German or Irish, their nationalities indentifiable by the shapes of their pipes which they lit almost in unison as they finished their cups. I was charmed by the mood of laissez-faire that permeated the cooperage, by the feeling of camaraderie, and by the old thrill which I always got when I worked with strong, well-seasoned wood.

All that first afternoon I toiled in a cloud of scented frenzy, my eyes and fingers gauging unerringly the requisite amounts and bevels to be trimmed. Here there seemed no compulsion to prove, nor any need to turn out a given volume. And I revelled again in an occupation that gave so much gratification for so little effort and which paid satisfaction in such limitless quantities.

I had given no attention to the number of casks I finished when the end of my first working day approached, nor did I see, in the dim light of approaching dusk, the gathering of fellow craftsmen opposite my bench, or notice the hollow ring of my tools in an otherwise silent cooperage. I had run a testing palm around the barrel's girth and rolled it to where the others lay, when the sound of heavy handclaps broke the silence. The sounds were unexpected, shattering. For a moment or two I remained motionless, disoriented. Then I emerged from the fierce concentration with which I had devoured five hours of the afternoon.

Though I saw the applause was mocked, I saw it was for me, and I tried to accept with an exaggeratedly good natured bow. Now that several came forward and examined my barrels – twice, even three times their own production – I sensed their admiration, read approval in the rough hands that felt my workmanship. There was no hint of envy in their open, frank glances, and gestures, but only an unmistakable current of professional esteem.

Brandy was produced and went the rounds. Now that the first day was over I was aware of a wall of stiffness in back and shoulders. I sat on my bench after a long pull at the brandy bottle and watched the others leave. Muscle knots dissolved slowly. The streets were dark, and here and there a lamp or candle burned feebly as I walked slowly homeward.

There was a light, too, in the cabin (originally a small store) when I arrived. Charles was in a jovial mood, and at the same time, curious to know what had kept me so late. He wished to tell me about the closure of the deal. I listened to him first, anxious to know how he had fared with the feelings of the town's founder.

"He rejoiced with me, Claude! I was amazed that Robidoux carried no grudge. He was pleased that a newcomer, without knowing anything about the town, would make such a profitable deal – and in so short a time. The turnover netted me just over five hundred dollars, and while I may not have made friends with the gentlemen whose conversation I overheard, Mssr. Robidoux approved of my tight trading. He's done a deal of it himself, you know, and with similar methods now owns many hundreds of acres around and in town. Now he is selling it off at enormous profit. He needs it too. I've been with him most of the afternoon."

Pan The Low Waters

Charles gushed on and on, telling about the numerous Robidoux tribe, about how Mssr. first bought his Blacksnake trading post from the American Fur Company; how we then saw towns and farms closing around the post and had the foresight to buy some three hundred sixty acres, which, over the years, sold for ten dollars a lot; then, how, when settlers and merchants began to form the nucleus of a community, he advanced his prices until a wash of wealth flowed in upon him.

"I don't believe anyone", said Charles," even he, knows the worth of his holdings. He claims to have sixty papooses – French Sac, French Kickapoo, French Potawatami, besides half a dozen white children. These, and another half-dozen brothers who live with the Indians or roam the continent west, seem to keep him drained of money. The wandering, squawing brothers know he is a soft touch and return to the parent source, knowing he will pay – if not for their wild and improbable tales of far-away places – at least the going prices for their furs. One, he says, keeps a post along the Platte, one works as guide on the Santa Fe, and one has been in Spanish California for over year. The others, he thinks, may be up in Blackfeet country – or dead."

I, too, related the events that had made my day – the ones that had planted my feet firmly at the mouth of the Blacksnake River – Le Serpent Noire. It was late when I had done so, and after we were deep in our cups of celebration. My tale was superfluous, of course, for the glow of Charles' own first triumph seemed to diminish the significance of mine.

I lay thoughtfully awake for many hours that first night of many nights – a newcomer in a newly-born town, and turned and returned to the events of the day. Besides rejoicing over both our initial fortunate circumstances, I saw a kind of happy complementing in our relationship.

In many ways we were opposites. Though I was two years Charles' senior, and felt a kind of fatherly feeling toward him, I believe this attitude showed only in my more thoughtful approach to all our problems: my tendency to wait and reserve judgement – as opposed to his more mercurial – though as keenly perceptive nature; he was much the extrovert; I the introvert; he tended to have a more urban outlook, because he had been raised in more cultured surroundings – his father was affluent, and his sister was something of a free-thinker, given to notions of social service not yet considered ladylike (a nurse in the Crimean War); I, happily, was easily satisfied with what circumstances provided me, and felt I could always make the best of any situation given me; Charles, by contrast, demanded more exciting fare, needed the stimulus of frequent business of social challenges, and went looking for them if they came not to him. My stimulation, for good or ill, lay in a far more basic and natural need – one which came so long ago with the learning of my trade: to do a good job in pleasant surroundings with flawless tools and fine materials in a mist of nature's aromas. This was, at the same time, both my goal and my task; it was my total required environment. In a word, I was easily made happy and satisfied with my kind of frictionless existence. It spelled security for me. I needed none of Charles' savoir faire, business acumen, or social gregariousness, although I admired these facets of his personality. They were the elements that made Charles the person he was. I was happy with my lacks; happy that my little was my all.

Chapter 23
Settler Meeting

And so the promising summer of '45 came to a close and a new and strange season began. It was a curious, almost foreboding autumn, one in which both human and natural element seemed to pit themselves against each other. It was a season in which, it seemed, there was a desperate bid for freedom among the ever-fluid settler population, and a counter-surge of inhibiting natural forces that toughened, made lean and desperate the populace, kept them off-balance and miserable, so that from the ranks of these cold, often hungry settlers, there was always a fringe, a kind of mad-cap froth, forever seething, forever manifesting a need for change. It showed itself at small gatherings which took place at odd intervals in stores and on the straw-strewn floor of the large livery stable, particularly on those afternoons and evenings after a bitter storm had come and gone.

I had need for change too, though I frequently relieved the icy tedium of those flat, white monotonous evenings by fishing in the Blacksnake and its nearby wide pools after work, and enjoying a sumptuous fish dinner, hot and bubbling on the slab fronting the fireplace.

Arnold F. Rothmeier

On a particularly keen evening, one day late in November, I returned from one of my fishing jaunts, I had, dangling from my belt, three large bass and several greylings. As I mounted to the main road, I observed signs of unusual activity at the livery. Lights showed through wall-cracks and animal-skin windows; wagons clustered unevenly in the street; horses blew their twin heads of steam; their bodies' warmth raised sweat-fog that gave off a gray mist which seemed, oddly, to dispel the growing darkness.

I paused at the wide doors and peeped curiously through the narrow space. The stable was lit by a half-dozen lanterns and candles, and on a platform of timbers in the most distant corner stood a man, cynosure of the eyes of a crowd, seated or lying on straw. The audience was immobile, seemingly entranced. They could have been dim cartons of warehouse goods stacked in rows across the stable, had it not been for the form of one, then another, who rose, shouted a question in answer to the speaker's words, or offered a bit of lame, local humor that stirred the crowd to laughter and movement. I entered.

It was some moments before the sense of the meeting became clear; before I heard, repeatedly, the words, "great valley", and "Californy", mentioned with understandable clarity and in context with other words so that I could gather a thought. Being a Frenchman, I still had much difficulty with rapid English speech, and if the words were shortened or nasalized, or if they were used with hasty reference to a regional situation, I often had to sacrifice comprehension of whole blocks of speech and begin again with only a murky idea of the foregoing verbal landslide.

Having entered late at an apparently open harangue, I decided to remain a short while and see if I couldn't make a bit more sense of the discourse. Many of the exclusively male gathering were seated on the straw strewn floor against the wall, clasping knees in folded hands. Some smoked or conversed with one another. All seemed engrossed with a central idea put forth by the speaker. When statements were made by him an invisible current would seem to touch his huddled or reclining audience, and an eddy or response – not unlike the slow circling and stir of fallen leaves in a vagrant breeze, would send his listeners into murmured rejoinders with one another. His words were stimulating, and through it all his listeners would absorb a thought or two, digest them for a moment, and effectively block hearing the next thought by shouting a half-formed rebuttal or quip. Occasionally the speaker resorted to an unnaturally rapid speech in order to voice a thought in its completeness before audience sounds blotted out its comprehension. For the most part it was fragmented and incomprehensibly presented, and one with far too much levity of response and disbelief expressed in what was said.

The speaker was a tall, bronze-bearded man of about thirty. His face showed the batterings of weather, but his slightest movements betrayed a suppleness that could only have been the result of a life spent in forest and prairie. Despite the interruptions he received, his voice rang loud and convincingly. Indeed, for the most part he seemed not even to hear the numerous interruptions, part jest, part query, and told, in a steady rolling baritone, of the life, the country and the climate of the area called California.

He was a keen, steady and intelligent young man, and, despite his unkempt appearance, possessed a bearing that radiated confidence. The sometimes jeering retorts he handled by seeming to ignore them, and yet, a few moments after given, his trend of thought would, somehow, bend to give precise and factual answers to the shouted queries.

One would shout a question about the route, for instance, while he spoke of an abundance of game in the country, appearing to ignore the query. Then, without referring to the questioner, and as though he possessed a memory receptacle into which he tucked the jist of the shout, he would begin another stream of information that led to the answer. There were, it seemed, a number of approaches to the country California, some of which he knew others had successfully followed.

This melange of shout and delayed answer went on for some time. Finally a loud, shout, half plea, half query:

"But they won't leave us cross the Mo!"

To this, there was such instantaneous chorus of agreement from so many quarters of the barn that the spokeman's voice was lost in the bedlam of shout answering shout. And though unanswered, the answer was tacit in the very atmosphere: There had been unauthorized penetrations, and there would be no stopping the tide of prying, testing pioneers.

The last shout seemed to mark an end to the evening's exchange, for there was a general rising, relighting of pipes, and movement toward the wide carriage doors.

I lingered where I stood, brushed by farmers and townsmen in the dim light. All were heavy with the odors of sweat and tobacco. Some pipes, by design or accident, sent small showers of sparks to the damp, trampled arena of a moment before. There was little conversation, but the exiting, silent throng seemed to mill and cogitate, and I caught the mood of a restless, surly and irresistible spirit that chafed at imposition of an arbitrarily drawn line here at the Missouri River – a line drawn in the wide water and buffered on the opposite bank by ragged remnants of tribes – a line which said, in effect: "You move no farther west."

There was a mood of unyielding rebellion, and here it was much more pronounced than I had noticed in the comparatively sprawling opulence of St. Louis. It was as though a more tenacious, insistent form of woodsman had somehow spread upstream to this outpost, here to await an opportunity to try the patience of the opposition, the law; to grumble and to wait out the inevitable moment when they and hundreds like them, would, by weight of numbers, break the federal cordon and flood toward the west. There was here a zeal for movement, any movement – even the verbalizing of it – by spirits like the tall, rawboned man of this evening, shouting himself hoarse before men who, least of all, wished to listen in a calm fashion to descriptions by a veteran of the trail. There was a mood of frustration in the burly, bearded figures who had sought so long for ways to circumvent the published edicts.

Most of the crowd had done some shouting and had not actually listened, but had, I sensed, an animal-like need in each shadowy figure to forever move toward the west. I sensed, too, the strength of that which pulled them, and turned at last, with a strange feeling of the same power.

St. Jo., in the winter of '45, was a river's edge village of a few hundred souls, a few dozen places of business fronting wide rutted streets which led at right angles from a busy waterfront up a swale of valley into the Blacksnake Hills. A short way up the Missouri the Blacksnake River flowed into it, as did numerous other streams on both sides. A small raft-like ferry was maintained to bring bands of trading Indians across. They had seemingly piled up in a great admixture of tribes on their west side, and came often, with many furs, to satisfy their newly manufactured needs. Rarely did women or children come over, and the returning ferry often carried white men – traders, trappers, and drovers with packs and boxes. They set out with considerable ostentation to barter with those across the river, but their barter was most often for the unpackageable young girls who met them on the far side, and who, with sloe-eye and subdued giggle strayed into the bushes with the men and their gaudy temptations.

During our stay at St. Jo, I became conscious of basic differences between Charles' personality and mine – though these resulted in little friction. Charles, in his new affluence, was becoming much more of a party-goer and joiner than he had been. I had always noted in him a greater dependency upon conversation, upon crowds. I noted how he throve upon association with people, as though movement among them were vital to his well-being. This need led him to make friends much more readily than I, and I often returned to the cabin to find him preparing to leave for an evening at cards or dance. Charles was a southern Frenchman, and though poised on the edge of the wilderness, and though surrounded by savages – both red and white – the need to move with those who had known gentler times remained strongly with him.

My Norman blood and temperament, while not as openly gregarious, prevented frictions that might have resulted from our close association. Just as Charles needed a listening post, just so my introverted mind needed his verbal fodder to chew over. I was well aware of the Norman in me, and could no more have changed it than could Charles. My ability to avoid a straight "yes" or "no" answer must have annoyed him, just as his garrulity occasionally piqued me. Happily, my native taciturnity and reluctance to make explicit statements fostered stronger bonds of understanding between us.

Often, when Charles returned home from an evening soiree or *partie de plaisir*, he would tell me, until I fell asleep listening, of the personages he had met, of the latest gossip, of his rare female dancing partner. He would tell of Mssr. Robidoux and of a man called Fremont, who had recently passed, with pack train, through Independence, and of others spilling over the arbitrary river boundary – without government permission.

A picture of a new frontier migration began to emerge from all that Charles told and from what I read in the small local paper. For, you see, I yet read and spoke English but haltingly, and I could no longer depend upon the juxtaposed French and English to compare, as I had in New Orleans *Picayune*.

Chapter 24
Enigma

But with Charles' influence I found my comprehension of English growing. He now rarely spoke French, and when questioned about this, replied, "If I am going to live in an English-speaking country, I may as well begin learning the language, and make my mistakes here, where penalties might not be so high", or "The people here in St. Jo don't want to waste time trying to understand French, so I have to stop thinking in French."

And so, under Charles' influence, I, too, turned to this endeavor and began consciously to translate my thought into English. My efforts had the almost immediate affect of drawing me into formerly closed conversation at the cooperage. Several workers who had respected my accuracy of my work now took pain to express their opinions and even flatter me with questions about how I accomplished my feats of fitting and tool-sharpening. The replies I gave were always more demonstrable then verbal, but I could do no less then try to answer. My willingness to demonstrate would have been neither requested nor accepted in any but an intimate circle of artisans such as ours. I was proud to share their workroom and to demonstrate my skill, not so much because they had accepted me, as because their actions demonstrated so much the opposite of the going attitude toward the Frenchmen. It was not current practice to thus admit inferiority – certainly not in a group – to the skill of a non-American.

Then there were the mid-day pauses when the tapping of hammer, the soft thud of oak, and the dry sough of drawknife halted, and the expulsion of breaths held over the tools gave way to contented munchings and easy talk. For an hour there would be raucous or barbed banter between Pole and German about one's waning masculinity or another's inability to bend a stave.

But frequently the talk would take a serious track, and each in his own way would hint of the depth of his news-reading and independent thought concerning the effectiveness of the federal prohibitions against movement west, or the reasons why all Indians couldn't adjust to farming, as had some of the huddled Pawnees across the river, or about the dwindling market for beaver pelts, or about wagons waiting at Independence for the greening of buffalo grass.

As the season wore on into early spring there was a general self-congratulation concerning the mildness of winter. Those who now saw the beauty of the burst bud and leafy spray, noted, with almost malignant eye, the huge stacks of unburned wood outside their neighbor's door. The new comers who had spread themselves about in rude shacks back in the little gullies, breathed relief at the mild winter. They dropped their reins or ax and trudged to town, as though here, in indolent gossip, they might find the reason for their good fortune – or lack of it.

On Sundays, Charles and I often took our guns – on the off-chance that we might see game. We followed the river bank toward the high-rising back land, or hiked along some recently cut wagon trail to see who had carved another homestead, what crops planted. This was one of the things which we enjoyed doing together. His eye was ever

Pan The Low Waters

on the dollar, alert for the chance of another coup. Though he shared, in lesser fashion, my love for sights and odors of the raw country and sometimes would gaze for a moment, or even exclaim over a striking or picturesque view, he seemed immune to the feast of odors which I inhaled – the crushed willow bark the heavy, resinous fullness that rose in invisible cloud from a sunny spot, and I never knew him to crush a pine needle for the aromatic pleasure within it.

The winter of '42 had first gathered its stormy skirts about itself, and blown out in a series of week-long icy storms. After wreaking havoc along the river in brutal sub-zero weather that threw a howling funnel-like gale through town, it settled down to a long, placid autumn that made riot of color. As spring unfolded, a mood of hesitant poise at the river betrayed itself. More men were employed at the cooperage; more wagons and families streamed into town; they came by road and by river boat; they came not to settle, but appeared to await something; they had not the air of seekers of permanence but of transients: they seemed puzzled, expectant. There was much talk about the trail.

Since Charles and I had arrived, almost a year ago, the town had expanded. Street ends, once only narrow paths ending in tree clumps, had become wide muddy arenas for the turn of wagons and deposition of goods now tucked into a maze of raw, new business houses, smithies, and store rooms. From the cooperage window I would watch the flow of life in our new town. In the street there was constant movement of rough wagons high with supplies, and of men, all bearing, behind dark beards, the stamp of seekers and of dissatisfaction. And I felt myself torn and swayed, for though my job paid in a feeling of fulfillment, there was always a pull, a rending inside me by unseen forces when I chanced to glance up and see the slow sway of children on a dray-load of family goods and catch the rough, throaty utterances of a drover.

One morning, as I rested from the completion of another cask, I glanced again at the lively street scene before me. I was seared by a question which suddenly surfaced. It was as though the sight of so many strange persons – walking, riding, driving – catalyzed a force within me, one that demanded an answer to the question, "What is it you want to do here?"

Strange that I should now hear such a query, one so loud and so insistent! Perhaps stranger still, that almost four years in a foreign land should pass before I should ask such a question. I had heard it asked on the *Zotow*. Then it had seemed only an idle question – one to be answered lightly as: "How are you?", or "Nice weather, hien?". Now it came as a serious question, and I looked unseeing at the rough, ungainly figures passing beyond the cooperage wall. Again, half-aloud, I asked myself the question: "What is it you want to do here?"

Obviously, the reply to my question was: "To make barrels". And yet I knew the answer to be purile, almost childish. It seemed to lack the content of a full, mature response. It was somehow, incomplete, fragmentary, almost without significance. But why should the question – which no one had asked anyway – suddenly arise to annoy me? I had come alone to a foreign land with only a single skill. I had fitted well into every little swirl and eddy of society where my travels had lodged me. I seemed to adjust and to thrive in a warm flash of pride. I acknowledged this. Yet now I was torturing myself with this "Why".

The afternoon passed in a frenzied play of skill that sent me home in a pet of fatigued exhilaration, and I was nearly drunk on brandy when Covillaud came in late that evening. I was too far gone to comprehend the significance of his latest business coup, and it waited for comprehension until a stabbing hangover awakened me the next morning.

Charles had not left the cabin as was his usual custom, and I awoke dully to the sounds of his breakfast putterings. I felt a sharp sting of remorse that I had let myself go the night before. My inclination to ponder what it was about the frontier that made a body live from one excess to another was cut short by Charles' cheery, "How's your appetite this morning?".

It was not so much a question as a statement, for at the same time he placed a tin dish of pork and bread beside my bed and went to the corner to pour a mug of wine. My senses refused to function without their usual tipple of burgundy, and I hardly gave thought to the rarity of being served breakfast in bed.

Charles waited – with masterful self-control, I am sure, while I munched the unsavory leather-like bread and greasy pork, washed down with wine. Then he approached his subject:

"I've been told there will be need for more barrels than Mssr. Mallot can supply this coming season". To which I assented with a slight head shake – all that my aches would allow. Needs for the next season had been mirrored in an attempted production increase for some weeks. But one doesn't make a skilled cooper overnight, and I was asked to do more and more remedial labor on the casks of the new employees. Yes, this was what caused my irritability and over-indulgence. I wondered, vaguely, why Charles should mention shipping needs. His concerns lately had been relevant to increased property values and sales in the town, and to the expansion needs of a small, cadaverous Jew to whom I had often nodded when passing his store. He was an anomaly here in St. Jo. I had felt, upon seeing him putter over his strange assortment of used wares, trying to make a knife or a grinder, or a pair of worn pants appear desirable. If the sun shone he would be seen scurrying about, placing things on plank counters and pegging used clothes high up on the store wall. If it rained he scurried in reverse, taking huge armfuls of the handiest and most valued articles, dumping them inside, then rushing outside to see if anything had been stolen. There was something ferret-like in his actions. Though everyone knew of light fingers and the thieving proclivities of the mixed bands of Indians, the little Jew seemed to remind one continually of this and to suggest we were all lusting after his worn and rusty objects.

I had been trying to attend to Charles, but my mind seemed oiled off its usual concentrating track by last night's brandy. The flow of my thoughts about the Jew merged, somewhat abruptly, into reality as I heard Charles mention the man. It was an odd sensation, the spoken word, "Jew", merging with the thought, "Jew", somewhat like the rough engaging of gears I had heard at Chouteaus's mill as water power ground his corn.

"The Jew", I heard Charles say, as I took the proffered coffee cup, "is moving on and wants to sell his store." Still the words made no impression; Charles continued:

"Do you suppose you and I might take his place and make it pay? I think he might sell very reasonably. It's a well-built store, and close to the area where lots are becoming more valuable."

By this time I was sufficiently alert to understand what Charles was saying, and just sufficiently irritated by my general physical condition and by my mind's picture of the Jew's paltry inventory to answer curtly, "If he couldn't make a go of it, why do you think we might do better?"

"We wouldn't take over his rags and broken tools, Claude. I see no more value in his stock than you do. But if we cleaned up the place and stocked it with new things and staples, I think we might do a good business – especially since there are only two other general stores in town."

In his answer to my annoyed question, Charles outlined a whole series of reasons, among which was the one that we would handle only those things needed by the new horde of new-comers – their necessities. Then, as I drank another cup of his hot coffee, I began to see how Charles' plans might profit us.

I was overdue at the cooperage, and, with a promise to look more closely at the store and lot on my way home, I put jerkey in my pocket and left the cabin with the good feeling of anticipation in my hands and muscles. For I truly loved my work. The whole environment – the mild, aromatic balms that enveloped me, the feel of my knife, hammer and adz; the way Mssr. Mallot showed his approval of my work; even the ill-concealed jealousies of the new, the so-called coopers. I lost myself in my work, and the morning melted away to lunchtime.

I will not say that all was without friction. By noon my energies were low and my head had increased in size. I was off-balance and irritable, and, in addition, I had inadvertently left home without my usual bottle; jerkey was tougher than usual. Irritated at my forgetfulness, I left the cooperage and stumbled up the street to buy my bottle.

When I returned the others were again working. There was a new face at the bench across from me. It was not a kind one, nor had it the lines and wrinkles of one accustomed to humor. What I saw was a brutal expression of ignorance, intolerance, and selfishness I had noted concealed behind the beards of many who feel themselves badly treated on the frontier. His was a rebellious, leering mask, and as I planed the staves, my hands had a puzzling, unnatural unsteadiness. I was awkward and fatigued. I laid it all to the previous night's drinking.

Toward mid-afternoon, I was further annoyed to see the area about me become increasingly glutted with rejected wet barrels. None of these were mine, but were the unskilled and slovenly work of help newly added to increase production.

As day drew on, I felt imposed upon; not a true cooper, but one called upon to repair shoddy workmanship and careless fitting, Then, as the quitting iron sounded, to add to my physical discomfort, I caught an unmistakable, leering grin on the face of the hulking recent hire.

The impression of my changing situation at the cooperage remained gallingly with me on my walk home. I tallied up the changes that had come about since the increased need of barrels and disliked the sum: it seemed I no longer left the cooperage whistling, proud of my skill and record, and proud of those who approved of my skill. I worked now not with aromatic white oak, but with worm-wood, and at the side of shirkers for whose mistakes I paid. There was an irritating slackness about the whole operation, and instead of an increased population of fine wet barrels, there was only increase in the number of rejects.

Charles was already home when I arrived.

"Thought you would like a pot of crawdads for a change", he said. "Haven't had any since leaving New Orleans. I got them from a little fellow on the dock this afternoon. He said he caught them with a piece of liver and a line up along the mill ditch. They fasten their claws onto the liver. The idea, he said, is to jerk the crawdad out of the water before it has time to let go. You have to be fast then, or they'll scuttle back."

He was in an unusually light-hearted mood, and the odor of the boiling 'dads' lent an element of security to the cabin. A pot of "dandylion" greens simmered on the side, and the odor of bay and thyme that Charles had added soothed my pricked spirits.

The 'dads' were succulent, the greens and the burgundy excellent. It was a fine meal, and when our pipes were lit and my defenses down, Charles spelled out the ridiculous figure the Jew had asked, along with the uses that could be made of the property. And as he talked I saw not only Charles' security, but also my liberation: The man wanted only a few hundred for his shop and land, but he wanted it quickly. The building was sturdy and in a prime location. The contents were little more than rubbish – a collection of worn tools, tins and clothing that only a desperate man would want.

Pan The Low Waters

As Charles talked, my thoughts bounded along on a track of their own, urged on by his enthusiasm, but controlled by my memory of the demeaning events at the cooperage and the leering face of my new co-worker. Then, as though forced by the intolerable situation, a solution emerged as the answer to my problem. Perhaps the idea had lain hidden in the back of my mind for months, and had needed only the present circumstances to appear. In a flash I saw myself in a totally independent role in St. Jo.

If the Jew's store met with Charles' needs for a store, then perhaps, with an addition in the rear, I might have my own cooperage. Here I might do a business, not only of supplying fine drums and barrels – which I knew to be in considerable demand, but I might branch into related items: white work, pails, tubs, and repair of spinning wheels.

Independence was not a thing I had sought. Indeed, I was a little fearful of the notion of managing and coordinating production in my own shop. The business detail and the costs of an independent start needed a boldness and discipline that awed me.

As the thought increasingly intrigued me, and as the conditions of my present work surfaced again, I interrupted: "Charles, I want to look again at Stein's store in the morning. Couldn't you and I have a combination store and cooperage, and at the same time use the building for living quarters?"

Now the look on Charles' face expanded and his eyes brightened. And I saw in his face an instantaneous elation. I knew immediately he had had the thought himself, but had known the discovery must come from me. I had sensed this subtlety in my friend before, but never had I observed it so skillfully used. These thoughts were lost in the momentary confusion and elation at my mention, and my thoughts leapfrogged ahead. I balanced momentarily between the status quo – the

Arnold F. Rothmeier

approaching intolerableness at the cooperage – and the risk and uncertainties of a new business, then slowly inclined toward the latter. We drank to the success of a new kind of relationship and business, and it was very late, when, at last, the wick was pinched and we slept. I was late for work the next morning.

The poorly fitted casks, the unacceptables, had been rolled to my bench and surrounded my working area so that approach to it was difficult. Perhaps I should have been proud of the recognition that I was the only cooper capable of bringing these rejects up to standard; perhaps it was the mending of the awkward mistakes of others, who drew the same salary as myself that now galled me. At any rate, I had tightened the shoulder cinch around one particular barrel for the third time in an attempt to bring its staves into alignment, when I was approached by Mr. Mallot. I was sweating and a little frantic to make the closure, having failed in three previous tries. As he drew near I was able to fix the primary hoop and to rest a moment as I inspected the seams.

"That was a hard fit, eh Claude?"

That was what I liked about this cooperage: Mr. Mallot was not all the tight, money-grabbing man of business one sees so much of in this town. In his world of business, somehow a light of kind concern seemed always to show. He, himself, had labored in the barrels, and he shared the reversals and discomforts of his men.

I rested a moment from my efforts now, at this tactic invitation, and our eyes wandered over the seas of rejected casks that we knew must be redone. In the back of my mind lay the anticipation of liberation from the damned drudgery that lay there, spead out; and in the back of his, I knew, lay the necessity to pacify me. It was difficult to conceal the irritation I felt at the moment.

The moment was not long in arriving, though I wished with all my heart it had not come, for I had become attached to my boss. I had worked with a minimum of friction – at least from him – and always present, like the soft tang of the white oak, a deeply satisfying residue of trust and confidence was always there. The moment came in a way which obligated me and sealed me to him and his cooperage for the remainder of the year.

"Claude," he began, "How would you like to have a new job – or, rather, a new title? You've been doing the job of company inspector for some time now, without being paid for it. I think it is time you got the title as well as the wages. So, from last Monday, you will receive ten dollars more per week, and you are now my inspector. Also, I wonder if you would help me in the matter of hiring. I want to avoid this kind of pile-up in the future. Probably the best way is to be more careful with the choice of help."

Without allowing me time to accept or reject his proposal, Mr. Mallot continued on with other ideas for changed improvement, and I found myself inclining more and more to the side of status quo and to the passive security it offered. The salary raise was indeed flattering; the new level of self-esteem to which his words raised me was a sincere compliment; and these and the picture of a new status with new responsibilities were so devastating to my new plans with Charles, that by the time I reached the cabin after a hard day's work I had almost forgotten the new plans Charles and I had made.

Not so with Charles, however. He burst through the door late, as I sat smoking an after-supper pipe, and was almost incoherently ecstatic. I had never seen him so beside himself over a success, and his words, as he told of his *fait accompli* tumbled over one another, mixing his thoughts so irretrievably with English, French, and a few Burgundian epithets that I grasped his meaning only be snatching a few of his phrases as they flew by. I had never observed him so highly elated at a coup; he was so beside himself it was as though he had consummated a deal for half the muddy lots on Main Street. As his

Arnold F. Rothmeier

hurricane of words subsided to a stiff gale, then to a moderate wind, he accepted the bottle, and in a little while his words fell into a smooth tale:

The Jew had succumbed at the sight of a few dollars – a pittance, really – and had agreed to turn over the large lot and store in the morning, upon receipt of the balance owed. Charles' funds would be severely depleted, but I would reimburse him for my part, and we would share the property as partners. The remainder of the evening escaped, as did the flow of good wine and the white, wispy strings of our smoke, into an agreeable sequence of plans. And with verbal paintings of a tomorrow as rosy as the deep burgundy in our cups, we fell asleep in our chairs.

I slept soundly that night despite the wine. Whether it was press of the new situation in which I found myself – accepting status, responsibility and a salary increase while plotting to leave, or whether it was the violence of the wind outside that drove the rain against the cabin in a surf-like flood, I could not tell. I awoke cold and staggered to the fireplace to rekindle a dying fire. My mind had fastened upon the events at the cooperage, and, like my dog and his bone, gnawed them and would not let them rest.

By morning I had decided to continue with Mr. Mallot, and at the same time, two-faced, assemble my own cooperage and business in competition with him. I was not happy with the new inner conflicts; I felt selfish and ungrateful, and yet pushed into an irretrievable position. After all, I reasoned, I had asked him neither for raise nor additional responsibility. I had simply done my cooping, as always, as best I knew how. I had not asked for the recognition or responsibility now placed upon me!

Chapter 25
The Storm

As I had exhausted myself with the subject the night before, so had the massive storm exhausted itself by morning. Charles slept on, undisturbed by my preparations of grits and ham. I was unprepared for the scene that met my eyes when, at last, I stepped from the door on my way to work.

The rain had come in such great quantities as to make deep gullies in the roadways. Earth and sand had deltaed over the wharf planking, almost obscuring it. The wind had ripped stems and branches and strewn them along the streets. The railing and balcony of Mssr. Robidoux' house hung at a grotesque angle. But there was other mischief done in the night, and at the cooperage news of the flood and of cattle drownings up along the Blacksnake was excitedly told – often behind half-hidden smirks of those who, in telling, felt a comfortable contrast between the nothing they had to lose and the all which others had lost.

Among the losers that night was Mr. Sweeny – not heavily, but mentionably: a full barn with several head of cattle, built too close to the Blacksnake, had been undermined and swept downstream. The now-bloated bodies of these and many others lay on high sandbars until removed by hungry Pawnees and Otoes opposite the town. For several days these scavengers could be seen picking through the low, brush-covered banks of the Missouri for canvas, harness, wheels and usable boards. Loss of life among the upcreek settlers was not heavy, but those who had lost their men or women to the flood, buried them quietly where they found space above the high water mark.

But little time was spent on recrimination of the elements. There was a kind of tacit acceptance of life compounded of uncertainty, misery, and monotony. A brand of hope existed that there was something new and bright and immensely alluring on toward the west – a kind of Christmas stocking filled for a Noel enticingly close in time; dismayingly distant in space.

By the end of the third day few remainders of the flash flood could be seen. Dust rose a little more densely from an increased activity over the drying delta of mud. The normally cloudy Missouri pulled a steady churn of viscous yellow solids past the site, and the town seemed to prepare for the next period of its wild existence. Along with all its misery and destruction, the storm brought an interesting benefit to Charles and me, one which had long-range effects on our lives.

The little Jew had vacated his store the day before the storm, and Charles had chain-locked the door – certainly more to prevent unwanted occupancy than out of fear that anyone would steal its pathetic contents. To Charles' surprise, the second morning following the storm, he was compelled, by a numerous crowd of the needy, to open, and by mid-afternoon had sold or given away most of the worn collection of garments and household articles that we had planned to discard in order to make room for a new inventory.

I left the cooperage early to re-inspect the new place, to formulate plans, and was greatly surprised to see wagons and horses tied along the store front and to see such late activity. The more was my astonishment when I entered. Charles stood near the door, urging a handful of articles upon a man and his wife. These were some of the settlers who had lost heavily. There was no attempt on Charles' part to coin money on the misery of the victims. On the contrary, as I stood there he refused, time after time, offered change for purchase, using the phrase, "No, Mr. Smith, we want to thank you for helping us to clear our shelves for new stock", or "Why should you not have this; it cost me nothing, and you certainly can use it."

This was a side of Charles' personality I had not seen before. I liked it. Perhaps I would have liked it even more had he not told me that evening as we ate, that he was sure he had made many good customers this afternoon.

The few remaining pieces of clothing and kitchenware stacked outside the following morning beneath a sign reading "PLEASE TAKE", were gone before noon.

Now began in earnest the stocking of our store – by Charles, of course, for I was yet working – and the laying of plans for my small cooperage. Though Mr. Mallot would have to know my plans sooner or later, I had not yet the courage to inform him of my leaving. I suppose I felt a coward, and yet I knew it would be infinitely better to tell him my plans than for him to learn them from another. Had he not lost so heavily in the flood, I should have told him of our plans much sooner. It was because I admired him, and because he had been so considerate, that I procrastinated. The situation in which I found myself annoyed me, galled me, and it was for days irritatingly uppermost in my mind.

Opportunity to inform him came excruciatingly slow. But when, a few weeks later, Charles left for St. Louis with a large part of our savings and an enormous list of general store items, I was able to casually let slip the fact that Charles and I were going into a mercantile business and would be making an addition to the Stein building. Of the projected new cooperage I said nothing, since plans were still forming and since it would be a month or more before I would be producing.

Charles returned one week later. I was summoned to the dock by a young messenger, for it would have been reckless to have left unguarded the mountain of boxes, casks and sacks he had purchased. It was too late to return to the cooperage when, with a rented wagon, we carted the material to the store.

Over a dinner of boiled beef, cooked in a makeshift corner of our new place, Charles grew ecstatic over his new bargains – most not from St. Louis stores, but from along the levee, where he had offered owners sums for unconsigned portions of shipments. Since we would be aiming, in large part, for the Indian trade from across the river, Charles had bought a quantity of the stock trade items: one, two, and three-point blankets, many pounds of beads, knives, awls, bolts of cloth in striking colors, sugar, coffee, and tobacco. But he had also paid our cash for many items he knew to be needed by the mountain men, trappers, and settlers, such as hats, lead, beans, bolted flour, rope, thread, several sizes of pans, saleratus, and medicines.

The costlier, smaller items were put on wide, deep shelves behind the counter which carried a sign: "DO NOT HANDLE". Bulky articles and supplies were stowed in the broad attic area overhead, and access secured by a loose ladder.

Our store was, in the main, to be Charles' enterprise, and I did little more than to help him transfer and arrange things to his liking before I set about building the rear addition that was to be my cooperage and our living quarters.

Of my necessary separation from Mr. Mallot and his cooperage, I

Pan The Low Waters

still said nothing, but work at the store caused me to become more irregular in reporting for work. Mr. Mallot said nothing about this, and by staying occasionally late, I was still doing twice the work of the other coopers. This fact was not lost upon my employer. Some mornings I reported not at all, knowing I could re-do the faulty barrels at my leisure. It became a most interesting, loose arrangement, almost as though I were part owner of the business. Indeed, since the termination of my nemesis – the menacing, bearded wood-spoiler, I excercised tacitly, a privileged position – that of occasionally teaching and demonstrating correct tool technique for those workers who could tolerate a correction. It was often a delicate matter to inject myself into this position, to correct a piece of work where patience threatened to disintegrate into explosive oaths.

Chapter 26
Independence

My time with Mr. Mallot terminated one afternoon late in March, 1843. As it turned out, there was no need for the months of apprehension I had forced upon myself – never had been. He simply called together his workers and informed us of the approaching sale of the premises to a group of men who would be concentrating on dry barrels, and asked us, as he introduced the group's spokesman, to stay on. I now no longer felt an allegiance to the concern, and, indeed, went back to my own budding cooperage with such a feeling of relief that I may have been quite as incoherently jubilant in the telling as Charles had been at an earlier celebration. I was not only relieved of an obligation I had been, of myself, unable to shed, but I sensed a possible stimulus to my own business (yet unborn) which would result from the news that the new firm's cooperage would produce only dry barrels. The feeling upon being relieved of responsibility for the correction of poorly made barrels was another ingredient that mixed well with my present *melange* of elations.

It was now imperative that I spend all my time furnishing and rigging the new cooperage. With Mr. Mallot's cooperage no longer making wet barrels, mine would be the only local source for these. If I could fill this immediate vacuum with my product before the demand was satisfied with barrel shipments from St. Louis, I could capture a steady and reliable local market. I was the only cooper then in St. Jo capable of turning out a consistently reliable quantity and quality of wets. The prospect and the need thus for quick action, drove me to long hours and overwork.

Mr. Jandu, the new manager at Mallot's having no need for several thousand wet staves, sold them to me at a reasonable price. And, to make sure I would have enough for future operations, I contracted with a farmer near the town's edge for the delivery of a number of his girdled seasoned white oak.

Then, to make my workshop as pleasant as possible, I chose the room's east wall for a four-paneled window, from which I was able to use an early morning sun for work. Past my window, especially in the early morning hours, rolled teams of oxen, wagons with oiled canvas tops, beneath which a few thin faces peered. And always – even on the coldest mornings – there would be the Indian, reeling toward the landing after finding nothing at the bottom of his jug but misery.

I suppose I enjoyed my window view of this parade of life because, for so long I had had a view at the Rouen Cooperage, where, each day, there appeared a parade of ships and laborers. My mind could tug gently at its many romantic leashes while the soft, feather-like shavings sifted from tool to the floor, and where the fine, aromatic pungencies of the oak never palled, but nourished. The odors were a healing, buoyant, spirit-lifter as appealing to my sense of smell as fine wine was to my palate.

I took to spending most of my time now in the cooperage, from earliest light until a dusk so late that I could hardly see fingers in front of my face. It was a busy period, that summer, fall and winter of '43. Charles' store did well, and our hours complemented one another's.

Arnold F. Rothmeier

At night he tended more and more to the social entrapments of St. Jo – mainly with Robidoux' daughters; I appreciated the warmth and the solitude I had built into the cooperage.

It was a time of honest labor and honest sales. Everything I made had a ready market. My barrels were sold in advance to the now two slaughter houses and a brewery; buckets and tubs were stacked on the floor in a number of sizes, each filled with damp shavings to keep their seal.

In addition, I was busied shortly with requests for wood repairs on wagon parts and on spinning wheels. Each was a challenge; each a task and a problem solvable in my medium – oak; each brought in cash – shiny gold tokens of an admission that I was a master craftsman, that I could make and repair anything.

It was a time, too, for appreciating the relative quiet of our town, which, though teeming with trading activity and news of impossible Indian exploits upriver and down along the Santa Fe, seemed somehow, shunted from the mainstream and eddied into our frontier.

Charles took almost monthly trips to St. Louis now – ostensibly to replenish stocks. During these times I tended both ends of the building, and, in talking with the customers, enlarged my stock of English. I now began to feel shades of meaning in the language as well as grasp the more utilitarian usages. Some days were spent lazily and recklessly listening to ruminant customers as they pawed over the latest rumors of national import, and who then, upon leaving, buried the news, like a clean bone, beneath shrugs and shallow generalizations. Always, I noted their penchant for getting on top of a situation, riding the wave, so to speak, and seeing the thing from vantage point, as though this verbal height lent sagacity to utterance, puffed one up, and stamped him with superiority. I, too, found myself generalizing, categorizing people with little evidence, save their words, into piles and stacks, like: ignorant farmer, clever investor, dangerous man, I wondered if I, too, was being categorized.

One of the liveliest subjects of conversation was that relating to the goals of numerous wagon parties now arriving, outfitting and departing in increasing numbers. I would listen in an idle fashion to the talk of these. Hadn't there always been wagons through town? And then, as I saw them jolt riverward, heavy with passengers and goods, I would muse over the reasons for the passage. Did they have nothing here? Was the simple act of moving their main goal? I had always thought that unhappy people moved. But what about my own case? I had been happy and secure in Rouen. True, I had left New Orleans because of Cholera and Bronze John, but then I had been in St. Louis. What was it that caused me to move westward? If I could answer that question, I could know what stung these men, prodded them now, dragging their covered nests of staring children.

But more and more, as the early spring days wore on, I found myself unconsciously uniting in spirit with these movers, these owners of canvas homes rolling toward the river and beyond. Sometimes I would leave my bench and walk to the store front for a better view. I would stand and calculate weight and sturdiness and pulling power, and try to fathom the mind of the man with the whip.

Then, suddenly, in the last weeks of a torrid August 1843, it was as though the road upstream was damned. There were no more wagons; somewhere the fountainhead had dried. Those who had read current sources of information about the trail took, at least, these two bits of caution: no early starts before the grass was up in fodderable quantities, and its correlative: no late start; the mountains showed a cold shoulder to late arrivals. The wagons, with their maddeningly lethargic ox teams and incoherent, cursing masters were gone. I returned to my bench feeling oddly stranded by their absence.

Arnold F. Rothmeier

Chapter 27
Tug Westward

The winter of '44-'45 rolled in with pretentious bluster. It began with short, violent storms that blew themselves out, trailing a drizzly dampness over the country. They were a series of rains that seemed to know no end. By Christmas time, the earlier and heavier tempests had cooled and a six-inch pad of snow blanketed all. Of river traffic there was none, but then there were no massive ice jams either, with their riverboat destruction. In the brief intervals between storms, Charles' end of the building was often the scene of a group of farmers and trappers. They would pounce upon generalities just as did my mongrel his deer bones, and tease and worry them until, like the bone, they shone bare and utterly depleted.

There was talk about the stiffening Mexican tolls on the Santa Fe and of a growing American colony in the Oregon Territory. It seemed to me that all who had anything to say about the territory spoke with a great deal of ignorance, for though some would quote the news of Fremont, or of a man named Marsh, few had been beyond the river. Few had returned to show and to tell. And yet, I thought, shoving skepticism aside, was not that the significant thing? –that those who had gone did not return? They did not return to Missouri, to former farms. Did they, indeed, find the new country the Eden of rumor? Or could it be they were unable to return?

My skepticism was dissolved one blustery February day when Charles returned with half a packet of supplies from St. Louis. I had been leisurely finishing a small order of whites, had a fine fire crackling. Just as I lit a pipe, with the intention of relaxing, a boy rapped and informed me of Charles' need for a horse and wagon at the dock. I was there shortly with staves siding the wagon bed, expecting the usual big buy of trade goods. But this time Charles' weightiest material was news. Instead of bags and casks, there were only half a dozen boxes and bundles. Charles met my puzzled eye with a nod and a suggestion that we load. He would explain shortly.

After signing the usual lading papers he found a seat, lit pipe, and with a kind of relieved look, almost as though anticipating relief through unburdening, he slapped the reins and began to speak.

"Claude", he said, "St. Louis and the country around it is filling with people waiting for the winter to pass and spring grass to sprout. They seem no longer to fear the west, nor to pay any attention to the government attempts to restrict settlement and travel to the other bank of the Missouri. They are gathering there and moving wagons, cattle, goods, and everything to Independence. You can have no idea—-", and here Charles broke into French, as he often did when he was excited, and spun another story of what he had seen at Independence on the return trip.

What Charles was trying to say, in his excitement, was that he had reached another plateau; that, despite his diversional trips and occasional dances and soirees at St. Jo, life was again becoming a tedium.

I, too, shared Charles' feelings, though I seemed to require much less diversion than he. I listened while he told what he had learned at

St. Louis – that the federal deterrents to movement west were dissolving; that hordes of wagons and teams waited only for the grass to sprout. It seemed, he said, as though the whole country was ready to move west.

In the end, I suppose I felt I was being left out of something alive and new, something occurring and passing me by. It created in me a feeling akin to mild panic, a fear of not being included; that here was being born a rare exodus, and that once it had passed, it would be no more. I was intrigued by an intangible. It was impossible to think about it rationally, for it was only a sensation, a mystery, a tug of a movement and a destination. It fastened itself softly and alluringly to my heart and mind and would not let me rest.

The something was akin to the promise of a secret Christmas present, its allure and anticipation all the stronger because its outlines and fragmentary descriptions and distances were so deceptive, and because these fragments contained nothing negative. It was generally accepted that somewhere out there where the sun set was territory virgin and fertile and beautiful, where no winter marred one's years; that there, beyond prairies and mountains was a marvelous secret and an ever-changing series of days filled with adventure; that once there, virgin land, rivers, forests, and much game was to be had. And, above all, a climate existed that was never hot and never cold.

In retrospect I saw that my life, thus far, had been filled with the satisfaction of a fascinating skill, an engrossing routine, and, at the same time, a kind of niggling fear of not being able to "make it"; of not having sufficient food and shelter – or means for their purchase. I could see that this is why I had striven so hard in the early days, then at New Orleans, St. Louis, and yes, here at St. Jo. how the thought of being part of a vast and mighty move to a virgin country gripped and held me.

It was not that Charles the salesman was talking me into a purchase. The thing had lain in the back of my mind like a fertile seed, as I often watched, like a boy being left behind, the emigrant wagons through the cooperage window. That seed needed only what was happening now – the excited, enthusiastic and sunny urgings of my partner – for its germinating.

I asked Charles many things – most of which were answered with unavoidably vague and passionate replies. He was literally possessed by a tide. I watched his face as he talked on into the early morning hours, and I seemed to see a man grappling with that tide. In a boat, I saw him, caught by the strength of the bore that once roared in past Rouen, and over which man's power was as a grass blade in a hurricane. I could feel the power of the thing that had gripped Charles, and I, too, was beginning to know the force of the thing that caused him to talk like a madman that night.

Frosty river mists hung like a veil over the streets of St. Jo the next morning. I had arisen early and soundlessly, dressed, and stolen out the side door to catch the town early and unawares; to possess fresh morning odors that seemed to vanish as soon as the sun struck. A soft melange of smells was in the air: the homey and acrid blanket of damp manure, the bitter sweet of burning oak, the heavy, stomach-enticing flavors of a fried pork breakfast.

Sights and odors seemed to cleanse my eyes and head, to sharpen those parts of me dulled by wine the night before. I strode the middle of the main street which Mssr. Robidoux had recently named "Valerie", and made slowly for the wharves. A golden pheasant rose in my path. The sky behind the Blacksnake Hills smouldered a dull red. The effect was a brief illusion. When, a moment later, my glance returned, the red was a somber maroon. Now the town emerged from sleep and frost to reveal a living, sensing thing: rugs were drawn from windows; slow smoke, pungent and cloud-white pushed into the frosty air; back in the brush oak a nameless bird scolded in arpeggios; a black emerging from his space between bales yawned generically on a note both defiant and relieved; St. Joseph uncurled for another day, and I sat on a piling and watched its uncurling.

    Whether I came just for the experience of another of those mornings, those witnessings, or whether I was driven by the memory of Charles' prolonged and passionate wordiness of the previous evening, I could not tell. I knew now not even whether I was the same contented cooper of a week ago. And I distinctly remember feeling that I did not want to succumb to another's wishes or ideas; that I must move and act in response to my own stimulation. For I had always been reticent to be swayed by another's enthusiasms; the thing we had had last night must be, in part, at least, of my own initiation.

    With the slow coming of light to the scene, as though the light of itself were some magic ingredient necessary for movement, light on the wharf unfolded and stirred in isolated patches until movement was everywhere. Vague bundles of rags stirred, then stood, aroused by other stirrers and standers; heavy food odors fought with that of bruised willow; teams approached for a share of the ship's bowels; ripe mule dung steamed and stung.

    I turned slowly and returned to the cooperage. There seemed no end to the orders for barrels. The thought that I had a timely, salable skill, that I was established, worked where I was surrounded by an eternal, passive excitement, and where all life seemed to hang in a delicate balance, piqued me. There had never been a morning like this, its odors and sights, its whispered promises.

    Though it was yet early – perhaps hardly six – Charles had breakfasted and gone. The post floor was yet stacked with the bales and boxes deposited the evening before. I lit fire and pipe and finished hooping the half-dozen wets fitted the afternoon before. Then I sat atop my stool, planing away at the marble-like stave edge, inhaling its sweet, aromatic balm, sensing the comfort and security of the place.

But now the view from my window caused a restless stirring, a kind of itch that defied scratching. I saw horsemen, and I swayed in the saddle, pulled a rein; I saw a plodding figure beside a yoke, and I strode beside him; I experienced an impatient stirring toward a new goal. That goal was clothed in a mystery of conflicting rumors, and I felt I must strive toward it. I must walk and ride toward the west and find its truth for myself. I had been dissuaded by Mssr. Chouteau from taking the river road to another beckoning wild and cold country. I had been dissuaded from taking the hot and sandy road to the Taos; from taking a portion of the riches that seemed to pour each year into Independence downstream. But now there was a third choice. And as a I planed and looked, my mind pondered the forces that drew the restless American, the Irishman, the German to the banks of the Missouri – though not to settle and build, but to dig and hedge through the winter, and, with the stirrings of springs, and the sprouting of grass, to fling himself, his family and team into limitless sandy wastes that spread out beyond the tree-lined Missouri.

Where, I asked myself, were these men with their federal edicts? For three or four years now, it was said, groups of wagons had entered the supposedly forbidden Indian lands, and yet no tale of penalty of trespass or rumor of massacre had come. There had been only the occasionally published letters of a man named Marsh – who seemed to have found what he sought – and the difficult-to-believe incoherencies of a few trappers.

I saw, then, there was truly no prohibition to fear. As long as one did not obviously flaunt the laws, no westering trespass was forbidden.

I resumed, mechanically, now, my barrel work. But then, it seemed, the delicious vapors of my white oak staves had suddenly gone flat; my fingers made unusual mistakes; a stave took the red smear of a slit finger.

I drank, and it was late afternoon when I heard voices up front. Charles and a leather-clothed stranger entered the workroom. I was relieved to have an excuse to lay my tools aside, for my mood fitted me more for the humming of society's voice than for the awkward scrapings of my tool.

"This is Mssr. Labadie", Charles began, by way of introduction, as he handed us both a tin of brandy. "He is interested in the post, if we might sell reasonably enough. He has only recently returned with a company from a profitable buffalo hide expedition, and is seeking a business."

I shook hands with the man, and in his eyes I saw the same intense wildness that had startled me so long ago in the eyes of the man in New Orleans.

It was not hard to see the reasons for Labadie's wish for a change. In addition to piercing eyes – the most alive segments of his body – there was about him a kind of warm decadence that whispered, "rest, rest". His left cheek bore four white plowed marks of an animal's claw, marks that began just in front of the left ear and disappeared beneath his greasy leather shirt. His right arm hung noticeably stiff. He was abnormally short even for a Frenchman, but the strength of his handclasp and depth of his scar lent him a stature far in excess of his physical measurements.

He spoke slowly and in French when questioned, and the resonance and fine, even richness of his voice lent authority to what he said: Yes, he had seen the blue western ocean. No, he would not reckon it far; he supposed, though, that if one were to measure each chain and mile, it would be long indeed. Since he had gone there alone several years ago, he had not reckoned days and miles. But there had been no tedium. The beauty, the newness of the world each day, the abundance of game, suddenness of storms, even the loneliness and an anxious few days of drought while crossing a nameless desert had been an adventure.

Under the spell of his voice and the magic of brandy, I began to comprehend the spell of the tug westward. The thought of a probing in the direction he had gone was heady medicine. Yes, hearing it told by one who had stridden the way, I knew the truth of the old French proverb: the <u>way</u> was the thing. To leave the bosom of security, armed only with confidence, to walk or ride into what experiences lay along the route, <u>this</u> was the great adventure. There would, of course, be a terminus – but then, even a terminus need not be an end to such a journeying.

We finished one bottle, then another before offering Mssr. Labadie space and robe for the night. It was he who spoke the last words before blissful effects of the brandy closed my eyes. But long after the log walls rang with our snores, I strode, in dreams across the muddy Missouri and into a western sun that never quite set, and on legs that never grew weary.

I was awakened gently by the fragrance of Labadie's pipe, then by a consciousness of a large, evil-tasting body within my mouth, which I quickly recognized as my own abused tongue still partially embalmed in spirits. A third and quite inexplicable sensation was that my legs and feet had recently carried me somewhere. Not only were my thighs achingly stiff, but the balls of my feet and my toes were cramped and responded to rubbing as though, in the night, they had tramped many miles instead of sleeping with the rest of me.

Charles awakened to the clatter of wagons and teams early on an icy road, and poured each of us a cup of his favorite burgundy to cut and cleanse the tongue. After a long and hearty breakfast we returned to our business discussion. Charles, the salesman, had done well with his estimates. Without – at least in my presence – having questioned Labadie about his resources, he had established a close estimate of what the man could pay, and had set the price just beyond reach. It was a breath-taking fifty-eight hundred dollars, which then slipped back to an affordable forty-five hundred after another brandy. My cooperage, which also was our living quarters, had value only for me as a business. Its stretchers, racks, and shelves were not even mentioned as of value, although their construction had not been easy.

All these things Labadie would, no doubt, use for kindling or for holding his stores after we were gone. I saw now they had been a stop-gap. The feint I had made in the direction of settling down now seemed ridiculous and futile. I suppose I had known for years – perhaps even as long ago as when I trod the worn St. Louis docks, where my being was tugged, and that the means would be those animals, who forever dropped their smouldering green there on the wharf planks.

It would have been foolhardy for me to meddle in the sale. I got no signal from Charles and needed none, for he had everything under control and needed no assistance. I listened and said little. I was not even present when they finalized an agreement over the furs and stores accumulated.

But I did go along, as a partner must, when the transaction was terminated at the new bank. Charles had asked Mssr. Robidoux to witness the signing. The latter, silent and inscrutable, had had several opportunities to observe my partner's business acumen since their first quick deal. Now he withheld all comment and simply signed. Though I knew him to be immensely wealthy, I could also imagine him glad to be rid of the competition that Charles represented. I admit frankly that I did not like or trust the man, for rumors of his craftiness and sharp dealing were, even then, a part of the St. Joseph legacy.

All present signed articles of transfer. Handshaking, It was done. The three of us, with property and money securely under lock and signature, adjourned for drinks at a new and freshly painted hotel up the street. Charles would work with Labadie for a few days; I would

Pan The Low Waters

finish my orders. It was agreed we would vacate the premises, leaving its contents intact, by the thirtieth of April.

I excused myself from the company to complete my last barrel orders. The day was fair, and through the cooperage window, as I worked, I paused occasionally to gaze down the main street. Though it was only mid-March, trains of emigrants were gathering; change was in the air. Charles and I had caught the fever. This year we, too, would be part of the crawl west.

Arnold F. Rothmeier

Mary
Part 1

Such a burned-out feeling I have today. I can't seem to stop hurting all over. If I could only feel close again, like when he would let me sit on his big bony knees and hold me. He always used to come in slouching and tired and smelling sweaty and horsey. But he always took time to sit and hold me. I guess I was his favorite, now that Sarah and Harriet have moved across the field with their own man.

Mama didn't tell us papa was that sick. I only thought he needed to rest more. Then they got the doctor from Springfield and mama came through the door crying into her apron and looking white and wrung-out. I'd have ran in to see him and I'd have made him well again. I know I'd have. Only none of us kids thought he'd just up and go sudden. And only after sis' told Harriet and their man came over fast in their buggy and saw mama – then they told me. And it hurts empty, and I know I can' t never sit there again no more.

I think mama feels worse because the Mormon man came late than because daddy went so sudden. I hate her and love her at the same time because I think that. But I know that won't do any good. It all changed so fast. I can't seem to fit myself into the different changes that have come. First, no more playing with my older sisters and their telling me how they feel inside when their men came over. Then I have to be more growed up with Lemuel and William and Simon, because Landrum is a boy and boys don't act growed up until they get whiskers like Pike and Foster. I don't know if Landrum will ever act growed up.

Pike and Foster told mama they would tend the farm for her. They're all talking about selling it because mama and us can't do it all. But mama only listens to them talk. All of a sudden she seems old, like that part of her that was young went into the grave with papa. She used to get after Landrum for being so slow, and after me for not being more ladylike. Now it's more like she don't care, but like she puts more trust in the Lord because that's the way it's going to be and none of us seem to understand why. She don't say no more about my being baptized into the "Saints".

I heard Pike and Foster talking the other day about us moving to Missouri. They've taken papa's mules and cows over to their own pasture so's mama wouldn't have to worry none about them. The barn looks empty now, with all the reins and fodder gone. Pike and Foster had most of their hay spoiled this winter because they didn't get it in fast like papa did. Now they need what's in the barn. Like as not they'll kill a few cows so the rest will have enough until the May grass.

I have a hard time getting used to things, they happen so fast anymore; papa dying, and no more milking chores, and not even no school now because the teacher up and went west without even telling anyone he was going. Now all of a sudden I have to do for mama and get the stew a boiling early and remind Landrum to bring wood, and I don't know what-all.

There was two men this morning to look over papa's farm. Mama was talking to Sarah and Harriet's husbands (they are both William, so she calls Foster, William, and Pike, Bill). They've about convinced her to sell out and locate with them out somewhere west. I guess that's all right. They say most all the Indians are away on the lee side of the Missouri River and don't bother nobody where they are now. I guess they mix up with white folk's ways when they see no harm comes of it. Our teacher – the one that left – showed us once a tomahawk and some Indian shoes and beads. That was before he skipped out and so we don't have no more school. He's not the only one, either. The teacher before him didn't say he was going neither, but just up and left.

I get the feeling since papa died that everything I do is kind of makeshift now. Mama is having trouble with her eyes again, and when she signed some paper for those two men she couldn't hardly see where to write, and Pike read it all legal to her. It's all kind of like Christmas, but without the surprise part. Everything is so unsettled and waiting for something, but when it's all over we won't go back to swinging, and friends in and my corner of the bedroom to myself. It's all going to change and be so different. I like this old house that papa built, but it's so different with him not here anymore. I wake up and think for a moment I'll hear him and mama talking across the hall and maybe he'll saddle up Rose and let me ride for a while, or just sit and read me. Then that empty feeling again, and I know today will be another yesterday when Will and Bill and Harriet and Sarah came over to get some more things to sell in town. Mama had me helping Simon read, and Sarah said why don't I be a teacher, I was so patient. I felt good after that. I like her. Sometimes I wish she was a full instead of a half-sister. Harriet is nice too, but quieter, but not so much like mama.

On top of all the getting ready to move and all, I saw blood on my nightgown this morning. And I shouldn't a been surprised but was, cause Sarah told me about her blood and how not to be scared, and how it only means you're getting' a woman now and so you should be thankful. That's all she would tell me. I guess it's all about what you find out after you get married. But seems to me sometimes a person can become a mother without having a husband. It's all so hard to figure out. It must be awfully hard to tell, or maybe it's supposed to be learnt and not spoken. Maybe that's why it's all a big secret.

I think I'm as pretty as Sarah or Harriet, maybe prettier. Sometimes I'm scared of life and the surprises that happen so sudden-like. Papa's going was one, but then when it's over it turns out not so bad you can't stand it – not if you pray and go to church when you can. Papa died a Baptist, but I think he would have made us *Saints* if he had of stayed a while longer. He hated to see the Mormons done to like the preacher said the long-ago Christians was. He said it's a sign of rightusness in the church when it shows such determination for it's beliefs. (1945, April)

Today mama sent me to ride over to Harriet's farm. We get our milk from them now that they took the cows to sell and milk. Its just over the next rise. The mosquitoes is bad now. Will don't seem to know what to do now, whether to plant or just to wait and see if mama can sell the place and then us all to get going to some place in Missouri. So many people moving there. Wil is so restless when he can't do something. Bill is the same way, always full of something that makes him get things done, and they both can't stand settin' still.

While Will was out in the barn, rubbing harnesses Sarah said, we talked about things like how many of the horses and cows we could run with the wagons if we went west. It all depends on if anybody will buy mama's farm. Papa sure put a lot of work in this place. Someday I guess I'll have a man. I hope he can make things and farm as good as Papa and Will and Bill. I wonder if Landrum will ever move like them. He's always been so slow, you'd think seeing his father work and Will and Bill would straighten him out a little. But he's always thinking or dreaming or something, and don't see how to get things done.

Sarah is beside herself because everything is in a state of not knowing what to do about getting ready for spring planting or packing, so, she says, she just sits and stews a lot, and it's hard on her. But this evening she says, her and Will are going to town with the Pikes and listen to a meeting.

The same horse and buggy was there when I got there. Mama met me at the gate and told me to go back and get Will and hurry. I could see she was excited. So back I went. He just threw a old blanket on Dash and followed me in. Sarah stayed, on account of little George. I wanted to come in and see what happened, but mama met us at the barn and said to keep Landrum and Simon outside while they talked. So we just sat and pretty soon the four of them came out and talked some more and made motions toward the end of the farm, and then they were gone.

Will and mama told us its all settled now. They took the place and mama was going to town tomorrow morning with Will and see a lawyer and then that's all, I guess. Will says they'll make room for us all at Sarah's and his house. That's asking a lot, but we'll make do. Mama want me to ride over the tell Bill and Harriet about the tent meeting tonight. Landrum is so slow, and with papa gone, mama depends on me a lot. But I don't mind. And I suppose some day my eyes will grow weak too.

Everything seems to be working up to moving west, and us along with it all. The immigrant meeting had so many people there they couldn't all get in the tent, so they had it outside on the courthouse steps, and everybody sat on the wagon beds or stood around with pitch torches lighting it all up. You'd think the whole town was wanting to leave, the way they went on about Missouri and the new land there. I don't think too many people have given their own farms here around Springfield a chance. It was all so noisy, and so many men all talking at once. Them that seemed to know about Missouri didn't have chance to say much because so many psaw-pshawed what they said. I never saw so many grown-ups yell so much and not say nothing. They teach us to be quiet in school so we'll learn, but they don't do it themselves when they get growed up. I don't know what to think.

Mama and Will and Bill said on the way back that they didn't hear anything that they hadn't already heard or read in the paper. Anyways, when we got to Will's and Sarah's they put all us kids in one room with George, my cousin, and went on talking about Missouri. It was awfully late when they finished, so Harriet and Bill decided to stay and leave early to get their cows milked. That made seven of us in two beds in George's room. But I don't mind, and we was warm sleeping together.

This was the first time we was away from sleeping in our home, cause now its sold, and we're either going to stay here of have a different home in Missouri. This last is what Will and Bill want to do, and Lord knows they've got plenty of push and gumption. They don't never seem to stop, only now Will don't want to put another crop ifn we're all going to Missouri.

I'm writing this later.

Well, we didn't stay long in Missouri either. Just like mama said: If Will and Bill offered their place cheap enough. And then we had the long dusty road to Missouri. And even after we pulled into St. Joseph and tired of traveling as we were, we got talked into another. But this was some weeks after we seed the town was, like Bill said, "too dam busy for its own britches". What I think he meant was there was no place a body could farm. People was everywhere an no room for cows if you had 'em 'cause people and wagons took up all the town.

But wagons came and wagons left, and mama, Bill, and Will finally found out what all the people was about. They was about a big movement of people to a place even farther west than we wanted to go. It was about a big country called Oregon Territory and another big place called California, where there would always be room for people, no matter how many got there.

Then while our poor horses rested, and we not knowing what to do, Mama and Will and Bill went to another tent meeting, and that was where it all started. But this time we didn't have nothing to sell, so we was like a ship on the ocean, and I never heard of no roads or streets on the ocean.

When mama and Will and Bill came back and told the rest of us about why St. Joseph was so full of people I wanted to cry. Alls they talked about was what the tent people said about the country west again: it was good weather all year; the Indians was friendly; it never snowed; it was a parydise compared to this country; there was good land for farming everywhere; there was trees for home building and all the grass the cows could eat. Then, like Bill hadn't had enough wagoning, he said him and Harriet was going to go for a look-see. They was joining; had already joined a big wagon train, and would mama and Will and Sarah go with them?

That was what happened at St. Joseph. And so we outfitted again like Bill and Harriet wanted. And so we all found us another trail – farther west again.

Our poor oxen! I feel so sorry for the poor beasts. They strain and pull a few yards and slouch there and bawl, and even Will's whip makes no difference. This morning I cut pieces from Bill's buffalo hide and tied it around their hoofs, but it was in pieces from the rocks before they had went far. Mama don't see good enough to pity them like I do.

We was all strung out across the prairie. We never see half the wagons together before we got to these hills they call the Wahsatch. Now it's all so slow and the wagons is all bunched behind the next waiting for the brambles and trees and rocks to be moved. Even the little girls help some and my brother William too, and then fall to eating the service berries. Some men work a while and then you see um hiding behind their piles of bushes and not helping. I try to help by cooking for mama and my dress is all tatters from trying to help clear the trail brush.

I lay awake at night in my blanket under the wagon and I think of the things that brought us to these stony hills they call the Wahsatch one.

Mostly I guess it was the tent meetings and the reading of those letters from California and Bill and Will's not having anything to do after they sold their land. They was both worse than us kids after they got the money – hid it sewed in the clothes they wore and such things as that. But they wasn't the only Murphy's that got excited about going someplace. They didn't have to argue with any of us. Even after we sold everything except what we could put it two wagons, and pulled it clear across two states, they still didn't want to settle down in Independence. They still kept going to emigrant society meetings whenever they heard of one, asking about the land and the weather, and was it really pretty and warm there like the Illinoise paper said it was. Mama don't try to argue with them like she used to. She says its like trying to argue against going to church or against eatin' or sleepin': everybody's doing it and it seems to do more harm than good, so long as its that way, she says, lets do it: so many people can't be wrong.

Then when spring rolled around we just were tired – mostly Will and Bill – of being firsted by all the trains, and joined up with the one that looked the biggest and had the finest wagons. And that's how we come to be here with the Donners and the Breens and the Eddys. Even Will and Bill are sorry now we came this way and didn't stay on the main road with the other wagons. The only ones we have seen coming this way was a bunch of men riding and packing mules, and they left us days ago and went on up the Webber River, which some said we should of gone and we went on hacking out a road to go west on. Don't' nobody laugh or joke anymore, just cut brush and roll stones and rest and roll more stones. Me, I don't' see the sense of making the poor oxen pull all this heavy stuff – boxes and barrels and the heavy wagons that only tire out the poor skinny beasts and cause us to creep along.

We are down out of the brush at last. But it seems we changed some back there. The people isnt' near as Christian as they was before we left the Big Sandy.

Mama don't go anymore to the big Reed wagon and sit and talk like she used to with the other women. Its like she wasn't invited anymore. And the men look at you with a kind of mean tiredness; don't talk. And the poor animals seem tireder before starting than when they got unhitched.

We came to the edge of the Salt Lake this morning and rested and I looked back at the big mountains behind and hoped we wouldn't never have to cut and dig and roll rocks ever again like that. I see Paty Reed and some of the other kids sometimes but mainly they stay to their wagons for fear of these thin Indians that Will says are around now. But I went with Sarah to a close by campfire last night, and its all just one big danger after the other cause now they're scared cause we've lost so much of the summer going up and over mountains and hacking rodes that maybe we don't have time or strength nor food. But then we don't have it to go back neither.

I had a funny dream last night and we was all stopped at the Soda Springs and was looking and pointing at the bloody colored mineral water and shaking heads. They was talking about the names of our people too and pointing and saying we shoul've been warned by names cause names have meaning. They said Graves was a bad sign. He just joined our train in the Wahsatch, and they is thirteen of em. And then there the Donners, and mama said that means thunder. Thunder is low and scary and always comes before a storm. And then they pointed to some of the others and said there was something hidden in most of their names that meant it was bad. Like having a living person carry around a word that was a sign or omen like. Keseberg was one of the funny ones. His name is supposed to mean 'cheese mountain'. Who could find anything bad about a cheese mountain? I wish I had some of the cheese papa made way back in Kentucky. I remember some one said Hardcoup means a hard job or a hard chore and that it meant a sign of something hard to get done. Wolfinger and Hook was two more that had a dark meaning without coming out and saying it. And I dreamed of eatin cheese and Reeds growing by a big lake and of a hard time I was having to catch fish while the thunder came across the water and drive the fish away. And then there was graves and sadness and in the morning Landrum said I kept him awake sobbing and talking in my sleep.

On that long dry drive across the Salt Desert they was no water for tears. I wisht I had the water for tears before we crossed the desert.

And we had a misery a-plenty in the desert. If I'd had tear water I'd a shed em mostly for the poor oxen. They could only pull and kind of waste away to hide and hoof. And then to see Breen's poor mare sink and smother in green slime and the mean look on Eddy's face and him not helpin.

But if I could've cried wet I'd a did it for the poor dumb things that pulled all that heavy trunks and anvils and stoves that wearried them down, and finally was thrown out anyways. And all the ox got for his trouble was a Digger arrow in the belly. I could never forget the big brown eyes that rolled in their big brown heads when they lay on their sides and bawled a little and jerked their hoofs and died.

But I learnt to look the other way or down at my feet because in the big desert crossing so much hurt happened and it did no good to feel it yourself no matter who it happened to. I just look away when a cruelty or a sad happened sos I wouldn't tighten up and tear inside. So many of em happened in the long weary time we was on the desert: the dying of Halloran with nobody really caring cause he was all alone; the dry stretches that went on and on – and then went on through the night; then the big fight between Reed and Snyder and him dying all cause of their tired and worry, but mostly tiredness cause that what all of us was feeling all the time.

They sent Reed away and we kept going through the long dusty plain, stragglin and nobody trying to keep together. And now that the poor oxen are near dead, they leave his big wagon in the desert, and they stumble on still low and plod hard like they thought they still pulled the wagon.

Will tells mama what he sees happen, but lately he is so tired he just lays down without hitching and no word. He told Sarah though that Bill Pike offered to walk back and look for old Hardcoop. But they wouldn't wait and nor Breen nor Graves would loan him his horse so poor Hardcoop was left. No body cares no more. No more pity to give. Its all been used so much now it hurts too much and easier to close your eyes.

I closed my eyes cause I couldn't do nothing for the poor beasts – the ones they wore down with their heavy wagons and then left to die – and the wagons too. I closed my eyes at the awful arrow wounds festering in the oxen that gave up and hunched in the trace when the whip hurt not as much as the arrow. I closed my eye to the look on Miz Donner's face when the Diggers ran off with the 18 oxen and I closed my eyes to the bloody feet I seen and the shrivelled-like whine the babies made; it was harder to keep from cryin over my own misery, but the hurt in my foot or stomach hurt less that the hurt in my heart.

It was like something pulled us all down into more pain and fear and death than we could bear, and if the hurt wasn't for us, then we had to feel it anyway. The heat and the tiredness of the day swapped for the cold and fear of the night, and both wore us down until it seemed nothing would change until we all died.

But it did change, but not for the good until after a sad thing happened. After Hardcoup came Wolfinger. They said the Indians killed him, and poor Miz Wolfinger didn't care about nothing no more, and the Donners put her few bundles in their wagon.

The change was the food that Suitter's Indians and Stanton brought. It gave us hope we needed bad, that it wasn't far now to where we was going - just over the mountains. And how good the new fresh bread tasted that mama baked and the dried beef. And then, when it seemed we had come to the end of the sadness all around us and the oxen had fine grass and we still had time to get over the mountains, and lots of water at the Truckee, and surely the seven mule train of food would last us, the worst happened. And then I couldn't close my eyes cause I saw and heard him get the bullet in the back. And I cried when he died.

We was resting in the meadows for a few days, and it come up evening, and most everything was tended to, and the Diggers was leaving us alone. Will and Bill was in good spirits and having nothing to do, and Will had nothing to do, so he was cleaning his favorite gun – a little pepper-box pistol. He was always helpful and when one of the party said the fire was getting low, up he jumps, turns around, and at the same time hands the gun to Bill. It happened so fast I had to think hard after about it as how it really happened. Maybe Bill didn't even grab the thing hard enough to fire it. Maybe Will himself pressed the trigger back when he handed it to Bill. The bullet did its work, and Will teetered and fell with a bullet through his back. He died in pain and in a hour. Such a senseless way for such a good husband and father to die, and after all what he's been through to get here.

But even Will's going, even the big empty place he left in the family didn't seem to sad us more than we was already. The snowflakes mixed with the dirt they shoved on poor Bill and Sarah had her hands full with little Naomi and Catherine and kept them in the wagon while the men filled the hole.

Then they just went to their wagons, and from then on I thought there was no more caring about what the other family did. On the terrible road there was wondering about how the next wagon was doing, and even some helping. Now there was too much fear over how much time was left before snow set in, how high was the mountains up ahead, and how many miles before help, and would we "do it"on the food we had left. I kept thinking – while we stayed and stayed there at the meadows – "It" to everybody was the big thing that was just over the mountains of snow we could see beneath the clouds; "It" was what we could reach even with our tiredness and the sharp bones of our poor oxen; and to reach "It" there was a awful fear we felt, with nobody leading and every wagon going off alone, weak and hungry, we might not have the strength to go on.

Nobody told us anymore the train was moving out. Some believed Stanton when he said the snow wouldn't be too deep until December. Some kept talking about the deep snow up ahead. After four or five more days we watched the Breens and some others go by. Their oxen pulled steady and they had more animals that the others did. Maybe they were more scared than most. Will couldn't stand it any longer, him being the only man we had left now, and feeling more sponsible than before. And next day we hitched up our few oxen and left with the Graveses, Stanton, and the Reeds.

Seemed to me the clouds and the sprinkling snow was trying to tell us something. It was cold, and the higher we went, the more often we came to little drifts around bushes and rocks. Then in a few more days of winding around hills, the trees got thicker. When the clouds rolled away sun shone on forrests covered all in white, like the sweet beat egg yolk mama used to make to put on pies. Only this white was bitter cold.

Sometimes I carried little Catherine. She was too little to miss her daddy I guess. We all walked now and Will was always up alongside our only two oxen left, slapping and switching. Sometimes Landrum or Lemuel carried little Naomi. We carried the copper kettle until Bill was shot, and then it was threwn away like most else except blankets and the little food. It was cold and we was always wet and stomach ache.

But the rain didn't wash the snow down like most thought. Instead it got deep and colder the higher we climbed. When the oxen and mules reached for their next step they would lay there on their belly, bawling and struggling with hoofs beating the snow until the driver dug under them or pushed them over to where the legs reached the ground. Then we knew we was nearing the end, and that in our heart we would not waggon through, and left it there like the others did, and tied bundles on the other animals. This was no good either, and in the end, after the bundle was shook off two or three times, it was left, and only the food was carried.

Stanton came back with news that him and his mules and the Indian had found the road and reached the top; but by that time most had either quit or couldn't make their legs move, and went into camp. Besides, it began to snow again and thick, and nobody wanted to keep working that hard even if they heard him tell how close we were to the top, which most didn't hear because of the dark and the cold and the snow coming down and need to make a dry bed. In the morning we wearried back to the wagons in all the cold white and grey world where there is something like the feeling of a home.

And then the longest, dreariest time of my whole life started. It was a time that had no beginning or end, and no fun. It had only thoughts of things like: how to get more food, and how to get warm and dry, and why did we have to leave our good farm. These kept going through my head like a dull knife cutting until it no more made pain because it was all the same, and there wasn't any more feelings like hope and laughing or surprises or any of the things like running or smiles or seeing the sun or things in the distance that made you feel like part of the world.

We gnawed on anything that had taste. I even tried bark. Chewing hides after the meat was gone took away my stomachache. All the good things were taken away quick in the first few days in the mountains, and the way most of us lived was like animals, and like not very clean animals neither. Weak was the thing I couldn't get used to, and after the fear of starving crept into camp it was always there, and I guess I just don't care any more about mama or Simon or little Catherine. Landrum always was lazy, but now he has reason to be lazy, and mama left off asking him to do anything, because, what was there to do? And besides, the smoke and the dark keeps mama from seeing what little she can still see.

No body here in the cabin tries anymore to keep the toilet place outside. Its too weakening and besides it got so that after one or two did it be side their bed so did everybody else, and then the smell stayed and no body cared anymore because that was not as strong as the stomach pain we got if we didn't chew on some toasted hide or down some of the gluey boiled hide.

I didn't know I could walk so far, and neither did mama. The snow has slacked off for two days now, maybe four or five. I can't tell for sure cause not going out much and trying to keep warm you don't know where the time goes or even if it is going. But his morning came a stamping of the mules and a lot of talking outside, and they're going to try for the pass, and mama and me are going too, but Simon and William are staying because they aren't strong enough yet and they want to wait for the horses.

Pan The Low Waters

With the Donners in a camp somewhere behind, Stanton is kind of a leader because hese been across the rocks. But he don't tell what to do, only lead out. Mama and me stayed back a way because we was so weak, but also because then we could go it easier over the trampled snow of the others or we could see where not to go because we was so weak. Part of the time we cold walk or slide on the crust, but the mules you could see up ahead was always sinking. Sometimes they was over their heads in the drifts and fighting mad when the snow would get in their face and nose, and rearing up when they got a hard whip.

Then that night in a camp in deep snow, after a big argument, with Eddy and Stanton almost fighting, they all gave in and quit trying for the pass. And no one argued to go ahead except Eddy. And I was so tired I didn't care anyway, not even if we stayed right there and not went back, which we did after the cold night huddled on blankets on the deep snow. Only it took til way in the night of the next day to slip and slide all the way back down. The hide mush was still in the pot, but cold, It settled my stomach pain some, but I lost it once before I made it stay.

I must a slept a long time. My stomach pains woke me. Bill was telling mama that Eddy and some of the others was going to try again. They readied and waited too long. Even while we was still getting some of our strength back from the try, it came on to snow. You couldn't hear it fall, but you could hear the change outside from quiet to dead quiet. That's when the snow is beginning. Then it came on to rain. In the morning the big hump of rock that was our back wall was running water, and all was slush in and outside.

More days and nights, and the storm settled in cold and snow deepened for days and days until you had to climb near straight up to get out. No body talked, no body even thought. Somehow it seemed wrong to move. The snow pressed us into huts but worse still, it kept us from doing the things we had always done – jumping, running, even walking. It shut out light, room space, seeing others, pressed us into sadness, kept us from seeing things to help others; made pain, and made us think only of ourselves; it took away any chance to help anyone because selfishness was always there and because what mama or little George or Cathy or Naomi needed just wasn't there but over the pass in the sun. And they lazed in their own muss and the days and nights melted into awful rotten smells and darkness and cold and no sounds

Nothing changed much after the snowshoers left – Lemuel with them – except that William, my older brother couldn't keep up with them and came back that night and cried a long time and then slept. I knew from last try I couldn't keep up, so I didn't try.

Then it began the dreariest blank time of my whole life. Days and even weeks grinded past, and I was like a little animal, with mama, William, Simon, George, Naomi, and little baby Catherine laying squeezed up on the damp floor around a little smokey fire that didn't do no one much good, but seemed to help drive the awful stink away or mix it with smoke which wasn't so sickening. I didn't envy the ones that left on snowshoes. I had tried to get out too, and knew how strong the snow was, how it clinged to you and gave under you and stole off with your warm, and wore you down with lightness that turned to water in the day and ice in the night. If Will got through on his shoes he would come back, he was sure he would. And until then, just lay here on a old cow hide, and cut off little pieces and toast them over the fire. (We wouldn't toast them too much because then the little fat that was in would drip away and that was the tasty part). The pieces gave me no strength, but my stomach ached so if it didn't have something on it. With Landrum and Eddy and Will and Sarah gone, William and Simon and me somehow kept the little fire going, and mama seemed to keep getting blinder and blinder. And after the bear meat was gone - which Eddy kilt with a lucky shot – she couldn't stomach the glue in the pot.

Pan The Low Waters

It came on more astorming and everybody weakened more every day. There was the same simpering and whining from the babies, the same awful smells and mama asking weak like what it was like outside. There was the same weak ache in my knees when I tried to move, and when I looked at mama or Simon or Landrum I wondered if my face looked like a skull and if my teeth stuck out of my mouth like theirs did – like the teeth had kept on growing while their face shrunk away from them.

I'm ashamed of my feelings when I'm awake. Something in me felt good when the teamsters said how bad it was at Donners; something in me didn't hurt so bad when I saw I could hold down the hides and they couldn't. Even I think I felt a little superior when Landrum took to calling out at night and saying nothing and just lying in his muss like little Naomi and Catherine whose mother was somewhere out there with the snowshoers and not here to scrape off their legs.

Even I think I felt no sadness when they told us about the Reeds' try to get out and Virginia's frost-bit feet: I still had mine. What shamed me most was how I felt when Landrum didn't move one morning after raving most of the night. I lay there and had to climb over him to get my glue, and touching him was like him a log instead of live. I felt the difference between him and me and almost my body boasted it was alive. And afterward I climbed back over him and turned my back, and still was proud or glad that I still <u>was</u> – though he was not no more.

William and Simon was too weak and sick to help and I pulled and shoved Landrum up the snow slant and got him covered decently in snow. Mama couldn't see no more and didn't know.

The time goes by by aches or smells or deaths. Its so long since Bill and Harriet and the snowshoers went. I guess the snow on top is what keeps this hole from cold. I don't know if I sleep or if it is night. Here its only one time and place – winter in a hole. William and Simon is both sicker'n me. They can't keep the hide mush from coming up. Mostly it stays down for me. If it don't I hurt. I never leave bed no more. Too tiring. But Breen came in. Didn't stay. I could tell he couldn't stand the smell in here. He says little Margaret Eddy died and Spitzer died. Then the next day he brought Jimmy for mama to warm. His mother died last night and they have too many children to feed in the shanty. But baby Catherine is too weak to even cry and I wish Harriet was here with her.

I must have slept when Milt Elliot died. Virginia and her mother tied a rope to him and dragged it up the snow bank. No one thinks dyin is bad no more cause you can't think its bad or scary when you can't remember no more the nice things about him cause the "now" around us is such a stink and a hungry and afraid and because you're so weak you can't think or care no more. Breen said Virginia and John Denton was sick too. I can't hardly remember or care. The Reeds was always so uppity because they had more than we had. Now they haven't anything – just like us.

I had not been out of the cabin for weeks when they came to us, hallooing and calling together to make us hear. Me and Simon thought it was maybe Pat Breen shot a bear or a deer there was so much noise up to his house. If it was a deer I wanted to get some to flavor the glue, and so I climbed out to daylight which was away at the top of the slanted snow that was higher than the roof. My back and legs ached and William walked like an old man, and called back, "Mary, it's strangers, it's no deer!"

I guess I thought food too much, and when William said "no deer", I felt only dissapointment at not having some meat flavoring and it took me a long time to find out there was some from California to help us. The others from Breen's came tagging behind as they came close. One held a leather bag and gave us a handful of flour from it. Another cut pieces of jerky to give, and wouldn't let nobody have only a little. I nearly choked on my flour, but sucked my jerky for a long while

Pan The Low Waters

because my teeth ached. The man took some of the babies and mama. They was too weak to come out. I stayed, now I was outside, but soon it got cold cause it was getting dark, and all the noise and cryin stopped pretty soon, and three of the California men stayed and curled up tired by our fire which they made big to drive out the stink. I remember they slept on their packs and I couldn't get at the jerky I knew was in em.

Four nights they was with us and we got more flour and jerky. I felt some better now, and I could think straight, and gittin out of the cabin didn't seem too hard now, and then some come back from Donner's camp and the leader – Rodes, they said his name was – told who would go out with them to California in the morning.

The hardest part was when Rodes said I would have to wait til next time cause I was too weak and hurt their chances. That was the hardest part of all, and I couldn't hardly stand to watch when they left. And I went back and lay down in the damp and the smell and I heard their voices and the slush of their feet getting softer and softer. And then there was waitin again.

The waitin for the rest of us to be took out was just more of sleepin and misery and storms. And sometimes thinkin maybe it could be worse, though I didn't think how. And I remember thinkin too, of how, long ago Will had said the man told him how nice the climate in California was!

The little flour and jerky left lasted a few days. After that the hunger was so big I ate some of Eddys baby that had been cut up and boiled. And while I ate I tried not to think of it. And most of it stayed down. That's all I can remember about those days until the hallooing came again and we had flour and jerky again.

This time they was more men. They was several of them. And they seemed kinder and cleaned up the cabin, though I could hardly stand the smell. And they dug holes and buried the remains of some. Then I followed slow and weak, and I can't remember if mama and Catherine and Naomi was with us or not.

The weather, come to notice it, was warm and thawy, like as if the rescuers brought it with em. And all the six from Donners loaded into our cabin, and Breens' and William and me got ready and hoped for no storm. Mama and some of the weaker ones – I was weak but tried to not show it – they had to stay. In the morning Rodes put Naomi in a blanket and slung her over his shoulder. I don't think he even felt he carried her, she was so thin. And mama knew now there would be other men rescuing, and winter couldn't last always, and she knew she would only hold em back, and Keseberg would be with her, and she had Simon to do for her, and there was no one to carry out little Naomi and Catherine. And there was Simon to get wood, and she had Eddy's James to take care of too.

Funny how the rescuers never said nothing about the snowshoers. They had went out so long ago most had almost forgot about them.

On the way out I know I was out of my head sometimes. I was crazy at the cabin, too. Later, William said I made funny chirping noises in my blanket on the trail. At the cabin my stomach ached, but I could glue it a little and then go to sleep. But now, with it so hard to keep up with the big man ahead, my stomach needed so much more, but it got less and less, and ached all the time. I couldn't go to the pot for glue and my stomach ached harder. I stold and et part of a snowshoe on the first night out. Part of the strings I kept in my pocket and chewed going along. I could stand the cold and the foot pain, but I could hardly stand the cut of the stomach pains, and the strings helped.

Poor William got his feet so bad frost-bitten they swelled and he couldn't hardly walk. And the worst was when we staggered into Bear Valley. I remember I had trouble understanding why they was so stingy when they had all them packs of meat, and I found out when

William Hook from Donner's went crazy over eatin. He snucked out to the food tree at night and ate a lot and got sick and was retched with tobacco juice. But that same night he stole more food and died of it in the morning. Just like you mustn't take too little, and you mustn't take too much. I couldn't understand this for a long time, but I could always remember how he looked – all swelled up and thin, and deader than those we left at the lake that had only glue.

My brother's feet – William's – was frost-bitten and he got to Mule Springs after us in a couple of days. I remember I looked at the horses and mules grazin and thought they should be tryin to get through to the lakers and mama.

This was the end of the stomach cramps and the awful tiredness and the cold wet. From then on when they put me on a mare – just like mine in Kentucky, I began to feel like before we started west. When I was hungry I could find crusts or pieces of jerky in my pocket. And not to have starvin pains was like heaven, and where everything had been sickness and hurt and cold, the sun came out and dried us. And William's feet hurt and he moaned, but there was no more of the dread and fear that being so weak we couldn't find food, and with no food, die.

The change from snow and hunger and pain to a full belly and feel of a even sway of my mare was like coming out of bad dreams. All around us was ground, and the sun shining through made a fine mist. And ridin through it made the rest of the ride seem soft and not real. There was no more pushing to get one foot in front of the other, or beatin your hands to get the numbness out, or thinking, "I've got to get up", after fallin. I didn't have a saddle, but that was good, and I laid my head on her neck and felt her big slow muscles carry me easy.

After one long sunny day on my horse, with my clothes dryin fine and me nibblin at bread crusts and jerky, come a sight I thought the most beautiful ever: a big wide valley and grass everywhere. The horses would stop to eat, but one of the men came back and used a switch to get them moving.

Only once I looked back and saw again the cold white line of high peaks I hope never to see again. Something blocked all my thoughts of mama and Simon and the babies still there. Whenever I would think of them, a shuddering-like something would come up and blow away all my tries to remember, and pretty soon it was easy not to think back on the misery and the smell and cramps and poor mama, and I thought only on the fine feeling of the sweating mare moving under me.

Late that afternoon we came up along a river through level fields with hundreds of cattle grazing (and geese in some swamps) to a ranch called "Johnsons".

Chapter 28
On the Trail

The decision of how to crawl west, and with whom, was solved for us in early April. Since neither of us – not being farmers – knew how to handle, let alone judge quality and endurance of oxen – we had decided to use mule teams to pull our wagon. We had even bought our beasts plus a spare team to trot behind, when we chanced to hear of a band of seven trappers who would be leaving on mule-back late in May.

Such a tardy start, if we might accompany them, would enable Charles to avoid a hasty perhaps unprofitable sale of his lots, and allow me to continue making, for another three weeks, a type of cask now coming into demand by the emigrants.

So there was a change in plans, an accommodation which helped us both. Labadie was agreeable, since he still felt we had not taken advantage of him in the sale. Also, upon mention of our change in plans, he spent some time explaining and demonstrating mule-pack cinching and criticizing our awkward efforts at the tight and double cinch. It is probable that had he not helped us with this and in the selection of sturdy, docile mules, our acceptance into the train of trappers might not have gone so smoothly.

The few weeks passed, and Labadie taught us well the art of mule coercion and of secure, non-slip packing; Charles and I were accepted – for a considerable fee – into the company of Metis trappers bound for California; we tied up the loose ends of our small sack of years in Missouri, and waited only for the starting word.

On a certain Tuesday evening all was in readiness for an early departure. Gendron, our leader, also had coached us in the art of packing, had checked our animals, anticipated needs. I was cleaning my gun, mumbling to the dog, and had a generally vacuous condition of mind when Charles entered with news.

"They want both of us at Mssr. Robidoux', Claude. The old man had some kind of farewell party for us, one with plenty of drinks, I think. Maybe he's so glad to have me out of competition he can't control his feelings of relief. I saw one of his men with half a beef out back, so don't bother with dinner."

I dressed hurriedly and we left soon afterward. Out on the trail there would be plenty of time for the mind to clear: There would be many a toast to our good fortune in California.

Toasts there were, and a plentiful disregard for how we would feel in the morning. The roast beef, fresh from a huge spit turned by sweating Indian helpers, washed easily with the burgundy and Bordeaux. Other foods, too, made the evening – and early morning – a gourmet's delight: gooseberry pies, candies, delicacies. It was an evening in which we followed the whims of the host. Clock was forgotten , and late, after much eating and drinking and songs sung without caution, there came a general backing and edging toward the door and away from friends we would never see again. Robidoux himself had drunk heavily, and, seeking gauchely for a last friendly gesture, insisted I take with

Pan The Low Waters

me a small sack of shelled almonds. At the time I thought the gesture somewhat superfluous, and both nuts and the words used to press them upon me were forgotten in the general stumble toward beds we would use for the last time in St. Joseph.

I believe we were one of the last parties to leave either of the three jumping-off places: Westport, Independence, and St. Jo. But we moved fast – at least we moved fast in comparison with others. We were a lean, small team of a nationality, and got on well together. We rode most often at a half-trot or a brisk walk, and before we were out along the Platte, we had passed several wagon trains that had cut in on the same trail. Their pace struck me as monotonous, dull, almost faltering. Not only was their's pedestrian and jolting, but oxen and wagons would lengthen their trip. In saddles we were kings with subjects under us to do the work. We enjoyed the scenery and had little responsibility.

But I had cause to envy the traveling style of the wagoneers when we caught the broadside of a bluff summer storm. Only the rubber ponchos, highly recommended by the Metis before we left, kept us from a complete sousing. As it was, when it rained, only our legs were soaked.

One evening, early in our travels, as we camped not far from one train of approximately twenty wagons, we had a chance to observe some of the contrasts between our mode of travel and that by way of wagon and oxen. Over pipes and coffee, after packs were slipped and hobbles adjusted, we watched the contrasting minutia of detail performed by wagoneers. The vehicles were regimented into an enclosure – like formation, tongue-to-rear. Oxen teams were unhitched and driven to water, chips hunted, fires built, food cooked, guards stationed. There was, I observed, no great difference between the ox-team way and ours, except in the matter of speed. Here we were, our beasts nibbling or resting, we smoking and chatting, while our neighbors mended gear, held meetings, jockeyed for place in line, and often rode miles to cut grass.

By contrast our routine was simple, and there were no wheels or gear to repair. Often we would camp near the river and away from the others. Here grass was untrampled and abundant. Hobbles were adjusted, packs arranged in a small circle, in the middle of which we would build a single fire – a job made easy by the many arms that shared in wood or chip gathering. A single person, chosen for the week's duty would cook a stew or roast fresh game. This chore, and that of night guard, were our only assigned train duties. We were of a temperament, spoke a common tongue, were all men, shared a common goal, and were well organized, energetic, and ran well together. Throughout the whole trek there was a minimum of friction – an element we appreciated the more as we had occasion to exchange experiences with members of wagon parties.

Early on the trail I had cause the venerate the judgement of our leader: at one time I had been annoyed at having to ride herd on the several spare mules. They seemed only intractable surplus, straying, sometimes, great distances from camp and becoming more wayward and wilder as we progressed. One morning my usually docile animal shied from his pack tree. I was knocked sprawling, and as I tied him to a willow, determined to give him a few good whacks, I saw the cause of his stubbornness: two bloody friction burns where his pack had ridden and pressed. I put away my switch and anger, and, after greasing the sores, caught and packed one of the spares.

Unlike most of the travelers of '45 whose lot was to plod monotonously week after week, we had, built into our mode of travel, an almost omniscient ability to inspect the conditions of others. What we missed by casual observations we often learned by visiting campfires. Often from a distance we shared their dances and songs.

One evening, as we set up camp across a small ravine from the circled wagons of a large train, we observed a gathering around a small wagon. Thinking this to be the beginning of some entertainment or news of the trail I went closer. There were no speaker, no planned entertainment, only two, who seemed to be the cynosure of all eyes. They were a buxom, carefully dressed young woman and a young drover. They stood, holding hands, in the center of a gay, almost hilarious crowd. I was puzzled, for though I caught some of the conversation and a few shouted sentence fragments, neither made sense for me.

One shouted, "She's got one now"; another, "Looks like she'd need two or more of 'em"; another, this time close by, confided in a friend, "I don't think the German boy has what it takes to satisfy her."

And while the girl stood in the center of the crowd and pointed, the young man repeatedly shook his head in response to questions and gestures I could neither hear nor interpret.

After a short period of this odd, rough jollity and an evident protestation by the young man, the crown milled and dispersed, going about their delayed unhitching and fire-building. Burning with curiosity, I returned to camp. There my inquisitiveness was satisfied: one of the Metis, also, had been attracted to the gathering and had gathered a full story from one of the drovers.

The young woman was a servant named Lucinda. Starting on the trek with one family, she had left them and had ridden and walked with so many different parties that she was actually not attached to any. The reason for her lack of a home wagon was due to a quality about her that all the other women objected to : she was a nymphet, and her behavior was apparently intolerable. Other women wished not to associate with her, since all knew she could be had without marriage. The Metis had gathered that her precocious sexuality was so abnormal as to be actually feared. She was the butt of many male jokes, but what she needed was a home wagon and a husband. What I had witnessed, during the hilarity, was one of her many attempts to get a steady bed partner. I reflected on how strange it was that people will encourage and make farcical a proposition that could only end in unhappiness for both parties and cause actual physical harm. The story was told by the Metis to the others in the camp and the reaction was the same as mine. Such behavior in a female was so rare as to border on the unbelievable. The contrast in reaction between young French and Americans to the phenomenon occupied my thoughts for many days on the trail.

Of all the months since leaving ship in New Orleans, certainly the time on the trail to Fort Bridger was the most idyllic. After the first few days, when legs and body were adjusting to saddle confinement, routine became carefree and effortless and the trip an enhancement. To ride with strong, experienced men who know the trail, how to get over it rapidly and effortlessly, and how to turn boredom into adventure or humor, is not only pleasure, but privilege.

I assumed early the duty of cook. A usual breakfast was slapjacks, cold from the night before, a slab of jerked beef, which we all carried in quantity, and coffee, cracked and boiled each morning. I had cooked for so long the duty was no imposition. Further, it had the pleasant effect of ingratiating me to my countrymen. They never ceased to show a bluff, reticent gratitude for this service. And even if they had known that between us, Charles and I carried several thousand dollars in gold coin, I believe it would have remained safe. The frontier, and especially the far frontier for which we were bound, was a place whose isolation demanded an exchange of personal values – bravery and daring – not bank accounts; skills in place of table manners; endurance in place of ego; adaptability in place of individuality. Belief in self was the religion of the trail.

So our days were interesting and varied, and after Fort Laramie we were never far from another party. Over these we could always feel a benevolent superiority: ours was the better led, the faster moving, the one lest prone to accident. Sometimes we led rather than rode

Pan The Low Waters

our mules – perhaps more out of consideration for out back-sides and joints than out of concern for the sweating beasts.

Route was plainly marked by hundreds of wagons during May and June. The dust, so easily avoided; the patches of grass so available a mile or so off the beaten path. Ours was a segmented ship, cutting its own path over, around, and through quagmires and obstacles often unavoidable for the laden, wallowing wagons, Though little of the trip was easy – its difficulties becoming daily more noticed by the stiff, aching joints and muscles – it seemed easier because of the distractions afforded by our high perches and our speed. We were not he only ones mounted. But among generally pedestrian and ox-pulled families we counted ourselves singularly lucky and carefree. Jules, the youngest Metis trapper, normally withdrawn, often heightened the carefree illusion with little swinging French folk songs. Time passed quickly, and our aches were hardly recorded.

And I sometimes wonder if Jules' rhythmic, sometimes bawdy tunefulness didn't account for much of the resentfulness shown both on the trail, and later on in California, towards the French. Did it not confirm, in the minds of those who were dedicated to the belief that all should suffer, the belief that we, on light, swaying saddles, and chorusing incomprehensible songs weren't guilty of some vague impropriety; did we not have access to some secret sins, which they, in their shrouded, slow-moving houses could not share?

Like several of the trains far ahead when we left St. Jo, we threaded the Webber and approached the Great Salt Lake. We had by now acquired a feeling of invincibleness, and had taken the cut-off of a man called Hastings. Cut-offs implied salvage of distance and time, and of all the smaller cut-offs we had taken, none, so far, had resulted in anything but benefit. But then, coming, one torrid noon, upon a wagon party deep in the Webber Canyon, we were given pause.

With apparent toil and bloodied hands, a new road was being hewn through thick brush and trees. We were inspected cautiously, though silently. There was little that would have been appropriate to say to these, for it was obvious that they had blundered into a morass of rocky, thickly forested defiles that had to be cut into, then out of.

Our impression was that the train had no leader, that they knew they were on a poor cut-off, but that going back would be worse than plowing ahead. Then two other impressions stuck with me as we sidled by: one was of the high proportion of children. They idled in the shade of the wagons and trees, inspecting us as we passed, or picked the thick, luscious service berries from the green wall that enclosed them. A small, singularly beautiful girl stared at us and clutched in her dirty bruised arms a tiny, hand-fashioned doll.

The road not far ahead – if it could be called a road – along the Beauchemin was rough and dangerous and wound through boulders in a dry creek bed. So, for several miles before reaching the valley of the Salt Lake we clung to the steeper, more thickly forested ridges above. Many times since that day I have wondered how the party fared in extricating themselves from those barriers.

I recall being impressed by the almost incongruous size of one of the wagons and the four yoke that pulled it. It stood out from the others, a bulky, awkward structure, somehow suggestive of both disregard for dwindling time and a smug, haughty tribute to past comforts. Both its size and finish suggested an opulence so foreign to the primitive surroundings as to be the subject of camp conversation far into the night, when, late that afternoon, we hobbled our animals in sight of the great lake. Charles, in pulling past, had caught glimpse of the wagon's interior. It was, he said, even more presumptuous than its exterior – with sheet-iron stove and stovepipe, beds and spring seats.

That morning our descent from the tangled mountains and rocky gorges was deliberate. The mules were given their heads to find the most acceptable paths. We threaded first brambles and thick brushes, then enormous, slick stream boulders where oxen would have broken their legs. There was no singing now. In the recent past we had felt our ride to be comparable to a summer outing on horseback. Now we reflected on the gloom and misfortune mirrored in the eyes of the men we had just left. We, too, had taken the cut-off. But our leader, who had been guided by massive markers like Pilot Peak, had aimed us like an arrow for the distant ridges where grass and easier going lay.

It was now the last week of a torrid August. For the first time, as we sat about the fire that night, Gendron expressed concern that there might be some snow before reaching California and the Fort. The time we had spent early in the trip, hunting and lounging at Bridger's post, had taken up much of the time advantage gained by our mode of travel. That night the reins of my thoughts stiffened: Could the Webber Canyon ox teams get through if, as Gendron said, we ourselves might be late? Then the reins of my mind slackened and I slept.

How I reached what I came later to realize as a kind of "Promised Land", is a tale better told in a hundred journals kept on the overland journey. One sad incident, however, seems worthy of the telling. All else was blended into a monotony of a hundred twenty days of saddling, trekking, unpacking; a period during which the landmarks ahead changed but imperceptibility.

It happened one parched noon in early September as we approached a spot of livid green that clung to a distant hillside like man-painted fungus. The light had beaten down mercilessly for hours and it had become easier to lead our mounts than to flail movement from them. Oddly, as we approached the green , our mules showed no anxiety to bolt for water, although we knew, from past experience, that it could be smelled.

From a rise before a narrow rocky gulch we caught sight of several pools of steaming water. Gendron had earlier spoken of these. They would be the surfacings of superheated water at a place called Geyser Springs. Its waters could be drunk only after being dipped and cooled. We would camp here, for below the pools grew a stringy, dwarfed kind of grass.

As we led our animals to the grass I was unprepared for the sudden bolting of my dog toward the largest pool, and called sharply to him as he raced to leap into an apparently limpid pool – a thing he had done so often along the Platte. One pitiful bleat, not unlike that of an ewe, rose from his throat. He thrashed once or twice before the furnace-hot water blinded, then seared life from his body. He was movement; then but a hairy thing, floating on the surface. It was over in a moment. His unnaturally puffy body twitched spasmodically, brown hair swirling, as steam rose above it. I tied rope to a stone, and carefully, lest I, too, slip into the scald, edge him to land. Tears clouded my eyes, and I asked Gendron to end his misery with a bullet.

Nor was death of my dog to be the last of the sadness on that long bone-jolting trail. Though on mules we were able to cut the angle off many a tedious square, slide through small swales too narrow, steep, or rocky for wagons, we did not escape to the moist greenness beyond that last barrier without paying a price just short of death.

Our ultimate trial commenced not long after reaching the Humboldt. Here we left its thin brackish trickle and unclean green sumps and faced, with cracked lips and seared eyes, the bright, light dust of the sink. Here all thrill of adventure ended, and time became only a persistent soft tug of sand in an eternity of desert. Had it not been for the occasional whinny of a mule there could have been no reality, no consciousness other than an intense craving for water and shade. These things we knew to be far ahead in mountains that tantalizingly receded even as we approached.

At bivouac that night, our leader offered little to palliate a growing hopelessness. When questioned about the next water he would only point mutely ahead, muttering words to the effect that their last crossing had been farther to the south, or that the weather had then been more cooperative. Whatever the reply, it provided slight comfort to eight men and twenty mules, and did little to slake cracked and burning lips and stinging eyes. And it was a miserably spent party that slogged, one noon, over a rise at the base of jagged, volcanic ridge and sucked warm, mule-muddied water from trembling hands.

By dusk, and by general agreement, we continued toward the darkening hills. Coffee, steeped in the cooled waters had revived us somewhat, but I swayed unnaturally in the saddle of my spare mule when shouts went up from several men ahead. With difficulty I pulled the animal's head form a small tuft of grass, urged him toward the shouting, and, sliding from the saddle, glutted myself in steel-cool river water.

Chapter 29
Savages

The ghost-gray morning was cool. The desert was behind, and the same grass and water that revived every train that summer now worked its miracle on us. The spot was the Truckee Meadows – a fine, broad steam of lively cool water bordered for miles on both sides by tall grasses and clover. Here there was no need to hobble the animals. Their trial in the desert and the surrounding green abundance would keep them close, And it was time to bring the body – wounded by a million sways and jolts – back into semblance of the order it had when trail was new. There was no talk of an immediate move ahead even though by the next day we felt revived. It was consideration for the beasts that caused us to delay our starting on what would be the last leg of the journey. And it was here, while lying and mending in the cool meadow grasses that we summed up all the experiences, fallacies and misjudgments of the trail.

So far – for we felt that our trials were nearing an end – there had been no annoyance from savages, although on the trail we had seen dead oxen with protruding arrows. Though we had seen their sign after leaving Shawnee country and near the Platte, none had even approached for barter or bother. Jules, one of the younger of the Trappers, had confided that their preference for horse meat might mean trouble.

Heavy wagons, all agreed, were an abomination for so long and unpredictable a trek. The heavier loaded wagons we had seen were the height of impracticality and waste, and the loads of sentimental furniture and stoves and other comforts were the slackest of poor judgement. Much heavy furniture – tables and excess staple foods had lined the trail near Fort Bridger: a loss, yes, but a sign that often judgement overrode foolish sentiment. But what struck us all early was that it was the oxen who pulled these foolish burdens – burdens which were discarded only when the lean animals could hardly stand. Through sentiment and pure bad judgment, and maybe a little stupidity, the oxen were yoked to burdens whose use and purpose became only a thing to wear down the animals. It seemed an inexcusable, even criminal practice, a ghastly act which ended in the exhaustion and death of the animal, and eventual loss of all goods hauled. It was as though oxen, on whom all depended, were assigned the task of hauling heavily laden wagons until they expired. Then the weights which they pulled were discarded. It was a kind of insanity to which I could never become reconciled.

But our trials were now nearly over. The promised valley was just ahead, over the high mountains. Jules had promised there was but another week of travel, that now water and game would become plentiful.

We caught our animals at dawn-light of the fourth day at the meadows, packed with ropes now coated with hoar-frost, and swung into the saddle. How good the feeling to be moving again, knowing the big tests of the trail had been passed! Never since have I felt so poignantly the exhilaration of life. I was renewed; I was without fear; I was revived and atop a sturdy animal; and now we climbed to a country of towering mountains and evergreens that spilled a cool shady fragrance.

Arnold F. Rothmeier

The mood of the country matched our mood of expectancy and its promise of fulfillment. Bear, deer, and squirrels were plentiful and the fact of their population added to my feelings that this was indeed a rare corner of the world and would never disappoint.

Toward end of the second day of our climb we skirted the north shore of Truckee Lake and came upon a large train at the base of a wall of immense granite boulders. Here we dismounted and camped, for the way up and across was blocked by numerous teams and wagons, Jules and several others went forward on foot; Charles and I, and three others prepared camp, hobbled and cooked, That the pass up forward was a difficult one was apparent and inadvisable to try during the remaining daylight hours. Even from our distance of nearly half a mile we could see that the train ahead had paused.

Jules and the others did not return until long after sunset; then we were astonished to see them approach from the opposite direction. By the time they had hobbled their animals and spread robes about the fire, each had imparted to us the things seen up forward. They had scouted out and found another, more gradual branch of the trail that led southwest around the lake, and all had announced that those leading ahead were dam fools. Instead of casting about, as Jules and Pierre had done, for an alternate route, the wagon trains ahead had seen only the high, frosty barrier, had repaired and used an old winch made by an earlier party, and were slowly lifting dismantled wagons and gear up the bulging rocky face.

Jules said little about the *yanqui* ingenuity. It was an admirable quality, and he was man enough to acknowledge it. At any rate we slept the sleep of the self-righteous, pulled camp next morning in a shivering pre-dawn cold, and retraced our steps to the route up a canyon east of the lake.

By the time sun was lighting the tall ponderosa tops we had returned to beyond the eastern end of the lake and were threading a comfortable, gradually rising canyon trail that carried us easily beyond the same high meadow sought by the winchers. More than once before, Charles and I had felt the glow of pride that comes from association with a superior team. Only the once – when crossing the hated desert – had my faith in Gendron faltered, and then, only for a day.

Two more days of rough packing brought us to a wide, grassy swale which Gendron had noted on his last trapping trip. We were now, he said, but a few score of miles from the great valley, our destination. Game was still abundant, and with the goal so close, we rested here at Grassy Valley – for we had so named the spot – for two days. The main emigrant trail ran along Bear River, far to the south. Gendron had departed from it because he was more familiar with the present route.

Upon leaving Grassy Valley late one morning for the last leg of our journey we came with increasing frequency upon Indian signs. Gendron was disturbed and told us why: At last passage his party had traded with them, and though his party had not visited their village – out of deference to the latter's filth and lice – the savages had been civil and friendly. Now, however, though a flitting figure was occasionally seen, none approached to trade. If there had been friction, if other parties of whites had changed that climate through mistreatment or unfairness, there might be trouble.

By nightfall we had slipped comfortably another twenty miles between a series of rolling, pine-covered hills – mere echoes of the massive intrusions behind us. Here, at our last camp in the mountains, on Wolf Creek, we celebrated by consuming what remained of our small stock of brandy, and lightening our packs of all unnecessary weight, including the pack trees of some animals. Then we fell asleep, confident of a short, comfortable trip to the valley.

Had the remaining stock of brandy allowed more than a taste for each, our response to the stompings, tortured bawls and wheezes of the hobbled animals might have afforded the Indians time to destroy them all. My head was none too clear as I grasped my hand gun and rolled further into the deer brush. Several of the men had fired to create commotion and to frighten away whatever was terrifying the animals. The sky to the east still supplied but little light, for it was then only changing to gray, and gun-streaks were slanted upward only to frighten. Further brushing noises from the trees and thickets. A single human voice, more animal than human, then a feeling that the intruders were withdrawing. Then a silence wounded only by an occasional threshing sound and a clotted wheezing.

All this could have taken two minutes – or half an hour. When there was no further sound in the direction our ears pointed, I saw the figures of Gendron and Jules crawl past in the growing half-light of the morning. Another minute and the need for caution passed, as they rose and ran toward sound of the tortured bawls.

Charles and I approached behind them. The scene was livid with curses and filled with the pathetic sight of several of our mules protuberant with arrowshafts. Hobbled tightly as they were, they could do little but stand in their own blood and strain toward the feathered shafts buried a few killing inches beneath their hides. Some of the mules thrashed in the brush in private agony; two lay still; four or five – including mine – had hafts in neck, belly, or ribs.

Gendron was beside himself as he told Jules which of the writhing, bloodied animals to shoot. There was no recourse. Those which he deemed to have a chance, we set upon with knife, carefully cutting and gouging, trying to avoid threshing hooves, while blood coursed our arms and clothing. I was deep in a wither of my best pack animal when Jules came up and put a ball into the head of the creature that had carried me nearly fifteen hundred miles.

A slow sun filtered a cool autumnal glow through the trees as we worked our butchery, and I received a vicious reflexive kick from one of the mules as I probed. I found the arrowhead, but the animal died from loss of blood without regaining his feet.

With nearly half our remuda dead or disabled, it now became necessary to walk and to lead the rest. And it was a tired French crew that stumbled out of the foothills that afternoon. Traveling south on their warm fringe, we arrived at the Bear River, along which most trains emerged from the Sierra. In the distance eight or ten dirty white-topped wagons clustered in the shelter of a grove of oaks that spread their limbs so wide they dwarfed the two adobe buildings beneath.

Chapter 30
Sicard

Our approach to this, our goal, turned jaunty and light-hearted despite our recent loss, and along the river we sang again "Le Petite Voillu" and "C'est un Pan de Feu" as we watched flocks of geese rise, circle, and settle again. Deer, singly, and once in a herd of a dozen, stalked off stiff-legged or leaped in proud annoyance. We trod a wide, loamy overflow plain beside a clear pebble-bottomed river. Grasses, heavy with seed, hid a soil that reeked with inviting fertility.

There was a soft, bittersweet drama about our entrance into the valley of California. We had arrived at Johnson's Ranch, and though fatigued, it was impossible to blunt the magic of the moment. Presently the memory of the journey was behind me; the hell of the desert, the thousand trials and annoyances enroute faded. Promise of a new existence same into focus in a broad valley of idyllic beauty between two mountain ranges – one behind, the other far ahead to the west. In the shade of a grove of fine, fat-bellied oak grazed several hundred head of cattle and horses. Deer intermixed and grazed with the cattle, seeming to enjoy the role of herd guardian.

Pan The Low Waters

We had entered the point known already for several years as Johnson's Crossing, but because of our approach from the north through the Grassy Valley, we had no crossing to make. The first habitation was that of a man named Richie. Gruff and bluff, he seemed almost annoyed at our appearance and offered no hospitality. Gendron said little that would encourage reply, and we spurred on toward another grove where it was apparent another brand of hospitality might be practiced, for tents were scattered throughout the trees, making a sizeable community.

This was the rancho of a Mr. William Johnson. Beneath the trees camped a dozen wagons, some still wet from their recent crossing of the Bear, which here flowed a comfortable two or three feet now, late in the season. We dismounted and hobbled, and at the invitation of the rancher, Johnson, accepted meat from the hanging carcass of a newly-slaughtered steer. Night was coming on, and as he had others about his campfire, we ate a hasty meal of the seared, fat and bloody meat, and left more social intercourse until morning. While I ate and tossed an occasional piece of meat to the dogs, I caught fragments of campfire gossip about me: "The beef was kilt so's we wouldn't go out and kill one and waste the hide"; "No Indian trouble here – yet"; "Sutter's is a good day's trip down the valley"; "At Sutter's a body can get almost any kind of work"; "Lots of good ground here, but mostly along the river"; "Some Frenchies up and across the Bear, it's called Sigur's Ranch".

I slept particularly well that first night in California. When awakened at dawn by the raucous braying of a mule, my first thougth was of the corruption of the name "Sicard". The name, I suppose, fascinated me because of its similarity to the French word "sicare", which means "hired assassin".

Charles was all for moving down the valley to Sutter's and investigating possibilities for trade and investment, so, after coffee and more beef rib he packed a mule and said he would leave with the others, each of whom had arranged to trade a mule for one of Johnson's half-wild horses. Our three wounded mules were turned out to pasture.

What it was, other than the name Sicard, and the news of other countrymen nearby, that led me to separate from the party here, I could not tell. And yet, had we not divided here, the split would have come later at the fort. At any rate, we had arrived and each felt the tug of his own personal goal now that the scene for those goals had been reached. That winter was approaching was apparent. Whatever that meant in regions far to the east, it could surely not mean eternally sunny conditions here. It was now almost November, and a fire felt good.

That afternoon, after separating Charles' money from mine, I said goodbye to him, to Gendron, and the others, and backtracking on my mule along the river, sought the man called Sicard.

My mind was at ease here along the Bear. New grasses had sprung up as though the soil expected another lively growing season instead of a dormant winter. I paused and scooped a handful of the dark loam. Its texture was that of moist humus, it contained little sand, and was rich with decayed matter. Back from the low banks this black soil covered hundreds of acres of overflow land on both sides of the river.

Small game and wild turkeys stirred in the sparse bushes; deer and elk nibbled the new grasses; far overhead a wide gossamer arrow of faintly honking geese wavered south. My heart expanded and I was glad to be here.

A few miles along the river, sound of wood chopping led me to a rise from which a low adobe was visible. Wedged between three of the mightiest oaks I had ever seen, lay the house, so squat it seemed a part of the grove itself. All about, swiftly moving clouds made changing patterns of sun and shade. The effect was elfin. Close by the man chopping wood struck me as one of the characters out of a German fairy tale book. His head was down, else I should have seen the gray canvas patch that covered his left eye. He was not a big man. I was five-nine, and Sicard was not that tall. But he had about him a quiet reserve of energy and a preciseness of ax-stroke that fascinated me. The murderous aim that broke each round caused a clean, reverberant twang.

Halfway down a slight decline my mule whinnied, and from a distance of perhaps fifty feet I met the incomparable Theodore Sicard. Like all of us, he grew a beard. But unlike most, he had managed to form it with knife or scissors into the shape of a *spitzbart*. The point of it and the absence of a moustache gave character to his face, elongated it, and added a joltingly sophisticated note to the wild and virgin surroundings. I sensed immediately a depth of character, and yes, behind his full, open face, a hint of guile. And his one majestic eye mirrored the same wild fear that had stuck me so forcibly in the man at New Orleans – he who had nursed me back from the cholera. I was immediately hypnotized by his voice, so level in tone, so inviting. His first words, after "C'est va", were "I need another countryman to help me make this soil bloom. It grows everything – and big. Can you stay a while?"

The cordial, unexpectedness of Sicard's invitation, the magnetism of his tones and the hypnosis produced by his physical appearance produced an effect so genuine and genial that I had no thought but to stay.

Toward dusk, and after I had staked out the mule, we sat upon logs in front of the adobe. Over hot oaken coals we suspended sticks piercing choice cuts of elk. From time to time he would toss upon these, a few green bay leaves from a bush near by. This smoke and its seasoning brought an immediate tear to the eye and seemed almost to lift the skull upon being inhaled. But if these senses avoided the trap, the taste buds were more than rewarded: no buffalo hump or tongue ever tasted more ambrosial. The sweet, succulent flesh was almost narcotic.

How easy it was to succumb to Sicard's invitation! It was not that he was lonely, for visitors, both whites and unusually friendly Indians were seen about. Nor was it that farming, until now, particularly appealed to me. True, the season was pointing a cool, moist finger toward winter, and certainly I needed shelter. I could never have told what force, what persuasion, or what allure drew me, held me at Sicard's rancho while all the Metis went on. But held me it did.

The rains came early – and supplied me with convincing reason for remaining here in the comfort and warmth of the roomy adobe. For several months there were periods of heavy rain. But on days when sun came out and clouds grew thin and were sent scudding to the east, Sicard and I would saddle mule or horse and ride along the rise paralleling the Bear or simply sit on the bank and admire the scene: the clouds, the subtle rich sycamore pastels, the flocks of fat geese, the tame and stately herds of elk and deer.

Sicard rarely boasted, but beyond his adobe rose the stubble of a fifteen acre wheat field that yielded him an average of fifty bushels per acre – farmed with Indian help. Of this he was inordinately proud. Here he also grew small, irregular patches of the vegetables he was fond of. And he would tell of the gardens he had kept for Sutter at the latter's Hock Farm. Sicard was the first and the only farmer in the valley – excepting Sutter – to harvest a field of grain. In the corner of his adobe were a collection of canvas and hide bags and barrels – all containing his recent fall harvest. Johnson, he said, and some other settlers up the valley – Gutierez, Keyser, and Smith – were much too prodigal with their land, and simply ran cattle on it.

Once I accompanied him to an Indian camp and waited while he entered what I assumed was the chief's hut. He carried in a bag of presents for the chief's daughter. I could only guess the purpose of his visit, for when he emerged much later, he no longer carried his bag; he liked his bachelorhood at the adobe too much to share it with an Indian female.

One evening, to the accompaniment of thunder and torrential rain, he told me his story:

He had jumped ship at Yerba Buena the summer of '43. Upon arriving at the valley he had worked for Sutter at Hock Farm, planting, building, and superintending the Indian workers there. He had learned their ways and befriended them. When, for payment of services, Sutter had given Sicard what he called his Nemshas Rancho, he found he could gain the services of the Nemshas tribe for making adobe bricks and for cutting and stacking an unexpectedly rich harvest of wheat. With a handful of Indians and a promise of a few bright beads brought from Sutter's farm, he had attached sharp wooden pegs to a log, and with this pulled by a mule, had scratched the surface of the fifteen acre plot. Wheat from the Fort was sown, and brush dragged over the area to whisk the seed into the scratches. The result was a bounty, which he shared so generously with his helpers that their chief had come, asking Sicard if he would like to visit his daughter.

On the few sunny days we would each shoulder a small hoe-like tool and walk the short pathway to Sicard's winter garden plot – a tiny corner of his fruitful acreage that stretched almost as far as the eye could see along the river's overflow plain. Here we would work a few pleasant hours, then share his bottle.

But the winter of '45 -'46 settled in early, and there were few days in early November when it did not rain heavily. During these shut-in days my one-eyed friend would ramble on comfortably about his South American travels, about his garden, and about the rumors he had heard concerning Spanish California.

We would conjecture, in our feeble, uninformed way what the

battles to the south meant and what it meant that Sutter's Fort was now held by American soldiers. We would putter about, scraping hides, enjoying an occasional bottle and pipe – for Sicard had early put in his stock of winter wines. Then we would stand outside, in the shelter of his enormous oaks and peer toward the white sierra peaks beyond the foothills. Sometimes we would stand and shiver as we noted the snow's low dusting upon the foothills.

It was on one of these days, as I returned form my morning squat in the bushes, that I came upon a camping area recently occupied by a family with children. I had not been over this spot, and now could not help noticing numerous discarded peach pits. I suppose I was looking for something to do, for there was no rain that morning and a dense river mist hung about, with the sun high above low, smoke-like clouds.

As I bent to retrieve one of the pits I was astonished to note that in the weeks it had lain on the ground, a network of fine root hairs had emerged, having made contact with the soil. The seeds were growing!

I hurried with a sprouted seed and its soil to the adobe, and, with Sicard as excited as I, selected a particularly rich and level bench of loam. Tenderly we transported all the partially sprouted seeds and tucked them in – more than thirty in all – in neat rows, each marked by a large stone. Watering was unnecessary for it began to rain before we had finished.

That evening, as I put on additional clothing against the night air, my hand contacted a sack of small, hard objects in the pocket. They were the almonds from Chouteau's farewell party at St. Jo, and I held them for Sicard to see.

"Now we shall have not only fine peaches", I predicted, "but almonds, too. Wouldn't you say we are getting quite civilized if we have both fruit and nut trees already started?" So the almonds, too, were planted to sprout, in a series of neat rows.

As the days of our weather-caused confinement increased, I learned more about my friend – how he had fought in the battle of Navarino and taken the life of an Arab soldier who had first gouged out his right eye. He told of bloody lashings he had witnessed on shipboard – his reason for skipping ship at Yerba Buena. And, as the days passed, his enthusiasm for the land infected me, and I found myself planning with him how we would plant greater acreage and greater variety; where we would dig the long, deep ditches that passed for fences to keep cattle and deer form nipping the produce. On rare good days we would saddle up, and, with a pocketful of jerky, ride south and west around the general definition of his grant, always seeing elk and deer, flocks of geese and duck resting from their flight south. If we went to the fringe of low foothill where new grass was beginning to shade the land from gray to green, we would meet the Nimshews.

Sometimes they crouched about a fire near a wattled brush hut, and sometimes we met them, bow on back, carrying a slain deer. There was always a shy but spontaneous greeting for Sicard as soon as he was recognized. Often a stretched hand was filled with flour or meat or a gee-gaw or beads. These were the hands that willingly worked at plow time and at harvest. Literally they were the subjects of the grant owner, though I'm sure they never thought of themselves as such. They seemed happy to have beings about, different from themselves, who, in some mysterious way mastered horses, grew things, made flour, could shoot and provide their village with so much good meat at matanza time – the time of the tallow rendering.

In time, I too, was greeted like Sicard and accepted as a friend. The Nimshews were all filthy – but only by contrast. Degree was the thing. Though they appeared to us more animal than human, they were somewhat educable, understood simple instruction and commands, and worked tirelessly when fed – if they could see a job's end in sight. It was, as with a child, the tired moment of successful completion that gave them their big satisfaction: to garner, in addition to this satisfaction, food and a shiny knife, or colored beads, or a red bandana, this as the extra. For these rewards they worked hard to complete a job quickly, for to be given a task whose end could not be seen, was to begin a hopeless task. Sicard sensed this and endeared himself by providing small jobs with a point, marking out the area to be worked, or clarifying with finger signs, the number of skins to be cleaned. I learned much from Sicard by watching him in his relations with the Indians. He never went back on his word and never failed to give a little more than was expected.

On one trip – a leisurely hunt on horseback and after a particularly drenching rain – I witnessed a facet of Sicard's personality I had not noted before:

Few emigrants had females about their camps. There was little need or inclination for "bundling": there were too many thoughts about their new life and how to adjust to it – needs for food; excitement for opportunities; adjustment to a new climate; considerations with one's status in a country where even the land's ownership was unknown or in question – to allow of thoughts of women. All fell into a limbo of concerns from which thoughts of the opposite sex were simply excluded. Thoughts of a lighter, warmer side of life gained no foothold in minds continually awash by tides of unknown and necessities.

It was a short while after shooting a young, fat doe, that we rode into a small Nimshew rancheria. At Sicard's suggestion I untied the deer and let it slide to the grass. He motioned to those gathered that it was a present. Immediately it was taken by young natives to an oak, skinned, splayed, and cut up. In the group was a particularly striking girl of sixteen or eighteen. She did none of the labor, but moved among her people, and, with soft, clear syllables and a few pointing gestures, directed the operation. I was so fascinated by her quiet authority and striking grace that I failed to notice Sicard's entrance into one of the wattled huts.

Presently he emerged, followed by an older male native whose handsome bearing, clear skin, and pleasing expression bore a close resemblance of that of the maiden now distributing the deer. There followed a little scene in which the girl approached Sicard, and, to my amazement, made little, stroking movements along his body, almost as one might stroke a pet animal. It was a pleasing, domestic sight, a kind of public declaration of affection, and one which seemed to cause her a slight, timid embarrassment. Sicard seemed to enjoy her slight discomfiture. The chief simply observed his daughter's actions, grunted, and entered the hut. I saw Sicard cup her face, and then, releasing it, stride after the chief. Few seemed to notice what I had observed, so busy were most of the Indians about their venison.

Sicard did not invite me to ride with him the next clear day, which was a week later, but saddled his mule and rode out in a line straight for the rancheria, saying, vaguely, that he wished to tend to some business. He was not back that night and did not return until the next day. By the time we had eaten some stew, the rain had resumed. I sensed some secretiveness about him, and did not commit the indiscretion of invading his private thoughts.

Arnold F. Rothmeier

Chapter 31
Eddy

I had been a working guest at Sicard's now for nearly three months, when my friend, on one of his short treks to Johnson's for some little thing, became trapped on the north side of the Bear by a particularly heavy rain. I did not worry particularly about the absence of my friend, though I did sometimes think of how much closer he was to total blindness than I. After fording the Bear some distance downstream he returned to tell me a pathetic story:

Shortly after he had left his adobe the rain had come in such quantities that, since he was halfway to Johnson's, he hurried on. I believe his business was, in part, to buy or trade some sacking material. Since the rain continued he had put up on the Johnson floor. The next day was sunny but the river was high, so he had decided to wait another day or two before attempting the crossing. About dusk, as he and Johnson were having pipe and coffee, one of the Indian helpers outside banged his hands on the wall, calling, in an excited blend of Spanish and Indian, "Hombre malo, muy malo!" then pointing upriver, "Richie", and repeating this over and over.

Pan The Low Waters

Not knowing what kind of "bad man" was being meant, they had taken guns and ridden to Richie's as fast as possible. There, on a pallet, in Richie's makeshift cabin, far from encountering any threat, they found the prostrate, half-clothed form of a man who seemed more dead than alive. His body was covered with sores now partially cleansed and dressed by several who yet bent over him, weeping as they cleansed him and as they squeezed a little liquid nourishment between teeth made hideous by receding gums. Since the Richie hut was small, even for the needs of his wife and daughter, Hariet, Johnson proposed that the man – found to have the name of Eddy – be taken to his own adobe, where supplies and room were more plentiful.

In the meantime, preparations were being hastily made to ride out and bring in another half dozen like Eddy, still fifteen miles back in the hills. Sicard and four other horsemen, packing food and blankets, rode away into the new moon, guided by the same Indians who had brought Eddy in, even as Eddy, shocked and confused, attempted to rise and follow. For the first six miles the five horsemen followed on the hoof-tracks of their predecessors and dark smears of Eddy's blood on the oak-leaf carpet.

Never had I seen my friend Sicard so caught up with an experience. Between sobs and eye-wiping he told how his group came upon the party, guided partly by the stench of vomit. The earlier packers had made the immigrants as comfortable as possible with fire, food, and blankets – food that made them heave. There was an air of shock and disbelief about the blanketed figures. Their eyes – deep gouges in sunken white faces – seemed the only live part of their beings. These moved uneasily, frantically about, never staying long on any one object or person longer than a second; seeming to fill up with fear, and move on to another object. All seven were women – excepting one man, and all were in the last stages of exhaustion and starvation.

Towards late afternoon, under graying skies, it was thought best to start in. One, sometimes two of the rescued figures were placed behind each rescuer; a blanket was wrapped about each. In order to keep them, in their weakened condition, from falling off, they were tied to the horseman. Sicard described the bodies of those who he helped onto horses as feeling like loose, sharp bones in a sack of skin.

In this way the caravan of horses, bearing nine men and five women moved slowly and painfully down to Johnson's and safety. Here Sicard had talked to the first survivor, Eddy, who was now feeling much better, and who told his story with such effect that already an Indian runner had been sent with a letter to Alcalde Sinclair near Sutter's, for there were others in worse condition yet, high in the snow covered mountains, A current of feeling was set up among the people of California – even among the lowly Indians – that nearly eclipsed the current struggles between Californios and immigrants over ownership of the country. For there were not simply these few – those now rescued and safe, but many more, chiefly women and children, still high in the sierra, and unable to leave through ten and twenty foot drifts. These were eating boiled cow hides to keep alive, and sure to starve unless soon rescued.

Plight of the immigrants was the subject of our conversation for many days as we tended to some business at Sicard's ranch. These were the same poor immigrants we had passed long ago in the mountain. The heavy wagons had slowed them and early snows had blocked their way to the valley.

I was not insensible to the mounting, threatening tragedy far away in the sierra. But I had not witnessed those first survivors, the snowshoers, and had little conception of their epic struggle. I had not seen what months of fatigue and starvation could do to a man or woman. All was hear-say and second hand, and words – even words of a countryman – fall short of a feeling for the reality.

But the efforts for relief of the Donenr Party were in good, if somewhat lethargic and selfish hands. Within a few days, clothing for the near-naked women and children arrived at Johnson's and by the time Sicard and I found it necessary to visit his ranch again, all five women and two men – Eddy and Foster – had removed to Sutter's, all riding in a wagon, since their feet were still unable to support them. They left behind a legacy of horror, half-imagined, but supported by their actual condition. There were gaps in their tale – such as what happened to their two Spanish guides. All had remained silent about these, and there were none who compelled a telling of what the fate of these had been.

While at the Crossing I had a chance to observe Johnson himself at first hand. So many immigrants had come through his ranch that he paid little attention to most of them. He knew and apparently respected Sicard, for both had come contemporaneously on the scene; both had acquired large tracts of land; had mutual interests; admired the other's endeavors: Johnson's cattle; Sicard's grain fields. But Johnson paid little attention to me – another Frenchman – aside from recognizing me as an inhabitant – probably a temporary one – of Sicard's Nemshas Grant.

Chapter 32
Assistance

I found Johnson to be a man who spoke curtly – a characteristic I had observed among sailors in general. He made no secret of the fact that he had jumped ship and had hidden out for some time among inland Californios, avoiding searching parties who sought to collect reward for his return. He was not an unkind person, nor a braggart, only somewhat harsh, self-centered and perhaps previous in many of his judgements. One of the reasons many of the early-encamped wagon parties chose to move on quickly to Sutter's was an observation made by the women – who came in considerable abundance in 1845 – that Johnson kept two Indian women at his adobe, one of them being particularly well-formed and attractive.

The few times I saw him off his horse, I noted the same carriage and stride of those who followed the sea – the unconscious spread of the legs, and the short, purposeful strides – as if taken yet on deck. By French standards Johnson would have been judged neither short nor thin. He was lean, however, and dressed usually in woolsey shirt, tight, greasy, deerhide pants, and thick, cowhide moccasins to which were sewed an ingenious boot-like extension. He seemed to wish to

Pan The Low Waters

stand tall, and seemed so when wearing his gray, weathered, floppy-brimmed hat. Strong, piercing eyes always cut just below that brim, and from them I swore I saw sparks each time he spoke to Sicard (He never addressed me). But he was almost always in the saddle, rifle in scabbard, hair riata flapping against the horse's belly. Occasionally, from as far away as Sicard's could be heard the report of a gun. Usually it was Johnson firing at wolves or cougar, for these were a frequent problem of the cattle owner. Each partially-eaten and rotting steer carcass meant two dollars less in hide and tallow at matanza time.

Two weeks after the arrival of the first pathetic Donner Party members (we were not invited to help with the actual rescue, and this was probably because there was no desire to share with anyone else the money raised at the fort), Sicard and I were visited by one of Johnson's Indians. By signs and by rude Spanish – probably learned at the missions, he let us know of some unusual activity at Johnson's. Sicard had been planning to exchange some of his wheat and barley seed and flour for a steel plow he had noted at Richie's, so, with this in mind we loaded sacks in his wagon, crossed where the Bear was fordable, and in half an hour arrived at the squat Richie shanty. A little later, though no direct trade for the plow was made, Richie's wife, in the absence of her husband, and for some flour, gave Sicard the use of his excellent tool for an unspecified time. She then directed our attention to the activity just barely visible in the direction of Johnson's adobe.

"My husband, M.D. is over there with the rest of em", she said. "They've got help from Sutter's, and promise of good rescue wages. A bunch are gittin ready to go help the Donners. They'll earn any money they're alive to collect if'n they git back from this one. Indians say it hasn't snowed so much up there for years." It was apparent she had little sympathy for the endeavor, despite the fact that her theshold was the first to be darkened by the blood of the earliest pathetic survivors.

Arnold F. Rothmeier

Under heavy, threatening clouds we reined our team into the well-worn grounds around Johnson's. The area was a ferment of acivity: several head of cattle had been slain. Two were being cut into strips; fires were being tended by Indians; long poles held strips of beef; wheat was being ground in mortars and coffee mills; some twenty mules and horses were being packed and saddled. A gruff, burly frontiersman by the name of Woodward went about in the milling crowd seeking recruits for a rescue party that would attempt the saving of women and children said to be starving in the sierra. Again, Sicard and I had arrive in time to help in the preparations, and did so without being asked. My heart was touched by the tale of suffering told by Eddy, but I had my reasons for not volunteering. Chief among these was a fear, actually – of the Pike, the man whose visage was behind a beard and whose thoughts I was unable to read. (I always kept my beard cut to a trim length for it made me feel unclean when it wiped food before I ate it). My experiences with men of the new world had begun with the brawl in New Orleans and memory of it caused me to seek out and remain with countrymen ; made me now reticent to volunteer. Too, there was no lack of enlistments, as they walked rapidly about from one task to another, with shout and shouted answer. Not only were these men forming a clique, and riding off to a task which some feared impossible – for a new storm was coating the foothills – but overheard were little intimatory remarks concerning pay for the adventure. Money considerations often made brutes of men of good intentions, and I did not want to work with those whose reason for chivalry was love of money. In short, I feared not the winter in the mountains, but human motives at the preparatory stage. I simply was not one of them.

Sicard (after a night and day working at preparations), seeing the slow progress made in wheat grinding, drove a buckboard to his ranch and returned with two bushels of flour we had made for our use. By the end of the second day, two men – a Sep Mootry and a man known only as Joe – two who did much of the calculating, as well as their share of the work – judged the preparations nearly complete. By midnight of the second night mules and horses were tied and packed for an early start. Many of the party had worked for forty or more hours, and some, to dispel fatigue had drunk coffee or a strong local whisky. These were surly now, or snored in a blanket on the damp ground. Sicard and I had had little rest and I was gripped by a most powerful need to sleep.

When I awoke and crawled from beneath one of Johnson's derelict wagons it was to a dreary dawn. From my damp bed and between the spokes of the wagon wheel I counted fourteen men. Each led a pack animal and, one by one, they disappeared below the riverbank. There had been no fire-building, no breakfast; only a few words of encouragement and exhortation from a man I later came to know as Alcalde Sinclair. It was his wife who had gathered underclothes for the five women – the first survivors.

Around mid-morning, as those who had helped arose and sought bushes and stoked smokey fires, one of the pack horses minus its pack came clattering back across the assembly area. A few moments passed before two of the fourteen horsemen appeared. They succeeded in retrieving the trailing line, jerked in most savagely, beat the animal about the head and flanks, and, after tiring of this, disappeared once more toward the hills with the animal in tow.

A light rain fell during the early morning. There was nothing more to be accomplished at Johnson's. Sicard and I breakfasted on a few remaining cold beef ribs and rode homeward, busy with our own thoughts, depressed by fatigue, apprehensive of the success of the rescuers, and harboring low feelings because our role in the action had been only that of lackeys. Our spirits were further dampened when, by noon the next day, the skies became a menacing iron gray. Sagging, low clouds disgorged such quantities of water that I had a momentary phantasy: What would happen if this powerful, drenching flood should displace the air necessary for breathing?

Arnold F. Rothmeier

The first relief – for so it had since come to be called – left on Thursday. It rained in a cold, monotonously thundering flood for two days and nights. On Sunday, we awoke to a morning stunningly bright, almost as violently bright as the storm had been violent. The Bear ran full and turgid, and a thin dusting snow had invaded the low foothills. I feared for the rescuers and their mission.

I knew I had neither the courage nor the strength for so long and severe a test, and that even if the rescuers had been countrymen, I would not have gone along. But I could sense the challenge felt by these rough and hardened men. Now, in the dead of winter, after protracted bad weather and indoor living, they needed an outlet for their energies. The combination of the expected great test and the meaner incentive – three dollars per day guaranteed by Sutter and Sinclair – gave it all the irresistible tug. I envied the spirit that pulled these men toward great hazard in mountains deep in winter snows.

All next day Sicard and I sat on his floor grinding wheat. My mind wandered up river to a rocky fall of the Bear. It was small at the side, even when the river was swollen by rains, but its volume, sluicing in a strong steady stream through a slick serpentine trough, suggested usable but wasted power. That night in the soft silence of the cabin, I built a dream mechanism for accomplishing the thing that was giving us both blisters. And in the morning I lay, recalling my dream:

It was of a wheel of oak, such as I had often seen near Rouen. It turned under the weight of that steady stream emerging from the cleft. It filled buckets on my overshot wheel; it groaned, then turned, despite the axle's friction drag. A belt led from another wheel, turned by the axle, to a mill on the bank. Here my mind wrestled with the gears of various sizes for the transfer of power from vertical to horizontal.

I must have looked foolish indeed, for I was startled from my reverie by Sicard's words:

Pan The Low Waters

"Claude, you had a look just now, as though you were miles away and couldn't find you way back."

"Theodore", I said, sucking finger where a blister had broken, "If next year's barley and wheat crop is as large as this year's, why not plan for easier ways of milling it? I was thinking just now of a set of grinding wheels that could be turned by water up at that little rocky fall we sometime ride by."

Sicard ground on, but listened as I explained my plan. And so we passed the month of February. Most of the time the earth was too wet to think of doing anything toward enlarging our barley land. I used the period to make a small model of the mill and its gears and levers.

Also, I found I harbored a growing desire to see the big fort downriver, about which Sicard had talked so much.

Occasionally Sicard would make an overnight connubial journey to see his Indian friends and the chief's daughter who encouraged his love-making. He would take with him flour, scraps of bright cloth, bead, discarded pots, and pieces of metal we had picked up on our visits to Johson's. He often came back wearing a present – usually clothes – that made me envy his appearance. His moccasins, fringed shirt and pants were of soft deerskin bleached to an off-white, and all fitted him well. I inherited one of his earlier gift shirts and wore it for many years. I envied his ability to make such friends. I subsequently tried, and did succeed, though not as well as Sicard.

Early in March, after another spell of rainy weather, one of Johnson's Indians came with the news that the band of rescuers had returned with some of the snow-bound immigrants. We immediately packed a quantity of flour, dried vegetables, bread, and rode.

At both Johnson's and Richie's we found pathetic sights. Almost a score of men, women, and children lay on the floors, softly moaning.

Arnold F. Rothmeier

A number of women cleansed bruises and cuts; in a basin, two men laved the feet of a young boy. Both his limbs were lacerated and swollen, and, as they worked on him, cleaning dirt and blood from deep holes in the bony pads, I saw the gray-black of frozen toes. These, I knew, would sluff off, leaving him a cripple.

Some of the eighteen or so pathetic survivors were nursed and billeted at Johnson's. The remainder were housed at Richie's and at the more distant shack of a man named Keyser. Both Sicard and I helped in many small ways. Those at Johnson's, where we found most of the men and a few of the children, had arrived in nothing but rags. Somehow we found a shirt and trousers for most men. Women of the area cut and sewed until all were suitably clothed.

Among those at Johnson's was one sad and quiet young girl, apparently sister to the boy whose feet had been partially frozen. They had arrived parentless because their mother had been unable to leave the mountains. She was now blind, too weak to travel, and would have endangered the party. In the dim daylight of the adobe, as well as in the candle light at night, it was impossible to miss the solicitude paid her by Johnson. Though he showed concern for the boy – William Murphy, who yet, after two days could not stand, it was the boy's sister with whom he most often conversed.

We returned to Johnson's several days later. All those who had been saved by this first relief party had been removed to Sutter's Fort – with the exception of Mary and her brother. These were being cared for by two of Johnson's squaws, and looked almost radiant in contrast to their previous shrunken, toothy mask. Mary, I could see, would grow into a beautiful young woman. At the time I was vaguely disturbed to note the subtle degree of familiarity that had developed between her and Johnson. She was a slender, frail young thing, perhaps fourteen, with long dark brown hair. Though she smiled now, her beauty was marred by a residue of the hell she had experienced. Echoes of sights and sounds of the dead and dying seemed to have carved sad holes in her face. She seemed a woman now, long before her time, and there was a stain of deep sadness about her face and form. Johnson had contrived to cloth her in buckskins that day, and as I mounted my horse to return, I turned and saw them walk toward the small corral where he kept his own special mounts. I loathed him for his concern for the girl.

The girl was saved; in this I rejoiced; she shone now, after only a few days of warmth, security, and plenty, with a rewarding radiance. But, I pondered, how could the girl, here alone in a raw land – among raw men – know what to do? And how, with a blind mother, now said to be dying a starving, sodden death amid others already dead – how could she know the time to say "no"; to even imagine the appropriateness of a "no"?

As I rode, my mind was occupied with a mixture of revulsion for the one and pity for the other. So engrossed was I with thoughts concerning the unsuitability of middle-aged Johnson and child-like Mary, that I took little notice of how the weather matched my black thoughts. By the time we had forded the Bear, sharp, stinging raindrops pitted the surface and we were wet through before we pulled off saddles and spanked horses into their corral. One of Sicard's Indians had been fishing, and soon the heady smell of bass and wild bay filled the room. We sated our appetites while our drying clothes sent up clouds of steam.

Though we had not taken part in the actual rescue operations, both Sicard and I could feel we had helped in our own way. That evening our conversation turned from the general to the specific. Sicard began saying what we were both thinking:

"What's to become of a girl like Mary Murphy, with no father or mother around and a squaw-man taking her riding about the country? Her brother even left her – went off to the fort. I guess Johnson arranged that. And her two married sisters left her too."

"Yes", I replied, "Girls her age get left alone to do their own will. They're too old to coddle and reprimand – with or without a parent around – and they're too young to know what's going on in the mind of a man like Johnson. I wouldn't want to meddle anyway in Johnson's business. He may be an old squaw-man, and pull too much cork for his own good, but he knows what he wants and lets no one change either his – or the girl's mind."

Our conversation went this way as we ate fish and drank wine. The rain grew heavier, and as our tired and wet dispositions turned mellow as the wine we drank, my friend turned the conversation to the vein of his own pleasures with the chief's daughter. Though Sicard had several times suggested to me the degree of success he had had at the little wattle hut of Moogay (he called her 'gay little cow', and said she liked the name), he had never gone into any amorous detail. Now, feeling no restraint, he lauched, with quiet confidential tones into some of their intimacies: she was now more fastidious than when he first knew her, and though the chief objection to any liaison with the Indians was their odor – and often their lice – Moogay had, somehow, wanted very much to understand these objections. She bathed frequently in the Bear, rubbing herself with sand and mud. She had cut off her hair in a bang-like effect, and, to assure the appropriate bedroom effect, had tried a number of natural odors she felt that Sicard would like: crushed willow, blooms from certain flowers, dwarf roses that grew in the higher foothills, the tiny filaree, and many others.

She observed his odor-likings and tried to vary their use. She had seen Sicard smoke his pipe and so had once incensed their hut by sprinkling the fire with tobacco; she knew that most whites were favorable toward whisky, and once Sicard had come to their love-feast and been almost overcome by the odor of alcohol: she had saturated the hut floor, for more enjoyable results, and he had been nearly overcome by the fumes.

That he was white – and one-eyed – and would not live with the tribe, seemed not to disturb either the daughter or her father. She was apparently strong-willed, and her wish for Sicard as a bed-mate seemed enough for the father.

These unusual, often funny, often outrageous accounts of Sicard's domesticities with Moogay blended into another pleasant wine-filled evening, and I believe I fell asleep without knowing it – or Sicard either.

In the wet but partially clearing dawn I sensed a change in the weather. It had been, all said, a most unusual winter. I, too, felt a change. Whether it was a restlessness generated in the groin by Sicard's bold and voluptuous narrative, I did not try to discern. I only knew that now that the weather seemed to be changing, I felt a more intense desire to again break away from the familiar, perhaps to see more of the country – in particular, the fort, its owner, his operation. One evening I voiced my feelings to my friend.

"You will come back, hein, when your curiosity is satisfied? Claude, you and I can own the Nemshas together. You come back when you are through seeing the country, and we will make just as fine a farm as Sutter's.

The lonely tone in his voice suddenly struck me forcibly, and I began to see a side of Sicard that had not been apparent until now. He was a desperately lonely man, and though he was only a few years older than I, he had more than the usual needs of a peasant Frenchman – that for much company, talk-talk, a feel of ownership of the land, and a quiet braggadocio about the things the land afforded.

Arnold F. Rothmeier

Chapter 33
Sutter's Fort

We had been here together for nearly six months, had wanted for nothing of consequence. Though confined much of the time by weather, I had never felt the irritation, the friction, nor the boredom that usually accompanies living in such close quarters. I had felt only the quiet results of a needed companionship. Our moods matched, and the need for silence was shared almost instinctively. In the candle-lit gloom of those winter nights, whether repairing a worn garment, moving a heavy grinding block over another handful of wheat, or turning a hock of beef, spitted and dripping over the fire, our relationship had been the same unabrasive, contemplative existence. And had I not known of another center – Sutter's Fort – where all went who had ridden or walked the emigrant trail, I should have remained here at Nemshas.

It was, then, this idyllic life, free from need, from competition, from all friction, that marked my time at Sicard's as a kind of gauge by which I measured all other periods – either before – or after those Nemshas days. But I knew I would return. For all else – all other human contact, all the other places I would see, all the valleys I would explore, the rivers, all the ignorance and greed I would witness – all would drive me back to Nemshas simply because of the contrast.

I left this Eden in late April amid a welter of spring signs and after promising Sicard I would return as soon as I had satisfied my curiosity about the country south. It was good to ride out again, to feel the thrill of expectation. My spirits rose virgin, like the red tips of the early spring willow shoots along the river. Pheasant started up before my horse, sending up their wild dark purrs of displeasure; gray squirrels with tail longer and more luxuriant than any I had ever seen, flowed down oak like gray droplets on a tilted straw. They flowed back, and leapt wild distances at impossible heights. They sagged and swayed on thin limbs – and then repeated their acrobatics.

Far overhead through the budding tree limbs geese wavered northward in wide, fragile lines trailing faint, wounded cries, and across, on either side of the wide valley, the mountains rose, blue and hazy, their summits yet coated with the white remnants of a wild and treacherous winter.

My mind back-tracked over events of the past season: After the first relief had returned with its pathetic cargo of souls there had been two more severe storms. Yet despite these, more reliefs had gotten to the trapped immigrants and brought them out, sent them down the valley to Sutter's. Relatives of those yet trapped had, themselves, hardly recovered before they had faced about and dared the snows again. I could not feel ashamed that I had not volunteered. Neither Sicard nor I had felt welcome. Better to leave the hope of reward – and glory – to the sturdy and durable Irish and German. There was no room in the rescue trains for the shorter men, for those of us who had not the hard eye-glint of desire for treasure still suspected as hidden in the death camps: For it was rumored that there had been wealth aboard the Donner train. I thought, too, of the young children who had arrived almost naked and without parents, and who had been thrust into a rude land with only the saddest of trail memories.

Arnold F. Rothmeier

Thinking thus, time and distance to the fort spent itself, and by late afternoon of the second day I arrived in view of massive fort walls so reminiscent of the large, moated ones near Rouen. The trail had taken on the appearance of a broad, rutted highway. Mounted Spaniards pestered herds of cattle, and wagons and emigrant activity clouded the area with dust.

The road diffused as it approached the fort walls. Horse and wagon tracks led everywhere and nowhere. Far beyond the gentle rise of the fort grounds the river lay like a silver snake. Now, down the swale, I approached a scattering of half-clothed Indians, their black, greasy hair reflecting a late and hazy sun. They were responding to tones of a bell within the walls. Throwing down their tools – the crude rake or club with which they had broken clods, they scampered as one for a spot near the wide palisade gates. Here another Indian spread a steaming mush in long V-shaped troughs. From these the workers ate, fingering the steaming mixture to their mouths. I was not close enough to note the process in more detail, but as I raised my eyes, there, high on a pine stake to the right of the gate, a whitening human skull could be see – a warning to miscreants?

Other figures and sights now commanded my attention: A small black bear chained to a tree a dozen yards from the west wall padded about, pawed and sniffed its chain, then resumed its padding. Through a veil of oaks about the fort acreage could be seen tents of emigrant families. A few Indians in ragged shirts and even more ragged trousers, slouched about, as though trying to fathom meaning of the large structure and of the fully clothed figures passing through the gates. Occasionally one bent, squatted, the true indolents in a land of plenty – the few who chose neither to work, nor share in the mush troughs. Off in the growing haze a baby sobbed, a dog yelped at some wild thing.

I rode through yellow poppies and knee-deep grass and the high fort gates. I dismounted, tied, and looked about. The enclosure was much as at Fort Hall. Walls were lined with slanting shed roofs and stalls; a center area was dominated by a single, large two-storied, block-like structure.

But I had no time for lengthy examination. Almost as though he had known the time of my arrival, the man of whom I had heard so much broke away from conversation with another tall, dark-suited man and approached me across the inner court. He had a quick, utilitarian stride, oddly inconsistent with the soft and leisurely German-accented speech with which he greeted me. His body and attitude, certainly his cheery smile, breathed an impression of welcome, His French was weighted lightly with a touch of the Swiss.

"I am Johann Sutter, and my fort is yours. Please tell me your name and what you do, so I may invite you to my table."

The hospitality and flattery of his greeting were disarming. I felt welcome indeed. As I supplied the words "Chana" and "cooper" his eyes took on an even brighter, more cordial gleam, and he led the way past lounging whites and Indians to the doorway of the large central structure. Once inside, I was offered a rugged but comfortable rawhide chair while my host used an odd mixture of Spanish and German sounds to coax activity from dark, loose-gowned domestics. Meat, the plentiful staple of California, was already brown and dripping in the fireplace, but I was unprepared for the variety of food and drink which quickly appeared on the table: corn, squash, beans, mutton, fish, and beets. It was as though I was being made obliged – though pleasantly so – to stay, to become part of Sutter's kingdom. He poured an excellent brandy, newly arrived on his launch, the "Linda", and he carried on an amicable conversation in French, for he seemed to want to exercise the language. Most of his monologue concerned his recent arms flurry with the Mexicans and the help he had given to rescue the Donners; the outlook for his corn and wheat production.

Many small farms had sprung up in the immediate several miles surrounding the fort. This was done, of course, by squatters, but Sutter, after his brush with the Spanish, encouraged it, indeed, he encouraged all settlement of both whites and Indians who were inclined to build, for he wished a buffer of like-thinking settlers between his fort and influences which once threatened his ownership.

Before we had reached the coffee and cigar stage of our dinner, Sutter offered me both a room for quarters, and work in the adjoining room as cooper and carpenter. Even if I had had other plans or obligations elsewhere, I could not have declined his offer. The famed Sutter generosity and persuasion were compelling. I had been fed and liquored and made pleasantly bereft of all other inclinations – if one had existed. I accepted both the room and the job, for, though wages were but one dollar per day, I was convinced that there would be little compulsion. Short pay would be made up in food.

At daybreak I was startled awake by the boom of the work cannon, which I was to hear each morning as long as I remained. Almost immediately there was a quiet surge of sound from the stalls, the inner court, and even from over the high fort walls. Chickens clucked, dogs barked, voices, indistinct and blurred, but imperative, rose and fell. Fast footpads, some booted, some bare, sounded in the court. I arose and stood in the doorway to observe the beginning of a new day at Sutter's Fort.

All was movement. Sutter himself stood straight as a general in his doorway across the court while fifteen or twenty brilliantly uniformed but poorly fitted soldiers with muskets scrambled and shuffled into lines. When all was nearly straight they turned to a muffled command by a tall, sworded and sashed Indian officer, and ambled in two columns through the huge gates.

Behind them the inner court came to life: in one corner of the stockade a burro began endless grinding rounds at the end of a thick pole, turning one massive granite wheel on another, pressing grain into flour;

beneath a wide, slanting shake roof came slushing sounds and a rank stench of leather preparation; large, high-rimmed vats received the stiff, dry hides which lay in wobbly seven-foot high stacks; numerous persons went about the enclosure – some with rifles, some with burdens; two kinds they were – those on business or at work, and those who had no present purpose, but simply watched, as I did, for purpose to materialize. This was it? This was the goal of all those reckless, monotonous months on the trail?

I breakfasted on food saved from the previous dinner table, accepted hot coffee from an Indian boy sent by Sutter, and, with tool sack on my back, crossed the court and entered the central building. Here, about a long, rough plank workbench in the center of the room, stood three other bearded workmen. One bent at sharpening a tool, another planed a spoke, a third – the one opposite whom I was placed – worked at replacing a new carding wheel.

All three worked silently, and none but I noticed the entrance of Captain Sutter until he spoke, stating that I was a cooper, just arrived from Rouen. The two farthest from me nodded, but continued their sharpening and planing. The man opposite whom I was to work and who, at the moment, was fitting spokes, leaned across, extended an unusually large and hairy hand, and said simply, "Howdy, Chana".

There followed a simple orientation period in which Sutter made known his little projects. These consisted mainly of repairs of tools and containers scattered in a pile in the corner. He then left and I went to work with the other three.

We made rakes, hoes, shovels, knives, and scythes; mended same; mended buckets, spindles, and shuttles. One of the men worked on guns – which esoteric occupation may have accounted for his aloofness – and perhaps for his feeling of superiority. I was accepted, but not with equality until one day when Sutter entered and made known his pleasure at the smooth refitting I had made on a certain cask.

Arnold F. Rothmeier

From then on I was post cooper, and looked up to for my skill in the profession.

The relationship we had with Sutter was one of equals. Though he did indeed own the fort and many hundreds of leagues of surrounding land, and controlled all activities thereon, his only apparent domination was over the lives of a few women and men who had come with him long ago from the Sandwich Islands, and, of course, the several dozen natives who soldiered or labored for him.

It was a curious confedercacy, and from the day when I first surveyed the fort from the knoll where hung the impaled skull, it grew more singular the longer I remained: first, there was the whole question of ownership of the fort. Possession was domination – domination not by any force or law – which was exercised by Alcalde Sinclair – an appointee of the now defunct Mexican government – but by the force of Sutter's presence, his genial personality, the simple fact of his presence – or, perhaps the absence of another dominant figure. He ruled his vast, loose conglomerate of fields, boats, cattle, fort complex, and the lives of a growing number of emigrants and natives by that in all of us which seeks and finds a source of decision making.

Now that California had shown fight, and it was inevitable that these vast lands would become a part of the United States, then it seemed also inevitable that at some future time the power of this man – or the strength of his personality and his little show of arms – would also decline.

It was all part of the evolving and changing of a situation much too complex for my mind. One face emerged and then remained eternally unchanged amid all the possibilities of change: it had to do with the first act of all those I had observed since I arrived – Johnson, Sicard, and now Sutter: They had all striven for and achieved ownership of the most valuable property possible – the land. Then they had seen to it that this land was described, built upon, lived upon, and used, so that custom and tradition and long original use – even if no valid, written trace of ownership existed – would establish possession.

These thoughts obsessed me and were uppermost in mind during my long stay at the fort. They often pursued me when I observed, both at the fort and outside, the degree of dependency most individuals had upon an employer. And it seemed to me strikingly inconsistent with reality and the times that so many emigrants should live so dependently on squatter land, and that they should not establish ownership of land as a first and basic requisite.

George Marshall, the tallest of the three workers, toiled steadily and seriously opposite me. From our first meeting he and the two others showed an almost fierce reluctance to communicate. Full-bearded as we were, it was always difficult to tell what a man felt or though by the look on one's face. My fellow workers were no exception. Each seemed to live within himself and to concentrate so completely on the job at hand that only strong physical needs – food, wine, and elimination – interfered. The job was a time of silence and steady production and of a kind of expectant waiting. It was as though all California waited for a great moment, a truth, for a culmination of some great event. I felt it sometimes in the audible silence of our shop; I saw it in the furrowed concentration of these men, and I watched it in the expansion of the fort population. Now that spring weather had arrived, more and more persons were put to work outside, as well as in the inner court. Indian women sat about in the sun carding from piles of lamb's wool, scraping hides, and sewing rough linsey sacking to hold wheat now greening in wide fields.

Then, one day in early June, before work, preparations began around Sutter's door for a special ceremony of some sort. Such was an almost daily occurrence, and thinking it possibly an Indian or an emigrant wedding, I gave it little thought, but turned to my work. An hour passed. There arose from across the courtyard sounds of cheering mingled with a few gunshots, and, since Marshall and the others left their benches, I trailed them to the doorway.

    Between the small sea of heads and waving hands that partially blocked my view, a new bride and groom emerged from Sutter's office, groom in wrinkled dark coat, broad-brimmed felt hat, and bride in what suggested something borrowed and the promise of delight – for the bodice was exaggeratedly tight, full and sensuous in contrast with a long, full skirt. Her bridal hat was weighted awkwardly with new spring lupins and tiny roses from the foothills. This floral abundance about the face concealed her identity until they passed our workroom door en route to saddled horses tethered nearby. Then there was no mistaking the pretty flushed face of Mary Murphy. Both face and figure were greatly changed since last I saw them on the pallet at Johnson's. Gone was the mask of starved death, the sunken sheen of eye rimmed with blue-black tissue, gone the sallow, cadaverous face. A flushed and child-like smile replaced the former ghoul-like openness caused by teeth made manifest by receding gums and starvation. She walked now with the bearing of a young woman, to her horse, and mounted unaided. I caught sight of the hem of her "second day dress" rolled behind the saddle. The groom, none other than the bantam-sized Johnson, already unsteady and weaving, accepted a proffered bottle, emptied it on the spot, mounted, and quirted his animal into a headlong dash through the fort gate. Mary's trailed.

    The scene took but a few moments, then they were gone. The fort grounds quickly resumed their restive but unfestive appearance. There were the usual male quips about the forthcoming wedding night. I resumed my cooping. But now stave edges lacked in smoothness of fitting, for my mind dwelt on the questionable future of those I had just seen; the real tragedy of a beautiful fifteen year old girl who had lived through one haunting tragedy only to pass into another through the portals of the altar. For it was well known that Johnson was a rounder. He had been a rough seaman, had already used two squaws, and apparently cared little for his new wife. He drank excessively and uncontrollably, and was more than twice Mary's age. I pondered:

Could there be a better formula for unhappiness?

    My mind was not on task; but neither was I ready to listen to the bedroom jokes of the two men who shared a workbench across the room. These knew only that another man had taken an emigrant girl to bed, would use her, make her old before her time with many children. I turned from their unthinking coarseness determined to know the man Marshall a little better.

Arnold F. Rothmeier

Mary
Part II

But then I don't remember papa ever being all cuddly and sweet-talking to mama either. But I'd have thought Mr. Johnson would sort of help me onto my mare after the wedding, like I see men do sometimes. Something about it gentles a body. It doesn't really help. I can get into the saddle by myself. It's just that a man's hand tucking your foot in the stirrup and holding 'round your waist when you push up, tells a woman he wouldn't let you fall – even if you could. It tells you, maybe, that you're a little, well, precious, that he'd like to protect you – even if you can do everything yourself.

And Mr. Johnson was like that, there at the ranch. His was one of the first faces I saw when we came out of the hills and snow. That was the day! Those men shining up to little Virginia Reed and Lavina Graves, and asking to get married to those babies!

I guess I was a sight. No wonder they paid me no mind. There was no fat on me and I know my face was all hollow and white from the months in the snowy mountains. And I was so scary thin and scabby. No wonder they didn't ask me. And even when I awakened and slept

Pan The Low Waters

and awakened again and was washed, I cried myself to sleep over mama being still up there, blind and cold and hungry.

But I came out of it slow, and came to know that I would never see mama ever again. I began to eat and walk about after the others left for Sutter's. Mr. Johnson seemed to like me a lot and looked after me and my brother, William. We were the only ones still at Johnson's when the third bunch came down out of the mountains, because we had nowhere to go. Then brother's toes got well and he left for Sutter's too.

Now it has been a whole year since we rode out along the Platte. Instead of riding in a jolting wagon, I have a horse, a different one every day, if I want. Instead of brothers and sisters around me there is Noo-Noo and Hoopa, Mr. Johnson's squaw women. (He wants me to call him William, but it's hard, he's so much older than I am).

One day while I was getting better and better, Mr. Johnson asked me if I would like to go riding to look up a herd that had wandered to the south side of the river. He gave me an extra jacket because it was a cool April day. We never found the cattle, but as we rode along in the new fields of purple flowers he said he wanted to marry me and protect me; that if he didn't, any number of things might happen to me. He said that was what his friend, Lienhard, thought too, because I was all alone now, excepting my brother William, and all women here on the new frontier needed a man for protection. So we talked on, and I could certainly see that I should do something. He told me he loved me and I could see he did, otherwise why would he want to protect me? Then we rode back without seeing the cattle, and I still didn't know what to do. My brother left to help with a furniture store that Foster and his new wife were starting in Yerba Buena. I really was alone then. And so I said I would ride to Sutter's Fort and wait for him there and, if he still wanted to marry me, we could do it there.

I stayed in the wagon I rode in when we reached the fort, but Mr.

Johnson came in the next day and told me he had made arrangements for a Mr. Sinclair to marry us. Mrs. Sinclair helped me with a new dress from some gingham Mr. Johnson got from someone near the fort. (She said I needed a second "day dress" – why, I didn't know). I was all mixed up about my new husband. I knew I had to have one because all the others, even the Indian squaws and the Kanakas who lived with Sutter had a man. Mr. Johnson said he loved me. I guessed that meant he wanted me to talk to and to help with the workings of his house. I never thought that I was supposed to love him, too. I know I didn't at first, but then what I felt toward him was a kind of pride that he should want me, just a young girl; a kind of thankfulness that he should want to protect me; and a kind of happiness that I could get a man too, just like my sisters, Harriet and Sarah. And I felt, too, a kind of relief that now, at last, after all that trail and starvation from Independence, and the not having a bed of my own, that now I could be sure of something again. I could have enough food and a fireplace and even two squaws to do most of the hard work.

It never bothered me that I knew I didn't love Mr. Johnson. How could it bother me? I was come up through the time of my life when there wasn't anyone around to sort of be skittish with. Then we ups and taken to the trail. Then we go through the months of dyin and stomach pain and sameness that no-one should have to pass through. Then, when at last we come out of the misery to the valley and the green grass, sisters go off on their own; William, my only brother leaves, and the men return from the mountains and say that mama is dead before she can be brought down.

I guess I can be a wife, too. Why shouldn't I? Sarah and Harriet both married at seventeen and I'm almost sixteen. I'm still mixed up about what I should do now that I am Mr. Johnson's wife. But, I don't' suppose it will be so very different. But I do wish Sarah and Harriet were here to talk to.

Mr. Johnson's horse clattered ahead of mine all the way back from the marryin at Sutter's. we forded the Bear near the cabin and arrived near sundown. I was thinking, as we rode along, that this country was so big that a person could ride for a day and not see anything but herds of deer and cattle. And I was thinking that all this country around the house now was ours. Not that I was going to do anything with it, but just by marrying me, Mr. Johnson made me owner of it, too. And now the buds and new leaves and the grasses were out, even the hills to the east didn't look as sad and cold as they did – even though there was still caps of snow.

Noo-Noo and Hoopa came out of the ranch house and stood by the door while Mr. Johnson unsaddled the horses and spanked them into the near corral, and then threw a deerhide over the saddles.

I've always liked Mr. Johnson's adobe because that first night I slept here made me feel safe. I remember stretching out my hand and feeling the rough warm and hard of the walls. Those first few hours, when someone helped me drink some soup or gravy before I slept that first warm, dry sleep I had had for such a long time. That was the smell of Hoopa's stew I smelled again. She gets bay leaves somewhere nearby. Its smell is like she has put her name on the food. I know by the soft, heavy bay smell that she has made it.

Instead of having me sleep by the fireplace like I did before, Mr. Johnson wants me to sleep with him in the big new bed of hides and blankets off to the side room. Noo-Noo gave us each a bowl of stew and then went out. They never say hardly a word. Sometimes they talk Indian to each other. Mr. Johnson says he makes them wash regular, and so they are cleaner and don't smell heavy like other Indians.

Mr. Johnson and I sat up a long time on our first marriage night. I cracked and ate the pine nuts Hoopa brought us. Mr. Johnson ate them too, and drank his brandy. After a while, he blew out the lamp and we pulled up the robes. Then for a long time he tried. It's such a strange thing to talk about, but he says all husbands and wives do it. But, the more he tried, the tireder he got. He's so big, he says, and I'm still a young girl. After a long time he just rolled away and went to sleep and snored with a little snifty sound. Off someplace I heard a coyote howl. I lay awake a long time thinking maybe I would grow bigger when I grew older, or that maybe Mr. Johnson wouldn't be so big if he drank less.

In the morning Mr. Johnson was up and away on his horse before I woke. Him riding by outside was what woke me up. He was gone two days, and I walked a lot down along the Bear while he was gone. Such a pretty river in the springtime, with the thick run-off swirling around rocks and fish jumping clear out of the water in the shaded places. The round white rocks on the bottom seem like a flooded cobblestone road. I walk like this because it's easier to walk than to sit at the ranch and think. The river and the sights sort of spread out thinner the thoughts I will have to think about Mr. Johnson sooner or later. I know he was disappointed on our wedding night, and I feel, somehow, that I disappointed him. But how could I have did different? I know so little about men and what they want or need.

Noo-Noo and Hoopa don't do much when Mr. Johnson is gone. They let the fire go out, or don't build one. They don't even bother to cook, and so I made a fire and put things in the kettle.

I was glad when Mr. Johnson rode in after sundown. He looked tired, but he was more than tired. He didn't even unsaddle, and he hardly noticed me or talked, and he smelled heavy of whisky. Hoopa lit a lamp and sort of scurried around for bread and stew. Mr. Johnson just sat near the fire and brooded, and when Hoopa handed him the bowl, he flailed out his arm and knocked it from her hand.

In the morning, the stew was still on the floor. I felt it slippery under my feet when I awakened early and started the fire cause it had turned chilly for early July. After knocking the stew from Hoopa's hand, Mr.

Johnson had gone to bed, called to me rudely, and then pawed all over me. His arms pulled me, but his whisky breath was like a fence between us. But I couldn't give him what it was he wanted, and he staggered up after awhile and went in by the fire. After that, he never slept in the new bed, and I was afraid to ask him where he slept, because from then on he got surlier and meaner than I ever thought he could be. I was pretty used to mean things, and seeing people and animals hurt, but at the ranch there was more.

At the ramada, where the cattle are roped and butchered for tallow and hides, I once saw Mr. Johnson go out in the dust with his knife and slit the front tendons of a roped steer. Then he cut the leg ropes and laughed and drank some while he watched the beast plow through the dust and not able to control his hooves. He laughed real loud to see it stumble stupidly about for awhile before its throat was slit. I watched from a distance, for if I was seen, I would be send back to the house. I watched only once, and I could not stand the reek and the bleats that slid down to a gurgle.

If one of the Indian ranch hands was slow, Mr. Johnson took to slapping him or kicking him. They got scared about coming close to him, especially late in the afternoon, after he had been drinking most of the day. None of the ranch hands could seem to understand why he all of a sudden changed. I began to wonder if, in some way, I had helped to change him for he had not been like this toward any of the emigrant and rescuers when I first knew him.

The ramada killing and hide drying and tallow cooking went on through most of August. It was hard to get away from the stench of drying hides and the heavy green smell of decaying flesh and offal. Far down along the Bear, the carcasses were dug, hundreds and hundreds of them. There they stank in the hot sun. You could see the warm night you could hear the howling and snarling of wolves and dogs fighting over their share.

I would always go to bed early at ramada time. The smells made the night seem warmer, but often on these howling evenings, if I stood by the door, I was cooled by a misty stir of air from the bitter-sweet smell of willows up river. These moments were like balm, for they brought scented cool air to take place of the heavy blood and offal stench; I could forget the brutality and blood and dying that, ever since papa died, seemed my lot.

It was on one of these cool and perfumed nights that I got up to enjoy the sight of the moonlit shadows of the oaks and stand cool and alone in the delicious river smells. I was there leaning against the doorway for perhaps fifteen minutes when I heard short, out-of-breath grunting sounds from Hoopa's little room. Thinking she might have eaten something that did not agree with her, I poured a cup of water for her and opened the curtain door. Moonlight slanted full on Hoopa's narrow bed. She was not alone; nor was she ill. My husband was crouched over her, and it was he who was making the sounds I heard.

In the morning I was not awakened as usual by Mr. Johnson's shout for breakfast and coffee. He had eaten and gone. Hoopa and Noo-Noo had been assigned some tasks outside, and so, through most of the day I brooded over what I had seen in Hoopa's room. I was too disturbed by that experience to think clearly either that day or the next. Then I seemed to get clear in my mind what was happening. My mind seemed to chase thoughts, but never to fasten them down. I would think, "Mr. Johnson is unfaithful. Leviticus Twenty says an adulterer shall be put to death." This cannot be, but neither does the good book say that my husband may have squaws. I know now I am at least partly to blame for what I saw the other evening. But then, how am I to blame? And I would think, "Hoopa must be easier to have". And the thought would end almost unbearable. And I would think, "Mr. Johnson has had his squaws for perhaps years before I married him". And I would see no answer to my thoughts, and I would sit for hours, as I was turning a roast or boiling clothes or mending, and I would think I would go mad to try to find an answer to the trouble I was in.

Then my mind turned to my religion, because I was baptized a Mormon before leaving Kentucky and I had thought nothing about a man having two or more wives. That was when I was younger, but now the idea hit me hard, for I indeed did have a husband who felt he had other wives than me, and I didn't like the idea one bit. But I was all mixed up, and with no one here to talk about it with, I began thinking of Harriet in Yerba Buena for I felt that I had to get help for all the questions springing up in my head.

The ramada was finally over, the hides stacked, and the tallow rendered and bagged. Mr. Johnson had free time now and took to drinking more and more. Now, when he was unsteady with his bottle, I was careful to avoid him and took to riding a lot. One warm evening as I unsaddled from a long canter along the river, I noticed that all the stacks of hides were gone and nearly all the fanegas and barrels of tallow were loaded in wagons.

In the ranch house there were sounds of coarse celebration and I knew the hides and tallow had brought a good market. I was tired and wanted to lie down. I hesitated on seeing so many men about the door and on the floor, some pouring whisky or brandy, some just making those baby-like lisping sounds that drunken men make. Mr. Johnson saw me and before I could step around the men, he grabbed my hand and held his full cup in front of my face. When I shook my head, his face became a mask of hate, and he poured the full cup of brandy on my head. Most of the men were drunk, but none seemed to think this was funny. I stumbled into my room and gathering my skirts, tried to dry my hair and face. I had no water and would not go through the main room again, and spent the night feeling the sticky brandy about me. Then there was no more loud sound and coarse laughter; I counted the sounds of the men's horses as they left.

But the person that rose from that bed the next morning was different from the one that had ridden horse along the river the day before. For seven or eight hours I had lain awake most of the night arguing with myself against staying here for any more abuse. Before Mr. Johnson or any of the snoring ranch hands were awake, I wrapped a few clothes in a bundle, tied it behind the saddle, which had not been taken off the night before, and headed south toward the fort.

Chapter 34
Marshall

It was not an easy task to "open him up". At the outset Marshall, like all men I had met in California – excepting Sutter and Sicard – seemed to become less communicative upon meeting a Frenchman. And this, I could never quite understand as I tried to talk with a Californico, an Indian, or a Pike. I never felt, showed, nor felt the same suspicion or distrust that most emigrants seemed to feel upon hearing me speak. And since I was going to live among them, I determined to anglicize myself by listening to and imitating their clipped Yanqui speech.

It was not difficult to draw Marshall into conversation, but it was hard to pursue with him, for long, a given trend of thought. If I questioned him I learned to open up with a subject to which I thought he could respond with confidence. If I succeeded only in causing him to grope, the result was often either a turning of conversation into one of his favorite topics – mechanics, or his recent participation in skirmishes with Vallejo. His chief characteristic, however, was a grumpy silence or an uncongenial display of frustration accompanied by flushes, a decided twitch over his left eye, or an irrational, rapid speech which had little or no connection with the subject proposed. Gradually, however, I grew to like him for his eccentricities and silent strength. He made his reactions with personal, emotional equipment available, and he did have an astute mechanical mind and a clever knack for levers, pressures, and weights.

I was witness to an example of the fertility of his imagination one morning in the hog killing season: after having tinkered for several days at his bench with a small chain, he announced that he was ready. We were invited to witness the first working of a contraption for hog killing. A large group of people had gathered, some distance from the fort walls, and surrounded a fenced multitude of grunting, nuzzling hogs wallowing in their deep stench. Between two oaks stretched a thick endless rope that plied upon two pulley wheels. A slow and docile mare, led by an Indian, furnished power which moved the rope. I learned later that her eardrum had been pierced so that she could tolerate the sounds anticipated.

Slowly, the swine were directed from the end of their pen into a narrow, gradually ascending chute. Here, unseen by the hogs, a crouching Indian youth shackled their hind legs, and at the same time attached shackle to a knot on the ever-moving rope. In a moment the chute terminated and the animal found himself dangling by his hind legs. In the only way that hogs have of expressing surprise and mortal terror, the one now dangling split the air with the loudest of prolonged squeals.

This intense sound lasted but a few seconds and ended in gurgles and a cessation of all movement, as another Indian, with quick stabbing movement pried knife into the throat and barbed a small bucket to catch blood as it drained. There followed considerable show of appreciation and clapping of hands from the crowd of watchers. Efficient as Marshall's kill-line was, there was yet more to be seen. Near the more distant pulley, the hog, now bled, was released from the line and fell gently into a large cauldron of water kept boiling by several

Indian boys. So now, with a few prods at the uncertain, deaf mare, and amid cheering drowned by the sounds of the continuing pig-terror, slaughter, blood-letting, and scalding, death came to the hog in a few brief moments. After another few minutes of scalding the animal was lifted from the water and rolled onto clean planking. Here Indian women and children picked quickly at the bristles, saving them in their pockets or in baskets as one would treasure. When the hog pen was empty and the last pig throat slit, the crowd melted away, whispering its appreciation to themselves.

The demonstration over, I returned to my work. Marshall's planning had shown considerable ingenuity. I congratulated him when he later entered with Sutter. He was beaming, but very drunk, and sat for the remainder of the afternoon smoking and drinking and accepting compliments from numerous workers and visitors. And I thought, as I completed several small tasks, how much easier it was to know and understand him in moments like these, than when he was in his usual, morose, and silent state. Perhaps he differs from most of us only in being morose longer.

As a result of Marshall's show of mechanical skill I found myself stimulated to think along inventive lines also, and I thought more seriously now, about the overshot wheel and the harnessing of the Bear for milling and sawing.

Sutter, too, had been thinking along these lines, for he had imperative need for sawn timber, and even before I arrived, had sent several parties up the American River to scout a suitable site for a sawmill.

Arnold F. Rothmeier

Chapter 35
Cordua

Most of my decisions, it seems, have been arrived at during the simple act of staring from a cooperage window at Rouen, New Orleans, St. Louis, and St. Joseph. It was almost as though I saw at these times, the paths I must travel to fulfill a destiny. Now I was at Sutter's Fort, and again I was peering through a window. But this time there would be no more travelled paths.

One fine morning at the workbench I contemplated another change. Aside from a few unconquered miles I had no more westering to do. Not far from Yerba Buena the land ended and sea began. Of the sea I had had a sufficiency. In a way I had come full circle. What now would satisfy the perennial "Pike" in me – the one who struck for new horizons as soon as he saw neighbor's smoke a mile away? I reflected that there is within each of us wanderers an ingenious force: no sooner is one mode of expression blocked than our mind, leaping ahead unbidden, has already sought and found a new answer. It is then left to one's conscious thinking to discover and hit upon that plan which the unconscious, the yearning part of each discovered much earlier.

Pan The Low Waters

Sutter had been good to me, seemed more than satisfied with my workmanship, and it was from him that I heard of Charles Covillaud's activities at the ranch of a man named Cordua. Sutter told me that Charles was now managing the man's herds and Indians with unusual success, that the Cordua Rancho was a large tract of land at the junction of the Feather and Yuba Rivers. Though Sutter, I could sense, was not anxious to have me find out too much about the country that might tempt me from my job, he was less apprehensive about letting me go when he understood that Charles and I had come west together and that I only wished to visit him. I could understand Sutter's apprehension more easily when I learned that Marshall would be leaving soon to direct construction of a sawmill in mountains along the American Fork: he had in me a good cooper, and would be badly handicapped with both of us gone.

Routine at the fort was always the same: soon after the evening cannon exploded there was an orderly closing of the huge gates and a gradual securing of the fort by trained savages. Indians, as well as whites plodded quietly, wearily down a path they seemed to know well, one that led to their food and bed. In anticipation of the evening guns, steaming kettles of mush were ladled into troughs where the Indians fell to with lip-smacks and throaty sounds of satisfaction. Next, suited overseers coaxed and pushed them through the fort gates and herded them into a long barred room on the inner east wall. By this time the sun had set, and along the wall, silhouetted armed guards could be seen, each taking care of his fort section. At each of the towns in which I had lived, I had been conscious of authority, of the office of gendarmerie, and of armed security. Here, now in the growing darkness, I also felt secure, but it was a wild and bizarre form of mind peace, made exotic by trained savages – themselves only months away from inherited wildness and violence. Here indeed was despotism. Here the lives of savages and whites alike depended upon the judgement and anticipation of one man. And I wondered what could occur if something were to happen to the man Sutter – a man prone to the same jealousies and passions as all those about him. It was, at the time, common knowledge that a man named Daylor, who lived south of the fort, had sworn to kill Sutter.

In the morning – which became visible morning only with the firing of the cannon as the sun came up – regimentation began again with a smart parade of uniformed Indians and an exodus to the fields. Doors were thrown open and those who had not escaped confinement stumbled outside and staggered toward the gate, grunting and yawning, to work another day, fill belly again at the gruel trough, and, perhaps this time, run to the hills instead of suffering confinement, and so break the cycle.

The day, for others, began with a few pieces of dried meat and a cup of thin coffee. Then the vaqueros strode, with blankets and rope, toward the south corrals, where, after saddling half-wild mounts, they rode to the hills in search of cattle suitable for the day's slaughter. The women, who daily filled large water kegs for the fort's use, left next, moving unsteadily toward the river, casks upon their heads. Others began work at well-greased spinning wheels and looms; hand mills ground the choicest wheat, bolted the flour for Sutter's table; and when most of the functions had begun, the most favored class – the one to which I belonged – rose and made its way to the work bench.

Almost daily, now in late September, Sutter hired more men from among arriving emigrant trains. The shelters and workrooms that lined the inner walls, so full when I began my stay, now held an amazingly large population. The ever-present odor of human feces, trapped as it was by the high walls, often stunned the senses. Its unpleasantness was multiplied by a warm and humid fall.

After seven months of seeing soldiers and trappers come and go, and new faces and new wagons, and new tales about a new state, I was gradually stirred by a desire to see still more of the great valley. I found it impossible to work at a bench and let the world go by. So, by promising Sutter to return, and by leaving my tools with him by way of a suggestion of surety, I left one fine morning on Sutter's launch "Sacramento", going upriver to Cordua's ranch at the juncture of the Yuba and Feather Rivers.

It was a quiet and uneventful trip, filled only with the sounds of motor and sights of a virgin countryside. Deer, elk, wild horses, cattle, and ducks were such a common sight that their absence would have been as striking as a landscape without trees. A large Indian rancheria appeared on the west bank as we approached the river juncture, and the launch steered so close it was possible to see the breasts of near-naked squaws. It was late in the afternoon, and the scene was made domestic with the smoke of cook fires and scampering children. Near some of the low, rounded, mud and wattle hovels lay huge woven baskets of acorns. A light breeze brought to all on board the sweet-heavy odor of cooked fish. In a few moments the peaceful, wild sight wound behind us and disappeared, and we approached a point of land that wedged the two rivers. Swirling into the cove, we tied at a small earthen dock near a large valley oak. A stiff wind blew. I shouldered my blanket and went in search of Charles.

Here, where the Yuba and Feather joined there was little to hint of a town that was to become Marysville a few years hence. Indeed there was little to distinguish the worn landing paths from the dozen we had observed from shipboard, and that led to rancherias or to small pioneer huts. A settlement emerged from behind a shield of willows as I climbed a short overgrown pathway, and, on a bank some fifty feet above the Yuba I found the headquarters of the man Cordua, for whom Charles had worked for nearly a year. Like Johnson, Cordua was principally a raiser of cattle. But unlike the former, his German industry and thrift gave an overall impression of neatness and order. With the help of Indians and others he had built comfortable living quarters and outhouses of adobe. Corrals abutting these held cows with full udders and sleek horses spoiling for a ride. Beyond the corrals many acres of now wilted bushes and vines showed the extent of his summer wheat and gardens. Behind another squat, shake-roofed building came the sound of hammer and anvil, and beyond its low roof a slope of hill was visible, filled with the bulbous yellow gold of a thousand pumpkins. It was a scene of industry and plenty, of care, thrift, and contentment, and I confess to a twinge of envy that Charles should find so delightful a spot and establish himself so well.

It was he whom I had heard striking the anvil, and as I approached the door I saw him hand his hammer to an Indian and guide a few of the boy's strokes against quickly fading iron. It was good to hear his voice again , and it seemed I could detect in it a fatherly quality. Had Charles' eyes not followed those of his pupil, who sensed rather than saw me in the doorway, I should have remained an undetected observer for many minutes. Only by peering and squinting into the comparative glare of the entrance and hearing my voice did Charles know it was I. He immediately dropped his instructing with a surprised "Claude!" and wrung my hand with both of his. The novice was dismissed, a young bellows-squeezer was directed to fetch a bottle of wine, and we drank and smoked while Charles pulled the past together into terse pithy plugs of important news. He had always had the faculty of plucking the important, the relevant, from a given situation and forming it up in tight round verbal balls. And in a few short minutes, there in the early gathering gloom of an approaching storm, he related all that had happened since we parted at Johnson's.

He had ridden west to the Sacramento River intending to boat south to the fort and work, but while waiting for the launch, had fallen into conversation with the man Cordua, who was also going there in search of a majordomo for his settlement. Both had agreed there was no reason to continue, and their meeting had ended the searches of both.

Charles' station was at first that of laborer. He built, as did Cordua, corrals and outhouses, made implements and tools, and cooped barrels as needed. Then, as Cordua's enterprise became a trading post, more emigrants and Indians were employed. Covillaud's job gradually became more that of overseer, with Cordua frequently absenting himself to bring in the supplies landed at Yerba Buena or at the fort. It was during these periods when Charles was on his own, that he realized the potentially strategic importance of Cordua's location. Here two large rivers came together at a juncture where there was little apparent flood danger, where there were long stretches of fertile bottom land, and where navigation made the area accessible to trade. It was a place so similar to that of Sutter's that its merits were startling.

In Cordua's absences, as was the case this morning, Charles was not only free to train Indians to take over many of his own duties, but he was able to inventory the land and its possibilities. He became, at these times, as he put it, another Sutter, and determined to own as well as oversee.

This was the Covillaud I had known: the irrepressible entrepeneur. That he should, in the course of events, become something other than the tool of another was inevitable. There was in him a pull that surged, where the urges of others were lacking. There was a thing about him that permitted vision, where others saw only an immediate chance for gain. And long after our hearty beef dinner with peas and squash and prime brandy, I lay awake in Cordua's fine thong bed and wondered why I had left Sicard's incomparable company and the rich land of the Bear.

Upon awakening to the sounds of Charles' breakfast making, I lay thinking. I was experiencing an accelerated pulse. I was infected by a new and potent virus, a vision, a desire. Secretly, I had known I would not be returning to Captain Sutter's. I knew now that I wanted what every true Frenchman has always wanted, that for which every pioneer searched, whether he knew it or not: his land; his inviolable acreage.

My earlier desires to simply travel and inspect became replaced with an urge to create lasting marks upon the land, not merely for their intrinsic value, but for the joy of turning the wild into form; the haphazard into the productive; the barren into growth and strength. I became infected with a deep need to carve my mark upon the land and to grow, prosper, and build. I felt I had shed an old, outworn Claude, had arrived, however tardily, at a changed station; that my earlier values – if they were indeed values – had been replaced by a matured perspective that would guide my thinking from now on. I would board the return boat to the Bear and never again enter into the tedium of daily work that netted me no lasting satisfaction. I would leave the launch halfway, at Altgeier's ferry, and work with Sicard to make the Nemshas bloom. I had labored for another the better part of my life, and was determined now to be the benefactor of my labors. My thoughts even investigated the possibility of ownership of farm land and buildings and the employment of Indians. My fellow emigrants were doing it, why not I?

My reverie and a heady kind of new resolve were interrupted by a call from Charles to eat, and by the soothing aroma of coffee filling the cabin. A new peace had taken possession of me and I confided a detailed portion of my new plan to him, asking about the trainability and dependability of the Indians; which articles of trade were most attractive; how, and in which month to plant corn and wheat; what to pay for a starter herd of cattle and horses. The questions about an agrarian life, into which I felt myself deliciously slipping, came in a flood. And more than once I noted in Charles' eyes the keen penetration of a doctor. My pulse and temperature were up, and all evidences – including questions, which tumbled one upon the other – must have seemed to Charles the evidence of one caught in the grip of a tremendous emotional change. He enthused over my new desires, and the coffee was boiled and re-boiled as he supplied answers and pointed out the way he saw California must go.

Surely this was the end of migration. There would be no further movement west. Wagons and their families would mill about now, like the buffalo after a stampede, and settle, and there would be a market for everything – especially foodstuffs. And in a few years those who had the tillable land and cattle - which bred so profusely – would grow wealthy. Commercialism, in itself, held not the attraction for me that it held for my friend. But I confess to a feeling of high excitement when I though of the fallow back soil that lined the Bear and the rich choke of grasses and berries that grew thick with promise, of the mill and the powerful river running close to the land.

I stayed at Cordua's Rancho for three more days, observing the ways of Charles with his Indians and his management of men and acreage and store. A pioneer name Nye, who had married Harriet Murphy the same day her sister Mary had married Johnson, was living with his new wife on land upriver and was having trouble with his old squaw and their newest baby. During my stay he spent several hours lounging about the store, telling any who would listen, the merits of his new wife and about how unreasonable the squaw had become concerning Harriet. Years later I was to learn that Nye's wife had given birth to three children, but that, like the two he had had by his squaw, they had both died soon after birth.

Charles never seemed to mind the self-assured, swaggering bravado of this man. Indeed, the two frequently had long talks about the value of the Cordua property because of its location. I stayed away from Nye's for I was yet somewhat fearful of the temper and nervousness of one who scowled as he did, fiercely spitting his quid, erratically jerking around at any new sound, and scowling furtively through his beard as though looking at another for the cause of his stomach pains. I had never quite gotten over the fear acquired long ago at the New Orleans eye-gouging, and there was in the fierce stares of many that which reminded me of the cat, cornered and spitting. Even when I chanced to see my own fierce image in Cordua's mirror for the first time since St. Louis, I could never quite lose the fear I had of the unknown that lurked behind the full beard, and which hid the intent that I must know. Few shaved, and often, were it not the expressive eye, I could not tell if a man held murder, or jovial good humor in his heart. With the Indian, of course, it was different, and his usually child-like intent shone full from his brown, hairless face. It was for this reason that I early learned to like the California Indian – and they me.

I did not meet Cordua since he was in Yerba Buena all during my visit. I could gather, however, from Charles' guarded references, that now, after many months of close association with the German, there was something less that full trust and mutual admiration between them.

Charles fully approved of the new enthusiasm I showed for working the Nemshas, and intimated that he would like to acquire a part of the Cordua Rancho. He said little about farming, however, and much about its strategic location for commerce, its position at the juncture of rivers, its being at the head of Feather River navigation, and of its growing popularity because of the trails out of the Oregon Territory which crossed at this point. He drew parallels between the location of St. Louis, Cordua's, and Sutter's. And as he talked about markets and settlers and future land prices, my mind sped easily ahead of his words and built its own small kingdom of farm and mill and growing things.

We said goodbye at the small dock. I wished Charles well, and boarded the Linda, which, the evening before, had loaded barrels and hides and was bound for Yerba Buena. Few were aboard, and as I stood and watched Charles disappear around the river's turning, I felt again the thrill of my new commitment. The old question I had asked myself so long ago: "What do you want to do?" was resolved. I would have questions, but never again would I ask this one.

Odd how a particular need will generate in objects or property around one: If I have need of a tool I will notice closely another's tool; if I must purchase horse or saddle, I see only horses and saddles; if clothes are my need, only they receive my attention. So it was on my return trip down the Feather. I saw only the massive live and river oak and the sycamores that lined the river and which spoke, with their pastels and vivid greens, of the fruity promise in that rich black soil. The confining rains that had washed over the countryside for two days had ceased, and the new December grasses made beaches of color that sparkled and shone in the morning sunlight. Though I felt I could make bloom anyone of a hundred stretches of that incomparable shoreline, there was but one to which I felt drawn, one river's shoreline that held both promise and suitability, and to which I felt strongly attracted. That river, the Bear; that land, the Nemshas. I felt I knew it as I knew the matching countryside of Rouen. Indeed, it was the Rouen long before Joan d' Arc, before kings and castles, before roads brought coastal hordes inland to settle, when the Seinne was the giver of beauty and life, and not the recipient of the refuse of the upper valleys. I felt strongly drawn to the Nemshas, and I resisted not the pull that took me to the beautiful Bear.

Arnold F. Rothmeier

Chapter 36
Nemshas

The short boat ride was refreshing and uneventful, and I debarked at the boat's closest stop to Sicard's - a small settlement at the mouth of the Bear called Nicholas. Here an old German named Nicholas Altgeier inhabited a hut of willow logs and ferried wagons across the river. Here the clear-flowing, but smaller Bear met and swelled an already broad and deep Rio de las Plumas.

In exchange for a little fort gossip, Altgeier sheltered me for the night and in the morning offered me use of a spavined mule and some jerky – I declined the former, but accepted the latter, and with a pocketful of dry venison, set out for the Nemshas. By late afternoon I was opposite the ranch houses of, first Keyser, then Johnson. A few miles farther along, and from a slight rise, I caught sight of Sicard's farm and paused to drink in the sight of our kingdom.

Beneath me in the cool waning light of evening flowed the Bear. From Sicard's chimney rose a steady white smoke that spread its aromatic blanket over the cleared acreage. Beyond the house, far to the east, rose purple haze of the sierra, with its coat of white that would always moisten our valley. I had felt drawn, as a by magnet, as I rode the miles from Nicholas. I watched the river's slow flow and surprised many a band of deer in the willows, and now, again, I caught a vision of the immensity that was California.

Atop the rise I broke off the spell that held me. The shout I made as I descended was answered immediately by my friend's appearance at the door. We greeted in a rough slapping fashion and danced around a bit before I smelled his stew. I had arrived precisely at supper time.

As I raised the proffered bottle to my lips – the best California burgundy I had ever tasted – I saw that we were not alone. In the corner, on a bed, sat Sicard's squaw, immovable but for dark, darting eyes. As Sicard spoke, motioning for her to greet me, she moved from the low bed with something of the wild, controlled grace of a cat and came close to her man. Through gestures and a few words, my friend helped her to know who I was. There was the usual nodding by both of us and the terrible silent challenge of communication.

A small deal table was set with bowls of stew, and the three of us ate the first of many meals together. Sicard was elated over my return and full of the past years' happenings. I sat and drank in both his news and wine and found them both excellent. He told of the past years' bumper wheat crop, his success with its harvest with the help of the chief's tribesmen; he told of several trappers – countrymen, who had erected huts just upriver; of his suspicion that Mary had left Johnson, since he had not seen her there for many months; the salmon, which ranged far up the Bear were running good this year; corn had been excellent; the rafters were strung heavy with venison jerky; and smoked goose and goose livers abounded.

Then, after I, too, had related my adventures, and just as rosy dusk bathed the Nemshas in a soft glow, Sicard led me down the river path to where we had burried so carefully our peach and almound seeds. There, in neat rows were the strong, naked switches of our efforts, each tied securely to a stake and each an amazing inch thick at the base.

I marvelled that a tree – in any soil – could come from seed to this growth in so short a time, and as we returned to the adobe we talked of our plans for larger orchards, of the art of fruit-drying, and of the possibility of obtaining cuttings from old mission vineyards beyond the western mountains. And, in my now stimulated state, I farmed far into the night and tilled many acres of the promising black Bear loam, and grew wealthy, indolent, and envied at my friend's Rancho Nemshas.

There was no thought now of retuning to the fort, to work indoors – and for another – though I would still have to retrieve tools left at Sutter's. Weeks of winter rain were yet to be expected before any planting could be done. Meantime, however, with Indian help, we cleared more bushy acres. After a day of labor our helpers showed their keen, child-like anticipation of reward. Sicard not only allowed them to sleep in a corner of his small barn, but after the usual supper of hot meal laced with venison or beef, he also gave them small presents. One day it would be knives, another it would be pieces of bright cloth or beads.

Some days we would be joined by three other Frenchmen whom Sicard had allowed to squat and build along the river to the east. They had been trappers before coming west. Now with wild game – particularly the deer and elk that had come to the valley floor to escape the cold, they saw no reason to labor. They lived hedonistically, the few pelts they gathered, going for whiskey and rum. Each had a squaw and seemed to want for nothing.

Occasionally Sicard and I would hunt. We saw Johnson but once. He seemed to want to avoid us and the other Frenchmen. Then one day in early February, Sebastian Keyser told us he had bought out Johnson and that the latter had left for Yerba Buena and uncertain parts. We never knew where his two squaws went and we never saw them or him again.

Chapter 37
San Jose

By mid-February, and with the help of the Indians, we could see vast improvements in the Nemshas acreage. Weather had allowed us many days of work in soil just right for grubbing. And as we paused occasionally – for we both labored alongside our Indians – the long, flat stretches suddenly filled with wine grapes.

I pointed out to Sicard the more elevated sunnier slopes where grapes would grow best, and we planned large acreages of wheat and corn. The peaches were already flourishing. There were never any differences between us. I liked his plans and he liked mine. We inhabited the same house, but were never obligated to the other for continual company. His squaw came and went as she wished, but seemed always near his bed when he had need of her. It was as though the Nemshas had two owners. Indeed I felt it to be part mine and would have been lost without its wild security along the rushing Bear, its heavy black loam, its promise for the spring. As though this life would go on forever, we broadened our acreage, planned in wide plots for more varieties of fruit trees, and, at last, sowed the winter wheat – the first to be harvested.

Pan The Low Waters

I was anxious to begin planting a vineyard and to make an improved wine, since not much could be said for those tasted so far. For this I would need cuttings. Cordua, Charles had told me, had secured his from old mission grounds at San Jose, and that many varieties had been grown there.

One crisp morning in March, Sicard gave me directions to San Jose. I left, trailing two pack mules, and riding a brown mare – the one I believe, that had carried Mary Murphy into Johnson's the previous year. It had found its way into Sicard's remuda in a trade.

Except for a late coastal rain squall, the trip was uneventful. I headed directly south past the fort and entered the coastal mountains at a point where a settler named Livermore ranched. Then, bearing south, with Pacific waters on my right, arrived at San Jose. Here, besides a mission with its seeming miles of weedy, unkempt vineyards and unpruned orchards, the town consisted of a few stores, a saloon next to the Webbers Hotel, and assorted shacks and corrals lining a wide, muddy street.

It was a bone-chilling morning, and I had been riding since before sunup, so, before going to the vineyards, I stopped for a plate of beef and a bottle. I seated myself at a table, but had some difficulty in getting the proprietor's attention, for another customer, several tables removed, was reiterating loudly and drunkenly some jumbled statements about a substance he displayed as being "sure'nuf gold", and about everybody knowing it was being found along the American fork at a mill site. What little coinage there was in circulation at the time, was only "bit" pieces, and I could certainly see the owner's objection to accepting the man's supposed "gold" as payment. Presently, however, the bill was settled when those present paused to listen to the words of another with a broad accent, who asserted that the material was indeed gold.

The man was in his cups, and when he was alone and the others had dispersed, I approached him, for I was curious to find out if his mill site was the same as that which Sutter had had my friend Marshal build upon. The man – whom now I belatedly recognized – was none other than Charlie Bennet. I had seen him many times at the Fort. I knew him to be a good, steady worker, and though inclined to puff himself up and boast a bit of his powers, he could be relied upon to persevere at a task until its end. This had been my earlier judgement of Bennet. I did not ask or pry, but it was obvious he had been sent on an errand. Inside a leather pouch he kept slung over his shoulder, and from which he had taken his bagged samples, he seemed to nurse important documents given into his care.

I was allowed to inspect the peculiar, dull yellow pieces. Some were pea-sized and some were but thin, rice-like grains. All appeared smooth and worn, as though gentled by the action of water and sand. And, yes, the gold had come from near Marshall's nearly completed mill. Presently he dozed, with pouch pillowing his head.

Early the next day I moved through an unkempt wild waste of what had once been thriving mission vineyards, cutting switches from the straggling vines. By mid-afternoon I was able to tie together, in four bundles, hundreds of slips for our new vineyards. I had chosen to prune only those vines which were overgrown and which, despite lack of care, had thriven and bore evidence of strength. I had come just in time, for the leaf-buds were swelling, and my slips would need to be planted soon.

While I tied my bundles, and indeed, during most of the return trip, there went through my head an unsettling series of thoughts – not unsettling in the sense of being annoying – but in the sense of producing change. I was fully committed to a farming effort. I wanted nothing that would interrupt this – certainly nothing that suggested money for money's sake, for money-grubbing was not a part of my nature. And yet, possession of larger sums than I had, would help me establish what was already confusedly forming in my mind – a wish to secure title to a piece of the Nemshas, where I could work out mill plans, build and farm, and bottle my own wines. These thoughts were heady ones, and filled my mind all during the return trip. They did battle, too, with memory of what Bennet had shown me. I was in a lather to get back, to plant the vineyards that rode there on my two mules. After planting I would go to the place called Columah and see for myself the mine of which Bennet had spoken.

Arnold F. Rothmeier

Chapter 38
Mine Test

I arrived back, at the Bear River valley in a few days to find disturbing changes. Neither Sicard nor his squaw were at the ranch, and only with difficulty could I get from his best Indian worker, Noontka, the news that Sicard had gone to Sutter's Fort. He had left no message and had evidently left in haste.

I wasted little time in setting out the hundreds of grape slips. They had dried somewhat during the four day trip, but I was confident that most would grow. I did the planting myself, as I felt that I could not trust this most important step to the Indians. Only in the watering did I allow the most careful to assist. This two workers did with skin bags, the other with a bucket.

But as we worked, I was aware of a behavior subtly different in the several Indians. Those not working were not inclined to gather about in an inquisitive fashion, as I remembered. They hung together in groups, more secretly talkative than ever before; they gesticulated excitedly among themselves, making motions suggesting rewards of sugar, arm-bands, knives, and all the while laughing like children expecting presents.

Slipping my new vineyard was not an arduous task. By mid-afternoon I could look down dozens of rows one hundred feet long. They curved over and around a low fertile dome of earth and made a design shockingly new in this valley of irregularity. Oddly enough, they resembled some of the stippled tattooed areas on the faces and bodies of the savages. Noontka was the first to note the resemblance, pointing it out to the others as we stood looking at the finished work.

I fed the workers and afterward gave each a lump of sugar from the bagful I had bought in San Jose. Then I went inside to pack again for my trip to the American Fork. I felt good about the new vineyard. It would, of course, grow much faster than even the trees which had done so well. I had no notion of what I would find at Marshall's sawmill and mine, but I suppose I thought I might work with him, or perhaps even buy a small share in it, if by now it was not all worked out. Such were the thoughts of a neophyte miner that night.

In the morning, as I saddled up, I was surprised to note that of the six Indians who always seemed to stay with Sicard and me, only Noontka was in the lean-to next to the house, with my usual signs and a Spanish word or two hitched to a questioning tone, I asked about the others. Noontka's signs in reply involved presents, and were so vague and impatient that I left off trying to plumb their meaning. I did ask him, however, if he wanted to go with me. In a flash the blank, questioning face turned to one of smiles, and with a few lithe, spare movements he caught another horse, inserted horse-hair bit, and was mounted. No slightest concern for clothing or food, only simple glee over the prospect of movement —and with Claude Chana.

As we headed southeastward toward the foothills I thought: How vulnerable! Armed with only a thin, rusty knife at his waist, a pair of rent cotton pants for clothing, and a possibly misplaced faith in white men, whom he had come to both venerate and fear!

Arnold F. Rothmeier

We struck directly south, following roughly the many wagon and deer trails that led in that general direction. I wanted, specifically, to avoid the fort and Sutter, since I had intimated, upon leaving him, that I would be returning to work. So, when we approached his newly planted fliel004s and could see his white walls, I reined eastward along the American. Earlier, I had not realized how truly vast Sutter's holdings were. Now, riding through them, I was struck by the size of his herds and flocks and by the black flatness of his tilled fields. They stretched in curved plats along the river, an undulating body of pregnant land above the silver American. But this, I know was but a tithe of the domain that was his, for his boundaries pushed as far east as the greening low bulge of hills below the sierras.

I thought I would not like to have as vast a world as did Sutter; I would like only a one-man farm, one that awarded me the satisfaction of seeing a measured growth in height, quality, and color, one that created no feeling of envy in my neighbor, but one that gave back in provision and enjoyment as much as I had expended upon it. I would like to watch and contemplate the growth I had encouraged and sit and rest from a day's work, enjoying a vintage that I myself had grown and bottled.

It would be difficult to tell precisely when the notion of my own private ownership of a portion of the Nemshas struck my fancy. I must have had subconscious desires for such an eventuality ever since Sicard and I first walked along the Bear. Now, riding with Noontka, I found the notion had ripened, that it was no longer a hidden and unfelt urge, but had emerged to become an idea, strong and urgent, one capable of clear and strident articulation: "I must own a Nemshas, and if not this one, then another. It must be!"

Noontka and I forded river many miles above the fort and its cultivated fields. Here, in the flat of the valley, bordering oak and sycamore grew close together and were strung with a mat of wild grape so dense as to give the effect of a deep green canyon. Through it the

American flowed full and deep. But now, as we mounted into the foothills, rocky ravines and then true canyons replaced the green and a transition so gradual as to be almost unnoticed took place in the nature of the soil. It possessed now a rusty red appearance, and I had not noticed precisely when it had first become so.

When it had grown too dark to see the wagon trail we slid from our horses, tied them in an open space nearby, supped on jerky and biscuits and slept to the rocky, wet sound of a small waterfall. I seldom dream, but this time the dream had to do with fishing and was so real that when I awoke the dreamed-of odors were coming from a fire and pan. Noontka had awakened early, and with one of several hooks he always carried in his shirt, had caught two trout. His face begged for appreciation, and I showed him my thanks with "Bueno" and back-pats and gestures. And we squatted there and ate on the soft river sand and amid a smoke that was as perfume. He used no dish but his hands, but, for my convenience, he had knifed a large section of bark from one of the trees. I sensed in Noontka a need to serve someone, and I would not have discouraged it, for I, too, knew the need for a companion.

We mounted then and wound along ascending wagon and horse tracks into the hills, The ascent was so gradual one could not have told of the change in altitude had it not been for the light crescendo of gurgles coming from the river as it coursed over its rocky bed.

Around noon of our second day Noontka pointed to a smoke. After a few more bends of the river we came within sight of the mill – a tall, open, box-like structure astraddle a portion of the river apparently detoured to provide power of manageable size. Farther up the wooded canyon several shacks leaned into the hillside. We forded the river and reined out horses toward the largest hut where several men lounged and whittled. From the door came smell of venison, and, as I was hungry, the thought crossed my mind that I might be invited to share.

Arnold F. Rothmeier

Presently metal, suspended near the door, was struck by a slight, aproned woman. In answer to this dinner summons, the loungers and whittlers entered, and from up along the river a muffled and indistinct call or two sounded to summon others farther away. After several minutes of waiting to see if my friend Marshall would invite me to sup, I recognized his tall form coming from the direction of the mill. He was alone and in no hurry, and, as he approached he glanced at me, then looked away, giving no sign of recognition. I felt an acute shun, for I had had high hopes of a flavorsome meal and perhaps a tour of the mill and a telling of the mine's prospects. In all of these I was disappointed, and I sat with Noontka on a boulder near the river and shared my jerky and parched corn.

As we ate I reflected on Marshall's lack of hospitality, for he had been outgoing with me at Sutter's. My thinking was interrupted once by the approach of a young man heading for the kitchen. He was happily whistling and had a purposeful stride. I put the question to him, "Is there any gold around here?" His answer was immediate and direct, "Oh yes. It's all along the river. Anywhere you dig you'll find some." Then, taking from his pocket several flat yellow pieces about the size of a cucumber seed, "I found these this morning. Most of the men are out looking now. Alls you need is a knife to pry it out."

"Well", I asked, still puzzled, "did you get the mill working?" Then, as though this were an irrelevant question, "Oh yes, they sawed a few boards, but then there was some rain up in the mountains and the millrace was flooded and that stopped it. And they're out looking now." He seemed to have nothing more to say and to be anxious to reach camp. I thanked him. He continued on, whistling his sprightly tune.

It was yet blustery March weather, and though I could see there was no great excitement here concerning gold, I felt I must search and dig for myself. Down along the rocky river bed we peered. I hardly knew the appearance of the substance I sought, having only twice seen the dull gleam of virgin gold. Besides this, I could not know where, other than in the general area, to search. Since I was ignorant of the whole matter – in addition to feeling disgruntled at having come so far for nothing – I was even disinclined to explain my search to Noontak. He followed me, haltingly at first, then, when he gave up trying to determine what I was doing, he cut a willow stalk and began to fish.

I removed my boots and waded along the river's edge, peering through the ruffled surface for a hint of the yellow. My first discovery was a speck no larger than a grain of Sicard's wheat. I pried it easily from a crack across the rocky bottom. A few others were likewise lodged, but came to my hand only with much prying. Then, a too-great pry-pressure broke the tip of my knife. I called to Noontka, showed him several grains and motioned toward the rocks. He too, found some flakes during the hour we searched, and brought them to me with the air of one who suspects another's sanity. By late afternoon, to show for two day's travel, several hours of hunched wading, we had, perhaps, half a thimble-full of metal. Long before I looked up and noted the presence of another miner downstream, I had decided that Columah contained no great riches. We mounted and rode toward the man. Presently he saw us, but then looked away as though to pretend he had not, and suddenly left the small cove in which he had been so intently working.

I had seen enough of the inhospitable Columah and signaled to Noontka we would ride homeward. It was nearly dusk, but we could cover a few miles before sunset closed the trail. I was cold, tired and disgusted with myself for having been gulled by false thoughts of riches. A kind of need to expiate my sin of secret greed kept me in the saddle until we could no longer see the trail. I had been unaccustomed to the bent position of prying for gold and the movement of my horse massaged and soothed away the aches. At dark we tethered horses, and after eating a bite of jerky, rolled into our blankets without bothering to make a fire.

Arnold F. Rothmeier

For the second time I awoke to the exquisite odor of fresh-cooked fish and ate my fill and basked in the warmth of Noontka's fine fire. I saw that what he did was not an act of servility, but a natural act of one who needed another, and I felt at that moment the same need.

Noontka was, from that morning on, and for many years, a kind of partner to me, a sharer in my endeavors, a recruiter, and an interpreter. There was never a feeling that he was my "garcon" or servant. Indeed, sometimes for weeks, in the months that followed our trip to Columah, he would absent himself from the farm. But when he was there, or with me in the hills, life was easier because of his knack of anticipating fire to be made, garment to be mended, or tool necessary for the moment.

As before, we followed the American's north bank through the foothills, this time to the fort. I was not anxious to see Sutter again, but felt that I should retrieve my tools, now that I was in the vicinity.

Sutter was in his office with another man when we arrived, but hailed me from his open door as I strode toward the cooperage. Since he was engaged I did no more than pass the time of day with him. He mentioned no lack of workers in the area of my employment, but I noted that he had about him an odd and uncharacteristic aura of distraction. This, at the time, I attributed to an engrossment with his visitor. It took but a few moments to sack my tools and to load them onto the extra pack animal. (None of the persons with whom Marshall and I had worked were there.) Then, perceiving the lateness of the day, I made known to Noontka we would camp outside the fort walls. We witnessed the usual evening pomp and the firing of the matin cannon. Noontka went to quiet the animals which were greatly startled by the boom. Then we slept until re-awakened by a repetition of the sound.

After an early start, and sometime around mid-afternoon of a cloud-shaded day, we came within sight of the serpentine of green trees that marked the flow of the Bear. We had emerged from a thick tangle of

Pan The Low Waters

vines and tall oaks on a flat rise. The valley floor stood out, sharply revealed in a pastoral detail I had not seen before. Far ahead the Buttes showed beneath high gossamer clouds. They seemed to grow from a pale gauze of vapor that obscured their detail. Far to the left I could see cattle – Johnson's, or perhaps Keyser's – as I had heard that Johnson had sold his western half. In an imaginary corral formed by steers nibbling at the periphery of a meadow, several young deer ducked and leaped in an idiotic show of wasted energy.

The sun, at this moment, threw a slanting wedge of gold light across the valley and my Nemshas. It was a soft but blinding sword. It pointed from a cleft space between dirty walls of dark purple clouds directly at the grove of tall oak beyond which I knew lay the Nemshas. I was entranced. I felt at the moment a kind of surrender as though there, everything awaited me. It was a moment in which I seemed to see the end of my searching. The feeling was akin to that which I had had when I returned to my parent's home after a day's work at Rouen. The strange, natural display, coming as kind of heaven-sent promise, contrasted with the disappointment and chagrin I yet felt over my useless trip. But now I knew my direction, and the feeling was good. With Sicard and his abundant Indian help, I was sure the rich overflow land would bring fine harvests. The Nemshas continued for miles to the west and east along the Bear. Perhaps Sicard would even sell a part of his large acreage to me.

The wall of dark clouds had moved closer as I sat thinking. In the distance a light veil of virga softly raked the Buttes and the valley to the south. But I had faced north and was not seeing the whole sky. Suddenly my reverie was dampened by a large drop of rain on my ear. Noontka, too, saw then the full, dark clouds behind us, and we made for the cabin as fast as the pack animals could travel.

Sicard had returned, stood dry and warm in the doorway while Noontka and I peeled pack and gear from the animals, slapped them into the corral, flung canvas over the saddles, and raced for the door

just as clouds shaded the landscape and poured down their chill drench.
   It was good to be back and to converse again with my wandering countryman. For more than half the night we ate, smoked, and drank. Sicard was in high spirits. He had much to tell me about the way he had observed others making money on lot resales. His Linda property and his lots at Nye's landing, he calculated, had doubled in value. He had also been to Yerba Buena. He took little stock in rumors of gold on the American, and we said little about it but fell to making Plans for a larger vineyard, orchard, barley and wheat fileds. Together we would make the land bloom; we would, with our vineyards, make a fine, full-bodied wine, one that would lay to rest the word that all California wines were bad. In the soft glow of the fire and the inner glow of a brandy-washed venison dinner I listened to Sicard spin out the thread of his pilgrimage to the coast, and studied a newness that had come over him. Though there was between us a firm resolve and desire to farm and to reap the fallow riches along the Bear. I was struck, unpleasantly, by a new and discordant note of fiscal hysteria in his voice. Sounds of money-making monopolized his conversation in tone, if not in content, and I could not help feeling that a kind of eager grasp for money now possessed him. He sped on, verbally, over the possibilities of money-making in burgeoning communities, and before I fell asleep in my chair, I recalled his sleepy and maudlin monologue in which he confessed to an inordinate desire to captain his own sailing ship. The abundance of liquor had made me relaxed and sleepy; in Sicard they had dredged up hidden desires. I know not how far his midnight voyage took him, but he left me there on the fecund, fragrant plains of the Bear.

   We slept late, and again there was the luxury of being awakened by the dark, narcotic aroma of boiling coffee. Only Noontka's furtive, pleased eyes and his perpetual business about the cabin belied the fact that he sensed our approval of his efforts. Sicard was amazed at my good fortune in blundering onto a man servant as efficient, quiet and faithful – and as free of vermin as Noontka was.

Chapter 39
Agriculture

Sicard had only yesterday returned to the Nemshas, and was as anxious as I for a look at our modest orchard and vineyard. But as the three of us trod the now overgrown path toward the river, I reflected on the change that had come over my friend. In addition to his more crass attitude toward money, it seemed he had also affected a kind of swashbuckling yanquiness to better meet the Kentuckian and Missourian businessmen on their own grounds. He radiated a growing business acumen. I knew he had been a sawyer in the coastal redwoods and had whipsawn timber for Sutter's mansion at Hock, but his emerging, speculative nature was, somehow darkly disappointing to me.

Neither of us were prepared for the sight that greeted us along the overflow plain. The incipient vineyard of slips that I had packed from the mission now trembled low in the morning breeze, transformed into cushiony pink and green rows full of promise. These, the more colorful and showy growth caught our eye first. Beneath the leaves of some of the larger plants the first preposterously ambitious and fragile clusters of tiny grapes showed, as though ridiculously anxious to repay the trouble of their planting. Downstream lay the new rows of an orchard that had grown so fast that pink blossoms showed on the two-year-old trees. Barring a severe frost or hail this bouquet would become fruit of the first orchards, save those at Hock Farm, to fill the valley.

It was a fine beginning, but to preserve our tiny start, which was already being nibbled at by deer, we would have to fence the acreage. Sicard had already observed various barriers on the coast, at Hock and in the northern part of the valley – rock walls, willow palings, ditches. Of these, the only practical fence for our use was the latter. I rode to the crossing, where I was able to borrow a few shovels and pieces of flat iron that would serve, and for three days the slow process of ditching continued. Sicard and I worked shoulder to shoulder with a score of sweating natives. Only the chief, who knew Sicard would pay well in flour, cloth and knives for his Indians, sat watching as the ditch, five feet wide and four deep, slowly encircled the small orchard.

Toward the end of the third day we had completed the three-sided fence – all but a short gap near the river. Since it was late, we would complete it in the morning. We built fires along the river, slaughtered a steer and gave our helpers their slab of red beef to prepare as they saw fit.

It was now early May, I thought, as I knelt there on a slick flap of cowhide, carving from the hams of soft flesh. Nine years ago I had listened to a sailor at Rouen; I had wrestled with an audacious plan and won. Two years ago, almost to the day, I had listened one evening to a trapper, and before a week was up, Charles and I had sold a business, bought an outfit and had launched ourselves far beyond the protection of civilization on a long dry road to California—.

The deep brown eyes of a native looked up at me, sharply, inquiringly. I must have paused in my cutting as I went on in thought. He was slavering and understandably impatient. I handed him his generous portion and then sliced for him a fist-sized section of the liver which I had reserved and would share with Sicard. When the last of the helpers had been served, I propped my own steak and liver against a rock and watched it slowly tan.

Chapter 40
The Gold Bite

This was the soft, appealingly beautiful hour of the day. My own labor had not been excessive—just enough to make me appreciate rest and the ravishing odor of a hundred pounds of fine meat bubbling and frying, and the slobbering grunts of enjoyment coming from a score of savages.

The liver, which I had sliced thin, was the first to be done to my satisfaction. I salted it from a small can which I always carried and motioned to Sicard that his portion was done. Then, placing my hot piece on a handful of willow leaves, I propped my back against a tree and ate, savoring the odor of bruised willow almost as much as the meat.

It was a moment in which unusually piquant sensations of the eye, nose, and tongue blended with a feeling of accomplishment and promise. There had been evenings such as this on the California trail, but they had had about them always an aura of movement and uncertainty. Not only was there here an intense gratification of the senses at the moment, but before me stretched a roseate future for the Nemshas.

Pan The Low Waters

With completion of the ditch fence, with vineyards, barley, and wheat fields sown, now was the time for planning the mill, extending vineyard acreage, and arranging for wine-making.

I ate my liver portion and rose to turn the thick steak I had placed on the rock for slow cooking. It had turned a golden brown and its underside floated in a lake of savory, clotted gravy. My back was toward most of the company of feasters. Twilight had made the heavens a soft, heavy blue. A "Ca va, mon ami" reached my ears from the trail that led to the cabin, and three booted, bearded, and buckskinned figures strode into the firelight.

"The meat! She we could smell halfway to Nye's Landing," the taller of the tree exclaimed, looking around. "Looks like you're feeding the whole tribe."

"We are," said Sicard, "and yours too. These are helping Indians. We'll be all through fence digging tomorrow. It's for the deer. Plenty of beef here for all three of you. Have some."

Bottles appeared from one of the new arrival's packs and a general introduction made the rounds through all hands, and to the chief as well.

The tall Frenchman was Pierre. He looked at home, and was, for he had hunted the area many years ago, knew it as he did his own gun and traps, and now had returned to California southward through the Oregon territory bringing two other trappers, Courteau and Eugene.

The three looked hungry, I divided my thick, already-cooked slab among the three, then stoked the fire and cut more meat while we ate and talked.

Of the three, only Pierre found his words more important than the tasty rare meat he held. Speaking slowly, but with deep emphasis, he expressed surprise at hearing of anyone digging a fence when there were diggings so much more profitable along the American! Nor was he dissuaded from his opinions when he heard of my recent trip to Columah. Stepping into the gathering shadows beyond the fires, he unwound from his saddle horn a small, snake-like pouch, and, hefting it, carelessly tossed it at my feet.

"This we pried out of the rocks up above Sutter's mill. They're scrambling all over the canyon up there now. Not many are talking about their findings, but here's real rush on to find where it's coming from."

He untied a thong at the end of the snake and urged a few slick, shiny nuggets into his palm. His eyes shone moistly. A palpable silence was eloquent on all lips. Noontka crept close to see, having finished his meat.

"They don't tell what they know up there at the mill, not yet, anyhow, but up at Nye's landing the levee is all a-buzz over seeing this stuff, and they're riding down or taking the boat to see for themselves."

He went on about how Marshall and Sutter had tried to keep their find quiet so they could get the mill finished, but how the news had spread anyway, and the mill workers had just quit and gone gold-digging.

I thought, here are Sicard and Claude, who had debunked the discovery without bothering to thoroughly investigate; here am I, who saw the site, but had not bothered to make a good search; and then here are three countrymen who believed, and had a modest fortune to show for it.

The sight and feel of Pierre's gold transformed me, I was profoundly unsettled by thoughts of the wealth and the power that sprang from the sight of so much gold. The low drone of Pierre's voice became the easel on which my mind painted pictures of a farm and mill and fine buildings – and a woman, lavishly kept. The tantalizing sheen of the yellow pebbles, their surfaces, though hard and large as marbles, possessed a seductive softness unlike any substance I had ever seen, and there was about them that which tantalized, lured my mind with vivid promises.

The golden pebbles were at last dropped into their leather sheath, and all crept to the shelter of his own bed. As I lay long awake, the wild speculations of my vivid imaginings drowning the snores of the others, I knew that I had been transformed, that I was Possessed of half-formed and vague urgings, and that a demon of change was overpowering me. In touching the seductive golden surfaces I had unwittingly acquired the symptoms of a delicious fever – not of illness, but of turbulent health, of feverish enterprise, and a new drive.

In the morning, although I had intermittently dreamed grandiose dreams, and though I had twisted and turned interminably, I awoke refreshed and rested long before the others. The soft spell of gold returned, and I recalled with chagrin the reticence and secretiveness of James Marshall and the others at the mill. I had been gulled by their silence and apparent unconcern, and as I lay there, sensations of regret and avarice played over me.

Presently Noontka rose from his far corner and made flint fire, blowing the spark until his nest of cupped grass flamed. I watched him pad silently between the others, and I thought of the fine, long ditch, and of the many hours the Indians had worked it it, without questioning, for few pounds of bloody beef. There was an instant of revelations between the picture of Indians shoveling sand, and one in which I saw the searching out and plucking the nuggets and flakes from the river rocks. And, in my mind's eyes I saw them happily surrendering this yellow weight to me for sugar, scarves or a handful of beads.

Arnold F. Rothmeier

Over breakfast of meat and coffee I tried out my Indian idea on Pierre, and we determined to take as many natives as would go, and search the streams near Columah.

There were four of us Frenchmen and twenty-five Indian helpers – all mounted : Francoise Pierre, Filibert Courteau, and a younger fellow named Eugene when we left Nemshas that sunny morning. Sicard himself had pressing business at the landing and would not be going along. We were a happy band, and, as we strung along, one would begin a song we all had sung in the old country. Then, after its juices had become cold, another would be started. My favorite was "La Bergere". It had many verses, and if one found lyrics unfamiliar, another supplied them. The rhythm seemed to match the horses' hoof-plops, and we covered many miles singing:

>   Ils Ete une Bergere
>   Et ron ron ron, petite pat a pon
>   Ils ete une bergere
>   Qui garde ses mouton ron ron
>   Qui garde ses mouton
>
>   Ils faite une fromage
>   Et ron ron ron, petite pat a pon
>   Ils faite une fromage
>   Du lait de ses mouton ron ron
>   Du lait de ses mouton.

Though to this day the mystery of "sheep-milking" puzzles me!

Then, too, we sang "La Marseillaise", and I was surprised to note how our national anthem could be sung at the same time as "Bergere", and how it seemed to fit with the anthem as a kind of harmony.

On my previous trip with Noontka we had not known the country and had blundered about before finding the mill. Pierre, now our nominal guide and who had been trapping in the west since '32, led us toward

Columah in a more direct route. His path was always south east, and often over hills which I would have gone around.

When by a hot mid-afternoon we stopped to camp along a stream shaded by cottonwoods and near a huge deadfall, I selected a tree close to camp, felled it, and set about chopping and carving several sections into crude, pan-like bateaus. They were cumbersome things, but had shallow hollows much like those I had seen at Columah. When I had finished there was one for each of us, and while Corteau pulled at a bottle and Eugene scouted for evening venison and firewood, I took my batea to the stream to see how I would manage the art of mining. Selecting a spot several feet above the water line, I filled my "pan" with clean, loose sand and gravel, and began the washing.

At Johnson's I had heard how it was done, how the pan was filled, dipped, shaken and swirled until the lighter pebbles and sand floated over the lip, and I was determined to learn to do the operation just as I had been told.

As I swirled and removed the heavier rocks, my eyes seemed to play tricks on me. Several times I imagined I detected a bright gleam; then it would disappear beneath a sand finer and blacker than that on top.

Some moments passed, and just as I was about to discard the half-panfull as a waste of time, I detected a large, yellow gleam; then another. These were sizable nuggets, and I removed them with my fingers, for they were almost the size of Chouteau's almonds.

I swirled more then, and slower, lest any remaining treasure be lost. When my pan was nearly empty and I had twice almost lost my remaining sand and gold- for my hands shook uncontrollably with excitement – I had, in the bottom, two more pea-sized nuggets and many fine flakes of gold beneath a thin layer of dark sand. In all I had four shiny, smooth, and amazingly heavy gold pieces.

Arnold F. Rothmeier

The trembling urgency of my voice must have alarmed Pierre and Courteau, for my cries of "Vite! Vite!", brought them to my side within seconds. There, in the gathering dusk of the ravine, we took turns fingering the four glossy, yellow pieces, one after the other until it seemed they would wear thin from handling. And we plucked from the black sand so many of the smaller flakes that it seemed their combined weight was almost that of the "almond" which had first winked at me.

When at length the sun set and we could no longer see the pans in our hands, we gathered around the fire and inspected the combined results of our first day's mining. Pierre had been the most successful. In addition to much fine gold, he displayed a nuget almost twice the size of my almond. Courteau had worked closer to the water and was able to pull from his pocket a small handful of shining flat pieces. My luck had been the first, but I was able to show only one more "almond" and about half the fine gold that Pierre had gathered.

Eugene had been hunting and showed his success by pointing to the fine deer which Noontka had helped bring in and skin. Then we and the Indians feasted the feast of rich men – or so we thought ourselves to be. And we drank most of the wine we carried, and built castles in air, for it was said that gold was worth thirteen dollars an ounce and, all told, we had mined at least fifteen ounces.

Now there was no question as to what we would do. We had chanced upon a rich find and it was agreed we would not continue toward the mill, but work this stream and its banks as long as they produced and as long as our secret could be kept. For two more days our luck held, and several of the Indians were put to work mining with us, or given the tasks of contriving gold sacks out of deer hide. Nootka made several stiff but serviceable "pokes" by peeling hide from each of the slain deer legs and turning them inside out. They dried hard and stiff, but were sturdy sacks for our purpose, Some helpers created other clever containers. One killed an owl, and into the larger, hollow wing quills, poured much of the finer spangle gold.

At the end of ten days our supplies of knives, beads, red handkerchiefs, and salt and sugar were running low. Without these even Noontka had great difficulty in keeping our large band of helpers in check and bringing in their fine gold.

One day, while our luck and supplies of Indian gee-gaws still holding, Noontka approached me and, with pointing, signs, and a few Spanish words, made it known that several of the Indian helpers had left during the night – just vanished. They had been seen talking to one another and had lately shown dissatisfaction with the necessarily picayune labor and our apparently dwindling supply of rewards.

Then, a day or two later, we were all surprised by a visit from the man named Sinclair. He had farmed a small acreage on the Bear about as far down river as Sicard's rancho was upriver. His air was secretive behind a heavy mask of beard, but very inquisitive, and though we, too, had learned to be chary of the mining information we gave, he seemed to divine something of our success, for he was soon seen mining down on the American with at least two of my former helpers. He had tried to talk us into combining our parties and working the area more thoroughly. But we had declined, for there was something about the man we did not like. Although he might have helped our situation with his store of trinkets, we were unanimous in our decision to refuse his offer.

At the end of perhaps two weeks we reckoned our deadfall mine had petered out to a point where gold was hard to find. And there were other searching parties now. Some were lone prospectors, their pans and picks protruding from pack animals; some were in pairs; and there was one well-equipped band of evil-looking men who settled down to mine above us and muddied the stream and were seen to spit and curse and use words like "Frenchies" and "Keskydies" when they looked our way.

They were three reasons for our determination to move: It was getting crowded with miners who obviously hated foreigners; our supplies – both of gee-gaws and wines were low; and our mine had apparently petered out.

But had I known then what I was later to hear – that the bank where I had first found my "almond", a hoard of gold, almost beyond belief, lay waiting – not all the horsepower tethered in that cottonwood grove could have pulled me from the ravine. We learned, only a week or so after we had settled on the Yuba, that others at our deadfall had panned fortunes amounting to well over one thousand dollars a day.

We were far from being discouraged, however. Our take, amounting to a little over three hundred dollars apiece, was far from paltry. Gold now flowed in our blood, was part of us, infected us. It was money, and money was not only power, but influence and a hundred items of ambition and comfort and security. In a word, we were bitten.

On our return to Nemshas (Sicard was yet away) there was a general noting of the necessary items: salt, sugar, suitable pans, gee-gaws, powder, lead, containers for our treasure, wine and tools. All these we found at Sicard's and Johnson's, though we saw that prices had increased at an alarming rate.

The mining band that set out again several days later, was not only well-equipped; it was tighter, more experienced. Eugene had left us at the deadfall, as had several of my Indians. At Johnson's, news of rich new diggins on the Yuba, to the north, had given us hope. We were buoyant with confidence. We had found it once; we would find it again. We know we would. Rumors of the riches to be dug were now almost beyond belief, but given half their plausibility, the mother lode – as it was coming to be called – and its gold was sufficient to spur us on. It was like a piece of ripe fruit, only asking to be picked and eaten.

Pan The Low Waters

The country was no longer a place foreign, mysterious, and formidable, but cordial, beckoning, welcoming. Prospectors could be seen wading and shoveling and panning at almost every stream we passed, and we often waved and shouted a greeting to them as we rode by.

By noon we were in the tan foothills, and by nightfall we had drawn north along their western slopes and pushed northeast to where Pierre knew the Yuba debouched into its slower glide by Cordua's and Nye's ranchos. By evening we had ridden perhaps thirty miles and had established camp on a bank above a long bar just below towering, gate-like walls, beyond which the Yuba became tame and wide.

In the morning not only were we alone on a wide stretch of sandy bar – except for a man named Inman, camped alone on the north bank opposite our camp. But after a breakfast of slapjacks provided by Courteau, I was able to raise a few colors in my first pan.

The contents of this pan were not dug, as my first at the deadfall had been, from sand on the surface, but from material a foot or so deep. For I had reasoned that gold, being the heaviest of river-bourne substances, must lie lower, undisturbed, perhaps. Even when the Yuba was raging.

I was careful not to divulge my finding – nor my reasoning – to Inman, when he visited our camp that evening. I had also cautioned Pierre and Courteau to do likewise. But the four of us sat at our fire until late, exchanging news of California and the state of the new emigration.

Inman was a husky young fellow with a decided limp. It transpired that he was a German of peasant stock from lower Saxony, and after spending a year – just as I had done – at Sutter's, had lost his wife to small pox. After helping Marshall at his mill, he had taken to wandering and prospecting from place to place. He was quite open and confiding about his luck here on the Yuba. He had been moderately successful at first, but for the past two weeks had seen little or no gold in his pan. Lately he had mined less than half an ounce per day and informed us that in the morning he was moving on – probably toward the south around old Columah.

When Inman was gone the three of us went to inspect his diggings on the off-chance that we might learn the cause of his failure. Here on the north side of the river, where the Yuba, emerging from the rocky walls makes a decided turn from northeast to west, he had dug in six or eight places on the long bar, penetrating, perhaps a foot or eighteen inches in each. Courteau said this was good reasoning, for at the inside of the bar there was always less current and less inclination for heavier material – rocks and gold – to be pulled along by the current; that gold must settle where Inman had dug – providing, of course, the area did indeed contain gold.

The decision was made, following Courteau's reasoning, to extend the depth of several of Inman's holes, so in the morning, after another of Courteau's slapjack breakfasts, our second mine was begun. It was a new kind of material through which we now dug, a mixture if fist-sized ovoid rocks and coarse, heavy gravel, and for several hours we sweated over the dense, dark mixture, throwing rocks about and working pan after pan until our backs and legs ached mightily.

Then, simultaneously, both Pierre and I shouted to each other the news from where we crouched and swirled. Bottoms of both our pans shone bright and yellow. Colors and larger pieces lay inert and heavy as we swirled the dark sand around them. And both of us knew we held in our hands promise of our golconda.

And we danced and clapped each other's shoulders and sang snatches of La Marseillaise, and we were indeed – for a few minutes at least – temporarily demented, for luck had dammed the tide of fortune for so long. Now the dam was breached and the flow of what had been dammed flowed sweet and golden through our imaginings.

Courteau came immediately, swished both our pans, and hastily dug a shoveful from my deep hole. The combined weight of gold in our now three pans totaled easily four or five ounces. Nor was this all of the day's take. By evening we had filled a deer-leg poke with almost half a pound of fines and nuggets.

Early the next morning, after a short breakfast – which we scarcely touched – we were at the mine again. A plan had emerged before we slept: The whole bar must be worked systematically, now that a gold-bearing layer had been found. The Indians must be shown how to help – and be rewarded according to the size of the pile of rock each carried out and stacked.

Therefore, we did not now continue to mine in the area of Inman's original holes, but commenced some distance toward the west end of the long bar, throwing our tailings downstream and letting the current float away much of the accompanying muck. Even here at the bar's tail, good, fine color showed at the same depth as our first find and, as the days passed, and as we slowly worked upstream, almost imperceptibly the panned color grew larger.

By the end of the second week we had done a thorough job of erasing the lower part of our bar. And in the evenings we would sit around a bright campfire and heft and admire full pokes before burying them again in the sand beside the large boulder we used as a backdrop for our fire.

As we approached the area of Inman's holes, cleared ahead of surface rocks by the Indians, many of our pans contained an unusual richness – often, but not always – small nuggets of strange and fantastic shapes – of faces or trees or ghouls. Occasionally a nugget emerged in a matrix of fine quartz, as though recently broken from a ledge and not subjected to the long, tumbling action of water and rock.

Arnold F. Rothmeier

In the richest portion of the bar, which was just upriver from Inman's holes, the going was slower, for surface rocks were much larger and more difficult for the Indians to remove. Pans here were so rich with their heavy gold that all began working with half-filled pans.

By early November we had been at our task for nearly a month. The bar, now a low area ringed by many piles of stones erected by our Indians, showed low in the Yuba current. This, when we arrived, had been split by our work. It now flowed straight and unobstructed.

Several parties of miners had paused, tested river banks, and moved on. We had kept our council, shown little or no color to them, and they had moved on in search of their own mines.

But nights were now becoming cool. We knew that the wet season was not far off, that soon, before it rained, or snowed, we must finish with our rich bar and leave the hills. As if to hasten our decision, one evening, just as we quit, an early storm with thunder and lightening, soaked us. It was not a long rain, but it brought to a head the decision to move quickly.

On the seventeenth of November, 1849, we unearthed pokes and jars for the last time, weighed them on the crude scales purchased at Johnson's, and divided their contents into three portions. Then we passed out the liberal trinkets and sugar rewards to our Indians, slept, and departed for Sicard's. Although Pierre and Courteau had determined upon a visit to Yerba Buena, there to spend some of their gold, we remained together for security reasons until nearing Sicard's.

I had in my saddle bags – as did Pierre and Courteau, something in excess of seventy pounds of gold. Our journey out of the hills was made slowly and carefully, for it was now as though each of the horses carried two riders. We avoided other parties, often making wide detours at their approach. Though we had not calculated exact figures, we know that each carried gold worth in excess of twenty thousand dollars. How often I congratulated myself that I had had the good fortune to join with honest countrymen!

As we rode, my mind turned to vistas opened to me by the heavy weight I carried. I had mined and been successful; had truly had a surfeit of gold digging. Let others do their digging, for I had had enough of it. In the long days while bent over my pan, many of the events of the past year recalled themselves – scenes like those at Johnson's of the pitiful remnants of the Donner Party; the feelings of the rejection I felt upon hearing the words "Frenchies" and "Keskydies" at the deadfalll; the happier feelings at the thought of the peach trees now flourishing; the vineyard now overgrown and in need of pruning; the overshot wheel that would do my grinding.

And now from these musings my mind leaped to another and grander thought: Could it be that Sicard, now engrossed in land-speculation around Nye's landing and Cordua;s, might sell part of his vast Nemshas? Neither he nor I had ever seen his boundaries. But he had once said, "Why worry about where my land ends? From the river south and east it lies out there for miles, and it strings along the river for just as far. And Johnson and Keyser own a grant just as many miles wide and long on the other side of the Bear. So why worry about where the land ends? There's plenty for all."

With these thoughts – and principally the latter one – we arrived at the point on the Bear from which we could just make out the Nemshas adobe across the river. Here we three said our au revoirs and parted. We were never to meet again, but in the fruitful years that followed I was to think often and fondly of them and their comradeship; of their honesty and nonabrasive diligence.

Arnold F. Rothmeier

Chapter 41
Nemshas Purchase

This time Sicard was at this adobe to greet me, and over our wine we unraveled the threads of both our stories since the vineyard and tree planting that seemed, strangely, so long ago. My story, and the showing of my saddlebags were an amazement to him, and he examined the gold intently and long. But he, too, had a fine story to tell: he had bought cheaply of the land at both Nye's landing and near Cordua's, and had sold small portions at an enviable profit. While I had been mining for gold, he had been mining the pockets of those looking for suitable lots, and had been nearly as successful as I, buying cheaply large riverfront tracts, dividing, and selling dearly.

Now, from Sicard, I got the idea, hard to visualize at first, that Johnson's Rancho was, very roughly, the shape of a boot, with the Bear comprising an irregular sole, and with the Crossing lying at an irregularity which represented the forward part of the heel. From the point, Johnson's property line ran for many leagues southwesterly toward the boot's square toe, and for approximately as many leagues northeasterly in the heel section. It was across the Bear, and south of the heel section, that Sicard's Nemshas stretched as far south as the eye could see, and as far to the east as the tawny foothills of the sierra.

When we had both finished the narratives of our adventures and were mellow with good brandy, I put my proposition to him: Would he sell to me his Nemshas – or a portion of it?

It seems that he, too, had been thinking of ridding himself of some of his holdings, for his financial ventures closer to the centers along the Feather and Yuba were proving profitable – indeed so much so that he should not be absent from his business for long. So, toward the tail of the evening we arrived congenially at a price – one which would afford me with considerable finanacial leeway to begin the new ventures I had long thought on: a house; an overshot wheel for power; a flour mill; a winery, and one or two dependable men to assist in erecting these and in caring for orchards and vineyards now flourishing.

My purchase of an eastern one half of Sicard's land was accomplished. On a borrowed and accurate scales at Johnson's, Sicard accepted six thousand dollars in gold, for which I was handed a detailed release of the eastern half of the Nemshas. Keyser, the new owner of Johnson's, and one of his helpers witnessed, and we were done.

Over our drinks, by way of celebration, I learned of two happenings – both surprising, but surprising in very different ways: At our old deadfall – now named "Dry Diggins" or "North Fork Diggins", a man named woods had taken sixteen thousand dollars worth of gold from five cartloads of sand, and in a neighboring ravine, others were said to have mined between eight and fifteen hundred dollars in a day. My old and dear friend Covillaud was yet at Nye's landing at the confluence of the Yuba and Feather. He was no longer majordomo for Cordua, however, but was now wealthy in his own right, with significant holdings along the rivers, and was busy, with other holders, laying out the plat of a new town. Most surprising of all was the news that he was now married to the same little girl I had seen at Johnson's and at the fort : Mary Murphy. She had received an uncontested divorce from Johnson nearly a year ago.

Mary
Part III

There was only my step-sister to run to now, for in the eyes of all I was a fallen woman. Harriet and her new husband, Michael Nye, were living at Nye's landing, and it was toward the west again, that I rode that day. I would follow the Bear to the larger Sacramento River and then turn north. I was in a vacant state of mind, a kind of Not-caring. Though Mr. Johnson had been brutal in most of his actions and drank to excess, he had not treated me unkindly. And his consuming need for the kind of woman who did things for him was, maybe, a thing I could understand. But I was a woman of almost seventeen now, and even though I could not meet his needs, neither could I stand idly by while another, a squaw, met them.

I nooned at the ranch of a German named Nicholas, and then, over his protests, rode on the same afternoon. I was helped, however, by his suggestion that I guide by the distant hazy buttes, for they would lead me almost in a direct line to the landing.

Evening saw me in the home of another rancher and his wife, and by noon of the following day I was seated in the adobe belonging to Harriet and her husband. What one could say to a sister about my reasons for leaving Mr. Johnson were said in private – and, I am sure, passed on to her husband that night. I was fatigued, and after a light supper, slept long into the next day.

It was many days before I felt my old self. Though my sister and her husband fed me well, and I was made to feel as one of the family, it seemed that neither of us had completely recovered from the experiences in the mountains. Harriet had yet a slight limp because of two toes that had frozen and sluffed off. We occasionally compared our vague stomach pains. On sunny days we would ride out toward the buttes and watch the myriads of geese wintering there, and exclaim over the high wavering "V"s they made against the blue and thrill to their lonesome calling sounds.

Harriet's man Michael had, in addition to ranch duties and the building of a new house for Harriet, taken a firm interest in affairs of the town springing up across the river. He often enlivened our supper talk with news of its progress, and tales of new gold strikes and improved methods of mining. He was sure it would not be many years before California would become another of the United States. Michael also had a trading post in town. And I remember long evenings of talks he had with a Mr. Sampson and a Spaniard named Ramirez over storage of mine supplies and the improvement of the town. These two, and a man named Charles Covillaud were interested in enlarging the areas bordering the levee and in laying out the town into wide avenues, for Nye's Landing had grown crowded, and river traffic had led to congested conditions on the wharf.

Mr. Covillaud, especially, was frequently mentioned at our supper table. He had, Michael said, some new ideas – French ones – about how the streets should look, and I was intrigued with the notion of how he, a Frenchman, could hope to build the wide avenues and plazas he proposed.

One evening, as chances would have it, the three of us were invited to a small soiree in town. It was a light affair, held to celebrate the wedding of one of Harriet's acquaintances and held in The Round House – an odd looking structure built of canvas around a large circle of posts sunk in the ground. I had protested both an inability to dance, and a lack of suitable dress, but had been overruled. After Harriet had shortened the hem of one of her several gowns, we rode away to the party in Michael's light trap.

We had not far to go, and from the road atop the levee the two lighted oiled fagots before the tent could be seen.

Mostly I just sat, enjoying the novelty of the scene the several dancers, the flute, fiddle, and guitar music, and a large piece of wedding cake. I was asked to dance, but gave my thanks and declined. Then, suddenly as a new schotische began, and while my mouth was filled with cake, I was approached by a handsome, broad-shouldered man in immaculate dress. Since I found myself unable to voice a polite decline, without choking, I was led a short distance to the corn-mealed floor and soon found myself pleasantly swaying in his arms to the soft pulse of the music.

Somehow, I was able to avoid the appearance of a total novice, for he led strongly and reassuringly. His name, he said, was Charles Covillaud, and though I must have said mine in return, I can only recall the strong arms and the desperate need I felt to concentrate on the placement of my feet, which seemed so big and clumsy. But yes, I can recall, too, his deep masculine voice and the soft purring of his French accent, and I was intrigued by the way he so often placed an unconscious stress on parts of words unaccented in English. Oh yes! And I can remember how direct his every thought was – as though planned reverently in advance of its expressing.

When I was led again to my seat we found it occupied by Michael, who immediately – and now unnecessarily – introduced us. I was easily coaxed into conversation, and heard then, from the lips of the man about whom Michael had spoken, the plans Mr. Covillaud had for Nye's Landing town. These were very ambitious plans, but, as Mr. Covillaud remarked, ones which should be made and brought to fruition soon, for all was in a state of thriving prosperity, and that now was the time of greatest opportunity to set out the town: The mines were bringing untold revenue; there was more than enough enthusiasm and support; and it did appear that the landing was destined to be the head of river commerce, here where two great rivers joined.

The soiree and dance had been history for only three days when the four partners – Covillaud, Nye, Sicard and Sampson – met at Harriet's adobe to discuss business. As usual, Harriet and I left them alone, finding sewing and mending to be done in an adjoining room, but not beyond earshot of the sounds of their discussion. We knew, of course, that they were conscious of our near presence, and that we would be in silent attendance at their discussion.

It was all about legal matters, anyway, and of no concern to us. Toward evening, after lighting lamps there was a silence and a shuffling of feet, and sounds of departing. Their confab was over, and Michael came into our room. He mentioned to Harriet to come with him. They left also, and I thought it strange, at the time, that not only should Covillaud's group leave, but that I should now be excluded and remain alone.

Then, at the instant of their leaving, I felt the presence of another in the room with me. I turned, and in the dim light of my lamps I saw that I was alone with the man Charles Covillaud.

What followed was perhaps the humblest, sweetest presentation of a man I had ever seen. His self-assuredness and the brusque business man had vanished, and there in the dim rhythmic flicker of the lamps, and in his stunning French accents, and with me holding a mended garment and needles, I heard him say, "I love you Mary and

Pan The Low Waters

I should be greatly honored if you would be my wife".

It was as though a thousand thoughts seared my brain simultaneously. Not only was the proposal unexpected, and a surprise that completely disarmed me, but I had never even give the slightest or vaguest thought to any such notion or arrangement. The thoughts that flashed through my mind were those of my bad time at Johnson's, and of the confident way Charles had held me in dancing. My thoughts were of a seeming inconsistency and yet humbleness in the mind of a man I knew to be deeply involved in trading, commercialism and plans for a whole town, a man whose mind, I knew, to run to shipping and boats and trading.

These and others were the thoughts which coursed confusedly through my mind at the time. And they must have taken some time in their coursing, for Mr. Covillaud was fidgeting now, and nervous, and stood first on one foot and then on the other, and his face took on the appearance of a small boy caught with hands in a pie, and I must have taken an inordinate, hesitating, and thought-suspended time to reply, for I heard his voice continue. He told me he knew he would have to wait until the legalities of my divorce were settled, but that he could wait any length of time, but could I at least give him a hope that my answer would be yes. For he had known, since the soiree dance that it was me he wanted more than the profit from his enterprises, more than the wealth from his holdings at Sacramento, and more than the plans now afoot for the improvements of a town in Nye's Landing. And would I honor – he used the term again and again - would I honor him by becoming his wife and sharing the things which he said meant nothing to him if he could not share them with me. And I still could seem to say nothing, so confused had I become, and yet so fascinated was I with the music of his voice, his endearing French accents and the sincerity of his tones.

It was while I was standing there in what I suppose was a state of shock that Michael and Harriet re-entered. And though I had not spoken a work in reply to Charles, indeed not given him the slightest hint of yes or no, both Harriet and her husband entered with a wild scramble and threw their arms about me and congratulated Charles, and took my answer for granted. And I remember no more of what was said at the time, for gracious Charles seemed to sense in me a confusion greater than his, after Michael had proposed a toast, we drank, and Charles left, and I fell into Harriet's arms and had a good cry.

Long after I had sifted through the soft sands of my feelings with Harriet that Night, and then lain awake more hours thinking of Charles and his sweet, soft French petition, I think I fell at last, and blessedly, to sleep. And I dreamed of a new life; of one in my own house, with warmth and a plenty for all to eat; of happy children, and of an end to all that had happened to me since papa's death in Kentucky so very long ago.

*   *   *   *

Now I could begin with plans that had proliferated and matured in my mind while panning. I took my leave of Sicard and Keyser, and as I rode slowly back to the adobe (Sicard had pressing business at Cordua's) through an early winter drizzle, I mused on a fate that had so well provided for three French emigrants: Here was Covillaud, just as I was, making larger plans – he, for the beautification and efficiency of a town, and I for a ranch and appurtenances that would complement the beauty of the Bear. Sicard was a secure and successful entrepreneur. My mining had been but an interlude. Now I might bring to fruition some of the things at which fate had seemed to hint-my orchards of almonds and peaches, a mill, a winery.

Of greatest importance now was the security of the remaining gold – nineteen thousand dollars – plus the several thousand in currency which represented five years of barrel-making and trading. I buried all but a few thousand in several elevated locations about my acreage, for there was neither bank for its depositing nor agency for its conversion. There was, of course, much exchange of it for property, but with the increasing influx of strangers, risk of keeping on hand such an awkward weight was great. I kept only a portion of the currency securely on my person.

With my burying task completed, I installed Noontka as majordomo and set about making plans for spring. It was now deep into the winter season of "49, and rains came often and heavy. On those cold but clear weeks in late January we would ride over my leagues. I would note the best level locations for Russian barley and place, in my imagination, the flour mill, the overshot wheel, the winery. I would see, as in a vision, the vistas of undulating ripe grain and would plan numbers of Indian helpers, how they would perform sacking, how I would install my grinding wheels and, best of all, I would vicariously taste the first fruits of the orchards and vineyards.

When closed in by the near-floods of late February, I would plan and sketch details of the mill; I would work out the method for the transfer of power from a small millrace just east of the wheat fields, where the Bear's flow tumbled from a high rocky shelf to a smooth flow.

Often, in the evening, I would engage Noontka in fragmented conversation, pointing repeatedly to objects and having him repeat, using the same words in a context of meaning to fasten more securely the words in his alert young mind.

By early March much of my overshot wheel had been built on paper; the eager Indian helpers had cleared many acres of brushland for Russian barley (for it had become increasingly dangerous for them to be around miners); additional ground had been planted with the prunings from my original small vineyard, and I had dickered with a group of disenchanted miners for delivery of rough-sawn boards for the construction of several small projects. Of these, the mill and overshot wheel would have to come last, for their erection and installation would have to await a season when the Bear's flow became manageable and a millrace had been dug to accommodate the needed water flow.

In addition to planning I had been to Nye's landing, where Sicard had invested cleverly and had joined him in several small city land purchases, then sold at a handsome profit. He and Covillaud now operated a profitable store at Timbuctoo on the Yuba very close to the scene of my rich bar – now called Rose Bar, and Covillaud even had interests in the town of Sacramento – an area which was burgeoning on the river landing on Sutter's property. Sicard's new store on the lower Yuba was also bringing him a handsome profit.

These were the days filled with news of wild and unbelievable rich strikes along the high range of mountains, canyons, and rivers stretching for hundreds of miles in both directions from Marshall's original discovery; of quick and profitable exchanges of property; of hordes of gold-seekers arriving at the stopping places around Johnson's, then moving toward the great central gathering place near Sutter's – now generally called Sacramento.

And when, in May, I was well embarked upon the planting and sowing of my first fields of Russian barley, and the new acreage of peaches and grapes began to show their first green life, I would look toward the eastern hills and behold whole caravans of white-topped wagons rolling toward the crossing. It was always a satisfying sight, this white wraith, peeling slowly, snake-like toward the valley, and I though often of their owner's motivation and their destinies. These late-comers were for the gold fields, of course, and for the wealth said to be for the gathering. But would they, too, as I had done, after the golden harvest – or its counterpart, disillusionment – was past, would they too, stay to build?

Pan The Low Waters

Chapter 42
Land Commission

By late May it was nearing time for the construction of the overshot wheel, for the installation of its massive oaken axle, attached cog wheels and for the setting in place of many hundreds of rock to form its wide solid foundation.

I had planned well for this construction and its erection, and for many days I had had the help of the chief and his natives. The Bear, now low and manageable, was shunted, with rock dam, into a wide shallow millrace parallel to the river. Then, while the current gouged and dug the race yet deeper and the old river level waxed lower, and more and more of the Bear tumbled before regaining its old bed, my gangs raced to the dam. In its now shallow bottom they piled two ever-growing rock foundations on which the overshot wheel would anchor and turn, scooping its weighted bucketfuls and turning and ever more turning to create the steady, plentiful and reliable power to grind my wheat.

It can be stated truly that my Nemshas dated from that day – the day in which I harnessed the might of the Bear. For all that followed, as I went from project to project, dated from that harnessing: the success of the flour mill, with its power received from the wheel; the water for house and winery; water for the truck gardens, orchards, and vineyards, which my Indians tended so well. For, you see, on a tripod was mounted a high trough which caught the water from each bucket as it emptied on the downswing, carried it to another trough on the bank, and so, became a system for irrigating – one that I was flattered to see imitated by several neighboring ranchers.

After erection of the sixteen-foot wheel came more building and the erection of a mill, with its stone floor over which rode, in tandem, two heavy and wide stone wheels to grind wheat to flour and meal.

All this took place at the time of greatest mining excitement. But though day after day my workers and I would look up to see another caravan arriving or another band of miners treading their way to the hills, I was never troubled by them but once – and then only indirectly.

All this time I had been living with Noontka in Sicard's old adobe. The fledgling peach and almond orchards and the vineyards were beginning their second year of growth and had yielded a few hundredweight of fruit. Some had been given to travelers – though some had been sold – for I was looking ahead to a booming market with the miners. I knew that in another year Nye's landing and a settlement thirty miles to the east, called Grass Valley, would be a ready market place for all I could grow.

Then one morning, as I surveyed my peach orchard from a distance, the trees seemed to have a slanted, trampled appearance. Stumbling and running, I hurried to examine cause of the change. All about my young trees lay, some stripped of their leaves, some trampled and lying flat. All about where the hoof-prints of a large herd of cattle. Though I had no way of ascertaining the owners, I could only assume that the destructive herd belonged to a neighboring rancher who had joined the thousands of miners; that he had simply abandoned his animals and left them to feed and to roam as wild cattle. Frantically I went about my young orchard, pruning broken limbs, propping fallen and trampled trees, carrying water to irrigate those most damaged. By nightfall Noontka and I had saved nearly all the trees. Though I lost a portion, my orchard had not been devastated, and I could yet count on a good harvest the following year. The ditch which we had dug as fence the previous year might have done its job, but while we had been at the mine its edges had sluffed in and it was no longer a barrier.

The winter of '49 passed, with the near-devastation of my peaches, and the true beginnings of my Nemshas. By the time winter had again arrived (1850), I was still in Sicard's adobe, but could now look with great expectation on the beginnings of what I felt would surely be one of the Edens of the great valley. With Indian help I had cultivated ground, sown a five hundred acre field, and reaped a rich crop of barley; I had erected my overshot wheel; I had a mill which ground the barley even as I sat, enjoying pipe and brandy; and I had crushed my first wine grapes in a small and crude, but efficient winery.

The winter had been plentiful as had been that of the season just passed, and nothing planted failed to produce in excess of expectation. I now counted myself a successful farmer. My volumes of wine were increasing and my Nemshas was the object of congenial and admiring visitors who sat drinking with me on the veranda. For, by the autumn of 1851 I had with the help of unemployed carpenters from Marysville (now changed from Nye's Landing), erected a three-room ranch house with encircling verandas, a large barn, and was already planning additions to it

It would be difficult to tell precisely when my plans, so well-ordered until now, began to go awry. But, I suppose, the first intimations of change were the initially small but increasingly longer notices in the fledgling newspaper concerning investigations of land grants by the

Arnold F. Rothmeier

federal land grant commission in session at what was now San Francisco – the former Yerba Buena. The articles spoke of the law, and how it had become necessary to investigate land titles and, out of fairness to all land claimants, to establish rights and issue new documents of ownership. But I reasoned these pertained to others, of course, and surely not to me. For, had I not received my personal papers from Sicard, and had he not received his from an original Spanish land grant through Sutter?

I was not only secure, but my ranch was already the envy of all who saw it, and when I had finished with the cultivation of another projected one thousand acres of peaches, almonds, and grapes, I would have, perhaps, the finest vineyards and orchards in all California.

I was, I knew, approaching the zenith of my success, for, by the summer of 1851 my orchards bore their first bumper crop. This was from acreages of peaches and almonds that stretched for nearly a mile along the bottom lands and were bringing an increasingly higher price in Marysville and Grass Valley. The vineyards, occupying a preferred higher and drier soil, stretched almost as far as the eyes could reach, shiny and lush in their green leaves. Beneath their stake-like trellises, seven varieties of grapes seemed to vie in their production of the heaviest and sweetest fruit.

And so, it was as though I was not to know precisely which of the twin blights would fasten on me first. Perhaps it was the ecstasy I felt over the burgeoning richness of my farm that blinded me to the approach of both.

Intimations of the Bear's treachery had shown themselves often enough in recent years. Yet so engrossed had I become with my exciting finds at the deadfall and on the Yuba, that I was blinded by that treasure. Now, with my overshot wheel a hostage and pawn, I viewed its might, in the spring rains of '54, with an uneasy eye as it tore at its banks and wrecked a small bridge erected over it to haul fruit up the Sacramento and Nevada Road, I viewed also, in the foam of its high crest, the near-destruction of my overshot wheel, Both these warnings I should have heeded, but did not, thinking the rainy excess to be but a seasonal aberration.

My winery's output, from an early few hundred gallons in '51, grew to a production of ten thousand in '56. And I often thought of what Chouteau would have said had he then known the fate of his small sack of almonds given at the farewell party so long ago. I thought, too, of the fate of the children of that emigrant party who, so long ago had spat their peach seeds upon the ground; seeds, whose growth into sturdy fruit trees had become the cornerstone of my Nemshas empire.

As I say, then it would have been hard to tell which of the twin blights first materialized. Certainly the print was the more subtly ominous, for the increasingly heavy floods were only seasonal, and as Noontka, or some of my many visitors and I sat on the veranda, while Noontka's squaw brought us food and wine, we would read over the growing and foreboding list of those whom the new laws had disenfranchised. At times like this I would think, with a certain smugness, how fortunate I was to have bought wisely and to find myself so well set up, so firmly in possession of my kingdom.

A storm was brewing. I could feel it in the moist breeze, smell it in the newly-scythed barley and see it in the late afternoon ripple of aspen leaves that ringed the yards. By nightfall its persistent thrum upon my roof contained a note of rarity I had not heard before. Since the near-swamping of the overshot wheel Noontka and my helpers had widened and deepened the race to divert more of the Bear's flow and to relieve pressure which, a few seasons before, had threatened the wheel. And we had on hand the large boulders which could be rolled into place to divert the flow.

Arnold F. Rothmeier

But it was not now the rising river's broad sweep which I feared that January evening of 1856, but a letter from the land commission. I was requested to be present at a hearing in San Francisco on the morning of February 10 at precisely ten o'clock in the morning. I was to bring with me all documents that pertained to claims of ownership of the eastern half of Sicard's land. I was to bring maps of survey, and boundary definitions, such as point of tree blazings, stakes and boulder placings. I was to be prepared to state and prove such things as worth of appurtenances, length of residence at Nemshas, in the state, and in the United States. The letter was a simple form, abrupt, commanding, oddly cold, and menacing.

Despite trepidation and a sense of threat that possessed me as I rode west that morning, I could not help feeling secure. The bill of sale was there in my saddle bag, along with a plat of the area and plainly marked upon it were the oaks and scrub pines and their blazings; the area corner with its quartz outcropping. Surely I had no cause to worry. I patted the leather pouch as I rode along.

Yet so engrossed was I with thoughts of dark possibilities that I took scant note of change in the country through which I rode. I seemed hardly to see the vast changes that had taken place beyond Nicholas – the numerous squatter hovels and fences and farms, the absence of game, the small settlements, newly raised, as though pushed, magically, through the earth's crust. And after I boarded the "Linda", one of the launches now plying regularly along the broad Sacramento, delta fog seemed to penetrate my spirits. When at last we crossed a wide bay and approached the city of San Francisco, I found myself still unable to shake off something evil and premonitory, and I longed to be at Nemshas with my Indians. I knew I would never be a part of a teeming city life, such as I now, for a short while, must endure.

My return to Nemshas, two months later, was one filled with despair. A veiled, impersonal threat had hung over the hearing, held in an enormous, empty, second-story room. Voices of the bespectacled, dark-coated men had had a curt and disquieting ring. Not one of the seven had smiled, as copies of all my papers had circulated among them, and I had stood and shuffled as one accused of some heinous crime. Not one had inquired concerning improvements I had made, how my land had flourished. None had asked me about difficulties encountered in causing my farm to prosper. And not one had concerned himself in the slightest with any of the trails or expenses entailed in causing raw land to smile instead of frown. And when the two hour grind of waiting at the docket was over and I was dismissed, somewhat as a child is dismissed after reprimand, it had been with a brusque and impersonal suggestion that I seek to employ the services of an attorney to represent me. A short list of these was handed me, a date noted and given me for a second audience, and another petitioner was called – the signal for my dismissal.

So confused had I become immediately after my "trial" – for I felt indeed as though I had committed some vague crime – that I cannot truly account for my wanderings during the remainder of the afternoon.

Nor did I drink at the nearby saloon. Nor did the brief, appointment-setting time spent with an attorney, dull the cutting edge of my growing apprehension.

Nor had I further recourse when, after three court appearances and three costly battles – with one, then three different attorneys – I was handed peremptory directions to relinquish all my beloved Nemshas with the exception of five hundred acres. Title to Sicard's original grant had been found flawed and my land rights were now reduced to those of a common squatter.

While I had been badly whipped during those costly months in court, I truly had not lost the land upon which my cherished orchards lay. My mill and the source of its power was yet intact; the security of my house and the promise of my fields and trees were still mine. What, in retrospect, I had lost was but the feelings of a king, feelings which daily I had experienced as I surveyed my impressive acreage and their fruits.

Such, then, were the rationalizations of a reduced king – which mullings-over lasted almost the entire journey home. And by the time I had hailed and passed Nicholas Altgeier I had almost learned to live with my dethronement. Long before I came within sight of Johnson's (now Keyser's) three adobes, the Indians who knew me trailed after my horse in welcome and followed me to the ranch house, shyly touching my boots, stirrups, and the sweaty horse's side.

Noontka, too, met me far down the Bear road, and it was he who brought me a glass of the fine, light wine of which I had become so immoderately fond. And I thought, as I greeted him and took the wine, "How truly wonderful it was to have the affection of them all", and, after passing through the mental hell of two months at court, to be seated yet, on my mare, drinking a superb wine of my own growing and making, and to look around again at all that was, blessedly, still mine.

All this was in '56, and now past, but had I known that in another few years I was to meet a challenge greater than that met at San Francisco, I would not have routed my life any differently. For was not the interesting life eternally filled with challenges to be met – and overcome?

Pan The Low Waters

Chapter 43
The Monitors

There were times during rainy-season nights when I was aroused by faithful Noontka. We would fight a muddy path to a fearfully rising Bear, and arrive just in time to see another of my year-old bridges float away on the foamy crest. Then there were times at harvest season when the Nemshas and I would play host to a half-dozen wagon loads of families from town. We would gather in the vineyards and trees and laugh and pick and eat, and then dine at the veranda on foods brought or furnished, and savor and discuss which lady or gentlemen preferred which wine.

These were the happy years in which my peaches sold readily in markets at Marysville, Grass Valley, Nevada City, and Sacramento, and when old Chouteau's almonds took first prize at California's first state fair.

But these were the days, too, when the first intimations of trouble with the Bear showed themselves in an unusual series of storms.

One morning in early January of 1857, at the end of a particularly heavy downpour, I chanced to ride with Noontka up along the river. It ran in an angry foaming tide, as it always did after rains. I knew it had been an unusually heavy storm a few miles to the east too, for now the Bear was full of fury and showed its teeth in foam and debris. Then, toward evening of the following day, when the waters had become more placid, we again rode the trail. The tide was tame, had lost its force and debris. But what startled me was sight of a reddish sand that now coated the river rocks normally swept clean in a few hours. This time the tide had not acted as a broom. In places near the banks, accumulations of the red sand and small deltas of rounded quartz clung like small bars along the banks; the bed seemed raised and to cause the river to flow at a higher level than was its custom, even after clouds had vanished from the uplands.

Sand and white gravel were the first intimation of change for my Nemshas. It was the effect of a cause about which I had been reading now for several seasons, but one which, though an annoyance, surely would pass – perhaps just as the land commission trouble had passed. I concerned myself no more over the excessively muddied water and the small white pebbles.

But as the comparatively calm winter and spring of '56 and '57 passed, with again, and then again, destruction of my bridges, and as the sand accumulations failed to disappear, one day in late summer, after harvest was in, I told Noontka to saddle up. We would ride into the hills to see the thing which newspapers and town talk were describing: the fearful destruction of whole mountain sides by a thing called "monitors". It was said, and often repeated (I thought with some exaggeration) that this new power was the tool of large companies – some even foreign – who, dissatisfied with the long tom and the pan, had organized in such a way as to finance the building of flumes. These, it was said, now brought to vast holdings of low-grade placers, streams of water that could, literally, cut a man it two. It was said that the streams of water were numerous and powerful, and were washing whole mountains through sluices, that this was the reason for

Pan The Low Waters

changes in the Bear, and that mining debris was even interfering with boat traffic on the Yuba and Feather.

It was now early September and the streams we passed were slowing to little more than healthy trickles. But all contained, inside sharp bends, and at flat, level stretches, the same curious pebble bars and dam-like accumulations of sand and river-worn rounded quartz rock. As we rode higher there was a gradual increase in choked accumulations of these, mixed with whole bushes, and even small trees, as though they had been torn whole from where they had grown.

By mid-day we had reached the upper Bear River basin. It was there we beheld the source of my alarm: It could be seen from a mile, this enormous white and brown-gray pastel-tinted scar against a three hundred-foot hillside. And, as we rode closer, seven streams of water from apparently unattended hoses were seen playing upon the scar, partially obscuring, with their mist, the work they were doing.

The closer we rode toward the monitors, the louder became the collective roar of the water, whose continual sound was punctuated by the undercutting and fall of huge sections of mountain and its mature trees. As we watched, an occasional boulder – some larger than my mare – would slowly detach itself from the scar and slide or bound to the wet floor. And always there at our feet were the sparkling white quartz stones, the same that had formed my small, clogging bars. Over all, wherever a small trickle of water ran, could be seen the deep, liquid mud and sand which had once been the mountainside, and which might one day reach the borders of my land.

These were the deep, auriferous gravels of a high, broad ridge. To uncover and sift fine gold hidden there had taken invention of the tool we were now witnessing.

We dismounted in shade at an unworked lip opposite the howling monitors and watched silently for hours as the mountainside scar slowly melted to red mud, and as the high trees above the scar – some four or five feet in diameter – suddenly lost root support and fell. There was no pause in the water's work, nor pause in the slow transformation of mountain to mud, the seven rivers of water playing against virgin hillside ran muddy and full into wide, iron-riffled sluices, then into streams, which, I knew fed the Bear. And in a kind of vision I saw nowhere the mountain could go but into my river. There, finally, to occupy the space where water itself should flow.

Noontka and I were as yet too astonished with what we saw, and too occupied with the scene's magnitude and novelty to talk. We were, however, reminded of the lateness of the hour when a distant steam whistle sounded. Thinking this to signal the end of the mining day, we were preparing to leave when, shortly, the rocky field below filled with a new crew. Monitors ceased their work and the heads of the riffles were cleaned by men wearing holstered guns, while others cut and rolled trees, stumps, and boulders. Teams of horses tugged and rearranged sluices. Then monitors began anew and boulders and trees resumed their fall. For the Dutch Flat Mine was not one which quit at a night whistle, but continued with a night crew. And when we could no longer see clearly, huge torches lit the area. It was time for us to go. We spent the night in a tent in town which advertised itself as the *Dutch Flat Hotel* and returned to Nemshas in the morning.

The journey had been a sobering one and had shown me the threat of a process already begun on the bed of the Bear. Since my five hundred acres abutted the foothills, I was the first local farmer to note these encroachments of hydraulic mud – *Slickens* – as they came to be called.

Chapter 44
The Bear

The winter of 1861-62 was one of serious flooding and of riverbed accumulations. It was the year in which presentiments became reality. Early in January, just as the furious Bear had receded a third time, a fourth period of heavy rains fell on already supersaturated earth. Weeks of steady downpour drenched the ranch until it seemed there would be no ceasing. From my veranda, I could only look through bands of water that coursed like waterfalls from the eaves, and it was as though the house was floating on a restless, pelted lake, though it had been built on a safe rise. Even as the storm periodically slackened, the whole world appeared to be awash in liquid, and I could see only a moving tide of water, hundreds of yards wide and moving through the bordering orchards so mightily that many of the mature trees were either bent under the tide or submerged.

There was no sleep that night, no relief from the conviction that my Nemshas was in the path of a force beyond calculation. That the worst had happened, I knew, even before the rains tapered off to a slow drizzle and before a fitful opaque sunlight showed through the low clouds that scudded from the south, yet black and full.

Arnold F. Rothmeier

When, by noon, rain had ceased and heavy mist hung like a shroud over the lake around the house, Noontka and I waded the lake toward the scene of my overshot wheel and mill. From a distance we could see only the rocky fall where it had once been. Even the huge mounds of stones – its foundations – were buried under sand and slime. My fine mill house, too, though erected on an adjacent rise, was tilted at an odd angle and had had its sides penetrated by the water's force. Grinding wheels lay downstream and half-buried in a pile of debris, sand, and rocks from the foundation.

The depression which overwhelmed me that morning was traumatic and lasted long into the spring. I had lost not only a fine mill, along with its source of power, but I had lost also much of the reason for the existence of both! Nearly the entire field from which my abundant crops of Russian barley and wheat came were sickened by a foot of sand and quartz pebbles, which lay, ironically, like a sparkling jewelled carpet amid the devastation.

My Indians had long since vanished from the valley, but in that sad winter of '62 there was other help. Squatters were available in all directions, excepting, or course, toward the eastern foothill boundary. I would not attempt rebuilding the wheel and mill because the reason for their existence had vanished. Though heavily silted with sand and debris, my higher vineyards continued to flourish, as though possessed somehow of a desire to console me; to make amends for the ruin which nature had brought to their neighboring acres. And all through these years they poured out such an abundance of grapes and such fine qualities of wine, that I could experience, at times, a palliation of the deep sadness I had felt at my mill's ruin, and looked at the green on their trellises instead of at the empty sand-filled spot where once the overshot wheel turned.

Now followed seasons exasperatingly the reverse of those just experienced. For three years newspaper ink ran heavy concerning drought, death of herds, property devaluations, and closed mines.

Anticipating other cycles of heavy rain, I used the time to hire a band of squatters to build levees and buttress against flood time. In a way, the three drought years were providential for they provided time for my army of squatters to harness their teams to fresnos – which I purchased at Sacramento – and raise sand from the Bear into higher banks. And for months during the drought, they filled the air with their "gee-haws" and whip cracks and coarse epithets. And when, after two summers of fresnos and dust and cursing were finished, all were confident we had in place a barrier over which the mad Bear could not climb. Each day, after we had done our stint and could see the levee grow with its promise of security, we would feed and water the animals and sit upon the veranda and feel our day's accomplishment, and my wine would wash away the fatigue in a bouquet of alcohol and blue pipe smoke.

When we had finished our long, rock-studded levees in the summer of '64. It was almost as though we had worked with an eye to nature's time schedule. The past flood had shown a need; we had suffered, but had survived the suffering and now could prevent further damage. Though the cost of the levee's erection had been nearly one half the large sum I had banked in Marysville, it was inconceivable there could be other seasons as destructive as that of January '62.

So it was with almost a feeling of smugness that Noontka and I welcomed the first rains of 1864. Had I but known at that date the vastness of mining debris then accumulated and waiting only the trigger of weather, my smugness would have vanished. For, though, during the drought there had been depression at the mines, and work at them had virtually ceased, there had followed a resurgence of activity at Red Dog, You Bet, and Dutch Flat. Now, immense stretches of tailings clogged the streams, poised for a tide that would sluff to the valley whole mountains of sand and slickens.

After the drought came good years, with above-average rainfall, but also with heavy and profitable crops; the crops I desperately needed to recoup a small fortune expended on the fresnos. On occasion heavy, pounding storms caused a repeat of the apprehension of '62, but the feeling passed when these ended with only moderate damage to the levees and farms. There was a general relaxing at all ranches and a feeling of confidence in the future. Tailings, for the most part, seemed securely contained in their basins and flats. Occasionally the papers sounded an ominous note about new improvements in mining equipment, about the invention of new blasting powder called "dynamite", used to loosen deep, cemented gravels, and about flumes hundreds of miles long. They would tell of the monitors that dissolved whole mountains in a day, of growing feelings that debris in many of the larger navigable rivers was causing cancellation of river traffic; that in the Feather, the Sacramento, and close by, in the Yuba, sediment deposits were visible. The paper showed, too, though guardedly and with restraint, some of the river damage done in the past. But this, too, seemed but a sop to the wealthy, for it was well known that many of the larger towns were forging much of the heavy equipment needed at the mines. I had read in the "Wheatland Enterprise" and "Marysville Appeal", in the week of my sixty-fourth birthday, of a new mining "artillery piece" called the "Little Giant". The paper had described its power: "With a ten-inch bore the piece can deliver a stream of water capable of reducing a mountainside from a distance of one hundred feet". The water, it was said was a force so powerful that it could tear apart deep, cemented aggregates formerly only loosened by pick or single-jack.

And so, the scene was arranged, the stage sets placed, and a script sketched, perhaps in Heaven, for a drama that would change many boundaries, fortunes, and lives.

Winter rains of '65 had peaked the Bear just short of my highest levee, then receded, mercifully, without a break. This time they seemed to test our work somewhat more thoroughly. There were minor lappings where the persistent, swirling river touched levee tops where now a hundred wet and cold sandbaggers built their fires and plugged threatened areas before the Bear could plunder. These were nights filled with apprehension and near-terror, of shouting relays of men on horseback and gangs of helpers held behind each levee in reserve, much as an army holds its battalions for anticipated attack. They were nights long and wet and full of cursing and black coffee. And in the mornings, full of unspoken thankfulness that the long earthen shoulders had again held.

But the strain was making itself felt. I do not mean these periodic night or day alarms, when the Bear came close to breaking confinement, for by the winters of '65 and '66, a flood routine had been established and most property owners within the river's threat could be counted on to send two or three helpers. The strain which now taxed me was that at the bank: by 1865 I had paid out for tools, sand sacking, labor and teams, almost twenty thousand dollars. The account sagged low.

Scenes along the twin levees were repeated in '66, and my helpers, once in December and then again in January, helped hold back the waters, although some minor flooding occurred through a hole in the south bank near the narrows where my overshot wheel once stood.

Returns from the peach and almond orchards were handsome the following summer. Though I think I loved these more than I did my vineyards and winery (perhaps it was a growing nostalgia I felt over their humble beginnings), it was the latter that enabled me to remain solvent. By the fall of '66 I had not only picked and sold fine crops of fruit and nuts, but I had bottled some two thousand gallons of wine. And although I had banked over ten thousand dollars, the need to find workers to strengthen weaker spots in the levee drove me to spend increasingly more time finding and hiring levee-building help, for now, in dry weather, they were busy harvesting their own crops.

One bright note in the late fall of '66 was the visit of Charles Covillaud and his wife, Mary, the thin and ravaged mite I remembered on the floor at Johnson's, where she lay resting after her rescue from the snows. She was a fine, even beautiful young woman now, when, with parasol, she stepped, with Covillaud's guiding arm, from their trap. Next came the nurse and two healthy children, both of whom closely resembled Charles. Our talk revolved mainly around Charles' fortunes, which I had followed closely, for many years, in the papers. He was now well-to-do and they attended mass regularly, even though he was a long-established Mason. Their ranch and home northeast of Marysville was yielding consistent bumper crops of the finest peaches on two thousand acres of choice land only lightly touched by any of the long series of floods which had troubled me. Their two children, William and Mary Ellen, had had the usual childhood diseases, but had not been seriously affected by them. And so went the visit with a pair whose association and fortunes had touched, and framed, mine.

Late that afternoon, when our reunion drew to its close, we toasted the new name of the town down-river from Johnson's – Wheatland – and liberally sampled my best wines. I could not help noticing the faint, almost invisible trace of anxiety or hint of apprehension, if that be the word, in the haunted but beautiful look in Mary's eyes, and the faint depression between her full eyebrows that told the sadness through which she had passed. It was the last time I was to see either of them, for Mary passed away early in '67, and Charles died shortly afterward. By then I was too engrossed in levee troubles to attend either of their funerals.

Chapter 45
Defeat

The years between 1866 and 1874 imposed an odd contrast of feeling – those of elation and apprehension. My orchards and vineyards were recognized throughout the valley as the finest, and their fruit and nuts often bore so heavily that limbs broke from the weight. My wines were recognized as premium and sold quickly to distant buyers, who came early at bottling time, without advertisement, and paid the prices asked. But despite my growing agricultural success and promise, the mighty Bear and its seasonal increments of sand and slickens continued.

On the debit side was the ever-growing expense of maintaining levees, which, in the early seventies, had to be moved, as well as enlarged. The river had become so glutted with slickens that its normal bed required widening. Half a mile east of my orchards the Bear, at average flow, was a flood plain many hundreds of yards wide. Then, in the heat of summer, it went almost completely underground, so all-pervasive had become the encroachment of mining sand.

Those neighbors from whom I had asked advice had recommended only higher, broader, and longer levees, and, since the only other option was that of leaving the Nemshas to what must be inevitable ruin, I chose to fight for my farm with continued levee-building and repair.

By 1870, despite the farm's generous income, it was necessary to mortgage all I owned – house, orchards, and winery – in order to prepare for even light winter floodings and pay for levee breaks. And even with this ridiculous sum, received over the jaundiced eye of a bank clerk, it became necessary to rent one hundred acres to a tenant farmer for two thousand dollars. So, the play, the final act, now had only to begin.

The early rains of '74 were hardly a curtain-raiser. They approached hesitantly, only dampening, but continuing to dampen, the valley. There was neither flooding nor hint of it, but there were many light rains. Hardly a week passed without a shower that kept the soil and sand saturated. Walking became a muddy task and breath itself seemed often more moisture than air.

Then, in late December, two warm, pounding storms bent orchards to the ground. Rivulets reminiscent of '61 and '62 formed about the house and for a period of hours, mad gusts ravaged the farm, ripping shakes from the roof and strewing veranda chairs in a heap. And as I peered through the front window to investigate the cause of the sound, I saw leaves, then whole limbs of peach trees being caught up in an insane whirl and strewn about until they were banked against the porch in a hedge of wild and stripped destruction. Even the glass against which my face pressed in amazement, seemed in danger of shattering inward.

I became conscious of the sounds of water dripping on the floor and hurried to contain it.

By noon the force of the storm had diminished, and an apprehensive Noontka and I were able to walk outside and repair some damage. That done to the roof was but slight and the shakes were replaced with ease. But sight of the wind's destruction to peaches and almonds, the mainstay and first love of my farm, was almost more that I could bear. The storm had bowed them almost to the ground, until they resembles something distorted and slanting. Each tree cowered as though from punishment. Limbs and branches were torn and strewn about. It was as though the whole orchard had been set upon by a band of scythe-yielding madmen, so complete was their destruction. And I recalled the near-demolition of my fledging trees by the abandoned and starving cattle so long ago, and felt the pathos of their fate – to be saved only to be destroyed by the force of a storm.

But I had yet to reckon with the Bear. I knew, even as I viewed this wantonness, that the river must be high and ravaging and so I sent Noontka again to gather neighboring helpers to work on the levees. Only then did I go to the river and watch the wild, mighty expanse that grew higher even as I watched.

It was an hour or more before Noontka returned. He had been unable to cross the Kearney side to raise workers, for the bridge was out. However, he had notified many others, who would soon appear. Not wanting to endure more the apprehension building within me, I turned back to the ranch house intending to begin coffee and food for the men when they arrived. But, to my surprise, then horror, I found the wide road to the house now under a foot of water that flowed with menacing force. It was then, I knew, that there was a serious break in the barriers; that I was faced with more than a destructive windstorm.

By the time help arrived from farms downstream, I knew that the Nemshas, as I had known it, was no more. A two-foot head of water, thick and strong with mud and debris, was even then pounding at the walls of my house. As Noontka and I raced to gather papers, bedding, and valuables, and to turn out the horses, I wept, and my tears mingled with a cold sweat as we raced to higher ground.

Arnold F. Rothmeier

All through the night, as we huddled, still awake, on the floor of neighbor Burtis' yet safe home, the rains continued with a distinct roaring sound. This time where was no interval of mist or high cloud, but a maddening seven-day stretch of hammering rain that permitted no one to go outside, except for nature's calls, after which it became necessary to dry all clothing.

The week did finally pass, but like a sentence, and when it was served and the prisoners were at last released, it was only to pay new and more severe bonds. I had expected, of course, to rebuild. That my house, like the wheel and the mill before had been swept away, or at least partially destroyed, was to be expected. But, even my most pessimistic expectations did not prepare me, during those seven days and nights, for what Noontka, Burtis, and I saw on the morning when we were at last liberated.

I now walked over my Nemshas as through a new and foreign countryside. The only recognizable points of orientation were cloud-rimmed foothills to the east and a few giant oaks close to where the mill and its wheel once turned. In the wide areas near where barley and wheat had once bent in a June sun, flowed the Bear, its roil half a mile wide. Beneath the surface, white quartz pebbles from the mines glinted like cheap sequins.

Of the house, no sign remained. Of my precious winery and its store of full bottles to sell, nothing remained but mounds of mine tailings – some ten feet high, themselves so deeply gullied that, after weeks, when the waters finally receded and I could walk over acres where all once flourished, I found it necessary to walk up one steep hillside of gravel and down another, and I could find nothing to show where my Nemshas began or ended.

That night at Burtis' house, I was visited by an uneasy dream. So mixed and confused seemed its import, that afterward, all that remained and capable of dim recall was the sad feeling that I must pay, somehow, for the gold which I had taken from a bar on the Yuba; that if I did not, then I must be destroyed by the very thing after which I had lusted. And in the morning I was awakened with a feeling that the destruction of all I had on earth, save my aging body, was being visited upon me by that very lust which powered the monitors.

EPILOGUE

Records show that Claude Chana, still a healthy, industrious, and enterprising man at the age of sixty-four, moved to Wheatland. There he began anew a seemingly shattered life, building a winery and purchasing grapes from neighbors and , in one of his remaining years, producing three thousand gallons of fine wine. The orchards around Wheatland are today's memorial to Chana. He died in relative comfort at Wheatland in 1882 and lies now in the cemetery of that town, next to his friend, Theodore Sicard.